BY J. R. WARD

THE BLACK DAGGER BROTHERHOOD SERIES

Dark Lover   Lover Avenged

Lover Eternal   Lover Mine

Lover Awakened   Lover Unleashed

Lover Revealed   Lover Reborn

Lover Unbound   Lover at Last

Lover Enshrined   The King

The Black Dagger Brotherhood: The Shadows
An Insider's Guide

BLACK DAGGER LEGACY

Blood Kiss   Blood Vow

NOVELS OF THE FALLEN ANGELS

Covet   Rapture

Crave   Possession

Envy   Immortal

THE BOURBON KINGS

The Bourbon Kings   The Angels' Share

BLOOD VOW

J. R. WARD

BLOOD VOW

BLACK DAGGER LEGACY

BALLANTINE BOOKS

NEW YORK

Published in the United States by Ballantine Books, an imprint of Random House, a division of Penguin Random House LLC, New York.

BALLANTINE and the HOUSE colophon are registered trademarks of Penguin Random House LLC.

LIBRARY OF CONGRESS CATALOGING-IN-PUBLICATION DATA
Names: Ward, J. R., author.
Title: Blood vow / J. R. Ward.
Description: First edition. | New York : Ballantine Books, [2016] |
Series: Black dagger legacy ; 2
Identifiers: LCCN 2016030520 (print) | LCCN 2016039795 (ebook) |
ISBN 9780451475336 (hardcover : acid-free paper) | ISBN 9780698193284 (ebook)
Subjects: LCSH: Paranormal romance stories. | BISAC: FICTION /
Romance / Paranormal. | FICTION / Fantasy / Paranormal. | FICTION /
Romance / Fantasy. | GSAFD: Fantasy fiction. | Love stories.
Classification: LCC PS3623.A73227 B58 2016 (print) |
LCC PS3623.A73227 (ebook) | DDC 813/.6—dc23
LC record available at https://lccn.loc.gov/2016030520

Printed in the United States of America on acid-free paper

randomhousebooks.com

2 4 6 8 9 7 5 3 1

First Edition

Endpaper image by freeimages.com/Pedro Simao

Dedicated to:

my Tatson, Dee.

With all my love,

xxx mummy

GLOSSARY OF TERMS AND
PROPER NOUNS

ahstrux nohtrum (n.) Private guard with license to kill who is granted his or her position by the King.

ahvenge (v.) Act of mortal retribution, carried out typically by a male loved one.

Black Dagger Brotherhood (pr. n.) Highly trained vampire warriors who protect their species against the Lessening Society. As a result of selective breeding within the race, Brothers possess immense physical and mental strength, as well as rapid healing capabilities. They are not siblings for the most part, and are inducted into the Brotherhood upon nomination by the Brothers. Aggressive, self-reliant, and secretive by nature, they exist apart from civilians, having little contact with members of the other classes except when they need to feed. They are the subjects of legend and objects of reverence within the vampire world. They may be killed only by the most serious of wounds, e.g., a gunshot or stab to the heart, etc.

blood slave (n.) Male or female vampire who has been subjugated to serve the blood needs of another. The practice of keeping blood slaves has recently been outlawed.

the Chosen (pr. n.) Female vampires who have been bred to serve the Scribe Virgin. They are considered members of the aristocracy, though they are spiritually rather than temporally focused. They have little or no interaction with males, but can be mated to Brothers at the Scribe Virgin's direction to propagate their class. Some have the ability to prognosticate. In the past, they were used to meet the blood needs of unmated members of the Brotherhood, and that practice has been reinstated by the Brothers.

chrih (n.) Symbol of honorable death in the Old Language.

cohntehst (n.) Conflict between two males competing for the right to be a female's mate.

Dhunhd (pr. n.) Hell.

doggen (n.) Member of the servant class within the vampire world. *Doggen* have old, conservative traditions about service to their superiors, following a formal code of dress and behavior. They are able to go out during the day, but they age relatively quickly. Life expectancy is approximately five hundred years.

ehros (n.) A Chosen trained in the matter of sexual arts.

exhile dhoble (n.) The evil or cursed twin, the one born second.

the Fade (pr. n.) Nontemporal realm where the dead reunite with their loved ones and pass eternity.

First Family (pr. n.) The King and Queen of the vampires, and any children they may have.

ghardian (n.) Custodian of an individual. There are varying degrees of *ghardians*, with the most powerful being that of a *sehcluded* female.

glymera (n.) The social core of the aristocracy, roughly equivalent to Regency England's *ton*.

hellren (n.) Male vampire who has been mated to a female. Males may take more than one female as mate.

hyslop (n. or v.) Term referring to a lapse in judgment, typically resulting in the compromise of the mechanical operations of a vehicle or otherwise motorized conveyance of some kind. For example, leaving one's keys in one's car as it is parked outside the family home overnight—whereupon said car is stolen.

leahdyre (n.) A person of power and influence.

leelan (n.) A term of endearment loosely translated as "dearest one."

Lessening Society (pr. n.) Order of slayers convened by the Omega for the purpose of eradicating the vampire species.

lesser (n.) De-souled human who targets vampires for extermination as a member of the Lessening Society. *Lessers* must be stabbed through the chest in order to be killed; otherwise they are ageless. They do not eat or drink and are impotent. Over time, their hair, skin, and irises lose pigmentation until they are blond, blushless, and pale eyed. They smell like baby powder. Inducted into the society by the Omega, they retain a ceramic jar thereafter into which their heart was placed after it was removed.

lewlhen (n.) Gift.

lheage (n.) A term of respect used by a sexual submissive to refer to her dominant.

Lhenihan (pr. n.) A mythic beast renowned for its sexual prowess. In modern slang, refers to a male of preternatural size and sexual stamina.

lys (n.) Torture tool used to remove the eyes.

mahmen (n.) Mother. Used both as an identifier and a term of affection.

mhis (n.) The masking of a given physical environment; the creation of a field of illusion.

nalla (n., f.) or *nallum* (n., m.) Beloved.

needing period (n.) Female vampire's time of fertility, generally lasting for two days and accompanied by intense sexual cravings. Occurs approximately five years after a female's transition and then once a decade thereafter. All males respond to some degree if they are around a female in her need. It can be a dangerous time, with conflicts and fights breaking out between competing males, particularly if the female is not mated.

newling (n.) A virgin.

the Omega (pr. n.) Malevolent, mystical figure who has targeted the vampires for extinction out of resentment directed toward the Scribe Virgin. Exists in a nontemporal realm and has extensive powers, though not the power of creation.

phearsom (adj.) Term referring to the potency of a male's sexual organs. Literal translation something close to "worthy of entering a female."

princeps (n.) Highest level of the vampire aristocracy, second only to members of the First Family or the Scribe Virgin's Chosen. Must be born to the title; it may not be conferred.

pyrocant (n.) Refers to a critical weakness in an individual. The weakness can be internal, such as an addiction, or external, such as a lover.

rahlman (n.) Savior.

rythe (n.) Ritual manner of assuaging honor granted by one who has offended another. If accepted, the offended chooses a weapon and strikes the offender, who presents him—or herself without defenses.

the Scribe Virgin (pr. n.) Mystical force who is counselor to the King as well as the keeper of vampire archives and the dispenser of privileges. Exists in a nontemporal realm and has extensive powers. Capable of a single act of creation, which she expended to bring the vampires into existence.

sehclusion (n.) Status conferred by the King upon a female of the aristocracy as a result of a petition by the female's family. Places the female under the sole direction of her *ghardian*, typically the eldest male in her household. Her *ghardian* then has the legal right to determine all manner of her life, restricting at will any and all interactions she has with the world.

shellan (n.) Female vampire who has been mated to a male. Females generally do not take more than one mate due to the highly territorial nature of bonded males.

symphath (n.) Subspecies within the vampire race characterized by the ability and desire to manipulate emotions in others (for the purposes of an energy exchange), among other traits. Historically, they have been discriminated against and, during certain eras, hunted by vampires. They are near extinction.

the Tomb (pr. n.) Sacred vault of the Black Dagger Brotherhood. Used as a ceremonial site as well as a storage facility for the jars of *lessers*. Ceremonies performed there include inductions, funerals, and disciplinary actions against Brothers. No one may enter except for members of the Brotherhood, the Scribe Virgin, or candidates for induction.

trahyner (n.) Word used between males of mutual respect and affection. Translated loosely as "beloved friend."

transition (n.) Critical moment in a vampire's life when he or she transforms into an adult. Thereafter, he or she must drink the blood of the opposite sex to survive and is unable to withstand sunlight. Occurs generally in the mid-twenties. Some vampires do not survive their transitions, males in particular. Prior to their transitions, vampires are physically weak, sexually unaware and unresponsive, and unable to dematerialize.

vampire (n.) Member of a species separate from that of Homo sapiens. Vampires must drink the blood of the opposite sex to survive. Human blood will keep them alive, though the strength does not last long. Following their transitions, which occur in their mid-twenties, they are unable to go out into sunlight and must feed from the vein regularly. Vampires cannot "convert" humans through a bite or transfer of blood, though they are in rare cases able to breed with the other species. Vampires can dematerialize at will, though they must be able to calm themselves and concentrate to do so and may not carry anything heavy with them. They are able to strip the memories of humans, provided such memories are short-term. Some vampires are able to read minds. Life expectancy is upward of a thousand years, or in some cases even longer.

wahlker (n.) An individual who has died and returned to the living from the Fade. They are accorded great respect and are revered for their travails.

whard (n.) Equivalent of a godfather or godmother to an individual.

BLOOD VOW

ONE

*T*here was a place in Axe's life for masks. Whether they were literal and hid your face, or figurative to protect your soul, he was supremely comfortable with camouflage. Knowledge, after all, was power only if it gave you insight into your enemy. If insight was applied to you?

He'd rather have a knife to his throat.

And everyone was his enemy.

Standing in a crowd of over a hundred sexually aroused humans, he was ready to feed his dark side—you know, toss some fresh meat over the chain-link fence of his sex drive and stand back as the meal was consumed, the gnawing hunger briefly satisfied.

It never lasted. But that was why he'd joined this club.

The Keys was a private, members-only gig, and there were only two rules. No minors. Always with consent.

After those conditions were satisfied? You could scratch the itch of whatever sin you wanted: glory holes, gang bangs, girls on girls on guys. There were rooms for fetishes, and pits for fucking, and every tie-up, chain-down, in-the-air you could ask for.

Especially here in the Cathedral.

Of all the spaces in the sprawling, multi-block compound, this was largest and the loftiest. Filled with swirls of white smoke, pierced by purple and blue lasers, empty of furniture and fixtures except for the altar, only the hardest of the hardcore were allowed in here.

And masks were always worn, even on nights when the rest of the club didn't require it.

Through the eye holes of his fitted skull plate, Axe looked up, way up, to the altar.

It was like a scene out of *The Silence of the Lambs*, a human body suspended high above the floor, arms outstretched, head tilting to the side, swaths of fabric fanning out like wings all around the torso. The Hannibal-arisons ended there, though. Not a man, a woman. Not clothed, but naked. Not real blood on the flesh, but a viscous wash that fell like rain from the ceiling, hitting her breasts, dripping over her stomach, licking down her thighs so that she glistened under the remote lights.

Not dead, but very much alive.

"Do you want that?" he was asked from behind.

Axe smiled and didn't bother hiding his fangs.

None of them knew that he was an actual vampire. And not as in a neo-Victorian Dracula-wannabe with cosmetically altered canines, high-heeled boots, and a fake black rinse through his already dark hair.

As in the real deal. Different DNA. Different traditions and language. Different biological imperative that, yes, involved drinking blood from a vampire of the opposite sex.

Different sex drive.

"Yeah, I'll take her first," he said.

As the staff member whistled loudly and put his hand up to summon the rolling scaffolding, a rush tripped and fell over the crowd, excitement building for the first show. And for a split second, Axe considered materializing up there just to freak them all out, just because he could, just because he liked creating chaos.

Instead, he scaled the front of the metal framework with the ease of a spider over its web.

When he was up at the woman's level, her body responded in a starving arch, her head falling back, her mouth opening, her eyes begging him. She wasn't drugged. She was achingly aware, the scent of her sex flaring, her flesh calling out for release.

She'd wanted him. Out of the many below, she'd wanted him specifically.

"Take me," she said. "Take—"

He reached out his gloved hand and closed her mouth with his fingertips. Bending over her, he bared his canines and went for her throat. But he didn't bite her. He ran the tip of one fang up her jugular.

With a jerk against the chains she had volunteered for, she orgasmed for him right then and there, the alchemy of the public display, the danger he represented, the kind of sex she needed, coalescing into a release that flushed her face and made her moan as she thrashed.

Down below, the pleasure she felt rippled through the teeming bodies.

And he was aroused, yes. But not like they were. Not like she was.

Never as any of them.

However, the screaming voice in his head that told him he was a piece of shit was dimmed down by the sex. The fire of his rage against himself was doused by the distraction. The packed house of recriminations under his real skull were, momentarily, displaced.

So yes, this worked for everyone.

Reaching up to his own throat, he released the cord of his cloak and dropped the heavy weight from his shoulders. He had black leathers on and nothing else but his tattoos and piercings.

Axe's hands went to her body and traveled, with his mouth, everywhere.

And the storm he was deliberately creating raked over the decimated landscape of his soul, obscuring the ragged, desolated mess he was.

She was getting what she required, and so was he.

Good thing. He needed to be at the Black Dagger Brotherhood training center in about an hour, in some kind of shape to continue his education. Being a soldier in the fight against the Lessening Society? Walking the line between life and death?

Now that was finally going to get him what he was after.

Inner peace through acts of war: Because he had to believe if you were facing off with the undead, surely you were too busy trying to stay alive to worry about anything else.

Fucking perfect.

STATE UNIVERSITY OF NEW YORK, CALDWELL CAMPUS

Elise, blooded daughter of the Princeps Felixe the Younger, smiled at the human male across the library table from her. "Of course I'd stay late. I'm not going to leave you to deal with all this by yourself."

"All this" was a debris field of final papers sufficient to cover every square inch of surface except for two feet in front of her and two feet in front of Professor Troy Becke. Although the submissions for Psych 342 had been filed electronically, Troy believed in printing them out for grading purposes—and after having been through midterms with the man, Elise had to agree. There was something different about holding the work in your hands and being able to write your thoughts down. It had to do with the lack of speed, she'd decided.

Too easy to scan if you were doing things electronically, and she was such a quick typist; having to handwrite things gave her time to really think things through.

Troy sat back and stretched. "Well, considering it's ten o'clock at night only days before Christmas, I'd say it's yeoman's duty."

As he smiled at her, she measured him. He was tall for a human, and he had bright blue eyes and the sort of face that was so open and friendly, it could make you forget that you were a stranger posing in a strange land, a foreigner who had come to visit and stayed because they were captivated by the freedom that was enjoyed by the natives.

"So that was my last one." She put the printout on her stack of graded papers on the left and twisted in the chair to crack her spine, a little sunburst of relief easing at her waist. "You know, this was a good group of students. They really got it—"

"I'm sorry," he interjected.

Elise frowned. "Why? I'm your teaching assistant. This is my job. Besides, I'm learning even more now. . . ."

She let her voice trail off because she was pretty sure Troy wasn't hearing a thing she was saying. He was looking around at the stacks that bracketed them in their alcove, his eyes not really focused.

As a vampire among humans, Elise was always a little twitchy, and she hopped on the scan train, glancing about in case Troy had sensed something she had not.

The Foster Newmann library was a place where students went to study even though print was dead and notes were now taken on laptops and chalk no longer existed in classrooms. Four stories high, and marked by stretches of shelving that were broken up by sitting areas, the facility was a place where she always felt safe, with nothing but her studies and her ambitions before her.

It was when she was at home, in her father's mansion, that she was hunted. Pursued. Threatened.

Although that was just allegorically speaking.

Noticing nothing, she rubbed her eyes, the reality that she was going to have to return to that big old house making her head pound.

Seven years into her studies and she was starting to get close to her goal. Thanks to an undergrad major in psych, she had been allowed into the Psy.D. in Clinical Psychology program without a master's. Her goal was to go into a private counseling practice for the race when she was finally finished, specializing in PTSD.

After the raids of two years before, there were a lot of vampires suffering from traumatic loss, and so few avenues for anyone to seek social workers and counseling.

Of course, the raids had also slowed her down, too, her father insisting that she cease her studies and decamp with her aunt, uncle, and first cousin out to a safe house far from Caldwell. As soon as they had come back, however, she had gotten on track again—although tragedy had struck once more, making it all so much harder for her.

She hated lying to her sire every night. Hated the subterfuge about where she was going and who she was with. But what other choice did she have? The small window of freedom she'd been granted had been slammed shut.

Especially after her first cousin had been beaten to death four weeks ago.

Elise still couldn't believe Allishon was gone, and her father, uncle, and aunt were likewise in a state of renewed shock—or at least, she assumed they were. No one was talking about the loss, the sadness, the anger. But they were reacting to it, for sure: Elise's father was so tense and grim, it was as if he were going to snap at any moment. Her aunt had been locked up in her bedroom for a month. And her uncle was a ghost who wandered around, throwing no shadows, casting no footfalls.

Meanwhile, Elise was sneaking out of the mansion to go to school. But come on. She had worked for years and years to get this far, and if anything, the way her family was handling Allishon's loss was exactly why the race needed good, well-trained psychologists.

Stuffing things under the proverbial rug was a recipe for interpersonal disaster.

"I'm just tired," Troy said.

Yanking herself out of introspection, she looked at the man. Her first thought was that he was hiding something. Her second was that she had to know what it was.

"Is there anything I can help with?"

He shook his head. "No, the problem's on my side."

As he tried to smile, she caught the scent of something in the air. Something . . .

"I think you better go." He leaned down for the duffel bag he'd brought the exams in and started shuffling stacks of papers into it. "The roads will be getting bad because of the snow."

"Troy. Can you please talk to me?"

He got up, tucking his loose shirt into his khaki slacks. "It's all good. And I guess I won't see you until after New Year's."

Elise frowned. "I thought you wanted me to do the syllabus planning with you for Psych four-oh-one, two twenty-eight, and the seminar on Bipolar Two? I have tomorrow night free—"

"I don't think that's a good idea, Elise."

What the heck was that scent—

Oh. Wow.

With a flush, she realized what it was. Especially as his eyes shifted away from her: He was aroused. Because of her.

He was seriously, sexually aroused. And he was not happy about it.

"Troy."

Her professor put his hand up. "Look, it's nothing you've done. It's not you, honest."

As he didn't go any further than that, she found herself wishing he would just come out with it all. Not because she was necessarily attracted to him, but she hated anything that was hidden. She had had more than enough of that from her family's perennial stiff-upper-lip way of handling life's inevitable unpleasantnesses.

Besides, it wasn't as if she wasn't attracted to him. He was appealing in an unthreatening kind of way. Smart, funny, and a heartthrob to his female students for sure. God knew she'd seen plenty of the humans he taught stare at him like he was a god.

And maybe she had thought about what it would be like with him. The touching. The kissing. The . . . other things.

She had no male prospects currently and that was not going to change anytime soon. Especially given the fact that she was fouled in the eyes of the *glymera*.

Not that anyone knew that, as the male she had lain with that one time had been killed in raids.

"I am of age," she heard herself say.

His eyes flipped to hers. "What?"

"I am not young. Too young, I mean. For what's on your mind."

Troy's gaze flared as if that was the last thing he'd expected her to say. And then he looked at her lips.

Yes, she thought. He was safe, this human. He would never hurt her or pressure her, as that kind of aggression was not in his nature—and even if it was, she could easily overpower him. Besides, she was never going to be mated, would never have a life wholly outside of her father's control, never experience anything more than the distilled life stories in her course books.

"Elise." He scrubbed his palm down over his face. "Oh, God . . ."

"What? And no, I'm not going to pretend I don't know what we're talking about here."

"There are rules. Between professors and students."

"You're not teaching any classes of mine."

"You're my T.A."

"I make my own decisions, no one else does."

At least that was true here, in the slice of life she had in the human world. And she would be damned if some rule in a society that was not her own was going to keep her from doing what she wanted. She got way too much of that in her species.

Troy laughed in a harsh rush. "I can't believe we're having this conversation. I mean, I've had it in my head with you a thousand times. I just never thought it would actually happen."

"Well, I don't care what people think." And that much was true. When it came to humans. "And I'm not afraid."

"I can't say the same. I mean, I've never done this before. I know it's a cliché, the whole teacher/student thing. But I've never crossed this line. I thought I was, you know, stronger than this. You're different, though, and because you are . . . you're making me act differently."

There was a curious helplessness to him as he stared at her, as if he had struggled and lost a fight.

Now she looked at his lips.

As she did, his scent flared again and she saw his chest rise—

"Professor Becke? Hi!"

The human woman who came up to him was petite and curvy and wearing perfume. With her makeup on and her blond hair curling around her shoulders, she seemed like she belonged on a poster advertising the university as an attractive and fun place to go.

"I'm in your survey class, or was in it, and my roommate—she's here also. Hey! Amber! Look who's here! Anyway, I was the one who had to go home because my parents were getting a divorce, and you let me delay my exam. Well, I . . ."

All kinds of nouns and verbs continued to come out of the girl, and then Amber, the roommate, bounded over like a puppy. Meanwhile, Troy seemed scrambled, as if the intimacy that had flared before the interruption was a place he had to travel back from.

Gathering her coat and her backpack, Elise pushed her chair into the table and lifted her hand in a goodbye. As he nodded at her, there was a desperation in his eyes, as if a gift he had long hoped for was slipping out of his hands and falling into a ravine.

Elise made the sign for call-me up by her ear, and then she was striding out to where the reception area was. The older man who worked nights behind the desk was bent over his computer as if he were in the process of logging out of the network, his blue parka and his knit hat already placed on the counter next to a thermos she guessed was empty.

"Good night," she said as she came up to the glass doors.

He grunted. Which was the best he ever did.

Outside, the wind was strong and cold as a slap, and she one-strapped her pack so she could zip up her coat. The walkway was illuminated by lampposts, and sure enough, delicate flakes were wisping in and out of the light as if they wanted to dance with each other, but were feeling shy.

For a moment, Elise glanced around and thought that Allishon would never enjoy the quiet night again, never walk among swirling flurries, feeling the warmth inside her coat and the chill upon her cheeks. And Elise wished she had spent more time with the female. The two of them had been so different, so opposite, the bookworm and the wild child, but still, maybe there could have been some kind of opportunity to change the outcome. Shift the destiny. Flip back the switch that had taken Allishon away from safety.

Not to be, however.

Elise stepped off onto the brown grass and strode away from the light, the parking lot, the classroom building that was close on the other side.

When the shadows fully claimed her . . . she dematerialized away, traveling in a scatter of molecules to her father's sprawling Georgian mansion that was miles away from campus. Troy was on her mind, maybe as a distraction, maybe as a legitimate curiosity. Probably some of both. Still, the trip didn't require much more than the blink of an eye and a wink of the will.

As she re-formed on her father's lawn, Allishon's death converged with memories of Troy staring across the table of papers, his eyes burning, his body sending off its scent of arousal. Life could change in a moment, and didn't that mean you should take advantage of however many nights and days you had?

Time wasn't so much relative as an illusion. If she'd known her cousin was going to die, she herself would have made different choices. On that theory, if she knew she had a week left, or maybe a month, shouldn't she see where things went with a male, even if he was just a human?

Troy had her number. And she had his. How did this work? They texted occasionally, but only about scheduling things.

A date was a "thing" to be scheduled, though, right?

Walking in the grand front door, she started trying out conversations in her head, ways of greeting and following up on—

"Where have you been!"

Elise froze. And realized as she saw a grandfather clock and a set of stairs that was right out of Buckingham Palace that she had seriously screwed up: She'd come in through the formal entrance . . . and walked right past the open door to her father's study.

With her coat on, and snowflakes in her hair, and her backpack on her shoulder.

"Elise!"

Through the open door, her father had stood up from behind his carved desk, his shock and horror more appropriate to someone having crashed an SUV through his mansion.

And actually, his pale face, his peeled-wide eyes, and his ruffled evening coat might have been funny. Under other circumstances.

With a curse, Elise closed her lids and braced herself for the onslaught.

TWO

"So what is that?"

As Rhage's daughter piped up, he froze with his gun halfway into his under-arm holster. For a split second, he decided to pretend that he hadn't heard her—but that was going to get him nowhere. In the two months or so that he and Mary had had Bitty, they'd both learned that she was smart as a whip and tenacious as flypaper.

Ordinarily, he got a kick out of those two defining characteristics. When it came to describing the technical specs of a forty-caliber killing weapon to his thirteen-year-old? Pass. He wished she had an empty skull and ADD.

"Ah . . ."

He glanced into the mirror over the bureau, hoping against hope that she had moved on to something, anything else. Nope. Bitty was sitting on his and Mary's new bed, the one in the third-floor suite that Trez had graciously moved out of so the three of them could have ad-joining rooms. The girl was way on the small side, her skinny arms and legs the kind of thing that made him want to move to the tropics instead of live in Upstate New Freezing-Fucking-Cold. Hell, even under a body weight's worth of fleece, she seemed fragile.

But the oh, dainties ended right there. Her brown eyes were direct as an adult's, old as a mountain range, keen as an eagle's. Her dark hair was thick and shiny, falling past her shoulders, nearly the exact color of Mary's. And her aura, her . . . whatever, life force, spirit, soul . . . was as tangible as her physical form seemed almost transient.

He took pride in the fact that the longer she stayed with them, the more she was emerging. Not like a flower.

Like a fucking oak.

Buuuuuuuuuuuuut that didn't mean he wanted to get into the nitty-gritty of his job killing *lessers* with her.

And nope. Really not interested in the whole birds-and-bees talk, either. At least they had another twelve years or so to prepare for that.

"Father?" she prompted.

Rhage closed his eyes. Okay, so every time she called him that, his heart got too big for his chest and this unreal, won-the-lottery feeling sunrised all over him. It took him back to right after he and Mary had been mated and he'd gotten to call her *shellan* for the first time.

Pure, full-bore awesomeness.

"What is it?" Bitty prompted.

That happy pink bubblegum glow faded as he seated the gun and clipped its strap over the butt. "It's a weapon."

"I know—it's a gun. But what kind?"

"A Smith and Wesson forty."

"How many bullets are in it?"

"Enough." He picked up his leather jacket and smiled. "Hey, you ready for movie night when I get home?"

"Why don't you want to tell me about your gun?"

Because if you're the audience, I can't separate what I do with it from a discussion of its specs. "It's just not all that interesting."

"It's what keeps you alive, though, right?" The little girl's eyes locked on the black daggers that were holstered on his chest, handles down. "Like your knives."

"Among other things."

"So that's interesting. To me, at least."

"Look, how 'bout we talk about this when your mom and I are both here? You know, like, later tonight."

"But how do I know you'll come home safe?"

Rhage blinked. "I am never not coming back to you and Mary."

"What if you die, though?"

His first thought was:

MAAAAAAAAAAAAAAAAAAAAARY!

His Mary, as a trained therapist—who had treated Z with all his demons, for godsakes—could deal with this so much better than some meathead fighter like him could. But his *shellan* was at Safe Place, working, and he didn't feel right about calling and possibly interrupting her with anything other than an arterial bleed or a house fire. Zombie apocalypse. H-bomb behind the compound.

And fine, maybe if they were out of cheesecake.

Except he needed to man up. What was going down right now? This was Father Shit, and not only had he signed up for exactly these kinds of hard conversations when he and Mary had started the adoption process, he really didn't want to admit this early that he couldn't handle the job.

Okay, note to self: Find an online course on being a father. Surely there had to be a curriculum for this kind of thing.

"I'm just worried," she said. "It's scary for me, okay?"

Jesus, it was scary for him, too. He had so much more to lose with her in his life.

Rhage went over and knelt down. Bitty had tucked her arms around herself and her eyes were steady as if she were not going to accept a load of bullcrap.

Opening his mouth, he . . .

Closed it. And wondered what he needed to do to jump-start his brain. Maybe bang it into a wall?

"You know my car?" he heard himself say.

As Bitty nodded, he had an image of Puskar Nepal–ing himself until he passed the fuck out from foot-to-forehead contact: Of all the things for his subconscious, or whatever was running his program, to spit out, he led with his GTO?

"Well, you know when I was teaching you to drive?"

Yeah, Bits, right before those kids attacked Mary and you found out that I have a dragon for an alter ego? Har-har, good times, good times.

God, he wanted to throw up.

As she nodded again, he said, "You remember when you were figuring out the gears and the steering wheel and the brakes? Going back and forth, again and again, until you could get it right?"

"Yes."

"You know how I drive that car?"

"Oh, yes." Now, she smiled. "Fast. Very fast and fun. It's like a rocket."

"So, someday, you're going to drive her just as well as I do. You're going to know where the gears are by feel, and you're going to work the clutch and the gas without thought. And if someone swerves in front of you, you're going to react so quick and so sure, you're not going to be aware of even thinking about it. If somebody slams on the brakes, you're going to shift lanes instinctually. You're going to feel the tires hydroplaning on the highway in the rain and you're going to know to slow up on the gas, but not hit the brakes. And all of that is going to happen because you're going to practice, practice, practice on a car that is kept in tip-top shape."

"I'm going to practice. So I drive better."

"Right. Even if the people around you drive dangerously, you're going to be aware and focused and trained to deal with whatever comes at you." He put his palm over his daggers, over his heart. "I have been out there fighting for a century, Bitty. And everything I take with me into the field—the weapons, the gear, the support in the form of my brothers—all of it is engineered to keep me safe. Is it a perfect system? No. But it's the best it gets, I promise you that."

Bitty's arms uncoiled and she looked down. The pink and green bracelet on her wrist was made out of faceted beads that sparkled like real gems. Moving the thing around and around, she took a deep breath.

"Are you . . . good at it? I mean, the fighting?"

God, he wished he was an accountant. He really did. Because if he were some pocket-protector'd numbers cruncher, he wouldn't be having to tell an innocent that he excelled at killing things.

"Are you?" she prompted.

"I'm very good at keeping myself and my brothers safe. I'm so good at it, they're having me teach younger people how to do it."

She nodded once again. "That's what they were saying. At Last Meal the other night. I heard people talking about you and the other Brothers teaching people."

"That's where I'm heading right now. While you hang here with Bella and Nalla, I'm meeting the trainee class out in Caldwell to show them how to stay safe."

Bitty tilted her head, her brown hair cascading over her shoulder. And he let her stare at him for as long as she wanted. If that made him a little late to work, who cared.

"You must be really good at it to be a teacher."

"I am. I swear to you, Bitty. I am effective and I take no more chances than I absolutely have to in order to get my job done."

"And the beast will keep you safe, won't he."

Rhage nodded. "You better believe it. You saw him. You know what he's like."

She smiled, sunshine replacing the worry. "He likes me."

"He loves you. But he doesn't love people who get aggressive with me."

"That makes me feel better."

"Good." He put his palms up, and as she high-fived him, he said, "You're never going to be alone, Bitty. I promise you."

In that moment, as he sought to relieve any and all of her anxiety—and his own, for that matter—he nearly came out with the one thing Bitty didn't know about her adoptive parents. Yes, her new old man had a dragon living under his skin, but her new mom had an even fancier secret.

Mary was a unique flavor of immortal. Thanks to the Scribe Virgin—and this remained true even though V's *mahmen* was no longer in charge—Mary did not age, and could choose when she went unto the Fade. It was a gift beyond measure, insulating this family in ways that other people's weren't.

Except Rhage stayed quiet on that front. Even though the knowledge might have helped Bitty in the moment, he really felt like it was Mary's information to share, not his.

"You're never going to be alone, Bitty," he repeated. "I swear to you."

As Mary sat behind her desk at Safe Place, she put her bag down and shrugged out of her parka. Extending her arm, she pulled the sleeve of her turtleneck up and smiled at the pink and green bracelet that twinkled at her wrist.

She and Bitty had made matching ones the other night, the pair of them sitting at Fritz's kitchen table in the mansion, a jewelry-making kit spread out everywhere, a huge array of clear plastic boxes holding a rainbow's worth of iridescent beads. They had talked about nothing and everything, and greeted each person who came in, and split a bag of Combos and a Mountain Dew. They had also made a necklace for

Rhage, a different-colored bracelet for Lassiter, and braid for Nalla to play with. And even Boo had come over and curled up to watch, the black cat's green eyes inspecting everything.

In a mansion full of priceless stuff? That time together had been the most precious, irreplaceable thing.

Looking across her desk, Mary reached out and picked up a photograph of Bitty from two weeks before, when the little girl had been taking selfies with Rhage's phone. Bit was making a crazy face, her dark hair back-brushed until she looked like something out of an eighties glam metal band.

And in fact, Lassiter was over on the left, doing his best Nikki Sixx impression.

Unexpected tears pricked Mary's eyes. In all her life, she had never expected to be a woman who had pictures of a daughter at her work desk. Nah, that hypothetical, blessed, stranger of a person, that lucky female who had a husband and a family, and holidays to look forward to, and homemade things on her wrist? That had always been someone else, a stranger whose reality was something you watched on TV or saw in Maytag ads or overheard at the table next door in a restaurant.

While you were eating alone.

Mary Luce was the nurse to an ailing mother who had died horribly and too young. Mary Luce was the cancer survivor left infertile after chemo. Mary Luce was the ghost on the fringes, the shadow that passed unnoticed through a room, an allegory of where you didn't want to end up.

Except life had corkscrewed on her in the best of all possible ways. Now? She was exactly where she had never even dared to dream of being.

And yup, this unexpected destiny came with a not-too-small dose of PTSD. Hell, sometimes, when she woke up next to her gorgeous vampire of a husband? And especially now, when she tiptoed into another bedroom to check on Bitty at nightfall? She expected to wake up, back in her nightmare of a real life.

But no, she thought as she put the picture down. This was the real stuff. Here and now was the story she was living.

And it was . . . amazing. So full of love, family, and happiness that it felt as though the sun lived in the center of her chest.

They were all survivors, her, Rhage, and Bitty. She of her illness. Rhage of the curse he had to live with. Bitty of the unimaginable domestic abuse she and her *mahmen* had suffered at the hands of her birth father. The three of their lives had started to intersect here, at Safe Place, when Bitty and her *mahmen* had come in seeking shelter. And then Bitty's mother had died, leaving her an orphan.

The opportunity to take the girl in had seemed too good to be true. It still did, sometimes.

If they could just get through this six-month waiting period, the adoption would be final and Mary could take a deep breath. At least there were no relatives coming forward. Even though Bitty had talked initially about some uncle, her mother had never mentioned having a brother or disclosed anything about any blood relations, either during intake or in subsequent therapy sessions. Notices posted on closed Facebook and Yahoo groups had yielded nothing so far.

God willing, it would stay that way.

On that note, Mary signed in to the computer network, her heart starting to bang in her ribs, a sick flush blooming in her body. As social media aficionados went, she was below amateur status, the anti-Kardashian—and yet every night, but only once a night, she hopped onto Facebook.

And prayed she found nothing.

The FB group she checked was one specifically devoted to vampires, its closed roster restricted to members of the species. Created by V after the raids, moderated by Fritz's staff, the clearinghouse was an opportunity for folks to connect about anything from safe-house locations—always in code—to garage sales.

Scanning the posts in the last twenty-four hours, she exhaled in a rush. Not at thing.

The relief made her office spin around—at least until she went to check the Yahoo group. Recipe for Crock-Pot. Knitting group having a meeting . . . snowblower for sale . . . question about where to get a computer fixed . . .

Also nothing.

"Thank you, God," she whispered as she put another small check on her wall calendar.

Almost to the end of December, which meant they were nearly two whole months down. By May? They could move forward.

As her heart shifted out of tachycardia, she wondered how in the hell she was going to face this IT gauntlet another hundred and thirty times or so. But she had no other choice. The good news was that she was able to stick to this once-and-only-once-a-night check. Otherwise she'd be on her damn phone every fifteen minutes.

She had to be fair, though, to whoever else might be out there. Extinguishing parental rights in blood relations was serious business, and with no modern precedents in the vampire race to follow, she, Marissa, as head of Safe Place, Wrath, the Blind King, and Saxton, the King's head counsel, had had to devise a procedure that provided an adequate notice period.

Emotions did not have waiting periods, however, and moms and dads who loved their kids couldn't toggle back the speed of their hearts.

As if Marissa could read minds, the female put her head in the open doorway. "Anything?"

Mary smiled at her boss and her dear friend. "Nothing. I swear, I have never been more excited for May to get here."

"I've always had a good feeling about this, you know."

"I don't want to jinx anything, so I'm staying quiet." Mary focused on the calendar again. "Hey, I'm not going to be in tomorrow night. Bitty's got her physical exam scheduled."

"Oh, that's right. Good luck—and it's too bad you have to go all the way in to Havers's."

"Doc Jane says she just doesn't have the appropriate knowledge base. Pediatrics for vampires is a thing, apparently."

Marissa smiled gently. "Well, my brother may be complicated for me personally, but I have never questioned his ability to provide good care to his patients. Bitty couldn't be in better hands."

"I'd really rather just keep her with us at the training center's clinic. But at the end of the day, what's right for her is all we care about."

"That's called being a good parent."

Mary looked at her bracelet. "Amen to that."

THREE

"Elise! Do not tell me you have been to university!"

As her father came charging out of his study, he looked as much like a raging bull as a whip-thin, utterly distinguished aristocrat could—which was, actually, not like a bull at all, but more like a European prince trying to flag his butler down. Felixe the Younger did have, however, a highly uncharacteristic flush to his face, and he had failed to button his evening jacket as he had rushed from his desk at her.

If he'd been a commoner, he would have been picking up pieces of furniture and throwing them around as he carpet-bombed the air with variations on an f-word theme.

And as she faced off at him, from out of nowhere, she heard that line from *M*A*S*H*: *Winchesters do not sweat, we perspire. And Winchesters do not perspire.*

Or something to that effect. You had to love Charles Emerson Winchester III.

"Explain yourself!"

There were a couple of ways to handle this, she supposed. Deny,

deny, deny, but with a backpack hanging off her shoulder, those pesky snowflakes all over her, and the fact that she'd previously told him she was going to stay in and read? Hard sell, for one thing; for another, she detested lies. Another option was walking away, but that was a total no-go—she had been raised properly, and that meant that she couldn't be rude to her elders.

Annnnnd that left her with door number three.

The truth.

"I'vebeengoingbacktoschool." As her father frowned and leaned in toward her, she put some volume into her voice and slowed things down. "Yes, I have been going to school again."

Her father fell silent in shock and she studied him as if he were a stranger. He had a patrician face, the even features distilled by good breeding to the point that you were aware he was of masculine derivation, but the sexual affiliation was at a whisper, not a shout. His hair was dark, whereas hers was streaked with blond, and his eyes were pale gray, not blue. But their diction was identical and so were their good posture, their moderated affect . . . and their sense of values.

So, yes, she did feel as though she had done something wrong. Even though she was past her transition, arguably of age especially if you applied a human standard, and had done nothing more reckless than sit in a quiet library for three hours grading papers.

"Are you . . . have you . . . how can you . . ." It was a while before her father could get through an entire sentence. "I forbade you to go there! After the raids, I explicitly told you that it was unsafe and that you were not to be permitted to go! And that was before . . ."

Elise closed her eyes. That last sentence wasn't finished because it was That Which Was Not Discussed.

Allishon's name hadn't been uttered since the night word had come unto the household that she had passed. They hadn't even had a Fade ceremony for her.

"Well!" he demanded. "What have you to say for yourself!"

"I'm sorry, Father, but I—"

"How can you possibly be so delinquent! If your *mahmen* were still alive, she would be apoplectic! How long has this been going on?"

"A year."

"A *year*!"

At that moment, the butler came scurrying in from the back of the house, as if he had heard the disturbance and was concerned some crazy person had broken in to the mansion for which he was responsible. When the *doggen* got a gander at her father? He backed off fast as a mouse before a cat.

"You have been going for a *year*?" her father hissed, his voice shaking. "How have you—you have been lying to me? For that long?"

Elise shucked her backpack and put it between her feet. "Father, what was I to do?"

"Stay here! It is dangerous in Caldwell!"

"But the raids are over. And even when they occurred, the slayers were hitting vampire targets, not human ones. It's a human school—"

"Humans are savages! You know exactly how much damage they do to each other! You see the news—the guns, the violence! Even if they were not targeting you as another species, you could get caught in the crossfire!"

As Elise's eyes drifted to the high ceiling, she searched for some correct combination of words to make this all go away.

"We're *not* doing this here." Her father's voice dropped. "In my study. Now."

When he jabbed a finger to his open door, she picked up her backpack and headed in that direction. Behind her, tight on her heels, her father fell into a full march, and she was not surprised when the carved door clapped shut, closing them in together.

The room was lovely, a fire crackling in the hearth, cheery light flickering over the leather chairs, the first editions on the mahogany shelves, the oil paintings of hunting dogs that her father had owned in the Old Country.

"Sit down," he snapped, though not loudly.

She knew exactly where he wanted her and she went to the chair across from his desk, lowering herself into its antique contours and being sure to keep her pack with her. The last thing she wanted was for him to take it away from her.

In the midst of this confrontation, the thing represented her freedom.

Felixe sat down and linked his fingers together as if he were attempting to control himself. "You know exactly what happens when a female goes out of the home unattended."

Elise looked up at the ceiling again and was careful to keep her voice low. "I'm not like Allishon."

"You're out in the human world. Just like her."

"I know where she went. It was not to university, Father."

"I'm not going to discuss the particulars and neither are you. What you are going to do is swear to me, right here and now, that you will not violate my trust again. That you will stay here and—"

Elise bolted up out of the seat before she was aware of moving. "I can't waste my life sitting here, night by night, going nowhere and doing nothing but needlepoint. I want my advanced degree, I want to finish what I started! I want a life!"

As he recoiled, he seemed as surprised by the outburst as she was. And to defuse the insubordination, Elise sank back down into the chair. "I'm sorry, Father. I don't mean to speak rashly, it's just . . . why can't you understand that I want to be free to live?"

"That is not your station and you know it. I have been more than lenient with you, but that time has passed. I will be entertaining suitable males for mating—"

Elise let her head fall back. "I want more than that, Father."

"Your first cousin is *dead*. After they already lost their son in the raids! You see the suffering of her parents nightly in this house! Do you want that for me? Do you care so little for me that you want me to mourn my only daughter after I've already lost my *shellan?*"

Swallowing a groan, she stared across the desktop. The objects upon it—the sterling-silver-framed pictures of her and her mother, the pens in their holders, the ashtray in which one of his pipes sat—were as familiar as the backs of her own hands, things that she had never not known. They were also part of the comfort of home, symbols of the security that she at once valued, but also wanted to escape.

"Well?" her father said. "Do you want that for me?"

"What I want is to talk about her." Elise sat forward. "No one ever speaks about Allishon. I don't even know how she died. Peyton came here and talked to the three of you behind closed doors—next thing I know, her room is shut up tight, Auntie has taken to her bed, and Uncle looks like a zombie. Nobody has told me anything. There's no Fade ceremony, no mourning, just this shut-off void in the midst of everyone suffering. Why can't we just come forward and be honest—"

"This is not about your cousin—"

"Her name is Allishon. Why can't you say her name?"

Her father's thin lips got even thinner. "Do not attempt to distract me from the real problem. Which is you lying to me whilst you put yourself in danger. What happened to your cousin is in the past. There is no cause for conversation."

Elise shook her head. "You're so wrong about that. And if you're going to try to use whatever tragedy happened to her to persuade me, then you better tell me what really happened."

"I don't have to explain anything to you." Her father banged a fist into his desk, making one of the framed photographs jump. "You are my daughter. That is a sufficiency unto itself."

"Why are you so afraid of talking about her?"

"This conversation is over—"

"Is it because you think she got what she deserved?" Elise was aware of her body starting to shake as she finally spoke what had been on her mind for weeks. "Is nobody in this house saying anything because you all disapproved of the way she was behaving, and the fact that she died because of it doesn't make you sad, but rather angry? Angry because you don't want the potential social complications for our bloodline?"

"Elise! You were not raised to—"

"Allishon went out at night. She dated males who were not of our class and consorted with humans—"

"Stop it!"

"—and now she's dead. Tell me, honestly, are you really worried about me getting hurt—or is it more about the potential embarrassment for you and the bloodline? One unconventional female with a tragic event may eventually be forgiven, but two? Never. Is that your truth, Father? Because if it is, that strikes me as far more ugly than my seeking an education."

Axe left The Keys with the scent of the human woman on his skin. As he stepped out of the sprawling, interlocking series of buildings, he breathed in the cold, fresh air and felt his overheated body steam under his cloak. Flurries were falling from a heavy cloud cover, and all around him the city was alive, sirens sounding in the distance, music from the club thumping in a hush, traffic on the Northway rumbling along.

He wanted to go home and take a shower, wash himself clean of the filthy, nasty sex he'd had all over her body, but there was no time.

Finding a thick of shadows, he whipped off that new skull mask he'd had made for himself and disappeared it into the cloak. Then he removed the great hanging weight from his shoulder, taking a black shirt out of another inner pocket, and putting the wifebeater on over his head. His weapons were hidden in still more compartments, and he retrieved them and their holsters from their Velcro strapping system. Arming himself, he gathered the voluminous fall of the cloak and folded it into itself until the outerwear appeared to be nothing more than a three-quarter-length coat.

A moment later, he dematerialized and re-formed in an alley eleven blocks farther into the worst part of Caldie.

He was not the first of his fellow trainees to arrive. Peyton and Boone were already there, the pair of them standing together under a fire escape. They were in black and as heavily armed as Axe was, but unlike him, they didn't smell like sex.

And Peyton didn't smell like weed or booze, either. Fucking miracle.

The male smiled. "Been busy?"

"Not at all." Axe clapped palms with him and did the same to Boone. "Where's everyone?"

Peyton smiled, flashing his fangs. The guy was right out of the Perfectly Bred Handbook—and so exactly the kind of bastard Axe hated on principle. Rich, blond-haired, with polished nails and an off-duty wardrobe that looked like something Zoolander would wear, Pey-pey was a pey-pain in the ass. The only thing that saved him? He was a helluva shot, and either too arrogant or too stupid to understand his own limits: In training, he fought just as hard as everyone else did, took way too many chances with himself and his safety, and was so out of control, all Axe could think of was a Lamborghini that had lost half of its wheels, most of its undercarriage, and all of its brakes.

As it headed for a brick wall.

So yeah, Peyton, first blooded son of Peythone, was the exception that proved the aristocrats-should-never-be-in-the-field rule.

But Axe still wasn't all buddy-buddy with the SOB.

Not that he went there with anybody.

Boone, on the other hand, was the anti-Pey-pey. Quiet, huge, and unusually physically adept, he was the crouching tiger of the group, the prowler who kept to himself and the shadows, the one who was most likely to pounce on your back and slit your throat with a knife you weren't even aware of him having in his hand. Axe was pretty sure the guy had been seriously fucked up by somebody or something earlier in his life. For all his outward calm, Boone was never, ever truly relaxed or at ease. Whether he was reading on his iPhone, listening to his music on the bus, or waiting for commands from the Brothers, you always had the sense he knew where everybody in a given space was.

As if he were waiting for an attack—and goddamned if he was going to let anyone get the best of him.

Watch the sleeper, Axe always thought. Before the cocksucker went Grim Reaper all over your ass.

Craeg and Paradise arrived next, the pair of them dressed in black and covered in weapons. The couple was as committed as a mated twosome, but they were not lovey-dovey in class or outside of it. And thank God for that.

After all, Axe hated vomiting—and if there was one thing guaranteed to make his stomach go evac? It was the sight of two people going baby-talk and gooey-eye'd all over each other. Back three years ago, when he'd been doing heroin all the time, his nightmare had been when he'd been too nodded out to change the channel on a Sandra-fucking-Bullock marathon.

Although he'd liked *The Blind Side.*

Axe acknowledged them and stepped back as the rest of the greetings rolled out. And then there was a lull, during which he amused himself by watching Peyton try not to stare at Paradise. It was the same thing every night, that weak pining after a female the guy couldn't get, and it was good to see the pretty boy who undoubtedly had everything he ever wanted get shanked by fate.

So fucking pathetic.

Man, that was one lesson Axe's moms had taught him. Never give a female power over you. That shit will castrate you faster than a pair of surgical scissors.

Hell, look at what had happened to his old man after Axe's mom had left them. Decades and decades of mourning. A life wasted at the altar of "love." An otherwise good male brought to his knees and kept there by an abandonment that was based on what someone else could fucking buy her.

As an old, familiar pain lit off behind his sternum, Axe bolted away from the sensation even as his body didn't move. Refocusing on the Paradise-Peyton-Craeg triangle, which wasn't a triangle at all for Craeg-adise, he found himself smiling. Yeah, the fact that the poor kid had won the girl made him happy. Craeg was the alpha of all alphas, the de facto leader of the trainees, but he came from nothing, just like Axe. Paradise, on the other hand, was the daughter of the King's First Advisor. You didn't get more pedigreed than that.

But she had picked the scrub over the Great Gatsby.

Attagirl. One more reason to like her. Aside from her hunting skills.

The last trainee to arrive was the kind of female that would have gotten Axe's attention under any circumstances. And yup, with nothing but black leather covering her from head to foot, he took the opportunity to admire the view—at a respectful distance. She was the cobra in the group, a sinewy, powerfully dangerous thing of beauty, with teal eyes, reflexes quicker than C4 exploding, and a subversive nature that Axe totally got.

But he'd never hit that.

Even though she was hot as fuck, he had a couple of reasons for his uncharacteristic restraint, the main one being that you didn't shit where you ate. Although Craeg and Paradise had somehow won the destiny lottery by hooking up without losing their edge or hating each other in the end, that was not a set of dice Axe was interested in rolling. Oh, and P.S., he was about as into relationships as he was aristocrats.

As Novo eased back against the brick tenement next to him, he nodded to her.

"Cold tonight," Peyton said to no one in particular.

"It's December," Novo muttered. "You want it to be eighty?"

"Yup, I do."

Novo had some choice words under her breath for the guy, including "arrogant" and "fucker," but nobody paid any attention to it. The pair of them had turned into conversational snipers, but only at each other, and hey, popcorn-and-Coke'ing the show passed the time.

A blast of wind shot down the alley like it was being pursued by an enemy, and Axe flared his nostrils, testing the rush for scents of Brothers or humans . . . or their enemy, the Lessening Society.

Nada. And that frustrated him.

After seven weeks of intensive training, that had covered everything from hand-to-hand combat skills and firearms to poisons, bombs, and stalking techniques, Axe wasn't alone in thinking they were ready for something other than fighting in the gym with themselves and studying hypotheticals. Each of them had their own reasons for wanting to get in the war, but the common denominator was they were all chomping at the bit to light some shit up.

And come on. They had been going in to the Black Dagger Brotherhood's hidden training center six nights a week, for six to eight, sometimes ten, hours at a time. And it hadn't been a case of a couple of seminars in classrooms and a paper typed up on your laptop. It had been hard, grueling work, and none of them had failed—which proved the brutal tryouts, that had weeded the applicant pool from like sixty to the six of them, had picked the right half dozen to go through the program.

Axe tested the air again. Still nothing. He'd been stoked when, for the first time, they'd been instructed to meet not at wherever the bus was going to pick them up to drive them in, but rather here in the field.

Maybe they were finally getting a chance to fight for real.

Ten minutes later, the checking of the watches started, the wrists popping up at first on the down-low, and later with increasing annoyance.

Axe didn't bother checking his. They were in the right place. They'd gotten here at the right time. The Brothers would show when they were good and goddamn ready.

Fucking hell, this shit was making him twitchy, though.

He looked down the alley. Snow was starting to fall on the serious from all that cloud cover, but the currents of wind that topped these tightly packed four- and five-story deserted cages for humans meant that nothing penetrated the maze of alleys between the abandoned buildings. Off in the distance, sirens continued to echo back and forth across the city like the ambulance drivers and the cops were playing hide-and-seek blindfolded. No humans were walking anywhere in this area, as there was nothing to come here for, not even a crack house.

Those were a little to the west. About three blocks.

He knew because he'd used them—

The gunshots came from all directions.

Up above. Down in front. From behind.

Axe dived away from the bullets that whizzed by his ears and his ass, and instantly regretted that he hadn't thought to have guns in his hands already. They'd been taught that. Goddamn it.

As he rolled across the pitted pavement, he fumbled to get his forties against his palms, but it was like trying to catch tennis balls while you were falling down a crevasse: His coat was flapping around, getting tangled in his arms and slapping him in the face, and his limbs were sloppy and uncoordinated as he tried to find a way to save himself from getting killed.

Somehow he made it to a shallow doorway in the wall, got his guns up, and then he was assessing whether the fire was a test or the actual enemy. He couldn't tell. He couldn't see anything, couldn't scent much. People were running everywhere. Bullets were still flying. He had no idea who to make a target out of, or what he should do, or what the fuck was going on.

The chaos was unexpected. So was the grind-to-a-halt-while-faster-than-the-speed-of-light dichotomy: His brain couldn't seem to decide whether things were in slow motion or going at a dead run—

And then a bullet came so close to his face that the tip of his nose felt the burn.

Fuck this, he thought as he pivoted.

With a violent thrust, Axe smashed his shoulder into the door, splintering the rotten wood. Just as he was falling inward, Novo streaked by, and he caught her arm, yanking her in with him. Together, the pair of them landed on concrete that had all the give of a morgue slab, arms and legs tangling, a split second of oh-fuck freezing them both.

Right away, they were back up on the vertical, and just as they had been taught, they went spine-to-spine with guns raised, forming the best defensive unit they could. Axe's eyes burned as they strained to see something, anything, but the darkness was too thick to penetrate. His ears stepped into the sensory void, however, isolating and droning out the sounds of bullets and bodies moving in the alley, focusing on . . .

There was something dripping over to the left. Novo was breathing as hard as he was. And he could hear the beat of his own heart.

Wherever they were smelled like old air and twelve kinds of mold, suggesting that the place hadn't been opened up in a—

"Click, you're dead."

As the soft words were spoken, a gun muzzle made contact with his temple. And given the way Novo gasped, he was pretty sure that she had a forty pressed up tight to her chrome dome, too.

"Motherfucker," Axe muttered.

"Yup," the Brother Rhage said without censure. "Neither of you are coming down for First Meal tomorrow morning. You failed your first field test."

FOUR

Sometimes it was better to just walk away.

Not that Elise necessarily *felt* any better about the confrontation with her father. But at least, as she sat up in her bedroom, staring at her reflection in her vanity mirror, there was consolation to be had that things hadn't gotten even worse.

Which, considering the stuff she'd said to him . . .

What came next? Her lighting their house on fire?

She'd meant every last word, though. None of it had been for show or distraction. And maybe if they'd been a different kind of father and daughter, the hard things she'd laid out would have opened the door to greater closeness, and forgiveness, and a mutual grieving.

Instead, there had been anger on both sides, and now her father was going to petition the King to make her a *sehcluded* female. If she'd thought she'd had problems before? Assuming the petition was accepted—and given his station in the *glymera,* why wouldn't it be—she would have less than no rights. She would be a physical possession of her father's, like a lamp or a car. A toaster oven.

A fricking couch.

As far as her father was concerned, the issue was closed. She wasn't going to university anymore, and she was going to accept punishment for lying in the form of that guardianship. Done and dusted.

In the background, the details of her room became oh, so glaring, the silk brocade drapes, the canopied bed, the French antiques and the hand-painted wallpaper like a set for a Merchant Ivory film.

You know, something Keira Knightley would be in, wearing a corset and a cascading hairpiece.

None of it was Elise's style. Hell, she didn't even know what her style was.

As her cellphone started to ring, she took it out of the coat she still hadn't bothered to take off yet and looked at who it was.

"Thank God," she said as she braced her head in her hand. "I need you."

"Hey, I'm in the middle of training. Are you okay?" Peyton's voice was hushed, as if her cousin had cupped his hand around his mouth.

"No. I'm not."

"Look, I can't really talk now. I'm playing dead in an alley."

"What?" She knew the guy was into some kinky things, but really? "Where are you?"

"Like I said, in an alley," he whispered. "I just got killed in a field exercise and I'm waiting for my punishment. Meet me in an hour."

As he gave her an address downtown, she shook her head even though he couldn't see her. "No, you don't understand. While you're playing dead, I'm under house arrest. I'm stuck here."

"What?"

Guess two could play at the surprise, surprise! game. "Long story. I can't get away to see you—"

"Of course you can. Just crack a window and ghost out. I'll see you in an hour."

The connection was cut off, and Elise took the phone away from her ear as if she could will her cousin back on her cell.

Peyton had been the one to come and tell the family what had happened to Allishon. And although Elise had been forbidden to be in the room or hear any of the details, he had visited her afterward and told her if she needed anything, she could always come to him.

He'd probably meant that more in terms of dealing with Allishon's death, but Elise didn't feel like she had anywhere else to turn.

When her phone rang again, she answered immediately. "I'm serious, I can't leave."

"I'm sorry?" a male voice said.

"Troy! Oh, jeez. I, ah, was expecting someone else."

"I just wanted to know . . ." Her professor cleared his throat. "You know, that you got home okay. And I was, I was sorry we were interrupted."

"Well, you're a popular guy." Elise took a deep breath and really wished she could go back to worrying about something as simple as when they were going to go out. "You're bound to be approached in the library."

"Hey, are you okay? You sound off? Is it because—"

"Home problems. Nothing to do with you."

"You know, you've never spoken about your family. I mean, I know you're not married—but other than that . . ."

He had a nice voice, she thought. And his human accent was exotic in her ear. But it was so hard to switch gears from the very real trouble she had with her father to something as frivolous as dinner.

Which was clearly where he was headed.

"I don't even know where you're from," Troy prompted when she didn't say anything. "I've never been able to place your accent. European, I know, but . . ."

As he went quiet again, clearly hoping she'd fill in the details, she said, "No, I'm not from the States, it's true."

"How long ago did you come here?"

Oh, I was born in Caldwell. Just into a different species from you entirely.

"Am I prying too much?" he said. "I'm sorry."

"No. It's just . . . my father found out I was going to school and he's really angry at me. I've been sneaking around behind his back, and when I came home tonight, I got caught."

"He doesn't want you to get your degree?"

"No, not really. He's very . . ." She tried to think of the human word. "He's very traditional. Old school, you know. The only reason I got to go at all was because my mother talked him into it, but she passed during my freshman year and there you have it."

"I am so sorry for your loss."

Elise rubbed her aching head. "I appreciate that. Listen, Troy, I don't mean to be rude but—"

"It is a totally different culture for you, then."

"You have no idea," she muttered as she bared her fangs at the mirror. "Completely different."

"So what are you going to do? I mean, are you going to come back at all? And I'm not just asking because you're my T.A. Is there anything I can do to help? Maybe I can talk to him—"

"No, no. Honestly, that would be . . ." If her father knew she was actively associating with a human? Maybe thinking of dating him? Chains in the basement. "I don't know. Right now, it's not looking good for me."

The problem with figuratively dying in the middle of a training exercise? At the end of the session, you got to experience literal death.

Or as close to it as you could come while still having a damn heartbeat.

Axe let out a groan as he lay flat with his legs raised and held off the floor of an abandoned rooming house. Next to him, Novo was in the same pose, back against the cold concrete, legs extended out with heels six inches off the floor, palms down and by the hips. Every muscle, in both of them, was shaking, to the point where Axe's teeth were knocking together and sweat was pouring off his face.

At least they weren't the only ones getting schooled.

Everyone had gotten "killed," even Craeg.

The Brother Rhage swung his flashlight away from Axe and Novo, the beam falling over to where Paradise and Peyton were doing push-ups, Marine-style . . . before moving farther on to Boone and Craeg, who were rocking sit-ups.

When it came to stuff like this, the rule was, you went to exhaustion, and no one wanted to *no más* first. Even as Axe's body was in a full-on fist of pain, he set his brain free, taking himself back to The Keys, to the scaffolding, to that human female and the audience. He embedded his memory in the particulars, the feel of her under his hands, the taste of her mouth, the driving thrusts of the sex. There was nothing emotional in it; if his last experience before coming to class had been rotating tires on a car, he would have been thinking about wrenches, radials, and hubcaps.

He remembered everything he could and—

The blinding light of Rhage's torch splashed into Axe's face like acid. "Bkdw nbh, koy dwn skfg."

Axe tried to squeeze out a *What?* but it was like forcing a city bus through a keyhole.

Rhage bent down and spoke slowly. "You can stop, son. You're finished. Everyone else has quit."

It was like releasing a rubber band after you pulled the thing tight. His body let go with a corporeal *snap!*, all parts of him hitting the floor, the back of his skull included. As pain red-lit his brain, he didn't have the strength to tell his lungs to get pumping. They were either going to or not, and he didn't particularly care one way or another what the result was.

In his mind, he had a passing thought that that was not normal. Not healthy. Not right.

But it was not the first time he'd had such a blasé attitude to his own life and death.

Conversation happened above him, Vishous and Rhage talking at the rest of the class, but Axe was too busy with the re-oxygenation process to follow any of it.

When he finally sat up, he found that it was only trainees in the tenement. The Brothers had left.

A lighter flared, and Peyton's face got washed with orange illumination as he lit up a cigarette. "It's one a.m. We need food and a drink. This was a cluster-fuck tonight."

Muttering. Cursing. And then Craeg stuck out a hand to Axe to help him to his feet.

"You coming with us?" the guy said.

"Yeah," Axe heard himself reply. "What the hell."

He was tired, he was hungry, and he was poor—and whenever they went out, Peyton insisted on putting the bill on his AmEx. Good enough equation for Axe, especially as this way, he didn't have to admit to anyone that he survived on ramen noodles when he wasn't eating in the training center's break room.

"Come on," Craeg said at his elbow. "There's always tomorrow night."

"I want to fight now," Axe muttered.

"Hell, yeah. This sucked."

Click, you're dead.

At this rate, the Brotherhood wasn't going to let them engage the enemy for months. Maybe years.

Back out in the alley, nobody was talking much, that refrain clearly playing in other people's heads. At least the cold air felt good, and shit, the snow was really coming down now, the fall so thick the stuff was making it to the ground even in the alleys.

As they headed over to Commerce Street, Axe replayed the cluster-fuck over and over again, imaging himself with his guns out already, better prepared for the ambush, more ready to fight. Next thing he knew, Peyton's favorite after-training haunt had somehow materialized in front of him.

The cigar bar was as pretentious as it sounded, the interior done in English Country Estate with all kinds of leather armchairs and a lot of dark, heavy coffee tables and stools. There were no TV screens, though, no human sports flickering in the corners, and the food was good—not that his noodles were much of a standard. The main negative? The human clientele were such arrogant assholes with their Mercedes and their Range Rovers getting valet-parked, and their women-as-accessories girlfriends, but at least the dipshits were so self-absorbed that they couldn't care less about the vampires who mixed in with them.

Although Paradise and Novo got a lot of attention.

And yup, that made the males training with them want to get their weapons back out.

The maître d' rushed forward to Peyton and started in with the welcoming act. Their regular seating area had been reserved, and Axe took a pass on the ass-kissing session, walking away from the group to the back, where the emergency exit was.

Novo sat down with him and he ordered two Scotches, one for each of them, as the others filed in and deep-seated in the stuffed chairs. There was a low table in middle with a humidor and a series of ashtrays, and soon enough, there were various cocktails and then plates of tapas filling the surface up.

". . . gun range tomorrow."

Axe rubbed his face. "What?"

"I said," Novo repeated, "you might want to chill on that club before sessions. You're out of it right now, and you don't want to look bad on the gun range tomorrow."

"What's fucking my head is my shit shab performance tonight." He swirled the liquor in his glass, coating the ice cubes with a wash of Scotch. "Hell, maybe I'd have done better if I had stayed at The Keys awhile longer."

"You going to bring me sometime?" She took a pull off her glass and eased back. "I want to see what it's all about."

His eyes traveled up and down her body. "Yeah, I think you can handle it. Wouldn't say that about most females."

"Sexist much?"

"Females have better standards than males. But you're one of us."

Novo threw her head back and laughed. "I can't decide whether to be offended or not."

"If I order you another Scotch, will that help you—"

It was like a car accident in his head. One second, he was cruising along the deserted highway of his normal state as an oversexed, self-shaming guilt-whore . . . and the next, all his thoughts, every ounce of cognition, even on his subconscious level, slammed into a five-foot-ten-inch blond female with eyes like an angel, a body right out of heaven, and the unusual combination of a spooked look and a jaw that was forged in iron.

Axe straightened in his seat like someone had jumper-cabled his ass to a Chevy, and everything went tunnel with her the light at the end, the glow around her created by his reaction to her presence—

Peyton got in the way.

That miserable motherfucker had the colossal nerve to stand up and greet whoever it was with a hug. And then he talked to her, his muscular body blocking Axe's view, the back of his head making an excellent target for a bullet or the claw of a hammer or maybe even a falling piano as far as Axe was concerned.

"FYI," Novo said softly, "shooting him is not going to get my second Scotch faster. Because the waiter's going to call the police on you before he gets me my drink."

"What the hell are you talking about?" Axe growled.

Except then he looked down, and—well, hello there, Mr. Shiny—his gun was in his hand and ready to go.

Unlike in the alley.

Great, now his brain decides to catch up with protocol.

Muttering under his breath, Axe put the damn thing away, and finished off the liquor in his glass. And then he made a show of trying to get the waiter's attention—when what he was actually doing was attempting to lean around Peyton's make-a-better-door-than-a-window routine.

The problem finally got solved when the SOB stepped aside and started making introductions.

But then shit got so much worse.

"This is my cousin," Peyton said to everybody, "Elise."

FIVE

The way Elise saw it, having already been caught sneaking behind her father's back, it wasn't as if she could get in any worse trouble by going out one last time before the *sehclusion* hammer fell and she was locked in. Besides, Peyton was going to be with his fellow trainees. What could be safer than joining him?

The bottom line was that he was the only person she could think of to go to. Maybe there was a way out, a way to . . . she didn't know.

"Let me introduce you," her cousin was saying as he indicated the people sitting in a circle of heavy chairs.

Elise would have preferred to catch him alone, but she wasn't going to miss her chance. Besides, they could always step off into a corner together.

"This is Craeg—and you know Paradise."

Elise lifted her hand to the female. "Hi, wow, hello."

Paradise was the daughter of the King's First Advisor, a high-bred descendant of a Founding Family—and yet she had somehow managed to talk her way out of traditional roles and into the Brotherhood's training program. As a soldier. A fighter.

Maybe she could give some advice?

"That's Boone, Novo . . . and Axe."

Elise nodded at each of the trainees—until she got to the last one. Then she wasn't sure what she did.

Maybe she had a seizure? Or a spontaneous concussion? Because sure enough, she forgot about everything and everybody the instant she met his eyes, with the cigar bar, the humans around them, and even her reason for coming out disappearing as if someone had hit the world with a dry eraser.

He was extraordinary.

Or maybe . . . extraordinarily dangerous was more like it.

However she defined the effect of him, she had a sixth sense he was going to change her life.

The male was sitting outside the dim pool of light that fell from the ceiling, shadows blanketing him as if protecting one of their own. He had dark hair, black hair, that was thick and spiky, and a huge body that was arranged like he could spring forward on an attack in the blink of an eye. The tattoos that ran up half of his neck and piercings that marked his left ear and brow made him seem even more sinister. And then there were his clothes, black and draped over him, suggesting there could be weapons underneath.

With his chin dropped to his chest, he was staring at her from under his brows, his pale yellow eyes glowing as they locked on her and her alone.

Her first cogent thought was that he was a predator.

Her second . . . was that she wanted to be caught.

"Elise?"

As Peyton said her name and stepped in between them, she shook herself. "Sorry, what?"

Her cousin's frown suggested he'd noticed the connection, and—no surprise—he didn't approve. Then again, with the way that male in the corner was looking at her? You didn't have to be a possessive blood relative to not want any female anywhere near the guy.

"Sit next to Paradise, here," Peyton said. "And let's talk."

Boy, it was hot in here, Elise thought as she started to unbutton her coat.

"Elise? Hello?"

Shaking herself, she forced a smile. "I'm sorry. What?"

"Have a seat," her cousin muttered as he pointed to a padded bench that he'd pulled over.

"Right. Yes, of course."

As Elise tried to get her brain back on track, she parked it and glanced at Paradise—whose smile was open and as beautiful as the rest of her was. Which was kind of a surprise. Most females with her sorts of connections were straight-up mean girls.

"So Peyton told me what's going on as we were walking over here." Paradise tucked her legs under herself and leaned on the arm of her chair. "And I won't tell anyone, I promise. But I get it. I so get it."

Elise shook her head and started to parse through what she was prepared to share and what she wanted to keep to herself. Talking about the pathology around Allishon? Not going to happen.

"My father's not a bad male, he really isn't."

"God, of course not. He's just a traditional one, who's worried about his daughter in a troubling world. It's not an issue of good and bad. What it is about is your right to live a life even though you're a female in a rigid social role."

Elise exhaled. "How did you get into the training program at all? I mean, I've heard that they'll allow females, but . . ."

As she continued to speak, some kind of split-personality thing happened—half of her plugged into the conversation with Paradise, the other part of her right with that male, sensing his body, his presence, his power.

The effect he had on her was nothing like Troy, she thought. With the human in that library, she'd felt as though she was in front of a banked fire, where you kind of thought, Huh, maybe I'll sit here and put my palms out and feel the warmth. Or maybe I'll just stay where I am and admire the view of the flames. Or . . . what the hell, let me pick up a book and read for a while.

A lot of pleasant, non-threatening, but certainly interested, reflection.

That male in shadows over there? It was more like she was frozen to the bone and starving because she had wandered off a trail in a December snowstorm, and seventeen days later she was still tripping through the drifts, on the verge of collapse, her lungs stinging from a lack of oxygen, her head spinning, her whole body aching . . . and there, there on the horizon, was an acres-wide bonfire set by a lightning strike in the forest, the flames eating up the landscape, the blaze overwhelming and terrifying, deadly . . .

But nonetheless the only source of heat with which to warm her tortured, half-dead, frostbitten body.

Oh, and actually, add a buffet of her favorite foods right in front of the giant hot mess.

With, like, four hundred pounds of Lindt chocolate on it.

And pasta. And champagne.

Yeah, that male was not any kind of pleasant reflection. Not even a choice, really. He was a compulsion to get to the beacon he was sending out.

And to hell with the consequences.

". . . talk to your father."

Elise kicked her own butt and replugged into Paradise. "I'm sorry?"

"Your father," the female said. "My father would absolutely speak with him."

"Speak to whom? My sire?"

"What better way to try and change his mind? My father worries about me, and he's from that old-school way of doing things, but he's evolved his thinking. If anyone can talk your father off the cliff? It's him."

"Oh, my God . . . that would be amazing." Tears made her eyes water. "But why would you—"

Paradise took Elise's hand. "Because I know how hard it is."

The unexpected empathy was a breathtaker, and Elise got jammed up on the kindness. It was so hard to battle alone the *glymera* and its restrictions on females, so impossible to argue with standards that she hadn't volunteered for and didn't believe in, but that were, nonetheless, running her life. And it wasn't until this moment that Elise realized she had given up before she had even started fighting because there had been no hope, short of running away, of altering her father's legal and social authority over her.

"But he's going to get me declared as *sehcluded*," Elise said. "If he does that, I'm finished. It's over before it starts."

"When is he making the petition?"

"Right now, I think. He's gone to the Audience House right now—that's the only reason I could leave to come here."

Paradise got her phone out and stood up. "Gimme a minute."

As the female went in search of a quieter place to make a call, Elise wiped her eyes. And when she took a deep inhale and shifted in her chair, she looked across—

The male was still staring at her, that massive body of his eased back in his seat, his knees spread wide, his drink in one long hand, the other up to his chin, his fingers on his mouth.

Like maybe he was kissing her in his mind.

Elise's body flashed with heat, the blast emanating through her veins in reply to those eyes of his, that erotic way he was lounging, that all-consuming intent he was spotlighting her with. But it was funny. As direct as his stare was and as unmistakable as the erotic tension was? He didn't make a move to come over and talk to her.

Even though she was very sure he was imagining them making love—

"This is all going to work out," Peyton said as he hopped into Paradise's vacant seat. "It's all gonna be fine."

Switching gears—badly—Elise met her cousin's eyes. "Ah . . . I hope so. And thank you for helping. I didn't know where else to go."

"I told you. Anytime, anywhere, I'm here."

Peyton puffed on his cigar, releasing clouds of gray smoke that drifted over his head. As he motioned with his hand to a waiter, and then circled the empty glasses on the low table, she had the distinct impression he came here often. Then again, maybe he was just sublimely comfortable and confident in the world.

Something to aspire to.

As he joked with the male Paradise had been holding hands with, and then laughed at something the guy said, Elise couldn't help measuring her cousin's face. Peyton was handsome as could be, the kind of guy everyone looked at and wanted to know . . . but he'd never been happy—at least not that she'd been able to see. And he certainly wasn't now. Underneath the snark and the sexy affect, she sensed he wasn't tracking, an essential detachment separating him from the world.

He was suffering in silence. Mourning alone. Rattled but pretending everything was normal.

What had his ties to Allishon been? Of all the people who could have announced her death to the family, why had it been him?

Had he found her or something?

"How are you?" she asked quietly. "You know, after Allishon's—"

"I'm awesome, are you kidding me?" He shifted forward and tapped the ash off the fat, glowing end of his cigar. "I'm spectacular."

His eyes were empty as he smiled at her, and abruptly, she felt like crying all over again. But if he could be strong, so could she.

And then Paradise was back and sitting down in the lap of the trainee she'd been holding hands with. "My father's going to talk to him right now."

Elise closed her eyes in relief. "Oh, thank you, thank you so much . . . I really hope he can help."

"My father has a way about him that really calms people down." Paradise looked at her male with love in her eyes and smiled. "And as traditional as he can be, he knows that that isn't everything."

No, Axe told his libido. No, absolutely not. You are *not* going to have that female.

Forget it. Drop it. Walk away.

F.F.S., it was like he was talking at a recalcitrant dog.

But what the shits. She wasn't just "not his type," she represented everything he despised about the *glymera*. He couldn't stand blondes, for one thing. And yeah, sure, she didn't have a lot of makeup on, and it wasn't like she was dressed in a bunch of highbrow, ugly shit that was supposedly "on trend"—whatever the fuck that meant. But that accent of hers? Come on, it was so patrician, she made that human Queen of England sound like a beer drinker from the Jersey Shore.

And her bone structure was even worse. That face of hers was so refined and perfect, he was very sure that she could trace her bloodline back to the beginning of time. And those eyes? Like sapphires. Those lips? Like rubies. That skin . . . like a pearl.

She was a goddamn jewelry store of beauty. But man, it was so frickin' easy to fill in the particulars of her life: she was going to live in a mansion in the very best part of town; her bedroom would be Barbie-meets-the-National-Gallery; her father would be all up her ass to mate a suitable male from a Very Good Family; and her biggest worry to-night was what set of diamonds to wear to Last Meal.

Good thing she had about four hours of deliberation time.

Phew. What a fucking relief.

She was exactly what his mother had hoped to become. When she left him an orphan and his father a ruined male.

So no. He was not having anything to do with that stuck-up, butter-wouldn't-melt-in-her-mouth, aristocratic breeding machine. Nope. Not going to—

What would she taste like? an inner voice whispered.

"Stop it," he muttered. "Just shut the fuck up—"

What would she feel like, naked and under him, with her legs spread wide and her sex his for the taking? Would she moan his name? Or would she gasp it—

"You know," Novo murmured, "you could make this easier on yourself."

"What are you talking about? And please don't answer that if you don't feel like it."

"Why don't you go over there and speak to her?"

Axe considered playing stoopid, but what the hell. "Not a good idea. She'd be naked the next minute, and then I'd have to slaughter anyone with a cock who saw her like that."

"You're a fucking animal." Novo laughed. "But I like that in a male. And I think so does that female."

"What female." Damn it, was he out of booze again? "I think you're seeing things."

"If you were any more turned on, you'd be doing something that would get you arrested in a place like this."

"Which is why I like The Keys."

"I'm serious, you need to take me to that club."

"Name the night."

And then he got quiet because Peyton's cousin was rising to her feet and giving the guy a hug like she was leaving.

Look at me, Axe commanded in his head. *Come on, look at me.*

The female had clearly been brought up correctly and she took the time to acknowledge everyone she had just been introduced to . . . including, at last, him.

A quick flick of her eyes in his direction and then she was lifting her hand in a brief wave, and off she went.

She walked like something he wanted to mount from behind.

Axe went to get up before he was aware of moving, but Peyton shot a live-fire glare at him, a big, fat, don't-you-fucking-dare coupled with some don't-even-think-about-it mixed with a whole lot of not-even-in-your-fantasies-asshole. But then saving grace walked up.

In the form of a set of DDs in a miniskirt so short it was essentially a pair of panties without the crotch. And the human woman was a blonde, Peyton's favorite.

All the bad shit and frustration that had happened in training, coupled with the bourbon the guy had been drinking, conspired against good ol' Pey-pey's cockblocking, protective instincts—and the next thing you knew, the DDs had taken a load off in Peyton's lap and her fake-tipped nails were stroking the hair at the base of his neck.

Cue the buh-bye's.

Axe was up and outta there faster than a marksman could lock and load.

Slipping through the dim interior, he moved like a laser sight through the crowd, slicing his way to the front entrance and out into the cold.

Instinctively, he knew she'd gone left.

And just as instinctively, she stopped at the curb the second he emerged.

As she turned around to him, a gust of wind caught her hair, feathering it out from her face. With the fat snowflakes falling in a swirl and her coat catching the winter's breath around her body, she was like something out of a fever dream, both real and illusive.

Axe walked over to her, aware that he was more like a love-starved virgin than the jaded sex addict he had become ever since he had kicked heroin.

Her eyes skipped around as if he intimidated her, and she put her hands in her pockets, although, he sensed, not from the cold.

Axe knew this because he caught her scent: This female, as skittish as she was, was far from indifferent to him.

"I knew you would come after me," she said roughly.

"And I knew you'd be waiting."

She kicked up her chin. "I wasn't waiting."

"If I hadn't rushed out here, you would have."

He liked the way her jaw set like he was pissing her off. But then she smiled. "If you knew I'd wait for you, why did you rush?"

"You're worth it."

She opened her mouth as if she had expected him to say something else and had prepared a line. Shaking her head, she smiled as she glanced away. "Isn't that a line from a hair ad."

"I wouldn't know."

"Not into women's magazines?"

"Not into women. Or females."

"Then what do you think I am?"

Axe didn't see how it was helpful to point out that he could be sexually attracted to people and yet have absolutely no other care for them whatsoever.

"How do I see you," he asked on a growl. "Name the where and when and I'll be there."

"What if I'm not interested," she drawled, and stepped off the curb into the road.

He stayed right on her tail as she crossed the street. And good thing there were no cars coming in either direction—or he might have had to throw them out of his way.

"If you say you're not interested, I'd call you on your bullshit. And really, why waste my time with that."

On the far side, she wheeled around and put her hands on her hips. "Are you always this arrogant?"

He leaned into her, and as he inhaled deep into his lungs, he relished the scent of her arousal.

On a whisper, right next to her ear, he said, "Do you really think something as flimsy as false denial is going to keep me away from you?"

At that moment, the door to the cigar club flew open and Peyton came out, all pouncing protector and then some.

"I'm not denying anything," she said dryly. "But my cousin most certainly is going to keep us apart."

"Only if you let him."

"Elise," Peyton snapped from across the street. "Go home."

"And this is the same male who was helping liberate me from my father," she muttered.

"Elise!"

As a couple of cars coming and going prevented the guy from crossing the road, she turned away. "Have fun with him."

And *poof!* she was gone, dematerializing into the December night.

"God*damn* it," Axe muttered.

Meanwhile, Peyton played dodgeball with a truck, and then broke into a run to close the distance.

"For fuck's sake," Axe barked at the guy. "I didn't touch her—"

Crack!

The right hook left him spitting blood out.

"You don't fucking think about it!" Peyton gritted. "She is *not* your kind."

"What, because I'm not an aristocrat like you, asshole?"

The two of them got right up in it, baring fangs even though they could be seen, grabbing at the front of each other's jackets.

Craeg was next out of the club, and Paradise was right with him.

"She's a female of worth!" Peyton started to wind up for another strike. "She's not like the trash you fuck—"

Axe caught the male's forearm and bent it out of the way. "Oh, and that human slut on your lap in there was some kind of saint—"

"Her cousin is dead, okay! Allishon was the one Anslam murdered last month—I had to go to Elise's household and tell them what happened! So no, you can't fuck her and leave her ruined, which is what you're going to do. There's enough pain under that roof already and she deserves better than that! Better than you!"

Craeg jogged across the street and wasted no time in hooking a hold onto Peyton's shoulders and dragging the guy back.

"Not here," Craeg gritted. "You two assholes are making a scene."

Axe cursed and walked off a little, pacing in the falling snow, his boots making tracks that quickly got him down to concrete. He spit out another mouthful of blood and tried to ignore how badly his knuckles were itching for payback.

But damn, they'd all heard about the killing. Anslam, the murderer, had been one of the trainees, one of the few to survive the induction night and get accepted into the Brotherhood's program.

No one knew, or could have guessed, that the aristocratic bastard had been brutalizing females and taking pictures of his handiwork on the side.

Peyton had gone looking for his female cousin after he'd tried to get ahold of her—and from what Axe had been told, the guy had walked in on a bloodbath. No body, though. Turned out she had died at Havers's clinic, but without identification.

Paradise had been the one to put it all together, and Anslam had nearly killed her when she'd figured it all out.

The sadistic bastard had ended up dead in her front foyer.

What a fucking mess.

"Not Elise," Peyton said roughly. "I'm not going to let you ruin her. And don't pretend that's not what will happen. Unless you want to ask her father for permission to mate her properly, stay the fuck away from her."

Yeah, like that was ever going to go down. One, because Axe would never ask any sire for that shit. And two, as if a high-bred father like the one she had would let a scrub like him even walk through the front door, much less entertain a mating proposal.

Hell, Axe wasn't good enough to vacuum the floor rugs on the guy's Rolls-Royce.

But what did it matter, Axe thought as he looked away again. It wasn't like he was ever going to see her again.

What was the saying? Ships in the night.

They were two ships in the night, passing each other, never the twain shall meet again.

"Fine," he muttered. "I'll leave her alone."

SIX

The following nightfall, Mary watched from the end of Bitty's bed as the girl mulled over which coat to wear out. One was a puffy parka that was red and black, a gift from the King that was, as far as Mary could tell, like bubble-wrapping the kid—Rhage had even joked that it was the Gore-Tex equivalent of one of those human hamster balls that people got into and bounced down hills. The other choice was a sedate, navy blue peacoat, the old-fashioned kind with the sailor buttons and the collar you could stand up like Dracula's.

A part of Mary's heart ached that this was the first time in Bitty's life that she'd had any kind of decision to make. Before, coming out of poverty, she had been lucky to have anything at all—and the idea the girl had spent so many winters cold was enough to make Mary nauseous.

"I don't see why I have to go to the clinic," the girl said as she put the parka back in her closet.

Mary had known all along that the wool coat was going to be the choice. Rhage had given the thing to the girl—and Wrath, son of Wrath, sire of Wrath, might have been the King of the entire race, but no one held a candle to Bitty's father.

And tonight was going to be scary.

"Do you think there's something wrong?" Bitty said as she came back from the closet.

"No," Mary said. "I don't. But it's better to know that for sure rather than simply hope that's the truth."

"I'm not sore, though." Bitty walked over to the dressing table and sat down in front of the three-part mirror. "And all pretrans are small."

"I agree." Boy, Mary hated to bring up the abuse. "The reality is, though, that your body has been through a lot. It doesn't mean that you won't get through your transition and be tall and strong. But what if there's something we can do now to make sure that happens?"

"Is it because of the broken bones?"

"Yes."

Bitty fell silent, picking up the hairbrush and running it through the long brown waves that fell past her shoulders—even though she'd already brushed them. And Mary gave the kid space, passing the time looking around the room . . . and wondering what else they could do to make the otherwise formal surroundings more what a thirteen-year-old girl would be into. Bitty didn't demand anything, though, and she seemed content.

There also had been a lot of new purchases lately—and it was hard not to give the little girl the world.

Hard, too, to stop the frickin' Brothers from spoiling her rotten. Bitty had arrived at the Brotherhood mansion with two battered suitcases, a doll head, and her old tiger, Mastimon—and within a night or two, her football team's worth of overprotective pains in the asses, better known as the BABUs (Bad-Ass Big Uncles), had been laying things at her doorway like offerings to an altar.

Actually, Lassiter called the uncle squad Baboons or Buffoons. And then the beatings occurred. But yeah . . .

Oh, and that fallen angel was the worst of the bunch when it came to presents. Just tonight, at First Meal, he'd given her yet another copy of the *Deadpool* DVD and a sweatshirt that had a red and black rendering of Dory with "Where's Francis?" printed on the front.

"I really don't want to go to Havers's clinic," Bitty said as she looked at herself in the mirror. "I'm scared."

Mary closed her eyes, recalling Bitty getting treatment there for what her biological father did to her. "Rhage and I are going to be with you the whole time. We aren't going to leave your side."

"Can't Doc Jane do whatever needs to be done at her clinic?"

"I'm sorry, but she can't."

"Can she come with us?"

"No, honey, she has her work to do here. But she's going to talk to Havers herself after all the tests come back. And so will Dr. Manello and maybe even V."

Bitty put the brush down and ran her palm over her hair. "Okay."

God, she was so small sitting there, and Mary would have given anything to be the one about to be poked and prodded and X-rayed and imaged. Bitty had been through so much, her poor little body absorbing blows and stress that most adults would have had trouble living through. And the actual experiences had been bad enough. The idea that she was still having to deal with them seemed grossly unfair.

"I think afterward," Mary said as she got to her feet, "Rhage is going to take the night off and hang out with us."

"He told me we can have ice cream and watch a movie, if I wanted."

"You got it."

When Bitty didn't stand up, Mary went over. "I'm not going to leave you."

"Promise?" came the whisper. "I'm scared."

Mary put her hand on the girl's shoulder. "I swear that I will never leave you."

Thank you, Scribe Virgin. And thank you, Rhage. When they'd decided to move forward with the adoption process, she and Rhage had agreed that even if he died first, Mary would stay with Bitty. Of course, they hadn't told the girl about all that. There just hadn't been a right time yet.

Bitty took a deep breath. "Okay, let's—"

The knock on the door cut her off, and then came Rhage's deep voice, muffled: "How're my females in there? We ready?"

"Yup."

"Yes."

Rhage opened things up and there he was, big and beautiful, his broad shoulders filling the doorway, his preternatural physical perfection the kind of thing Mary still did a double take on every once in a while. With blond hair that was thick and wavy, eyes that were the color of the ocean in the Bahamas, and teeth so white they looked like bathroom tile—even though they'd never been bleached—he was a legend in the race with the females for a good reason.

He was also totally and completely devoted to her and her alone.

It had taken Mary some time to get used to that, to trust it. After all, he could have had anyone or anything he wanted in a mate—someone blond and tall and gorgeous like him. Instead . . . he only had eyes for her, a brunette with a nice enough face, and a body that had been rendered infertile thanks to chemo.

Rhage thought she was a beauty queen, however, and funny, when she was around him and he was staring at her the way he did? She sure as hell felt like one.

As Bitty burst up and rushed over to him, he got down on one knee so he was closer to her height. And he took her hands, his larger palms engulfing her smaller ones.

"You ready to get this over with so we can watch *Deadpool* again?"

Mary shook her head. "You guys are in a serious rut."

" 'So what's it gonna be?' " Bitty quipped. " 'Long sullen silence or mean comment?' "

"'You got me in a box here,'" Rhage shot back.

"Yes, yes, yes, yes . . ." Bitty curled up her fists and pumped the air as she turned in a little circle.

"Promise me again," Mary cut in, "that you don't look at the adult parts."

Bitty and Rhage both covered their eyes as he replied, "Nope. We assume the position and wait till the ugliness passes."

Pick your battles, Mary reminded herself. You gotta pick your battles.

As the three of them headed out of the suite in a clutch, Mary said, "You know, you could try watching some other things? There are some wonderful documentaries out there on social issues that . . ."

She let the pitch trail off as the two of them turned around and stared at her as if she'd suggested spray-painting obscenities all over the foyer. Or firing Fritz. Or off-loading Rhage's GTO on eBay for scrap metal.

"How are you two not blood relations," she muttered. "But at least you might grow out of this, Bitty."

The girl came in close and gave one of her hugs, tight and quick. "Maybe."

As they headed down to the second floor, Rhage said, "Bit, you know we're not leaving you, right? It's not appropriate for me to be with you the whole time, but Mary will be, and I'll be in the waiting room or just outside in the corridor—"

When they emerged out of the stairwell, they stopped on a oner.

Right outside of the King's study, there was a group of people waiting: Doc Jane, in her surgical scrubs; Manny, in his white coat; Vishous, dressed for war; and Zsadist, in Adidas, with weapons all over him.

Oh, and Lassiter.

In a hockey mask and football pads.

"Well, this is a sweet send-off," Rhage said as he went to clap hands with his Brothers.

"We're not sending you off." Lassiter pounded his pads. "We're your entourage."

Mary blinked. "I'm sorry?"

Jane smiled and focused on Bit. "We're coming with you."

"Not that the 'rents can't handle it," Lassiter volunteered from behind his mask. "But let's face it, I'm working on my defensive tackle position and this will be good practice. That pencil-necked nightmare of a doctor gets too pokey and I'ma turn him into a splatter painting."

Vishous put both hands up to his face and rubbed hard. Like in his mind, he was throwing a beat-down in the angel's direction, but he knew he couldn't draw blood in front of the girl—and the self-control required was killing him.

"You can stay home," V muttered. "You really can totally f-in' stay the f home, you f'ed-up mother-f'ing f-twit."

Lassiter clasped his breastplate, and swooned like Julie Andrews. "Don't you love it when he can't swear? Warms my cockles—it's like watching a drunk on roller skates try to play dodgeball in the dark—"

Zsadist, who rarely spoke, cut the metaphors off. "We don't want you three going alone. So we're coming with you. Some things you need your family for."

As Rhage cleared his throat like his emotions were getting the best of him, Mary said roughly, "Thank you so much. I really . . . we really appreciate this."

Z stepped forward to Bit, and if you went by appearances alone, any parent would want the Brother as far away from their child as possible: with his tattooed slave bands and his scarred face and his enormous warrior's body with all those weapons on it, he looked more like an abductor than a loving uncle.

Without saying a word, he put out his hand.

And without missing a beat . . . the little survivor took the big survivor's palm.

Bitty and Z had always had a special connection. Then again, when you had been forced to endure the cruelty of another for years, there was always going to be a separator between you and the world, no matter how much time had passed or how many good things happened to you since.

That common ground united the pair of them. And although Mary would have wished for something else to bring them together, she was always glad—especially on a night like tonight—that Bitty had Zsadist in her life.

As the pair of them hit the grand staircase, it was as if a bell had been rung and the gates to the race opened, the assembled masses following them down to where Fritz was waiting outside with his black Mercedes.

The great thing about family, Mary mused, was that they showed up.

When it really mattered, your family, be they blood or by choice, were always where you needed them to be, even though they had busy lives and jobs and children of their own.

"Hey," Lassiter said as he opened the way through the vestibule, "will anyone slap a puck around with me to pass the time?"

"No," everybody, including Bitty, shot back.

"But I will slap the f-in' crap out of something else," V said under his breath.

"I love it when you talk dirty to me. Gimme a hug. C'mon, you know you wanna. . . ."

Nothing.

Elise knew nothing about where she stood: not whether she was able to keep going to school, or if she were stuck in proverbial jail, or even if she still had a roof over her head.

After she had gone to see Peyton out at the cigar bar, and had the collision-as-meeting encounter with that trainee as she'd been leaving, she'd come home and waited for her father's return. On the bottom step of the carved staircase right across from the front door. Like a lost child.

Three hours later, he had walked in, his head down, his shoulders slumped, his spirit as deflated as a fragile balloon.

He hadn't even looked at her—or even seemed aware that she was in the foyer. He'd just gone directly to his study and closed himself in.

Well . . . good talk, Dad, she'd thought. Breaking all kinds of new ground, aren't we.

But really, how could she have expected anything else?

After an internal debate about the merits of interjecting herself into whatever process he was working through, she'd gone up and gotten into bed. No sleep for her during the day, but that hadn't just been about her father and the *sehclusion* petition.

She couldn't stop thinking about that male . . . his tattoos, and his piercings, the way he'd looked at her, what he'd said. She'd spent a lot of time replaying that scene on the sidewalk. In her head? They were still back there in the falling snow arguing, the sexual tension so thick it was like a rope she could pull on.

It was a shock, given the very real issues she was dealing with in her life, that she had any interest at all in making things even more chaotic. But she wished she'd given him her number. She was, however, glad she hadn't—because if he did call her? She would see him again, and what a recipe for disaster that would be.

You didn't need to know the specifics about a male like that to be fully aware he was a Taylor Swift song waiting to happen.

Or worse—

"Enough," she said as she stood up from her bed. "Enough with the stewing."

Her father would be downstairs in his study by now. So it was time to go face the music, as her mother used to say, and talk with him.

As Elise stepped out of her room, she pulled up short. Her father was just emerging from his suite down the hall, and he paused, too.

Clearing her throat, she said, "Father, I—"

He turned away without a word, his hand rising over his shoulder in classic *stop* fashion. "Not now."

"Then when," she demanded.

Her father did not respond. He simply kept going, striding down the hall to the formal staircase and disappearing on the descent.

Short of throwing herself in front of him, she didn't know how to force him to engage. And even then, he was likely to just Conrail over her.

"Son of a bitch," she hissed.

Maybe it was time to move out. But undoubtedly, he would cut her off, so how would she pay for anything?

The only reason she was able to go to university now was because of scholarships she'd earned. And they didn't cover things like room and board.

A sudden urge to throw something had her turning her head toward an antique side table. That vase of flowers would be perfect, the thin neck at the top fitting easily in her palm, the weight of the water and the imported roses heavy enough to make her feel like she could do some damage, but not enough to hinder distance.

Shifting her eyes across the way, she stared at the closed door of the suite where her aunt and uncle stayed.

Her uncle would be out and about soon, but her aunt was no doubt still sleeping. Usually the female stayed in bed until after Elise got back from uni, rising only long enough to do her hair and makeup before returning to her satin pillows. It was no way to live, but after what had happened to her daughter? And the loss of her son?

Elise cursed . . . and then found herself on the move.

The next thing she knew, she was standing in front of her dead cousin's door. From a distance, she watched as her hand reached out, clasped the knob, and turned it. When she pushed inside, she caught a whiff of the perfume Allishon had always worn. Poison by Dior— old school, to be sure, but it had fit so well on the female.

Elise had always thought that if the color purple had had a scent, that fragrance would have been it.

Without a sound, she shut herself in and flicked the light switch.

Illumination bloomed in the room, emanating from the crystal chandelier in the center of the high ceiling. The bed was across the way, strewn with pale blue linens that had white and gold accents, and sporting enough pillows to put a Macy's display in the shade. The walls were papered with handmade Stark, the French scene of peach-and-yellow birds frolicking between blooming fruit trees something you could see down in the gardens during the good months. On the floor, the carpet was thick and of a cream that was so pale, it was nearly white, and the drapes framing the windows were the pale blue of a summer dress and just as diaphanous.

The decor was perfect for a young female of worth.

And yet Allishon's possessions were the off-notes in the room: a black robe that was part priest, part demon worshipper; a crystal skull on the mantel over the fireplace; books with black and blood-red leather covers scattered in the far corner by a tapestry-covered pallet. There were also chunky black boots that were tall enough to go up over the knee . . . a high-heeled shoe without a mate that had a gun for a heel . . . black duffel bags filled with God only knew what else.

It was hard not to see the evidence of her cousin's other life like potholes in a perfectly paved road. But how judgmental was that.

"No way to think," she groaned as she rubbed her stiff neck.

The reality, though, was that something evil had come across Allishon's path as she had searched for herself on the wild side. And that was Felixe's point, wasn't it.

Elise frowned as she thought about that trainee with the tattoos. He was everything that her sire was worried about her finding. Except she hadn't met him at university—and that was her point.

"Just as well," she muttered to the vacant room. "I'm not going to see him again."

SEVEN

The Brotherhood's training center was a state-of-the-art, hundred-thousand-square-foot bunker of holy-shit-how-is-this-not-the-government–level facilities and equipment. Located underground, and preceded by a gating system of gradually more secure and intimidating G.T.F.O.s, the place was off-limits to vampires, humans, and *lessers*.

As well as the trainees who were technically allowed to be in it.

When the "school bus" slowed again at yet another checkpoint, Axe could tell by the angle of the descent that they were getting close to the entrance to the facility. The blackout windows next to him didn't offer much visual, but he imagined the last couple of stop-heres to be like something out of *Jurassic Park*, all concrete walls that were as tall as the Hoover Dam and topped with miles' worth of barbed wire.

For the last month, the trainees had been meeting at designated locations in and around Caldwell and getting on this nothing-yellow-or-schoolish-at-all tank with its bulletproof body plating, thick-as-your-arm windows, and deep bucket seats.

Yeah, sure, Fritz, the old *doggen* at the wheel, could have worked for Caldwell Central Schools. But that was about it for comps.

And what do you know. Tonight's ride in from a deserted factory in the old industrial part of town had been about twenty-five minutes of Peyton glaring a hole in Axe's skull.

Good times, good times.

Everyone else was minding their own damn business. Novo had her Beats on up in front. Boone was reading—Kierkegaard's *Enten-Eller*, whatever the fuck that was. Paradise and Craeg were trading an iPhone back and forth like they were searching for PokéStops on the way and getting bad reception.

Peyton, on the other hand? He apparently had nothing better to do than steam like dog shit laid fresh on a snowbank.

Axe had done a damn good job of ignoring the glares, however, and he intended to keep up the brick wall for the rest of the night—

"I mean it," Peyton snapped.

As Axe let his head fall against the rest, he knew he should have moved farther back when Mr. Boundaries had sat across the aisle from him. Course that would mean he'd be riding in on the rear bumper.

"You made your point last night," Axe muttered. "And I agreed with you, if you remember."

"You didn't say shit."

"Fuck you, and I'll repeat myself now." He turned his head lackadaisically to the male. "I'm not going to touch her."

"Then why did you follow Elise out like that?"

"Fresh air, man. I needed—"

"I'm fucking serious—"

"Hey, I have an idea. Let's not play Emilio Estevez and Judd Nelson circa Maine North High School."

"What the fuck are you talking about?"

Boone spoke up but didn't look up from the row ahead. "*The Breakfast Club*. Widely considered the best high school film ever made. Filmed at Maine North High School in Des Plaines, Illinois, in 1984. Judd Nelson played the role of the stereotypical degenerate—"

"FYI," Axe cut in, "that's my role. You're the wrestler, Pey-pey. The judgmental fuck with the please-daddy complex."

Peyton cocked an eyebrow. "Him"—he motioned to Boone—"I'd expect to know that. You?"

"I haven't been a sex addict my whole life, you know. I used to be a druggie who specialized in nodding out in front of the TV. And will you do us both a favor and drop this shit. I'm not going to bang your pure-as-the-driven-snow cousin. She's not my type."

Okay, fine. He might have spent all day staring at the ceiling, reliving the way she had turned to him on that sidewalk. Looked at him. Spoken to him.

And yeah, there might have been some palm action. But it had been a case of either he took care of the perma-rection he'd developed or he came to class with a baseball bat in his leathers.

But that wasn't about her. Nah. That was just a sign he needed to spend more time at The Keys.

The bus came to a stop, and the ancient butler retracted the partition while opening the door across from his driver's seat. "We've arrived! Have a lovely evening!"

The *doggen* said the same thing in the same cheerful voice every night, and as Axe got to his feet and walked down and off before anyone else could, he realized it was kind of a ritual. The verbal equivalent of rubbing a rabbit's foot for good luck.

The parking area had a number of vehicles in it, including an RV that was actually a mobile surgical center, a new Hummer that was being bulletproofed, two pickups that sparkled like they were just off the Ford lot, and an earthmover of some CAT variety. There were other levels of graduated asphalt rising upward, but Axe had never bothered with them.

Even if he'd been allowed to drive in, it wasn't like he had a car or any prospects of getting one.

Nope, no whip for him. In his world, there was no money for anything other than the clothes on his back and the human property taxes on the little house his father had built for a female who had never given a shit about him. Oh, and those ramen noodles. Axe's electricity had been turned off again and this time, he wasn't going to bother to pay the bill. He could live in the dark—it was better than crashing at the training center like a homeless human. Besides, gas and sewer were municipal, so he had hot running water, and the fireplaces worked well enough to keep him warm.

He'd survive.

As he approached a steel-reinforced door, he didn't have to wait. It was opened from the inside, the *Dhestroyer* shoving the heavy weight wide like the thing weighed as much as a sheet of paper.

"Evenin'," the Brother Butch said. "We're in the first classroom."

Axe nodded and walked down the long hall, passing by interrogation rooms and other teaching areas, and then the new lab where they were, literally, blowing shit up.

The classroom they used was your typical set-up—or at least what he'd seen on the TV during his heroin days. There were two rows of long tables with pairs of seats facing an old-fashioned chalkboard. Overhead lights were banks of fluorescents; the flooring was speckled linoleum.

No readin', writin', and 'rithmetic taught here, though.

Try hand-to-hand-combat theory, military maneuvers, basic first aid, group dynamics.

Axe sat in the back and—thank you, God—Peyton parked it down in front. The others settled in, ready for the night.

The Brother Butch closed the door and sat on the desk that was off to the side. He had a Red Sox hat on, a shirt that had a stencil of Big Papi's face on the front, and set of Adidas track pants in black. Running shoes were Brooks and in a pink and red neon.

"Tonight," the Brother said, "we're going to review how badly you each performed in that mock attack. Which should take us eight to twelve hours. Then, if there's time left, we'll keep going with poisons, focusing on aerosols and contact poisons. But first, I have a job opportunity for someone."

Axe frowned.

Money, he thought, would be good.

"The position is one that will require the utmost discretion and tact." The Brother leveled a deadly stare at the group. "As well as an intimate knowledge of personal defense."

Rhage absolutely fucking hated Havers's clinic. Yeah, sure, the underground facility was secure, and even though he didn't like the guy, no one could argue with the healer's treatment of his patients. But as Rhage sat in the corridor outside the exam room that Bitty and Mary had been in for, like, a hundred and fifty years, pretty much everything was getting on his nerves.

First of all, he hated the synthetic "clean" smell, that fake lemon disinfecta-stench burrowing into his sinuses. Hell, it was so bad, he kept imagining all kinds of tiny yellow minions with pickaxes and spray bottles of the shit paying personal attention to his nostril regions.

Second, the productive hush of everything bugged the fuck out of him, even though it was arguably a good thing. All the soft-soled shoes shuffling along, the quiet voices, the carts of medical supplies and equipment whispering along the hall.

But the worst thing? He really couldn't stand the attention he got.

It wasn't that the nurses were popping their bodices and going grind-on-it all over his junk, but damn, he didn't need all the lingering glances and the unnecessary multi-walk-bys and the twittering and giggling.

He'd dealt with versions of this all his life—at least since the split second he'd made it through his transition. And pre-Mary, he'd taken advantage of the sexual attention to the point where he didn't leave a reputation so much as a religion of fucking in his wake. Post-Mary, though, he had no interest in other females. In fact, he'd begun to think of his face and body like a sweet-ass whip that his brain drove. His core, his soul, his heart, didn't have anything to do with how he looked.

And there was the issue.

When your daughter was on the other side of a thin door, dressed in a frail little hospital gown, her eyes big and wide from current fear and past trauma as her personal space and her body were invaded by third parties, the last thing you wanted was a bunch of people falling all over you because they thought you were Channing Tatum and Chris Hemsworth's frickin' love child.

Maybe he should put a paper bag over his head—

As a hand came down on his shoulder, he jumped—and was equally shocked to find Zsadist sitting down next to him on the hard floor of the corridor.

Across the way, V and Lassiter were still on their feet and arguing, the pair of them face to hockey mask, the brother putting a hand-rolled between his lips—and then whipping it out as if he remembered he couldn't light up—the angel more than holding his own, talking a mile a minute.

Rhage didn't have the energy or the focus to spare on them.

All he could think about was . . .

"She's just suffered enough," he heard himself say. "God . . . how long have they been in there?"

Looking into the eyes of his brother, he saw that instead of that stare being yellow, Z's peepers were jet black.

But yeah, Rhage was being pretty annoying. He'd been bitching about the same thing for how long now? No wonder his brother was getting frustrated with him.

"Sorry." Rhage rubbed his face. "I've got to shut up over here. Don't mean to piss you off."

Z looked at him like he'd sprouted a horn in the middle of his forehead. "Not you. I just want to dig up that sire of hers and kill him all over again. If Nalla had been abused like that? And had bones full of past breaks?"

The brother stopped talking at that point. Just as well. Rhage felt like vomiting again.

"When it's your kids, it's just a whole different level." Rhage started to bang his head against the wall, and then worried that it might disturb Bitty and the doctors. "You know, I wasn't prepared for this. I mean, I thought the hard part about being a dad was going to be the arguments—like her bringing some knuckle-dragging mouth breather home and expecting me not to slice off his smooth criminals and plant them in the yard. But this? I want to be the one going through it for her. It's just not fair."

Z held his stare, solid as a rock, about as far from psychotic as the brother had once been knee-deep in the crazy. "You are a tremendous father, you know that. You're the real deal."

Rhage looked away fast. Cleared his throat. "I feel like I'm failing her."

"You're right with her when she needs you most."

"No, to do that, I'd have to be on that exam table. I'd have to have my body there instead of hers."

"Not possible and you know it." Z cursed softly. "The hardest thing about being a father is not being able to make everything all right for them. Sometimes the best you can do is just show up."

"There has to be more to it."

"If there is and you figure it out, let me know."

"Ha! You're the best father I've ever seen."

"Tell you what, I'll call your ass the next time I lie awake wondering how I could have screwed things up worse."

"But it's different for you."

"Why." When Rhage didn't fill in the blank, Z didn't let the unspoken remain silent. "Why, because Nalla is biologically mine? G'head, say it. 'Cuz when you hear that shit come out of your mouth, you'll realize how stupid it is."

"I just . . . I wonder if I'd be doing something better if . . . you know, I were really her sire."

"Oh, like her biological father, you mean? Like the motherfucker who put her on that table? You want to be like him? Yeah, that's a real improvement over a guy who's been here in this corridor, looking like he's going through open-heart surgery without anesthesia 'cuz his little girl's having a hard time."

Rhage rubbed his hair so hard his fingers were fuzzy when he stopped. "You wouldn't understand. You're never going to be in my shoes."

"That's my point, though. Whether you had a hand in birthing them or you volunteer to take them in, we're all in the same shoes."

Rhage stared at the closed door in front of him. "I'm scared, Z. I'm just . . . fucking scared. What if there's something permanently wrong? That's what Doc Jane is worried about, you know. She's worried Bitty's transition will ruin her arms and legs so badly . . . that they're going to end up having to amputate them."

The image of Bitty dancing through the foyer made his eyes sting. She was so active now . . . he couldn't imagine her in a wheelchair that was operated by her blowing into a tube. It just killed him.

"What the . . . what the fuck are you talking about?" Z demanded.

"Something to do with growth plates. There were breaks that oc- curred right along"—He motioned to his thighs, his forearms, his calves—"you know, Bitty's growth plates, and they healed wrong? So when the change hits her, they're liable to bust open and be unrepair- able."

"Shit."

"Mary doesn't know." Rhage went back to trying to pull his hair out. "Yeah, I should have told her before now, but I just didn't know how. I told Doc Jane I would. But I'm a fucking coward for both of them. I was hoping . . . for good news, I guess, but the longer they're in there, the more I think—"

Across the way, the exam room door swung open, and Doc Jane emerged.

One look at her face and he knew that the worst case had rolled out in there.

"How bad is it?" Rhage gritted as he jumped to his shitkickers. "And is there anything we can do?"

EIGHT

Turtleneck.

Hours later, as Axe sat silently in the back of the "school bus," he tried to think of where in the hell he could get a turtleneck.

Reaching up to his throat, he massaged the side that he'd had tattooed and wondered if he could find one in his father's shit. And didn't that make him want a stiff drink . . . or maybe even a syringe full of lights-out.

He hadn't been anywhere near his dad's room since the death.

"Fuck," he said to the blackened window.

To get out of his head, he looked away from his reflection—and hey, what do you know. Pey-pey had gotten bored of the don't-touch-my-cousin routine, and was back in his primary mode of staring at Paradise as she sat beside her male.

No one had had a good time tonight, not that training was ever a party. But yeah, it stung when you were forced to meet your failures head on. What was fun? Seeing Peyton all castrated across the aisle from that female, wishing he could get in her head and help her out, be the savior he felt she needed. You could practically read the thought bubbles floating around.

Sorry, champ. She had all she required.

Novo stood up and walked down to Axe, shoving him over so she could take a load off. "I'm going at two a.m. When is your interview?"

"In a half hour." He rubbed his tattoos, thinking they were probably going to work against him. "I gotta hustle."

"Good luck."

As the female put her palm out, Axe shook it. "You, too."

"Guess it's just you and me going for the job." Her voice took on an edge. "Peyton already has enough money, and far be it from him to let gainful employment get in the way of his smoking up. Boone doesn't need the cash, either—and Paradise and Craeg are already providing extra security at the Audience House on their nights off."

Shit, Axe wasn't crazy about competing with Novo—he would have much rather gone up against another male, and yeah, guess that made him sexist. Then again, the joke was probably on him. She was just as good at the fighting and the shooting as he was, her strength nearly that of his own, her brains a little ahead of his. She also didn't look like a serial killer.

But hey, he would take his piercings out. Bam. Nearly normal.

He also had zero personal skills. So she could very well beat him in the interview.

"You want to have a friendly wager?" Novo drawled.

"On what?"

"Who gets it? Loser has to pay for dinner."

He wasn't in a position to buy her a Kit Kat. "How about winner buys dinner?"

"Deal."

Twenty minutes later, the bus came to a stop and everyone filed off. The night was bitterly cold, and no one lingered to talk. As Axe dematerialized to his father's cottage, he thought it was weird that he'd never called the little place his "parents'"—but then again, there had been no "parents" involved with the damn thing. It had been built for his mother, and hadn't done its job to keep her in the family.

So the roof and four walls were nothing but a monument to his father's weakness for a female.

Going inside, he was glad there was no electricity, no lights to turn on. He couldn't stand the kitchen, hated looking at it, and he steamed right through the shallow space. The stairs to the second floor were short and steep and he took them two at a time, proceeding to the only open door.

He kept his father's room closed off.

His room was a mattress on the floor, clothes in piles, and not much else. Hell, he didn't even sleep up here, because the fireplace was downstairs and he had to stay warm. In the spring and summer, though, he'd move back to the second floor—or maybe he wouldn't. Who cared.

Axe went through his own "wardrobe" of muscle shirts, black jeans, and the occasional leather jacket or cloak, although not because he expected a turtleneck to have miraculously appeared courtesy of the Look-More-Normal Fairy Godmother dropping by. It was more because he had to brace himself to go through his father's stuff.

Ten minutes and no turtle-for-his-neck later, he was down the hall and opening the door. With no lights on anywhere in the house, the shallow space was nothing but shadows and shades of gray . . . kind of like his self-hatred had sucked the color out of everything.

He couldn't even look at the bed, which was still messy from the last time his father had slept it in two years ago, and he certainly didn't spare all the pictures of his fucking mother a glance, and no, he didn't dwell on the layer of dust that covered everything or the fact that one of the windows had sprung from its sash and let in fallen leaves and even some of the snow.

It seemed colder in the room, his breath condensing in puffs of white.

Maybe his father was haunting the place.

As a shiver went down his spine, Axe marched his ass over to the bureau and went through the things in it with rough, agitated hands. He found what he was looking for in the bottom drawer.

It seemed so fucking weird to think the thing had been worn and used by the male. And as he shoved the drawer shut, and beat feet out of the room like he was being stalked, he vowed never to go in there again.

Back in his own space, he stripped off his muscle shirt and pulled on his father's turtleneck. Heading over to the mirror above his cheap dresser, he leaned in and made sure everything on his throat was covered up.

Just before he turned away, he reached up and removed, one by one, the black piercings that ran from his lobe up to his cartilage on the same side as his tattoos. Also took out the one on his brow.

Next move was to arm himself. Slipping on a shoulder holster, he tucked the pair of forties he'd been given the week before into both sides. The way the Brothers saw it, they were investing time and money into the trainees and the last thing they needed was for anyone in the program to wake up dead because they had shit equipment: Once the class had all been vetted properly at the gun range, the Glocks had been handed out—and although you were not permitted to bring the weapons into the training center, you sure as shit were expected to have 'em with you outside of it.

And use them properly if necessary. Unlike what they'd done the night before.

Out of the house, didn't bother to lock the door—after all, there was no electricity to power the alarm, and besides, he didn't really care about anything under the roof.

Hell, it'd be a relief if somebody broke in and lit the place on fire.

Not that that was likely. He lived in the sticks; his nearest neighbor was a quarter of a mile away and probably took a donkey in to work.

Axe knew before he even dematerialized to the interview location that the house—or mansion or castle or whatever—was going to be huge. Even poor kids raised outside of the human world knew where the big estates were, and the zip code the place was in?

Yeah . . . okay, he thought as he re-formed.

Wow.

Axe shook his head at the stone structure in front of him. The thing had to be at least three stories high, and the front face of the slate roof alone seemed big as a football field. With about seven hundred black shutters and a front door that was more like the entrance to a parliament or a maybe a municipal library, he couldn't actually believe a family lived there.

Then again, it wasn't just a momma bear, a papa bear, and a baby bear. There were probably dozens of *doggen*.

It was exactly the kind of place his father would have been called on to work in.

Precisely like the sort of fancy home where the male had been killed during the raids.

Before he blew the job interview before it even started, Axe swallowed his bitterness and hiked it up the snow-covered lawn until he stepped over a low hedge that skirted a circular ring-around and proceeded to a series of steps to the front door.

There was a huge brass door knocker that was big as his arm, and also a discreet intercom off to one side.

He was reaching for the button when the heavy weight was opened by—oh, snap—a uniformed butler who looked alarmingly like Sir John Gielgud.

In his *Arthur* years.

"Are you Axwelle, son of Theirsh?" the male said with perfect diction.

For some completely unhelpful reason, Axe's brain coughed out

Dudley Moore doing his best drunk impression: *You're a hooker? Jesus . . . I forgot! I just thought I was doing great with you!*

"Sire?" the butler prompted. "Are you Axwelle?"

Shaking himself, he almost answered with a *Yeah*. "Yes, I am."

"Please, do come in." The butler backed up and indicated with his hand. "I shall let my master know that you have arrived in a timely fashion."

"Thanks. Thank you."

Something about the guy made him want to be less of a schmo. Fuck that, everything about this whole damn thing made him—

Axe stopped where he was. Flaring his nostrils, he breathed in as the butler in the penguin suit said a few things and then turned away to walk over to a closed door.

Wait a minute, Axe thought.

Pivoting slowly in a circle, he continued to test the scents in the air. The big open reception hall, foyer, whatever the hell it was called, could easily fit three of the houses he lived in and still have room for a bowling alley, a swimming pool, and maybe an ice-skating rink. And the stuff that was placed around the open, cathedral-like space looked really old and really expensive: The floor was white and gray marble and there was, like, crystal shit hanging everywhere and oil paintings mounted on the walls. Oh, and there was a fireplace, but not like the one that kept him warm during the day. Theirs had, like, black marble and gold carvings around it, and the hearth was so big they didn't have logs so much as tree trunks in there.

But he couldn't have cared less about all that.

What he had caught on the air, after filtering out the woodsy pitch of the crackling fire and the soap of the *doggen* and a distant aftermath of some kind of meat having been served somewhere on the first floor . . . was the scent of that female from last night.

Peyton's cousin either had visited here very recently . . . or she lived under this roof.

"My master will see you now," the butler said from behind him.

Yes, Axe thought as he wheeled around. You're damn right he will.

Sometimes nightmares happened in front of you and hurt people you loved, and even though you prayed to wake up . . . you knew that there was no alarm clock about to ring, no eyelids to lift, no rollover and reposition about to save you.

Mary was in one of those loops of suffering now.

Bitty was lying on an exam table, a white sheet and blanket folded off to the side, her thin, pale limbs reflecting the light from the massive fixture above her. She was so pale, her face was the color of a Kleenex, and she was trembling, a twitchy, wrung-out shell of the vibrant, happy little girl she usually was.

As Mary stood next to her, the details of the clinical environment, the beeping equipment and the white tile, the stainless-steel everything, the people in blue scrubs and masks, were at once crystal clear and utterly diffused—and as in a dreamscape, the two extremes on the awareness scale alternated, the scene going in and out of focus randomly.

She'd known it was going to be hard to get through the night. But she'd assumed that would be because of Bitty's memories of abuse getting triggered. Or the fact that the girl was having to go back to the very clinic at which she had watched her mother die. Or even due to the claustrophobia of the MRI, the discomfort of the examination, the tedium of waiting for the test results to come in.

Not. Even. Fucking. Close.

Each one of Bitty's major bones was being broken and reset. Even on the leg that had a shin made from a titanium rod. Without anesthesia because she was allergic to it.

It was indescribable, the horror, the pain, the terror. And it was hard not to rail against God in this moment, cursing whoever was up there for this perfect storm of bad news: growth plates compromised by badly healed breaks; possible amputations after the transition; her being a non-viable candidate for general anesthesia due to her previous reaction to it.

What little pain relief that could be given didn't go nearly far enough.

"One more," she heard herself say. "You can do this."

Bitty didn't seem to comprehend the words. She was lost to the haze of agony, and Mary just wanted to break down in tears herself.

But she couldn't afford the trip to insanity.

Mary leaned down even closer. "Last one, okay? This is our last one."

Bitty's eyes opened wide, tears making them luminous, the great purple smudges that had appeared underneath making her seem like she was on the verge of death. "I can't do it. Please . . . make them stop. . . ."

"One more. I promise you, just one more." She brushed back the bangs and kissed Bitty's forehead. "Hold my hand. Come on. Squeeze as hard as you have to."

"I can't do it . . . please, Mommy . . . help me. . . ."

Sobs racked the little girl's body, making the hospital gown seem as if it were caught in a breeze, and Mary began to cry, too, the tears rolling down her cheeks and dropping onto the thin mattress of the table.

Sniffling, praying for strength, utterly lost, Mary made a mental note that the next time someone looked at her and told her that she had all the answers, she was going to kick them in the ass.

"Havers, can you give us . . ."

As she looked up, she found the physician and his two female nurses standing back. And the look he gave her was so full of compassion, it was nearly impossible to reconcile it with what she knew he had done to his sister Marissa.

But no one had ever faulted him in his profession.

"Let's just breathe," Mary said to Bitty. "Come on . . . breathe with me. . . ."

The MRIs had shown that the girl was at risk of catastrophic deformity when she went through her transition. For vampires, their growth pattern to maturity was compressed into the singular explosion that occurred during their change. It was as if, in the human parallel, a fourteen-year-old became twenty-five physically in a matter of six hours.

In Bitty's case, there were a series of subtle, and not so subtle, curves in her long bones because of the previous fractures. And Mary had noticed them, but hadn't really dwelled on the reasons for them or their implications. The issue was that when that explosive growth happened, those deformities were liable to separate completely, snapping because the force of the expansion would be off-angle.

The end result? Amputation. Of all or most of her limbs. Because for about six months after transition, the bones in vampires were not capable of fusing breaks.

The decision had been made to fix them now.

And Bitty had made the choice. She didn't want to come back in a month or a year or two years or five years to get it done. Nothing was going to change and there was no reason to have the prospect hanging over her head.

But this was just too much.

"I can't, I can't . . . I can't do this. . . ."

Mary couldn't agree more. She couldn't do this anymore, either. Too much. Tapped out. Over the threshold.

Yes, there was a larger goal here, but they'd done enough. Hadn't they?

"Can R-r-r-r-rhage come in?" Bitty stammered.

"Absolutely. Do you want the others?"

Anything to have this work.

"No, because I'm crying." Bitty sniffled. "I'm not brave. . . ."

"Oh, yes, you are." Mary blinked back more tears. "Sweetheart, you are the bravest person I know."

There was a tradition in vampire culture whereby the males of the species were not a part of medical interventions for females—and there were times when Bitty's modesty had been compromised out of necessity. Now, though? All bets were off.

Mary wasn't even going to ask Havers for permission. They needed something else to help the girl finish this.

"I'll get him," Doc Jane volunteered.

Rhage came in and Mary couldn't help it. The second she met his eyes, she choked up so badly, she couldn't breathe. And typical of a bonded male, he went to her first, hugging her tight, whispering something in her ear the words of which did not register, the strong, steady tone of which meant everything.

And then he was all about the little girl, his face losing color as he looked down at Bitty, his hands shaking as he reached out and pulled her into a hug.

A lot of medical people rushed forward, and Mary tugged him back. "Her arms and leg need casts still. Be careful."

Rhage laid the girl back down as if she were made of glass.

"I'm not brave," Bitty moaned up at him.

"Yes, you are," he said, brushing her hair back. "You're so brave and I'm so proud of you and I love you very much."

They talked for a spell, and then there was a pause.

As if sensing the time was now, Havers said gently, "Just one last one. And then you're all finished."

Rhage's brows sank down low, and Mary knew without asking that her *hellren*'s fangs had descended and the protective part of him was considering ripping the doctor's throat out. But that was instinct, not logic.

She stroked Rhage's arm. "Shh, it's okay. One more and this is over."

"One more . . ." He rubbed his face. "We can do this."

Rhage nodded at Havers, who was looking apprehensive. And then the medical staff stepped up to the table again.

Bitty's pelvis was strapped down again and her opposite leg was likewise immobilized. What Havers had to do was grip the thigh and apply pressure until there was a snap. And then he had to pull at the knee until he visualized correct alignment through the skin—something that was relatively clear given how painfully thin and under-muscularized the girl was. An X-ray would be taken to ensure that all was as it needed to be and then the casts would be put on so that the bone regenerated and reconnected itself correctly.

The break and alignment was so primitive, so brutal, that in the midst of all the high-tech machinery and state-of-the-art everything it seemed below the modern standard of care. But there was an undeniable mechanical side to the body, and this was nuts-and-bolts stuff— and again, Mary had to give Marissa's brother credit. He'd done this a number of times for his patients before, and he'd been quick, decisive, and gotten it right with each of Bitty's limbs.

To give Havers room, Rhage went around to the other side, his tremendous height and girth like the Great Wall of China had suddenly taken up res right beside Bitty. Taking the girl's hand, he had looked both stricken and strong.

"We can do this," he said to both her and Mary. "We're all going to get through this together and then we go home to movies and ice cream. Right? Before we know it, we'll be out of here, we'll be free, and we're going to set this behind us."

Mary nodded and so did Bitty.

"Do it," Rhage ordered.

Havers moved the little hospital gown up, exposing a pair of knobby knees that were too big compared to the circumference of the calves and thighs.

Oh, God, as long as Mary lived, she was going to remember the sight of those blue-gloved hands gripping Bitty's thigh, squeezing into her meager flesh and—

Bitty started to scream in pain.

And no more than a split second later, a brilliant light flashed through the exam room, as bright as an explosion.

At first, Mary thought the overhead fixtures had gone out, but then her brain made a horrible connection.

Ripping her eyes away from Havers, she looked at Rhage in horror. "No, not now!"

But it was too late.

The beast had been triggered.

NINE

Enough was enough, Elise thought as she finally descended to the first floor. After stewing in her cousin's room for what felt like hours, she knew she was just putting off the inevitable.

If her father wouldn't entertain a civil audience with her?

Then she was going to get uncivil. Because what was truly unacceptable to her, what she refused to live with for one moment longer, was this familial equivalent of a media blackout.

Besides, what was her father going to do? Turn into a great snarling beast or something?

It wasn't a surprise to find his study door shut, and as she walked across the foyer, it was impossible not to have an attack of the couldn't-possibly's. She had never once interrupted him when he was working on the family investments—but as an image of her beautiful mother came to mind, Elise used it as a battering ram. Even as her upbringing tried to hold her back, she pictured her *mahmen* and what the female would have done in this situation.

Elise didn't even knock.

No reason to give him an excuse to deny entrance.

She just went for it, pushing her way inside—

That memory of her mother was power-washed out of mind as the tableau at the desk sank in: Her father was at his chair, presiding over the masculine room, his dark suit and tie his informal attire. 'Cuz formal was white tie and tails.

That wasn't the shocker.

There was, however, a male sitting across from him, a male who had a pair of bulging shoulders and long, thick-thighed legs that dwarfed not just the seat, but the study as a whole. His hair was dark, shaved up the nape, and his turtleneck and leathers were black. As were the holster and the gun she could see under his arm.

The male slowly turned around to look at her. But she didn't need to see his face.

It was him. From the cigar club.

Elise's body roared with heat—and her brain roared with fury. How had father found out she had seen the trainee? Had there been another vampire around when they'd argued at the side of the street? But come on, they hadn't even had much of a verbal altercation. And Peyton had interrupted—

Peyton. That son of a bitch.

"Father, I—"

"And this is my daughter," her father interjected. "Please excuse her interruption. Elise, this is Axwelle."

The male she had been thinking about non-stop rose to his feet and towered over her. "Pleased to make your acquaintance."

Elise looked back and forth between the two of them as Axwelle bowed at the waist. As an unmated daughter of high blood in the *glymera*, even though there was a witness, it would have been impermissible for him to offer his hand to shake, much less for her to touch him in any way. And he knew that.

And it was just as well. Even though she was confused, what she was crystal clear on? The effect of that male on her had only gotten stronger.

The hours she had spent thinking about him had distilled that initial attraction into a compulsion.

But what the hell was he doing here? If her father was upset because she'd met the guy the night before, he certainly wouldn't have introduced her to Axwelle as if they were strangers.

Well, they were strangers.

Elise looked across the desk at her father. He had slumped in his chair, as if he were too tired to adhere to his posture standards.

"Elise"—he indicated the vacant seat next to Axwelle—"do sit down."

She complied instantly, crossing over and lowering herself into the seat. In her peripheral vision, she noticed that Axwelle wasn't looking at her. His eyes were focused forward on her father.

Yeah, boy, he was . . . okay, she hated the word *hot*. As if someone you found sexually attractive was like a plate of food out of the oven? But in fact, that was pretty much the first and only thing that came to her mind. That black turtleneck so worked for him. Where had his piercings gone? He had removed them.

What would his hair feel like? Soft and thick—

". . . and that's why I've brought him here."

Shaking herself, she blurted, "What?"

"After my discussions with Abalone, the First Advisor, I have come to that perhaps unmistakable, although uncomfortable, conclusion."

Great. She had missed on the whole thing. But chances were good that none of whatever he'd said worked in her favor.

"Well, I don't think I need to be *sehcluded*." Elise crossed her arms over her chest. "I think that is a backward way of handling—"

"Which is why I believe a bodyguard is necessary if you're going to continue to pursue your studies."

Cue the screeching tires.

As she recoiled, her father nodded at Axwelle. "He is here applying for the position. He is a trainee in the Black Dagger Brotherhood's program, and comes highly recommended by the King himself. There is another candidate coming in in an hour. A Novo, I believe the name was. He also comes with the very highest of accolades."

Bodyguard?

As in this male would be guarding . . . her body?

Elise swiveled her head in Axwelle's direction as the implications started to her occur to her—but then she snapped her attention back to her father.

"Wait . . . so if he's with me, you'll let me attend classes on campus and do my teacher's assistant job? You'll allow me to complete my degree?"

Her father cleared his throat. "That is correct."

"You . . . I . . . we . . ." She stammered some more. "Father . . . what has changed your mind?"

Felixe closed his eyes and took a deep breath. "The First Advisor is a male of worth whom I respect greatly. He made me realize . . . if he can allow his blooded daughter into the training center program? I can most certainly permit you to—"

Elise burst up out of the chair and was around the desk in a heartbeat. In her family, physical displays of affection were eschewed in favor of formal interactions such as bows, curtsies, and the very infrequent air kiss on both cheeks. But it was impossible for her not to express herself.

As she threw her arms around her father, he stiffened even more than usual, although after a moment, he did reach up awkwardly and pat her on the arm. "That's fine," he said in a rough voice. "Yes. Fine. Indeed."

He wasn't dismissing her. On the contrary, she had the sense he was equally emotional—it was just they didn't come from people who had any ability to handle intimacy. For the pair of them, this was the equivalent of embracing, holding on, and sobbing as she apologized for lying and violating his trust and he vowed to try to be the father she needed and deserved, as opposed to the repressive force she was coming to resent.

Straightening, Elise pulled her cashmere sweater down and glanced at Axwelle.

His yellow eyes were on her, his lids low, his expression remote. From her father's perspective, he no doubt appeared to be intense in a professional way. But she knew better. There was fire in that stare, fire that would consume her.

If she let it.

"I think this is great idea," she heard herself say. "The bodyguard thing."

As Elise spoke, Axe shifted his eyes back to the female's father. One guaranteed way to lose the job before he even got it? Undress the daughter in your mind right in front of the guy.

Even a poor kid like him knew that was "tacky."

Plus, the truly odd thing, considering the way he typically related to members of the opposite sex, was that he felt as though pulling a leer was just plain wrong. The world was a dangerous place, and this female was extraordinary. Males, human or vampire, coveted things like her. And then there were the slayers.

She needed protection. Deserved it.

He was here in a professional capacity, and there was nothing professional about being the very thing he could be hired to keep her safe from.

"Okay, dear," her father said as he shifted in his chair. Like he preferred her to go back around and be at an arm's length. "All is well."

And that was kind of sad—then again, he'd gotten his fill of parental rejection, hadn't he. At least she didn't seem to mind, though, as she returned to the chair beside him.

"Now, is there anything you should wish to ask of him, Elise?"

Axe felt her glance over, and damn it, he liked it. He wanted her eyes all over his face, his throat, his naked body. He wanted to be sprawled out in front of her on some bed . . . maybe the floor . . . fuck it, he'd lie flat on hot coals for her if that turned her on . . . and he wanted to have his hand on his cock as he looked in her eyes and begged her to ride him.

The submission fantasy, with him as the sub, was a new one for him, but what the hell.

It wasn't like it was actually going to happen.

"Yes?" Axe prompted her.

"Um . . . so I go to SUNY Caldie. I attend class at night and I work with one of my professors as his assistant. Will you be able to . . . blend in?"

Axe could tell she thought the answer was no, but he wasn't sure she exactly cared. Then again, she had narrowly missed being all but shut indoors for the rest of her life if a *sehclusion* petition had been filed.

If he were her, he'd take a hall pass to the university in any form it came: Santa Claus . . . asshole in a Batman suit . . . him.

"I will do whatever is necessary," Axe said—and he directed the response to her sire. "I will be as visible or fade-to-black as required. I will not hesitate to use force, but I will not provoke the humans. And yes, I am prepared to take a bullet for her if I have to. Nothing scares me and I do not run—from anything. Even my own death."

Next to him, Elise recoiled, but he couldn't help her with that. He'd gotten a modified dose of reality last night out in the field, and he knew all too well exactly what her father was worried about.

Felixe the Younger cleared his throat. "That's just fine. That is . . ."

"What you need," Axe finished for the male. "That is what is necessary if you want to protect your daughter. The goal is to let her do her work and make sure she comes home alive every single night. I can give you that peace of mind because when she is in my care, she will be my only priority, above even myself. Nothing and no one will matter except for her."

Felixe exhaled like the elephant that had been sitting on his chest had gotten up for a drink at its water source.

"You can trust me," Axe said.

"Well." More of that throat clearing. "That is just fine, son. Just . . . fine."

Annnnnnnnd that was when he knew he'd been hired.

Meanwhile, Elise was quiet and tense next to him, but then she was telling him what her schedule was like—which wasn't going to be a problem, because now that the trainees were heading out into the field, the Brotherhood's classes were going to be starting later.

He listened to it all, and then her father told him what the salary was.

Holy shit, Axe thought.

Steak-for-dinner money. Electricity. Repairs to his father's house.

"What is your family like, son?" the father inquired.

Axe started to jerk back and caught himself. He hadn't been prepared for anything personal.

At least the answer was easy: "My parents are dead. I have no mate and never will. I have no ties to anything or anybody aside from the training program."

"Did you lose your family in the raids?" Elise asked softly. Like she was having a moment or some shit.

He narrowed his eyes at her. "All you need to worry about is whether I can keep you alive, and I will. That's it."

As her spine straightened in that chair, he kept his smile to himself. She might be a female, but she was a fighter at her core. And she clearly didn't like doors shut in her face, literally or figuratively.

An image of her holding his arms over his head and putting all her weight into keeping him where she wanted him made an erection threaten behind his fly.

Axe cocked a brow back at her, challenging her to let some of that heat out. But she wouldn't. Not in front of her father.

Man, he couldn't wait for his first night on the job. She was going to give him an earful.

And he was, absolutely, hired.

Even if Axe hadn't come across as the deadly force her father was looking for, Felixe had wrongly assumed Novo was a guy: There was no way this genteel chauvinist was going to stand for a female guarding his daughter, no matter how spectacular a soldier and professional Novo was. And that was just fucked up.

But it worked in his favor.

Because he wanted her—

The job, he corrected. He wanted the *job.*

"So I'll be in touch," Felixe said as he rose to his feet.

"Yes," Axe murmured to them both. "I think you will be. And I'll give you my answer right now. I accept the position and I can start whenever you two are ready."

TEN

Complete. Chaos.

As the beast broke out of Rhage's body, triggered by Bitty's suffering, Mary covered the little girl on the exam table with her own body—although not from any fear that the dragon would hurt her.

Parts of the ceiling were raining down, chunks of plaster falling from where the great dragon's head had slammed into the panels. And then that barbed tail was slashing back and forth, splintering cabinets and scattering equipment, smashing into the sink and springing the pipes.

As a spray of hot water golf-sprinklered all around and lights flickered, Havers and his staff had the exact wrong idea. Instead of freezing, they made themselves targets by bolting around, trying to get to an exit that was blocked by something that might eat them.

But come on. Like any of them had dealt with this before?

"Stop! Don't move!" Mary barked.

And that was when the beast roared.

Mary turned her head to try to get one of her ears protected, but she wasn't going to use her hands. Bitty was so exposed—

Behind the dragon, the door to the exam room broke open, Zsadist, V, and Lassiter crowding in.

"Close the door!" Mary yelled. "And stay out!"

Her best shot for this not turning into complete carnage was to make contact with the dragon, soothe it, and keep the thing trained on her and Bitty. As long as she could get and keep its attention, no one was going to get hurt—

The dragon's jaw snapped closed. And then the beast seemed to shudder as its reptilian eyes swung around and focused on Bitty. Chuffing noises came out of its throat, and it took a step forward, the clawed foot landing heavy as construction equipment.

Mary slowly straightened, letting Rhage's alter ego see the child. "She's okay. Come on, investigate for yourself."

The massive head of the monster lowered slowly, as if it didn't want to spook the little girl, and as Mary backed off, the muzzle snuffled over Bitty. Worried sounds of inquiry came out, part nervous purr, part aching chest rattle.

Bitty lifted her hand up and stroked the purple-scaled cheek. "I'm okay. . . ."

Her voice was surprisingly strong, and then she smiled, as if the room wasn't a wreck, and people weren't scared to death, and she hadn't been through torture.

Mary put her palm on the bulging neck of the beast, feeling the muscle and the power. "It's all right . . . shh . . . that's right, snuffle over her. . . ."

Without moving her head or even eyes, she whispered to Havers, "Tell me you got the bone reset."

In her peripheral vision, she saw the male straighten his horn-rimmed glasses, which had gone cockeyed and a half. "I'm s-s-sorry—what?"

"The bone," Mary repeated in the same quiet, even tone. "Did you do what you needed to?"

"Y-y-yes, I believe . . . yes. I n-n-n-need an X-ray to confirm."

"Okay, let's not try to do that now."

The nurses clutched together even tighter, as if they were afraid of their boss challenging that.

"I . . . no," he said, "I agree it would not be advisable the now. Permit me to inquire—how long . . . ah, how long does he . . . ?"

"It all depends. But we're going nowhere until Rhage comes back."

Bitty and the beast were still communicating with touch and sound, and as far as Mary was concerned, considering the distress that the girl had been in, the two of them could spend the next six hours together and the rest of the adults in the room were just going to have to suck it up.

On that note, Mary glanced around and winced. This was going to run into some money, she thought, as she checked out the ruined floor, the battered ceiling, the debris field of glass-front cabinets. But then she looked back at her *hellren* and her little girl. The beast was a big part of their non-linear, freaky family, and deserved to be counted—

The door opened a crack, and then Lassiter, in his game gear, stepped inside the room. As he held something out, Mary couldn't see what it was—

Wait a minute, was that a *Snickers* bar?

"What are you *doing*?" she blurted as he cautiously approached.

The beast snapped to attention, its jowls curling up in a snarl at the angel. But Lassiter was undaunted—so not a shocker.

"Here," he said. "Have a Snickers. You're not yourself when you're hangry."

There was a heartbeat of a pause. And then she couldn't help it.

She had to start laughing. "Really. *Really?*"

And it was funny, as Lassiter looked over at her, his expression behind the open grille of the hockey mask was goofy—yet his eyes were anything but. That pupil-less, glowing stare was dead serious, offering her a kind of lifeline through the painful reality that she loved a child who had been horribly mistreated and that was something she was going to have to deal with for the rest of her days.

"Thank you," she whispered to the angel as the beast reached out and sniffed at the brown wrapper.

"G'head," Lassiter said to the dragon. "Take it."

And what do you know, with a precision that was impressive given the dagger-size of those chompers, Rhage's alter ego took the tiny little candy bar between its front teeth and munched it down.

A split second later, there was a *poof!* and Rhage was naked and shivering on the floor.

"Am I good or what!" Lassiter proclaimed. "Yeeeeeeeeeeeeeeeeeeeeeeah."

Rhage came back from the far side of Beast World blind, freezing cold, and in an absolute panic. As he flailed around on a floor that seemed slippery, he was petrified there was blood everywhere—but no, he didn't scent any carnage. What he did smell was electrical burning, plaster, and astringent, and he was dimly aware that he wasn't nauseous, which was another good indicator that he hadn't eaten anyone—

Wait, why did he taste peanut and chocolate? And something plastic-y?

"Mary . . . !" he called out into the darkness. "Bitty—"

"Everyone's okay." Mary's voice was close to him and utterly calm. "Everything's all right. . . ."

As her hand smoothed over his forehead and brushed through his hair, he mumbled, "Bitty?"

"I'm right here, Father. The beast just wanted to make sure I was sorted. . . ."

Rhage exhaled—and then realized he was lying on a bunch of debris. And there was rain hitting his face?

Oh, God, how in the hell had the beast fit into the exam room? It wasn't like the damn thing could ratchet down on its size.

Talking. Footsteps. A light weight being drawn over his lower body. A loud scraping noise like some big piece of a wall or the ceiling or part of a tall cabinet was being moved out of the way. Meanwhile, all he could do was lie there like a planker, drowning in a pool of aches and frustration.

It fucking sucked.

Vishous's voice came up close. "My brother, we're going to put you on a stretcher, okay? Then get you out of here. Fritz is coming in the Mercedes because we can't fit you in the GTO as easy."

Fuck me, Rhage thought. He was so fucking tired of this shit.

Bitty had needed him, and what had he offered her? A fucking mess. What the fuck had made him feel like he could be a father? He couldn't—

"I want to go with him," Bitty said.

Doc Jane spoke up. "We need to set your limbs, sweetheart."

"I'll wait!" Rhage barked. "I want to wait!"

Bitty's voice grew strident. "Put the casts on and we'll go. But we want to be together."

Rhage closed his lids even though it didn't change how much he couldn't see. The last thing the girl needed to worry about was him—

"You got it, Bit," Vishous affirmed. "That's why I asked for Fritz to come."

"I have to take care of my father."

"Of course you do." Vishous was talking in as gentle a way as he ever did. "And you got it right, kid. He'll do better with you."

No, Rhage thought. He was supposed to support Bitty.

This was a total fucking nightmare.

But at least things moved fairly quickly after that. Havers cleared a path and rolled in a portable X-ray machine, and the image confirmed the thighbone was where it needed to be. Then there was a flour-and-water kind of smell as fiberglass casts were put on both of

Bit's legs and her arms. Rhage refused to leave her, staying on the hard wet floor until everything was dealt with.

And then they were off.

Bit had a wheelchair. He was a slab of meat on a gurney. And the grim entourage of Z, V, and Lassiter fell in step behind Mary.

Talk about the halt and the lame.

"Hey, Rhage?" Lassiter said softly.

"What?" he mumbled.

"If your career as a trained killer doesn't work out? Don't go into interior design. You don't have a knack for it."

Rhage had to laugh. "You are such a fucker."

"Yeah, and you're a good male. Even if you just caused about two hundred grand of damage back there. Don't worry, I think we can write it off your taxes. You know, as a demolition deduction."

There was a squeeze of his shoulder and then Rhage sensed the angel fade back. Taking a deep breath, it was a case of holding it together until he and Mary could get some privacy.

Then he'd fall apart.

Onto an elevator. Slow rise. Slight jerk as they came up to the surface.

The cold, dry air of the night was fantastic in his lungs, but it did nothing to relieve the ache in his chest. And he and Bit both moaned and groaned as they were moved, by other people, into the back of Fritz's S600 4Matic.

Which was brutal for Rhage and not just because every joint and straightaway of his body was killing him.

He wanted to be the one lifting Bitty up and settling her in the back bucket seat. He should have been folding up the wheelchair and putting it in the trunk. He needed to offer support to her as they bumped their way over to the paved road.

It was he who should be carrying her up to her room when they got to the mansion.

"Rhage?"

As Mary said his name, he looked in the direction of the front of the sedan. "Yeah?"

"You ready?"

"Yeah."

Or at least those were the words they spoke. What they had actually communicated was:

Rhage, I know you're not doing well. Can you make it home so we can talk about it then? I'm really worried about you and I'd go into it here and now, but I'm aware that you don't want to do that kind of thing in public.

Oh, God, Mary, this was horrible. I feel awful. Will you still love me even if I'm the worst father on the face of the earth and I never, ever get any better at it?

You are not the worst father. We all have limitations, and we all have things that we wish might have gone better. But please remember. Being a dad is a lifelong commitment and you're just starting out. Don't generalize, okay?

As the car started to move, Rhage took a deep breath and—

Bitty reached across the seat and took his hand. "Thanks for coming with me."

He turned his head. "What?"

"It meant a lot to me that you came—and that you were in the room with me."

Rhage recoiled. "Bitty . . . no offense, but I made everything worse. I mean, I trashed the place."

"I never could have done that last one without you." Her voice was both shy and lovely. "You know . . . my birth sire? He never did anything like that for me. He never . . . he didn't even want me to go to the clinic. You know, even though I was hurt. . . ." She cleared her throat. "So thank you. You're the best father ever."

And then her head went down on his shoulder.

Tears welled into his eyes, stinging them, and making him blink in the midst of his blindness.

"Bitty?"

"Yes?"

He squeezed her little hand and cleared his throat. "You want ice cream when we get home?"

"Yes, please. Mint chocolate chip? We can all have some. We'll get three spoons."

Closing his eyes, he couldn't believe how powerful Bitty's forgiveness was. He felt positively resurrected, while at the same time, he couldn't fathom the generosity. How could this little girl accept him even though he hadn't been the Gibraltar he'd intended on being?

He'd been far closer to Godzilla.

From up in front, he could sense Mary staring at them both. And then his female murmured, because she always said the right thing at the right time, "Isn't it wonderful not to have to be perfect to be loved?"

"Yes," Rhage replied roughly. "And three spoons sounds like heaven to me."

ELEVEN

*T*he call came in to Axe's Brotherhood-issued cell phone at around four a.m., and he answered it as he sat in front of the fire in his father's cottage.

"Hello," he answered.

Sure as if he had conjured her up out of nowhere, the female he had been thinking about non-stop said, "Hi, it's Elise."

"Did I get the job?"

There was a pause. "Yes, you did. The other bodyguard that came was a female, and my father—"

"Would never have hired her. Yeah, I guessed."

"Um . . . is there any way you could come back to the house? My sire would like you to sign some documents and then I thought we could talk a little more about the next couple of nights? I'm not sure we ironed out how many evenings—"

"Give me ten minutes."

"Ah, okay. All right. Thank you."

Axe ended the call and sat there with his phone in his hand. And three . . . two . . . one—

Sure enough, the call from Peyton came in next. And Axe didn't bother with a greeting, he just accepted it and kept the phone where it was, down by his thigh.

Through the tiny little ear speaker, the male went off, his voice all treble. "Are you fucking kidding me? What the hell kind of lies did you tell them? You have no business—none!—guarding my cousin. You are—"

Axe put the phone up to his ear. "Not your decision, Peyton. Sorry—"

Bang! Bang! Bang!

Axe cranked his head around to the front door. "Are you kidding me."

"Open your fucking door!" came the demand.

Axe ended the connection and got up, his knees cracking. Muttering under his breath, he went over, cranked the knob, and opened up.

"FYI, I don't lock this place," he said in a bored tone. "Next time you come to rant at me, just walk on in."

As he pivoted away, he had every faith that Peyton would ride his ass, and surprise!, surprise!, that's what the aristocrat did, marching through the little room toward the fire.

"What, you can't turn the heat up?" Peyton snapped. "And it's dark as a cave as well as cold as fuck."

"Are rich people like you bred to be judgmental? Or does it just happen because of all the money?"

"This is not a fucking game, asshole!"

Axe pivoted and rolled his eyes at the guy. "Do I look like I'm playing Monopoly over here?"

Peyton got right up in his shit. "Tell them you're not going to do it. Or I will."

"Who the fuck do you think you are? Coming in here and trying to order me around? You don't know me, we're not kin, and what I do on my free time is none of your fucking business."

"Deny that you want her. Go on, lie to my face and tell me that you don't want her—and then you can piss around a whole lot of bullshit that you're going to be even halfway professional in this!"

"FYI, Richie Rich"—Axe jabbed two fingers into the SOB's chest—"I've spent all my life around things I can't have. So I'm really fucking used to it. And you should feel pretty cocksucking good about that. That's what you people do, right. You look down your noses at commoners like me."

"You're a male. This has got nothing to do with where you come from."

"Ohhhh, okay, right. So males can't have any self-control. None at all."

"They can't! Don't be a little bitch—"

"So you're fucking Paradise, then. Behind Craeg's back. Got it. Good to know."

The guy frowned. "What the hell are you talking about?"

Axe smiled coldly and leaned in. "You want that female. You want her so fucking bad you can taste it. I see you looking at her, pretending like you're smooth and shit. But you ain't. So, yeah, if males can't exercise self-control, then clearly you've got your dick in her mouth—"

The right hook came flying in at a perfect angle, and you want to talk about a light show? As contact was made, Axe's head snapped up and over, his brain going loose-cannon in his skull, his vision briefly browning out.

"You're fucking deluded, man," Peyton spat. "You're totally—"

Twice. In less than twenty-four hours. The douche bag punches him twice.

Axe pulled the gun he kept tucked in his waistband out and put it to the guy's temple so quick, Peyton didn't have time to step back. "The safety's off. And I have nothing to lose. So how 'bout we start with you never fucking hitting me again. You got two shots on me. The third will put you in a grave."

Peyton blinked. A couple of times. And Axe met him right in the eyes just so the male knew how dead serious he was.

"Get out," Axe said in a low voice.

"You're wrong about me and Paradise. She's with her male. She picked him. I've never been with her and I never will be. So you just drop that bullshit—and if you don't call Elise's father right now, I'll go over there myself and tell him you're out. You are not getting into that house—"

Axe moved the gun to the side a thin inch and pulled the trigger. The pop was loud; the impact of the bullet in the wall was louder.

Peyton shouted and covered his head, dropping to his knees. But Axe was done. Reaching down with his free hand, he grabbed the fuck-twit's expensive jacket and spun the male up and around, punching him back into the wall by the fireplace so hard the plaster cracked.

"You want to know why it's so cold in here?" Axe gritted out. "It's because I can't afford heat. And that's the reason there are no lights on, too. You may have the luxury of not worrying where your next meal or your next Mercedes is coming from, but I'm pinching pennies and eating at the training center as often as I can. You have no right to tell me to do shit—and my not taking a job just so you don't have to face the fact that your other cousin was recently murdered is not my fucking problem. Oh, and P.S., fuck you—don't stand there in your fancy loafers while you're not with the female you want, and maintain for one second that just because I'm poor, it doesn't mean I can't do the same. We can't help who we're attracted to, but thoughts are not actions. Even for commoners."

Axe punctuated his little speech with another *bam* into the wall. Then he released his hold and walked off, prowling around the tiny living room with its haphazard furniture and the drapes that were all wilted and the threadbare rugs. As the silence stretched out, he hated the fact that he was ashamed of his father's house.

It was yet another betrayal of the male. And more than that, Peyton and his platinum-plated double standards were hardly anything worth living up to.

"I'll pay you," the male said grimly. "Whatever you're making, I'll double it. Triple it."

Axe twisted around and stared at the guy.

Peyton put his palms up. "I'll give you a year's worth up front. Right now."

Axe opened his mouth. Shut it.

In the end, he just grabbed his leather jacket and walked out of the room for the front door.

"Where are you going?" Peyton demanded.

"Shut the door behind you. Or don't. I don't give a fuck. But if I don't leave now, I'm going to have to explain to Elise why I killed you, and I'd rather talk about her class schedule."

Elise's heart was pounding as she paced back and forth over the gray and white marble squares of the foyer's floor. Her father had left for a meeting across town with her uncle. The butler and staff were working quietly in the rear of the house—which, considering her family's mansion was over twenty-five thousand square feet in size, meant they were nowhere to be found. And her aunt was upstairs in bed.

Looking across at the French ormolu clock on the bombé chest by the grand door, she double-checked her watch. Then she turned to the antique mirror next to her and stared at her wavy reflection. The distortion seemed apt. She wasn't sure what she was doing, what she was going to say.

Fiddling with the collar of her cashmere sweater, she made sure her wide-legged Donna Karan slacks were smooth over her hips. Her shoes were nothing special, just Tory Burch flats.

She wished she were in jeans, but her father didn't approve of them.

As if the house were a country club with a dress code—

A rattling sound made her frown. Her phone, which was on vibrate, was going off over by the clock and she rushed to the thing.

It was Troy—

Great thunder rolled through the open space, the front door knocker being used by a strong hand.

As she put the phone back down without answering, she thought, Well, wasn't that a revealing choice.

Her heart skipped behind her rib cage—and then she jumped as the butler came out of the library.

"Oh, I have it," she told him with what she hoped was an easy smile. "Not to worry."

The *doggen* shuffled to a halt as if a polite dog fight between his sense of duty and her direct order were jamming his circuits.

"It's all right," Elise said. "Do return to your more important duties."

He hesitated for another moment, his eyes going to the big brass handle as if he had to go through at least a mental projection of doing the deed before he could leave. And then he bowed to her and returned to whatever polishing, dusting, or inspection he'd been performing.

Elise took a deep breath and opened the heavy door. Bracing herself to look up, she—

"Oh, my God!"

Axwelle was still in the clothes that he'd worn to the interview, the turtleneck and simple black slacks just as appealing on him. Hair was still thick and black and cropped. Face remained as rugged and compelling as it had been.

But he was bleeding.

Underneath his left eye, or maybe it was off to the side, there was some kind of cut, the skin broken and leaking. There was a bruise coming up, too, the cheekbone beneath the laceration swelling and turning red.

"You told me to come," he said with a frown.

"Your eye." She pointed to the injury. "You're hurt."

He put his hand up and touched his face, but rather than being alarmed, he merely seemed annoyed.

"You got a Kleenex?" he asked.

"What?"

"Tissue? Or toilet paper will work just fine. Point me in the direction of your bathroom."

"You're serious."

"Excuse me?"

"Oh, for God's sake." She grabbed his hand before she knew what she was doing. "Let me take care of it."

There was some initial resistance as she shut the door and tried to walk off with him, but then he followed. At least until she got to the foot of the curving staircase.

"We're going upstairs," she said, pulling on his hand. "I have a first aid kit in my room. And I also have my schedule for next semester up there."

"You don't have it on your phone? And come on, we don't need to make a big deal about this—"

"Scared?"

Axwelle stopped short, and the glower that hit his face made his eyes glow. "Of what."

"You tell me. Because I can't figure out why you don't want to go upstairs."

With a curse under his breath, he took the steps two at a time, and Elise found herself smiling a little as she jogged behind him.

"So what happened to your face?" she asked his huge shoulders.

"Nothing."

"FYI, if you're going to lie to try to get me off the scent, at least make it believable. We're not heading for a Band-Aid because 'nothing' happened."

"It's none of your business, how 'bout that. And Christ, I'm getting really tired of telling you people that."

"What's that supposed to mean?"

"Big house," he commented as they came to the second floor and he looked at the hall that went off in both directions. "How many rooms?"

"Really." She put her hands on her hips. "That's your next best?"

His stare locked on hers, and as he leaned in, his incredible size and power registered—but not in a threatening way.

More in a way that made her eyes flick down to his mouth for a split second.

"I'm not talking about it to you," he said. "If you want to play nurse, that's fine. But just because you're insisting on mopping me up, doesn't mean you're due some kind of explanation. Are we clear?"

Elise looked at him for a long moment. They were dangerously close to getting off on a seriously wrong foot. And if she lost him? If he decided to walk out on her?

She didn't want to give her father an excuse to rethink his decision.

Answer the damn house question, she told herself. Get on neutral ground.

"I don't know how many rooms we have." She cursed under her breath as she went to the left. "Maybe forty? Fifty? Something like that. My father built it in nineteen ten."

She was very aware of him behind her, sensing that body of his. His presence. His aura.

In fact, she found herself walking differently, her hips moving from side to side more, her shoulders shifting. She had no idea how she knew this . . . but she was sure he was measuring the shape of her ass, her thighs. Then again, it was exactly what she did—what she was doing—to him.

"Here's my room."

Opening the way in, she resisted the urge to Vanna White the exotic objects in the room, like *the bed!, the vanity!, this beautiful desk!, the wallpaper!*

What was it about physical attraction that turned even the smartest people into babbling idiots?

"My bath is in here." She indicated the way through the open double doors. Like he might have no frickin' clue what the marble space was. "Come with me."

Inside, the mirror over the double sinks gave her a wide-angle view of him as he stopped in between the doorjambs and proceeded no farther.

"Just give me something to wipe the blood off." His eyes moved over the claw-foot tub, the glassed-in shower in the corner, the banks of windows that were dark. "I'll take care of it."

His huge mass and all the black clothes were completely out of place among the pale marble and the crystal and gold accents—and a shiver of thrill went through her. He was standing in a place she was naked in on a regular basis.

She wasn't sure why this occurred to her or even seemed so erotic. But it did.

Elise pulled a monogrammed hand towel off a gold bar and cranked on the gold faucet. Putting her fingers under the rush, she waited for the water to—

"It doesn't need to be warm," he muttered.

It seemed silly to argue with him. So she just stood there until the temperature was right, and then wet the terry cloth.

"Just give it to me," he demanded as he held out his hand.

Squeezing the excess free, she went over and put the towel into his palm. "Be careful—whoa! What are you doing?"

Well, that was obvious. He was trying to scrub off that whole side of his face.

She grabbed his forearm, and as he recoiled, like she'd surprised him, she took advantage of the reaction and snatched the towel back.

Yanking him farther into the bathroom, she pushed him down onto the bench by the tub. Stepping in close, she batted his hands out of the way and went to work properly.

"How'd this happen?" She dabbed with care. "It doesn't look dirty. Who hit you and is he still alive?"

Axwelle's response? A jaw that ground his lower molars into his top ones—like he was having a conversation with someone in his head. Her? Or the person he'd fought with?

Probably her.

"You can tell me, you know." Elise went over to the sink again and rinsed out the towel. Came back. "I'm not going to judge."

Leaning in still closer, she focused on the laceration. "I think this is going to need stitches. It's deep and wide? Can you see out of this eye?"

No answer. Just more of that tightly locked and ever-rotating lower jaw.

"Okay, Mr. Chatty, let me see what I can cover this with. And then you need to go see Havers. You're obviously healthy, so you're going to heal, but this might get infected before it closes itself."

Elise patted the area dry with the other end of the towel and went to her cabinets, bending over the center drawers as she pulled them open one by one. The first aid kit was in the last one by the floor.

Rifling through the Band-Aids and gauze patches, she took one of the big squares out. "This'll do."

She shucked the wrapper into the wastepaper basket and headed over to her silent, morose patient.

"So, yes, thank you for asking," she murmured as she got in close again. "I love going to school. I'm really good at it, but just as important, it's where I get to be myself. No assumptions or restrictions because of where I come from. Nothing but my own actions and words defining who I am. It's freedom to me."

She peeled the backing off the two adhesive ends, pinched the gaping hole in his flesh, and covered the laceration, making sure that the bandage squeezed the wound tight. Crushing the little tabs in her fist, she stepped back. Axwelle was staring straight ahead, as if he hadn't been able to stand her getting near him.

Cursing under her breath again, she felt like her chance to keep going to that human university was disappearing in front of her very eyes.

"Look," she said with exhaustion. "I know you and I are doing the oil-and-water routine here, but I really need this to work. I need to finish my doctorate. It's years of my life. I mean . . . if you don't want the job, just back out now and let me try to find someone else, okay? Hello? Are you listening to me even in the slightest?" She threw up her hands. "This is ridiculous. Why did you come here at all?"

Maybe she had gotten him wrong. She could have sworn he'd been staring at her because he found her attractive. Maybe it was the other way around—

Abruptly, his hands gripped his knees and squeezed.

"Are you stroking out or something?" she demanded. "Because my medical expertise stops at Band-Aids."

When he just stayed where he was, she put her hands on her hips for the third time in his presence. "Will you just tell me what the hell is going on here? Do you need an ambulance? Did they hit you so hard you have a concussion? Whatever it is, you better tell me right now or I'm going to drag you out of this house and leave you to die on my front lawn."

His upper lip curled up off his fangs and he shook his head.

"You really are a coward," she muttered. "Big tough guy like you, but you can't talk about anything—"

"Coward?" he bit out. "You think I'm a coward."

"Yeah, I do. What's the other explanation?"

"Coward, huh. Fine. How's this for a problem."

With that, he rose to his full height, mirrored her pose with his hands on his hips—and just stood there, like that said it all.

Elise shrugged with a frown. "Yes? And? You want to remind me that you're six-six? Six-seven? Dressed in black? What—"

Annnnnnnd that was when she saw it.

It was a very big *it*. A very . . . erect *it*, straining the front of his pants.

TWELVE

How's that for communication, Axe wanted to say.

Instead, he simply let the female get a good hard gander at his little coward, which was neither little at all nor cowardly in the slightest. In fact, his cock was really damn bold, completely unapologetic, and seemed to be twice the size it usually was.

And Axe hadn't been a grower to begin with.

But fuck him, this was not the way he'd wanted to start out with her—and yeah, you could rewind that empty wish right back to him showing up at her father's mansion bleeding down his face. The problem was—well, *one* of his problems was—that he'd been so fucking riffed at Peyton's criminal sense of entitlement, he hadn't even thought about any injury—and then this female had taken him up here, where everything smelled like her, and sat him down, and stepped into his personal space and . . .

Yeah, he'd gotten hard.

The entire time she'd been doing her first aid thing, he'd been hoping, praying, to will himself back to flaccidity. No luck. It was like yelling at a pig. You looked like an idiot and the pig didn't give a shit.

So here they were, standing in a bathroom that was like something out of *The Devil Wears Prada*—if Miranda Priestly had had a Jacuzzi scene—with him ridiculously aroused and Elise standing in front of him as if she couldn't decide whether to cover her eyes and run . . .

Or find out what he felt like.

"This is a bad idea," he muttered as he turned around, rearranged himself, and stalked out into her bedroom.

Great, all he could stare at was her bed . . . and imagine what she would look like naked on it.

"Wait," she said. "Don't go—"

He pivoted on her expensive carpet. "You need someone else."

She kicked up her chin. "I don't want someone else. I want you."

Axe closed his eyes and tried not to read all kinds of bump and grind into that.

"Did you lose your mate?" she asked.

He shook his head to clear it. "What?"

"Your mate. Has it been . . . a while for you? Or something? And yes, I know that that's a personal question, but come on," she muttered dryly, "it's not like we aren't already there."

For a second, he thought she had to be fishing for compliments . . . but her face was open, her eyes guileless, her affect as honest as a sunrise.

She literally had no idea why she affected him as she did.

Without meaning to, he focused on her lips—which had been the original problem for him: While she had been nursing him, doing so much better a job than he had with the cleaning and Band-Aid action, he had made eye-to-mouth contact and been instantly lost in wondering what she would taste like, feel like, be like. And not just with kissing—with everything.

As in naked bodies and desperate, hungry sex on repeat until they both passed out.

"The raids cost a lot of people their family," she whispered. "It was a hard time for all of us."

"No one needs to tell me that."

She went quiet as if she were waiting for him to continue. When he didn't, she shook her head. "Well, I'm sorry for whatever losses you had. I know . . . what that feels like."

"Do you."

"My cousin was murdered last month. It's . . . been horrible. Especially as her brother had already been killed in the raids."

From out of nowhere, and for no good reason he could think of, a fleeting pain lit off in his chest. "Death is always horrible. Unless it is your enemy."

"I wouldn't know . . . much about the war."

"I'm going to go."

After all, his head was now completely fucked, a debate raging between his rational side, which felt strongly that having sex with her on the job while at the same time confusing her with the ice-cold aristocrats who had killed his father would be totally unfair . . . and his batshit crazies, which were maintaining that sleeping with her while being paid for keeping her safe and tarring her with the same brush as those other *glymera* assholes was utterly logical.

"What exactly are you afraid of?" she murmured. "I find myself asking that again."

He leveled a glare at her. "What?"

"Well, that's just what I'm wondering. I mean, there's nothing to be lost by sharing information and opinions and concerns as a means to a productive end—namely, you and I making it possible for me to go to school. You can ask me anything and I'll tell you. I'm not afraid—and I guess I'm trying to reconcile this tough-guy, protective-exterior thing with how incredibly cowardly it is not to express yourself to someone else."

Axe blinked.

Are you kidding me, he thought. Twice in one night?

"Let me ask you something," he said.

Elise put her arms wide. "Anything. I'm an open book."

"What is it about rich people that makes you believe you have a right to anything and everything? Not just material shit, but people's lives, emotions, thoughts. You tell me it's no big deal to talk about things? That I'm a fucking coward if I don't reveal stuff about myself on demand?" He shrugged. "You don't have any conception of my life or what I've been through, but unless I choose to give you that access, on your terms, on your timeline, suddenly I'm the one with the defect. You're a stranger to me. I don't know you. And I don't have to get to know you. I don't owe you any part of me."

That shut her up.

And just as he was congratulating himself for putting her in her place, she pulled the rug out from under him. Again.

"God . . . you're absolutely right."

She walked across to her vanity, her graceful hand drifting over the silver brushes and the few compacts and lipsticks that were on it.

"I'm really sorry." She looked over her shoulder at him and laughed awkwardly. "And to think I'm going for my doctorate in psychology. I should know more about interpersonal relating, right? Guess theory and practicality don't always go hand in hand. I apologize."

Annnnnnnnnd Axe blinked again.

Fuck. He hadn't expected her to get his boundary. Much less respect it.

At a loss, he sat down at the foot of her bed.

Running his hand through his hair, he put his elbows on his knees and thought, Yeah, he really needed to get out of here and away from her.

But instead of leaving, he said, "I've never known anyone who's gotten their doctorate before."

All things considered, Elise thought, Axwelle had been right to call her on her shit: The thing that she had forgotten—and this was especially true when it came to new people—was that you had to meet folks where they were. Arousal aside, he'd never given her any indication that he was an open book, and she had pushed him too far because she had ascribed her own characteristics to him.

But she was encouraged that he hadn't bolted out her door.

"Yes," she said, clearing her throat. "My studies have been years and years of work. That's why—well, that's why I got ahead of myself just now. It's been a huge investment of time and effort, and if I don't complete my dissertation, I feel like it's all been for nothing? And my father can be so hard for me to deal with. The fact that he's given me this opportunity is a miracle, and I guess . . . I just don't want to lose my shot."

As she fell silent, he cracked his knuckles one by one. "I can't help it."

"Being defensive? Why wouldn't you have been. I put you on the spot."

"No. Being attracted to you."

Elise tried to look calm as her heart skipped in her chest. But Lord help her, she nearly let out a giggle.

Straightening her spine, she decided to man up. "That's okay. I can't help being attracted to you." As his head whipped up, she rolled her eyes. "Come on. It's pretty damn obvious."

Axwelle cleared his throat. "So you're the psych pro. Don't you think that means we shouldn't work together?"

"At least we know what the issue will be instead of having to discover it." There was a pause. "Okay, that was a joke. You're supposed to laugh."

When he didn't even chuckle, she—

The snort he let out was probably one of the most unattractive sounds she'd ever heard in her life, part wounded gopher, part grizzly bear, part old car backfiring. And then he cursed and slapped a palm over his mouth.

"Oh, my God," she blurted, "that is frickin' adorable."

Across the way, on her girlie bed, with its pretty coral bedspread and the framing drapes of fabric that hung from a medallion on the ceiling, the fighter in his black clothes and bandaged face and his kill-ya-soon-as-look-at-ya affect turned the color of a stop sign.

"I burped. That's all." He stretched his back and rolled his shoulder as if he wanted to remind himself he was packed with muscle. "Look, I've never done this bodyguarding thing before, so I don't know what to expect with any of it. I think the question for you is, are you willing to bet your life on me? 'Cuz that's what it all comes down to. We could go a hundred nights without anything happening, but it just takes one where something does. And then you're not screwed—either in a sexual or a bad luck sense—you're fucking dead."

"Do you doubt yourself?"

He frowned. "You want the honest truth?"

"Always." She held up her forefinger. "I want to go on record right now and say this loud and clear. I always want the truth from you. That's more important to me than anything else—for reasons that you'll no doubt come to understand."

He cracked those knuckles again. Rolled his other shoulder.

"Personally, I think my attraction works for us—I mean, you. It increases my protective nature and will make me more lethal. I'm not bonded to you, and I won't ever be, but I am male, and in fact, I'm so much more raw than the overbred pansies you're used to dealing with. So, yeah, anyone tries to so much as brush the ends of your hair with their elbow, and I will kill them four times over before I light their corpse on fire."

"Well, isn't that something to put on a Valentine's Day card." Except he probably had a point. "And listen, I firmly believe we aren't what we think, we're what we do. You and I will keep things professional on a physical level and all will be well."

Axwelle got to his feet in a rush. "Okay, text me when you need me tomorrow. I can work until one a.m., but then I have training." He nodded, in a way that made it seem as if they had shaken hands, and then he went for her door. "I'll show myself out—"

"Wait, so my schedule—"

"Just let me know."

Boy, he'd had it with the conversating, hadn't he.

"We can do this, you know," she told his strong back. "It's all going to be okay."

"You say that now." He opened the door wide. "Let's hope at the end of it, however long it lasts, you feel the same."

"Wait, I need your cell phone?"

He spoke the digits over his shoulder like an afterthought and then he kept on going through the jambs without seeming to care whether or not she caught them.

But he did care.

Underneath all that hard-as-nails exterior, he wasn't as blasé as he wanted her to believe. Otherwise he wouldn't have sat down and talked to her at all.

Heading over to the bank of windows that overlooked the front of the mansion, she pulled back the lacy privacy curtain and waited. A moment later, Axwelle emerged from the grand entrance, marching off down the slate walkway.

"Look at me," she whispered. "Come on . . . you know you want to."

In the back of her mind, she was oh-so-aware that self-righteous speeches about professionalism and self-control to the contrary, a part of her really wanted the male to pull a John Cusack on the front lawn.

Which was nuts.

And not as in clinically insane.

More as in a road she shouldn't go down, given their circumstances.

The good news? As he continued to stride away from her house, he clearly wasn't going to—

Axwelle stopped about fifteen feet past the third lantern on the walkway . . . and he stayed where he was for the longest time. Years, it seemed. Just before she was going to either give up or go down to see if that head injury she'd asked about had finally decided to make an appearance . . . he pivoted on one boot and glanced back.

His chin lifted as if his eyes were traveling up to the second floor.

With a squeak, Elise jerked back out of sight and let the curtain fall into place once more.

Her heart thundered behind her sternum and a hot flush made her take off her cashmere sweater like it was a medieval hair shirt.

As she turned away, she looked over at the sunken impression in the duvet where he'd sat on her bed. From out of nowhere, she wanted to go over and run her hand over the spot.

"What the hell am I doing?" she said into the silence of her bedroom.

THIRTEEN

The funny thing about watching a movie marathon while you couldn't see anything was how much you could in fact picture.

Of course, in Rhage's case, he had essentially memorized *Die Hard* from the moment John McClane got the advice about taking off his shoes on the plane, all the way until his wife hit that obnoxious newsman right in the piehole.

"How you doing, Bit?" he said.

Hours before, he and Bitty and Mary had taken up res in the reclining leather ass palaces of the mansion's movie theater for two reasons: one, Bitty was more comfortable sitting up with her legs extending out; and two, the never-ending parade of cinematic distraction, which he'd curated from his repertoire of greatness, had been exactly what they'd all needed to cleanse their mental and emotional palates. They'd seen *Deadpool* first, of course.

One had to keep current, dontcha know.

And then it had been *The Devil Wears Prada*, out of deference to Mary, who, in spite of her preference for valid *Palme d'Or* stuff, loved Meryl Streep as Miranda Priestly. After that, they'd gone back to the ass-kicking with *Guardians of the Galaxy*—Bit loved Zoe Saldana in that one—and finally, *Central Intelligence.*

The Rock was probably one of the few humans who you'd want at your side in a fight.

Rhage had had to end with an oldie but goodie, though. Plus it had been at least three weeks since he'd seen Hans Gruber fall off Nakatomi Plaza, and it was Christmas.

#seasonallyappropriate

"Bit? You okay?" When there was still no answer, Rhage turned his head in the other direction. "Is she out?" he asked Mary.

When there was no reply on that side either, he smiled and felt around. He found Mary's hand first, and as he took it, his mate snuffled and curled in his direction, one of her legs crossing over his, her sigh as she fell back into deep sleep one of total contentment. Then he located Bit's much smaller version of same, and just as with Mary, the little girl turned to him, her head coming to rest against his bicep, her hair falling forward to tickle his forearm.

Rhage smiled and resumed not watching the movie.

Even though he couldn't see anything, he felt strong as an ox, big as a mountain, deadly as a cobra—you name the he-man metaphor and he was rocking that shit.

It wasn't chauvinistic to want to protect your females. It was appropriate, and not because they couldn't be smart and protect themselves. Females were simply more important than males and always would be, and in the very deepest part of his marrow, he was proud to be in service as a mate and a father to them.

God, he felt so totally whole, his *shellan* and his daughter bookending him, giving him all his strength and purpose, stabilizing him even though he hadn't been aware of feeling wobbly.

Funny, the experience was a little like falling in love: a revelation that made everything more beautiful, more precious.

Right on cue, as if fate were determined to give him A Moment, his sight slowly returned, the flickering of the screen, the contours of the seats and the dark theater . . . his beautiful females . . . coming into a soft focus.

Like his view of life had taken on a Merchant Ivory filter.

And to think, without his Mary, he wouldn't even know what that was.

Dearest Virgin Scribe, though, it pained him to see those casts, the reminder of Bit's suffering and his spectacular flame-out taking him back to a place he didn't want to be. But he did smile. Bitty had insisted the leg casts be blue and the arm casts silver, for his bloodline's colors. And everyone in the house had written on them with a black Sharpie, the signatures and messages blurring together, the King's overlapped by a *doggen's*, brother sharing space with Nalla's scribble, even Boo and George adding a paw print thanks to an ink pad that had been brought up.

Bit was fine now, he told himself. Safe here with him and Mary and the other members of the household.

It was all going to be—

Just as Argyle was getting down in the back of the eighties-era limo, head nodding next to the teddy bear, Rhage saw that he and his family weren't alone.

Lassiter was over on the left, leaning back against the fabric-covered wall, the light from the film moving over his face like flame from a fire.

His blond-and-black hair was down around his shoulders, the simple muscle shirt and track pants the kind of thing that a normal person would wear—which meant they should have been completely outside of the fallen angel's wardrobe hangers.

Even from across the way, and in spite of both the dimness and Rhage's iffy eyesight, it was very obvious Lassiter's expression was grim.

He wasn't even looking at the movie.

And that made Rhage wish for the inconceivable.

"Tell me you're here because there's a *Beaches* joke you want to share," Rhage said roughly. "Or maybe 'cuz you got a *Little Mermaid* sleeping bag for me?"

Lassiter stayed silent for what felt like a year, but was probably little more than a heartbeat or two.

Which, considering Rhage's ticker was on a broken field run in his chest, was a helluva commentary on the whole time-is-relative thing.

"I want you to remember what I told you," the angel said . . . in a voice that made Walter Cronkite sound like a falsetto with his nuts in a vise. "Keep your faith. It's all going to work out."

Rhage's eyes snapped back to the casts. "Havers told us the reset bones would heal in about six weeks. And after that . . . I mean, the transition is scary for everybody, but her growth spurt should be tolerated. Even if there has to be some physical therapy afterward, or an operation, at that point, she has different anesthesia and painkiller options and—"

When he glanced back, the angel was gone.

Frowning, Rhage twisted himself around.

Lassiter wasn't walking to the exit; it was as if he'd never been in the theater.

"Rhage? You okay?"

As Mary spoke up in a groggy voice, hc cranked back so he was facing the movie. Opening his mouth, he—

Shut it again. Shook his head. Tried once more. "Ah, yeah. I'm fine. Hey . . . ah, did you see Lassiter just now?"

"No? There's no one in here but us?"

Rhage blinked and pulled an optical sweep of the dark space. Was he even seeing this? Or had he imagined everything. . . .

Was he still blind, and was he dreaming?

"Ah . . . okay. Yeah. Sure."

"Do you want me to get you something to eat?" His Mary Madonna leaned up his chest to smooth his hair back. "You don't look well. Should I get Doc Jane?"

All Rhage could do was stare at her beautiful face. In the history of the world, there might have been females who other people thought were extraordinary beauties, whose bone structure and curve of the lip, whose eyes and brows, equated in the minds of third parties to earth-shattering attractiveness.

Nefertiti had nothing on his *shellan* as far as he was concerned.

To him, Mary was the gold standard that made all others base metals.

"I'm getting Doc Jane right now—"

As she went to get off the recliner, he caught her hand and gently tugged her back to him. "I'm okay. Just been a long night and day. What time is it?"

The distraction worked as she looked at her watch—which was his yellow gold Rolex President and about the size of a car on her slender wrist. "It's seven o'clock. Are you sure you don't need help?"

"Everything I need is right here." He moved in and kissed her lips. "And good, that means in another twelve hours, I should be ready for First Meal."

"It's happening right now. That would be seven at night. So, really, how about food?"

"Nah. I'm tight."

"Rhage, what's wrong?"

He resettled into the recliner. "Nothing. Just a bad dream."

Yup. It had to be a dream.

Lassiter without neon zebra stripes and an Olivia Newton-John "Let's Get Physical" headband in silver and hot pink?

Figment of his imagination. Abso.

"Are you sure?" Mary asked softly.

As he nodded, he was relieved when she eased back with him and put her head on his shoulder once again. Across his pecs, she looked at Bit, checking on the little girl and brushing a lock of that deep brown hair back.

"So brave," she murmured.

"The bravest."

"God, that was awful last night at the clinic."

"You mean before or after they broke our daughter's arms and legs again. Or . . . wait, when I put a sunroof in something that was underground?" He scrubbed his face, and then took her hand. "I can't believe we got through that."

"Neither can I." But then she smiled at him. "That's what makes a family, though. We persevere. We come out the other side of whatever it is stronger. The laughter and the fun, the good times, are wonderful and part of life's great joys. But the hard stuff . . . the challenges you just squeak by, the reentry into normal life that shakes your capsule and steals your oxygen and makes you think it's all going to be over in a flaming wreck? That's how you get the ties that bind."

Rhage thought about his brothers. His King. The other people in this house.

Then of his Mary and Bit.

Blinking quick, he kissed the top of her head. "You always know just what to say."

She rubbed her cheek against him and pressed her lips to his sternum. Then she looked at the big-as-a-drive-in screen in front of them. "So . . . is *Die Hard* your favorite movie?"

"Yeah, I think so." He squeezed her hand. "Either this or *The Godfather*. Shoot . . . I really like *The Wrath of Khan*. And then there's Ryan Reynolds setting the new standard. I don't know. It's like ice cream flavors—too many to choose from and depends on my mood, right?"

"Mmm-hmm. Are you sure you don't want to eat?"

"I like sitting here more."

As she yawned, he trained his eyes on the movie and tried to find his way back to where he had been. He couldn't get there.

Like a glass shattered, he couldn't put the feeling of safety and security back together again.

Lassiter loomed even though he wasn't anywhere to be seen.

FOURTEEN

In the dream, Axe was back in Elise's bedroom. He was in the clothes he'd been wearing when he'd gone up there, and he was sitting where he'd actually parked it at the end of her bed. The double doors into that bath of hers were wide open, and everything was as it had been in terms of furniture and decor—but it was all so hazy, like there was a smoke machine in the corner coughing out wafts of white fog.

He couldn't see Elise, but he could hear her voice. She was talking to him from her bath, her voice coming and going out of earshot as if somebody was adjusting the volume on the world and had a bad hand tremor.

He was aware of being seriously aroused.

Really. Fucking. Hard.

And that was before she came into the jambs of the arched door-way.

Elise was incredibly, spectacularly naked, not one stitch of clothing keeping his eyes from her skin—and yet the specifics of her body were lost to him, that haze airbrushing out her breasts, the plane of her stomach, her clefted sex.

"Do you want me?" she said in a distorted voice.

"God, yes, fuck yes . . . I ache. . . ."

"Tell me you want me."

Spreading his knees wide, he put his hand on his sex and squeezed. "So bad . . . I'm dying. . . ."

"Say the words."

"I want you . . . ," he breathed.

Elise came to him like a summer breeze, walking across the fancy rug with a graceful stride that had him moaning in the back of his throat. And then she was in front of him, and he was reaching out to touch her, to caress her warm, vital skin. As he pulled her in between his legs, her scent filled his nose and his cock roared, his fangs descending in his mouth.

"Elise . . ."

Looking up at her, he moved his hands to her upper arms, urging her to kiss him. But the more he tried to get her to lean down and let him take her lips, the more she slipped from his grasp, her body becoming ether as she disappeared before his very eyes—

The alarm went off next to his head like a gunshot, the shrill electronic beeping goosing him in the ass as he jumped up and panted.

The fire was long dead, not even embers remaining, and the cottage's living room was cold as the inside of a refrigerator. He'd crashed in the clothes he'd been wearing after he'd left Elise's, only a leather jacket pulled over his torso holding any of his body heat in.

His joints were stiff.

And what do you know, they weren't the only thing.

Rearranging himself, because it was either hands down the pants or he was walking like Quasimodo, he went up to the bathroom on the second floor and cranked on the hot water. Backing out, and shutting the door so that shit would warm up in there, he got a change of clothes, remembering everything from the socks to the combat boots— and then only started to strip when he was locked in with the humidity.

The first thing you learned about living in upstate New York during the winter with no heat was that you made sure you had what you needed before you got yourself wet. A dripping trip back to your room for a forgotten whatever was like cozying up to an electrical fence.

As shower stalls went, the one he stepped into naked was approximately the size of a salt shaker, its narrow plastic walls—which were about as structurally reliable as a Barbie playhouse's—offering shocks of cold if you didn't watch where you stood. The water was bliss, though, and he lifted his face to the roasty-toasty rush, letting it fall down his shoulders and his chest, his back and his ass.

It didn't take him long to find the soap.

And where he went with it wasn't good.

But his erection was killing him and it was getting worse instead of better as the caressing sensation of the spray got magnified and modified in his head, his faulty gray matter translating it into Elise's hands, lips, tongue.

He was thick and heavy in his own palm, hard and unyielding as he gripped himself, and on the first stroke, he saw Elise's face clear as day in his mind. And yeah, he told himself he should feel guilty for this, and he did. There was something nasty about jerking off to her when they had both drawn the line the night before.

His need for an orgasm was so strong, though, it wasn't going to be denied.

Leaning to the side, Axe got a pump going and had to put his head into his bicep, his fangs scoring his own flesh as he went faster and faster. Heat roared through him along with more images of that female from the cigar bar and even her father's study.

Which was so wrong.

But good luck trying to stop a speeding train with nothing except hand motions.

Hardy-har-har.

The pleasure was razor sharp, nearly unbearable and impossible to deny at the same time—and the release, when it racked through him, bent his spine back so hard, he hit his head on the rear shower wall.

He said her name. Loudly.

And he couldn't stop after it was through.

Before Axe could even recover, the tide was rising again, his hand continuing to work himself out, the sensations surging until his teeth were gritted, and his neck was straining, and his entire body was clenching up. . . .

Wonder what Axwelle was doing? Elise thought as she stepped out of her shower and wrapped herself in a towel.

The heated marble floor turned the sparkling-white bath mat into a toasty foot pad, and she took her time drying off, wrapping her hair up, and drawing on her thick terry-cloth robe. Aware of an excitement bubbling under her skin, she put on leggings and a different cashmere sweater that was blue as the ocean; then not only hit the blow-dryer, but also the curling iron.

She even threw a little eyeliner and mascara on at her vanity.

About a half hour later, she was wearing her coat and backpack and heading out of her room, spring-in-her-stepping it down the corridor—

When she came up to her cousin's closed door, she hesitated. And wondered whether or not a bodyguard would have helped Allishon. Would being guarded by a soldier have kept her alive?

The answer to that would be easier if Elise knew what had killed the female.

There was no time to get into a cognitive lock about all that, though. She hurried down to the first floor and all but tiptoed past the open door to her father's study in case he decided to recant the whole with-my-blessing thing. But then she remembered. It was Wednesday night. He had his long-standing bridge tournament.

Just as well.

Outside, the night was unseasonably warm, the kind of thing that made her think that the humans with their climate-change theories might be onto something.

And Axe was right where he'd texted he would be, standing just outside the circle of illumination of the second lantern down the walkway.

She went toward him.

"Hi," she said softly. "I'm glad you came for me."

He coughed a couple of times and shifted his weight in his boots. "Yeah. I said I would."

"Let's do this. Right to the library. I sent your phone the link to the address?"

"I know where we're going."

It took a little longer than usual for her to dematerialize . . . because he had clearly just showered and he'd come with his hair wet, the soap he'd used tinting the night air with something spicy and delicious.

God, he smelled amazing.

With an inner curse, she forced herself to focus and was off, reforming miles from her house, in the shadows next to the library's main entrance. Axe traveled right with her, his massive body materializing next to hers a split second later.

"We're going in over here," she said needlessly.

"I'll be staying back, but not out of range."

"Okay—wait, why are you here?" She waved her hand around. "I mean, what should I tell my professor?"

"Why do you have to tell the old guy anything? It's no one else's business."

"Like people aren't going to notice you?" She laughed a little. "You're about as invisible as a semi."

"Doesn't mean you have to explain anything."

As she looked up at his intractable face, she respected how unconcerned he was with what others thought. It was a nice change from all the *glymera* group-think she lived with. "You know, growing up in my family, everything had to be proper, and anything that wasn't—"

He walked by her, cutting her off. "Come on, let's do this."

With a frown, she caught up with him. "You don't have to be rude."

"I don't have to be your friend, either. I've got a job to do, and that's keep you alive. I'm not here to socialize."

So much for starting off on the right foot, she thought, as she pushed open one side of the glass double doors and strode into the library's lobby.

In spite of the fact that she had been using the facility for years, she looked around with fresh eyes, noting that the place was the color of oatmeal, everything from the short-napped, wear-like-iron rug, to the washed-out color of the reception desk, to the anemic drapes by the card catalogues like something you'd find in a breakfast bowl.

"We usually meet down here."

Leading the way, she took her bodyguard past the banks of computers over on the left and then down a distance of stacks to the third open area of tables and chairs.

Troy was back again where she had left him with those two female students the night before, facing away from her, piles of finals papers fanned out everywhere, his scarf and parka shoved into the chair beside him.

Kicking her chin up, she strode in his direction, and when she came up to the table, she put on her widest smile. "Hi."

Tory did a double take as he glanced up. "Ah . . . hello . . ."

For the first time, he shoved his chair back and made like he was going to stand up to greet her—but she motioned him to stay where he was.

"So I'm happy to report that I'm back in business," she announced as she put her things down across from him and took a seat. "You're not getting rid of me after all."

"I don't . . ." He shook his head as if he were clearing it. "I don't want to get rid of you."

She flushed as he didn't look away from her. "Yes, my father has seen the light. So what do you need me to help with tonight?"

"I . . . um . . ."

Elise made a show of fishing into her backpack for her red pens and notepad. "I think we were close to your being done? If that's true, maybe we can talk about my concluding chapter? And then I think I'm ready for a final review of—"

When Troy continued to stammer, she glanced up to see what was wrong.

Oh.

He was wide-eyed and pale as he looked up at Axe.

Who was standing over the human like he was measuring her professor for a death shroud.

FIFTEEN

What the hell kind of professor is this, Axe thought as he loomed over the human waste of space with the hipster clothes, the full head of hair, and the come-hither-you-college-coed eyes.

Professors were supposed to be old, bushy-browed, tweed-wearing anachronisms, the kind of males where, even on a deserted island with the fate of the race in jeopardy, no female would ever look twice at them, much less consider procreating with them without a loaded gun to the head.

Oh, and then top off all the totally-not-old-and-elbow-padded with the fact that the miserable bastard had been staring at Elise like she was the single most gorgeous female on the planet?

Which, fine. Was true.

But still.

He needed to kill the bastard right here, right now—

"Oh, I'm sorry," Elise said quickly. "This is my, ah, he's my—"

"Bodyguard," Axe snapped. "I'm here to keep punks away from her."

And how'd you like a demonstration, you pencil-necked psychology-

spouting whatever-the-fuck. How 'bout I break both your thighbones and use the splintered end of one of them to clean my teeth—after I rip your throat out with my canines—

"This is Axe," Elise cut in as she shot him a glare. "He's just here to make my father feel comfortable. I am well aware there are no real threats against me."

"Well . . . ah . . ." Mr. Professor pulled at the collar of his shirt. "So, um, actually, there have been a number of shootings on college campuses in the last couple of years. I, ah, I can see how . . . um . . . that would be distressing to a father. . . ."

Distressing?

This guy actually used the word *distressing*.

Yeah, you want distressing, Axe thought, *how about I hang you out a third-floor window from your cute little pair of Merrells until you scream like a soprano and your libido falls out of the top of your head—*

"Axe," Elise hissed as she jumped out of her chair. "Will you come with me?"

Grabbing him by the elbow, she smiled with determination at James Franco–lite. "Will you excuse us for a moment. We'll be right back."

Axe was more than happy to follow her, because he had a few things to say, too.

She frog-marched him back farther into the stacks and shoved him against a line-up of books on the American Revolution.

With a jab, she shoved her finger in his face. "Lose the attitude or you can leave."

"Excuse me?" he ground out. "I'm not the one who's dating a human. If you'd been up front with me in the first place about why you wanted to come here, I would have appreciated it. Especially after your holier-than-thou 'honesty is all I want from you' bullshit. Or, wait, maybe you're like your cousin Peyton and believe commoners like me are so second class, there actually is no hypocrisy when you lie to us."

"I am not dating Troy!"

"Troy. His name is Troy."

"What's wrong with that? It's a perfectly nice name!"

"I'm not touching that one—"

"Don't be an ass! And there is nothing going on between us!"

"Oh, come *on*. I saw the way he looked at you. And this . . ." He motioned around her face. "With the hair and the makeup? It's all for him, isn't it. You got yourself dolled up for your little boyfriend, didn't you."

"I did not! And he's not my—"

"Where's that honesty, sweetheart—"

"Okay, you did not just 'sweetheart' me—"

"What do you want me to call you, 'Professor?' 'Cuz that title's already taken by *Troy*—"

"You were growling! You were standing over him and growling!"

Okay, that got through to him. And she was not finished. Leaning in so close that she was practically rock-climbing up his chest, she nailed him with that forefinger again.

"You were about two inches and one giant testosterone surge away from baring your fangs and killing him!"

"I was not!"

They were both screaming at each other—at stage-whisper volume. Which was ridiculous, but at least they were alone back here.

"Show me," she spat.

"What?"

She grabbed his upper lip like he was a horse and cranked it up over his head. "See!" More with that damn finger. "Your canines are totally descended—and let me tell you, the last thing in the world I need is for my bodyguard to rip the throat out of the very reason I'm bothering to put up with his sorry ass! You back off or I will get someone else!"

Axe ripped his mouth out of her hold and jacked forward on his hips. "Don't put your hands on me again."

"I didn't want to touch you in the first place—"

"Liar."

She recoiled as if he'd cursed at her. But she recovered quick. "You're jealous."

"What the *hell* are you talking about?"

"You didn't like the way he was looking at me. Admit it. And if you try to deny that you want me, may I remind you of your 'attraction working in our favor' speech last night. You remember, you were sitting at the foot of my bed? You were quite articulate about it all."

As she arched a superior, pure-as-the-driven-snow brow at him, Axe seriously wanted to shoot something. Maybe her. Maybe himself. Very definitely "Troy." "You know, right now, I'm seriously reconsidering your cousin's offer to pay me to stay away from you."

Elise opened her mouth as if she were going to stay on her roll— but then clamped it closed as if the words he'd spoken had sunk in on a delay.

"Peyton did *what*?"

"He came to my house last night and told me I wasn't allowed to take this job, and when I told him to fuck off, he said whatever your father is paying me he'll double, triple, Powerball the salary."

"Why would he do that?" she mumbled as if she couldn't fathom any kind of "why."

"Because people like me are only allowed to fix your house or your car or work in your garden." Okay, now he was getting worked up again. "We don't matter to people like you. We're just another commodity to be bartered back and forth over—"

"That is absolutely not true!"

Before he could stop himself, Axe sneered, "Oh, really? Well, would you like to know how my father died in the raids? I'd be just goddamned *thrilled* to tell you, given that you're all about the fucking talking. My father is dead because the aristocrats he was working for locked all of the staff and the carpenters out of the safe room. So when the slayers came, the riff-raff were all slaughtered, even though there was plenty of room for them. They pounded on the fucking door, begged to be allowed in, but your people let them die. That's how my only family was killed. And that's the exact same attitude that makes your fuck-twit of a cousin think he can buy me off and allows you to preach honesty while you're blowing smoke up my ass about what you're doing with your professor over there."

There was a long, tense silence.

And then Elise cleared her throat. "I am sincerely sorry for your loss. That is an unbelievable tragedy."

He laughed with a harsh curse. "Did your fancy psych degree give you those two sentences on a card to memorize during your Grief Seminar? Or was it your Placating the Lower Class survey course."

Elise crossed her arms over her chest and just stared at him. And the longer she did, the more he felt like turning away from her and leaving.

He wasn't really sure why he stayed.

"I don't think this is going to work," she muttered.

"Yeah, I think you're right. And it's probably the only thing we're ever going to agree on."

As she turned her head away from him, he had to ignore how perfect her profile was. But then she opened her mouth again . . . and laid him out flat on the floor.

Even though she didn't make any physical contact with him.

"The makeup was for you. Not him. And congratulations, you're fired. Hope you enjoy wallowing in your misogyny and self-righteous prejudice. Clearly, you get a lot out of both."

On that note, she lifted her chin and waltzed off. Like she owned the place. Naturally—

Wait. What had she just said about the makeup?????

• • •

As Elise marched away from Asswell—Axwelle, she corrected in her head—she couldn't figure out who she was more pissed off at.

Which, considering how badly he'd behaved, was really saying something.

The award for Biggest Douche Bag on the Planet was a toss-up between him and Peyton. Him, because he was so outrageously offensive she really wanted to call on what little self-defense she knew and knee him in the balls—on the theory that the ranting and raving he'd thrown around back there could only be improved upon with the addition of a helium voice. And Peyton, because it was so completely inappropriate for her cousin to try and buy off anyone, much less a fellow trainee doing a job for somebody else.

Although, really, it wasn't like it was going to work—

Axe materialized right in front of her, so much out of thin air that she yelped and jumped back.

And then she realized what he'd done. In a human place.

"Are you insane?" She glanced around to see if anyone had caught the ghosting. "You can't do that in here!"

"Like the books are going to have an opinion?" But he shook his head and cursed. "Look, I'm sorry, okay. I'm really . . . sorry."

He met her eyes without flinching, and he had the grace to seem seriously sincere. "I'm not good at . . ."

She waited for him to finish. And when he honestly seemed to struggle, she debated just leaving him where he stood. 'Cuz he deserved it.

"Go on," she muttered. "I'm listening."

"The whole relating thing. I'm not a social creature."

"Really. You don't say."

"It's true."

There was a pause. And as it turned into a serious stretch of quiet, she wasn't going to help him out. Either he proved, right here and now, that he was more than a hotheaded thug with poor impulse control and the aforementioned self-righteous misogyny, or she was going to find another solution.

Hell, maybe Peyton would do the job.

And yes, she was going to have a happy little conversation with him, too.

Axe's eyes focused on something over her left shoulder. And when he finally spoke, his voice was flat. "I need this job, okay? I have to find work. So I'd . . . appreciate . . . a little leeway when it comes to social graces."

She laughed in a tight burst. "A little leeway? You need, like, a football field on that. Maybe more. You are one of the most offensive people I have ever met."

He shifted in his boots, something she was beginning to recognize he did when he really wanted to leave but was making himself stay.

"This is on you," she said. "I'm not going to help you here. If you've got something more to tell me, get on with it. Otherwise, I'm going to get my things and leave."

Axe looked around, and then he muttered, "I live alone, okay? And the training program isn't about making friends, it's about life-and-death—which doesn't exactly play to my interpersonal strengths. Unless it's killing. And yeah, you just saw what that looks like. So I don't really know how to make conversation. But I am sorry, all right?"

Elise shook her head slowly while meeting his stare. "I can't have you getting aggressive with Troy. Yes, I'm aware he finds me attractive, but we've never been anything but professional with each other."

She judicially edited out the details about their momentary lapse the night before. But she didn't feel guilty about that even with Axe having thrown the honesty thing back in her face.

Okay . . . maybe she did.

Whatever.

"You need to be tantamount to invisible." She put her palm out.

"And before you go there, that isn't because you're a commoner. That's what bodyguards do. Or . . . well, from what I've seen in movies, that's what they do. I have real work to do here, and I've already had to justify my efforts to my father. I owed the explanation to him. I do not owe it to you."

Axe nodded. "Agreed."

After a moment, she took a deep breath, and then indicated the space between them, moving her hand back and forth. "We're not walking this stretch again together. Am I clear? We're done with this. If you can't be up front without being abusive, and you can't do this job without being out of control, I'm walking away and not looking back. Again, not because I think I'm better than you on account of my bloodline, but because I don't deserve to have some male going ape-gorilla and pounding his chest in front of me all the time. I will *not* have this discussion again."

Axe blinked a couple of times.

And then the strangest thing happened. Or at least . . . she thought it did.

The right corner of his mouth seemed to lift ever so slightly, and not in a mocking way. More as if she had impressed him and the respect he had for her had been the last thing he'd ever expected to feel around a female aristocrat.

"Deal." He stuck his hand out. "And I'm sorry we had to run over the ground rules twice. It won't happen again."

Elise released the tension in her shoulders and accepted what he offered, shaking his much larger palm. "Deal."

When they dropped the contact, she leaned to the side and looked around his huge shoulder. "Shoot. Now, we have to try and smooth this over with Troy."

"Don't worry. I got this."

"Somehow that doesn't inspire confidence."

"Watch me."

As Axe headed back to where her professor was still sitting, Elise rolled her eyes and cursed under her breath. And then ran off behind him.

This was like *Groundhog Day*, she thought. With Jason-damn-Statham instead of Bill Murray . . .

SIXTEEN

As Axe headed back for the professor, it was amazing how much less he wanted to kill the guy. In fact, as he came up to that table with its banks of papers, he didn't even feel like hurting the human. Mostly.

The man bun had to go, though—and in fact, Axe did have a nice serrated hunting knife on him that could do the deed. Somehow, though, he doubted that was within the scope of his professional duties.

Troy shrank back in his seat, but that didn't last. Axe reached into the man's brain and erased the short-term memories of the aggression that had been thrown the guy's way. And then Axe stuck out his hand.

"Hey, I'm Axe. I'm Elise's bodyguard. I don't want to interrupt you two, so I'll just camp out"—he glanced around—"over there in that chair. You do your thing, I'll do mine, and we'll get along just fine."

Provided you keep your hands off of my girl, he tacked on.

Not that Elise was his.

Shit.

The human winced and rubbed his temple like something hurt up there, but he got to his feet and shook Axe's palm. "Pleased to meet you. You can't be too careful these days—remember that shooting down near Manhattan last month? And then there was another out West in California."

Axe nodded. "You got it. Dangerous times. So I'll just be over there. You guys get to work."

As he walked over to a low-slung chair that had almost as much padding as a piece of toast, he was very aware of Elise looking at him like he'd sprouted a horn in his forehead—and he couldn't resist arching a brow at her.

Parking his ass, he steepled his fingers and watched her.

'Cuz that's what bodyguards did, right?

But he also kept an eye on everything else, too. Without moving his head, he constantly scanned where they were, tracking the movements of the few-and-far-between students who wandered around like zombies, all hollow-eyed and worn out. A skeleton crew of staff were on duty, too, and he ID'd them based on their age demographic and the fact that they didn't look like they'd been living off of coffee and vending-machine dinners.

The library was so quiet that even though Troy and Elise spoke softly, he heard their convo just fine. Lot of discussion about passages in the final papers. Debates about certain students' trajectories at the university. Questions about whether something had been plagiarized or properly cited.

Whatever that meant.

Man, Elise was so smart, he was intimidated. She threw around terms he didn't recognize the way a pro tennis player covered a Grand Slam volley. And then it came to her desertion . . . distillation . . . dissertation?—and everything was ratcheted up even higher on the IQ scale.

Her thesaurus . . . theory? . . . thesis? . . . was about bipolar treatment in adolescents and whether or not kids could appropriately be diagnosed with the mental disorder during puberty. Whatever that was. And how they should be treated, both pharmacologically speaking, and in terms of talk and art therapy.

Big stuff, and Troy was clearly impressed.

When Axe checked his watch a little later, he was surprised to find that three hours had passed and the pair of them were starting to pack up. Axe got to his feet and stretched, but kept his distance because he wanted to show her that he wasn't a wild animal—and it wasn't like he couldn't hear what they were saying, anyway.

And yup, he knew Troy was getting ready for some kind of ask because the guy started looking over at Axe, his eyes jumping around like he was a kid about to put his hand in the cookie jar.

Axe glanced at Elise. The female had looked over in his direction a number of times, and he had to admit, he enjoyed the attention. At the start of the night, it had clearly been because she was wondering whether he was going to fuck off the new-leaf routine and pounce on her little human buddy—but later, he got the impression it was something else entirely.

Which again, made him warm up even more to good ol' Troy.

When there was an awkward pause, Axe smiled at them both. "Anything you want to say to her can be said in front of me. I'll take it to my grave."

Elise had to give Axe credit. He'd not only backed off, he'd functioned with perfect professionalism, staying out of the way, but keeping close enough so that if anyone approached the table or tried to do something, he could respond in an instant.

It gave her a lot of hope.

What was difficult? Hell, nearly impossible?

The feel of those eyes of his on her. For some reason, his yellow stare made her feel more alive, her skin prickling with sensation even though he wasn't touching her, the urge to check and see if he was still looking at her a constant, underground buzz in her head.

"So . . ." Troy glanced back at Axe. "Ah . . ."

Of course, Axe telling the man he was free to speak had helped override the awkward sooooooo much.

Not.

"Yes?" she prompted Troy. "I mean, if this is about Christmas, I told you, I'm totally fine to work. We'll just have to meet somewhere else."

"Um, yeah." Another glance at Axe—who was standing right there, a little smile on his face like he was enjoying how antsy Troy was. "I think we're done with the finals, though. And your dissertation is about ready."

"I'm feeling good about it."

Troy cleared his throat. "Are you prepared to help me with my winter-break seminar, still?"

"Absolutely. You want to plan that out tomorrow? When do the classes start?"

"Ah . . ." The human took out his cell phone and fiddled with it. "January third. I have thirty students signed up, almost all non-trad professionals in the field."

"Great. I can't wait."

As she zipped shut her backpack, he blurted, "How'd you like to have dinner with me tomorrow night."

Elise jerked her head up. Blinked. Tried to process the invitation.

Which was nuts. She'd been well aware of where things were headed the night before. Funny, though, meeting Axe had changed so much. Too much.

And she refused to look in the male's direction.

Then again, she didn't need actual eye contact to get a load of the arrogant pleasure on his face: He was assuming she was going to turn Troy down, and he was going to be happy about it.

You better slow your roll, buddy, she thought with uncharacteristic rancor.

"I'd like that, Troy." She formed a smile with her lips. "That would be great. But it needs to be after eight? Is that too late?"

The fact that Axe bug-eyed gave her a gotcha in the center of her chest. Not that she was proud of it.

God, what was she doing here?

"That's perfect." Troy grinned in a way that made his eyes glimmer. "Would you like me to pick you up?"

"Ah . . . it's probably best for me to meet you. Where were you thinking?"

As they discussed alternatives—seafood was out for her, he liked Thai, she preferred Chinese, how about that Brazilian steakhouse, Ignacio's, fantastic-it's-a-date—she kept her peripheral vision on Axe.

He was not happy.

"Well, I'll see you then." Elise drew on her coat and one-strapped her backpack. "And thank you again. I'm looking forward to it."

"Can't wait."

Troy had a dimple on one side. Who knew, she thought as she pivoted and started walking off.

Axe was silent as they left the building. But he didn't need to say anything for her to know what their next argument was going to be about.

Out on the lawn, she turned to him and put her hands on her hips. "You're not coming with us."

That brow of his went up. "To where? Ohhhhhh, on your date. Yes, I am."

"No, you're not."

"Wait, let me get this straight. You want me to be professional, except when you don't?"

"I would like some privacy. And we're not going to school."

"You don't think your father would want you covered on a date with a human? I'm very sure he will."

"It's not necessary." Okay, that sounded lame even to her own ears. "I'll be fine."

He was silent for a moment. "Okay. As you wish."

Uh-huh, right, he was going to agree with her on this one.

And as she waited for more to come at her, for the electric sparks to keep flying between them, she prickled with heat, roared with awareness, watched that full lower lip of his in anticipation of it moving again.

"Come on," he said. "Let's get you back. I have to go to training now, and I need to change into combat clothes."

Wait . . . what?

Axe motioned forth. "After you, m'lady."

Elise blinked. And then told herself that it was insane to be disappointed they weren't going to keep fighting.

"Do you have something else to say to me?" he prompted.

"No, I don't," she muttered as she closed her eyes . . . and willed herself back home.

SEVENTEEN

The following evening, Mary tried to make sure that Bitty was all set in the billiards room. But even after providing the girl with a bowl full of freshly popped and buttered popcorn, a bag of Chips Ahoy! chocolate chip cookies, a ginger ale, a bottle of water, the remote to the huge TV over the fireplace, copies of *Cosmo for Girls,* the *National Enquirer,* two weeks of *People,* and a partridge in a pear tree . . . she still felt as though she were leaving Bit in the wilderness alone in a snowstorm.

Which was nuts.

But that was a mom for you.

Sitting down on the sofa by the twin leg casts, she stroked Bitty's soft-socked foot. "You sure you'll be all right?"

The smile she got back was easy and happy. "Oh, yes, very much so. Bella and Nalla are coming down after Nalla's bath. And Lassiter promised he would come watch *Saved by the Bell* with me."

"He's a good soul, that angel."

"He also told me he was going to color my hair—"

"*What*—"

"Kidding." Bitty smiled even further. "I couldn't resist."

Mary clutched the front of her silk blouse. "Jeez, you'll give me a heart attack."

"Father came by, too. He said he was going to get off work early and make me a special Last Meal."

"He's at the Audience House tonight."

"Is he not in the field because of what happened at the clinic?"

"He needs a little more recovery time."

"Good." The girl got quiet. "I worry. . . ."

"About what?" Mary switched to the other foot, massaging the little toes in their cushion of fleece. "Tell me."

"What if something happened to him? I mean, I know the beast protects him, but . . ."

"He's specially trained, honey. His equipment is the best. He doesn't take any undue risks."

"That's what he said."

"He'll never lie to you." Mary frowned. "Are you sure you don't want me to stay with you?"

"The other kids need you. I get to be with you during the day."

You're so beautiful, Mary thought as she stood up.

"You can always call me." She took her cell phone out of her purse and waved it back and forth. "This is always with me."

"I know. Have a good night, Mom."

Mary closed her eyes briefly. Boy, that was one word she just couldn't believe was being applied to her. And right up with *shellan*, it was her absolute favorite.

"See you soon. Call me, okay?"

"I promise."

Just as she was leaving, Lassiter came into the room, his blond-and-black hair nearly down to his ass, his white robing like something out of *Animal House*'s toga party.

Dropping her voice, she said, "Tell me you are not coloring that girl's hair."

The angel assumed an innocent look. "She likes pink, you know."

"Lassiter, are you serious? You need to talk to us before you—"

"I don't see anything wrong with her having pink hair."

"I don't either. The issue I have is what you're going to have to do to get it that color. Bald is not going to work for me, okay? And if you melt that child's hair off her scalp, I don't care if you're a deity, Rhage will find a way to kill you. She's already got casts on her arms and legs, she doesn't need to lose her hair on top of it."

"Not for long," Lassiter murmured.

"Excuse me?"

"The casts."

Mary looked back at Bitty. The girl seemed perfectly content, reclining back and reading a magazine.

"Six weeks seems like forever," Mary whispered. "But you're right. It isn't."

The angel put his hand on her shoulder. "It's all going to be okay."

Something in his voice reached her at her heart and eased the ache there sure as if he had given her a Tylenol for a sprained ankle.

"Go," he told her. "I'm not leaving her side."

"I love you, Lassiter," she said without looking away from her daughter.

"I know."

Mary glanced back at him. "Did you just quote Harrison Ford to me."

"Yes, Leia. And it's also true. Go on, Mother, she's safe."

Mary gave the angel a quick hug and then she left the mansion, going out through the vestibule to the Volvo station wagon she used. As she was getting in, her phone went off and she dumped half her purse out trying to get to the thing in case Bitty needed—

It was a text from Rhage.

Can't wait till coast is clear today. Meet me in tub?

Mary laughed. "Coast is clear" was the code phrase they used for making love. And it was funny, ever since Bitty had come into their lives, the sex had gotten even better because it had to be planned, snuck in, kept a secret.

It's a date, she texted back. *But I'll fill the Jacuzzi so the level is right.*

Nobody wanted a repeat of the deluge that had happened the last time they'd tried to have sex in a bubble bath. Besides, Lassiter had already purchased all of the *Little Mermaid* merch in the United States. And where the hell would he get a second stuffed tarpon the size of a Volkswagen?

Then again, that was a question best left unanswered.

Mary was still smiling when she pulled up to Safe Place about twenty minutes later. As she headed in through the garage, the feeling that all was right in her world was like having sunshine pouring down over her body, her step light as a breeze, a little tune humming up and out of her throat.

"Hey, everyone," she said to the group making gingerbread men in kitchen. "Oh, this smells amazing in here."

She greeted a couple of the kids and their *mahmens*, glad that the human Christmas tradition she had passed on was being put to good use.

"Nice work," she murmured to one little guy who was covering his cookie with enough frosting to put a red and green blitz on half of Caldwell.

The stairs to the second floor were in the front of the rambling house, and she was still humming as she ascended to the top landing. Her office was not far from Marissa's, but when she put her head into her boss's work space, the female wasn't there.

It felt really good to prioritize in her mind the work for the night: the reports she wanted to finish up, the meeting with the intake supervisor, and then the community meal right before she would go back home.

So much easier than dealing with the trauma of what had gone down at Havers's clinic.

She was behind her desk, answering email, talking on the phone, about to transition into her report-writing mind-set, when she realized she hadn't kept up with tradition.

". . . think that is a really healthy solution," she said to the female on the line. "Your being close to your family is a good thing. You need extra help and support during this transitional period."

The survivor she was speaking with had been in the house for about eight months, the victim of an abusive boyfriend who had threatened to kill her when she'd told him she was finally leaving him after twenty-two years. Fortunately, she had had Safe Place to come to and be protected in as she had gradually unpacked all the damage from decades of abuse.

Now she was out on her own, and as for the boyfriend?

He was doing better, too.

Although that wasn't a result of personal introspection and growth. That was because Butch and Rhage had paid him a visit one evening right before dawn.

Mary hadn't asked a lot of questions. Actually, there had been only one: Was the bastard still breathing? When that had been answered in the affirmative, that was all she'd needed to know—and it went without saying that the male wasn't going to be bothering his ex anymore. Not if he wanted to keep his arms, legs, head, and testicles where they were supposed to be.

"I'm always here for you," Mary said, meaning every word. "Okay, great. I'll look forward to it. Bye, now."

As she hung up, she opened Facebook on her computer and signed in to the closed group for vampires only. She hadn't checked the night before, and her buoyant mood meant, for once, she didn't have a stomach ache as she went through the postings that had absolutely nothing to do with Bitty in the slightest.

"Nailed it," she said as she went to—

She had almost signed out when she noticed the red-flagged number 1 by the messenger icon.

For some stupid reason, she looked around the room. Like maybe the person it was actually intended for might materialize behind her desk or maybe walk through her open door.

Mary had never gotten a message before on her account. She wasn't a frequent FB user at all. In fact . . . the only post she had ever made had been the one asking if anybody was familiar with Bitty's family—specifically that uncle the girl had talked about right after her mother had passed. The one who had supposedly been imminently coming for her, in spite of the fact that her *mahmen* had never mentioned him or given any forwarding address for any family whatsoever.

The one whose name Bitty wasn't even sure of . . . Run, or something.

It had to be spam. Like the president of Nigeria asking her to fix a money problem of his in return for 3 million USD deposited directly into her bank account. Or an offer for Viagra or Cialis. Maybe a porn site.

Telling herself to get a grip, she was nonetheless shaking as she moved the little arrow over to the red flag and double-clicked the mouse.

When she saw who it was from, her breath stopped in her throat and the world spun.

"Ruhn" was the name of the sender.

EIGHTEEN

When Elise re-formed in the parking lot of the Brazilian steakhouse, Ignacio's, in Lucas Square, she checked her hair and smoothed the skirt she was wearing. There wasn't much of a breeze, thank God, so things were still where they needed to be on her head and she wasn't Marilyn Monroe'ing the lower part of what she had on.

Which was handy because Troy was just getting out of his car and locking up.

"Hi," she called out, stepping free of the shadows.

His smile was so immediate, she felt a tinge of guilt.

"Hey!" he said. "You found this place."

"I had to look it up on the Internet. I don't get out much."

Troy met her more than halfway across the lot, even though it meant he had to double back to escort her to the entrance. "Well, considering how much you work, I can see how that would be true. And wow . . . you look . . . amazing."

"Thanks." Oh, God. "So do you."

Troy had left his hair down, the curling lengths just touching the shoulders of his wool peacoat. His pants were cream corduroys and he had his Merrells on. The scarf he had artfully tied around his neck was red.

But he wasn't Axe. And that should have been a good thing.

Holding the door open, he indicated the way in with a gallant hand. "After you."

"Thank you."

Inside, the scents were heavenly and thick, and her stomach rumbled in approval and impatience. She hadn't eaten much since the night before. Too distracted.

Not with Troy.

Unfortunately.

The hostess was a beautiful young human with dark eyes and hair that was out of a Garnier Fructis ad, and after she took one look at Troy, she didn't bother sparing a glance at Elise. "Do you have a reservation?"

"Two. For Troy? Somewhere by a window?"

"Right away."

Taking two menus, the woman sashayed through the completely empty restaurant. Well, almost completely empty. There was an older human couple on the far side, a group of three way in the back . . . and one other couple.

"With it being almost Christmas," the hostess said, "we're having a light night."

"Thank you," Elise murmured as she sat down and accepted her menu. "I'm surprised you're open."

"I'm getting paid. That's all I care about. Your server will be right with you."

The hostess walked off, glancing over her shoulder to see if Troy was watching her go. He wasn't. He was smiling at Elise.

"I'm really glad we're finally doing this." He drew a hand through his hair. "And I'm glad you and I talked about what . . . you know, if something comes of it . . . I, ah, I think your switching to a different T.A. position makes sense. I wasn't going to be on your doctoral committee anyway because of my advising you, so that's also taken care of."

He had texted her late in the afternoon and brought up the whole professor/student thing, and Elise had agreed with him on every point—while knowing, the entire time they were going back and forth, that they were never going to be in a relationship.

There was way too much Axe in her head.

Not that she was going to end up with him, either.

"This is not to pressure you," Troy rushed in, putting his palms up. "I'm not taking for granted this is going anywhere. I'm just glad I've got a shot."

Elise smiled and opened up the heavy menu, because she wasn't sure what she should say to that. "Oh, look at all these choices."

Okay, that was basic, granted. But the reality she couldn't escape was that she'd spent all day thinking about Axe, remembering the way he'd met her eyes, that little half smile he'd sported when she'd called him out, the sound of his voice.

The way his body had lounged in that chair in the library—

Stop it.

She'd already wasted an entire day's sleep on the guy. She wasn't going to disrespect Troy by ignoring him in favor of a male who wasn't even with them. Especially because what she really needed to be doing was figuring out how to let the human down gently.

What a great first date. Crap.

And P.S., she was never, ever going to give another person a hard time about opening up and expressing themselves.

"What are you going to have?" she asked.

"Steak." As she looked up, Troy laughed. "You?"

"I don't know. Probably . . . steak."

This time, they both chuckled, and it was amazing how easy it was.

Sitting across from Troy, looking into his kind eyes and his handsome face, she wasn't jumpy or insecure. Wasn't spoiling for a fight. Wasn't thinking things that belonged in an erotic novel.

Being around her bodyguard, on the other hand?

"Elise?" Troy prompted as their waiter came up to the table. "Would you like a glass of wine?"

"Yes," she blurted, even though she didn't drink. "White, please."

"I'll have red."

The man in the black and white uniform nodded. "And may I suggest for an appetizer the blah-blah-blah . . ."

As whatever he was saying went in one ear and out the other, Elise shifted in the banquette seat and stretched her back. Fidgeted with her skirt. Her left shoe.

And then she realized the men were both looking at her as if they expected her to yea or nay something. "Well, yes, that sounds lovely."

God only knew what she was going to end up with, but like it mattered? Trying to focus on Troy, she let him start talking, his hands and face growing animated from the story he was telling. But it was as if she couldn't hear him, even though he was right across the table from her.

Boy, it was hot in here.

Pulling at the collar of her blouse, she realized she'd forgotten to take her coat off. That was it. She was having a hot flash because not only did she still have on a couple of yards of wool, they were flame-grilling steaks across the way, and—

Wait a minute.

With a feeling of dread, she leaned out around Troy and looked down to the very far back of the restaurant.

Right by the emergency exit, at a table for two, a lone figure dressed in black was sitting in the very dimmest part of the place, nothing but a glass of water in front of him.

Axe's eyes glowed in the darkness.

As he lifted that glass in salute to her.

Son of a bitch—

"I'm sorry, what?" Troy said with surprise.

Oh, God, had she said that out loud?

Axe sat back and silently counted down how long it took Elise to make an excuse to use the ladies' room and head his way with her hair on fire.

Ten . . . nine . . . eight . . .

Bingo, he thought to himself as she got up and came steaming in his direction.

As she arrived at his table of two for one, he was glad in a perverse way that he'd gotten under her skin. He'd hated seeing her walk in with that human, sit down with him, and laugh at whatever joke he was sending her way.

Especially looking like this, with her hair down and her skirt up above her knees.

"What are you doing here?" she gritted out.

"Having dinner." He indicated his knife and fork, and put up the napkin he'd laid in his lap. "Guess what I'm having? Steak. It's going to be steak."

Hell, he should order the stuff raw just so he could tear it apart with his fangs.

"You can't be here right now."

"Oh? Is there a law of physics I'm not aware of? You know, I learned how to blow up cars this week and also how to make a grenade out of a can of Coke, a toothbrush, four inches of duct tape, and a Little Debbie snack cake. But there was nothing about why I can't be where I want to be at mealtimes. Do enlighten me, Your Highness."

"You. Need. To. Go."

"Okay, fine, I lied about the grenade. I can assure you, however, that I'm having my dinner here." He pointed to the table. "Right here."

"This is not—"

"Professional? I'm not on the clock. So being here is not outside of the scope of my duties because it is not within them."

"You are insane."

Axe cut the shit and just stared up at her. "And you are . . . seriously beautiful tonight."

That stopped her in her tracks. And he took the opportunity to linger on her full lips, and her sweet, creamy throat, and the curve of her breasts . . . and those legs that were covered in black tights that did nothing to hide her smooth calves and dainty ankles.

"You are *so* beautiful right now," he murmured, refocusing on her lips. "And I know that tonight it's all for him. That's okay. I accept that. But the least that you can do as I sit here and watch you with that man is leave me in peace to enjoy the sight of you. It is all I have."

Elise crossed her arms over her chest. Dropped them. Looked around.

But she didn't leave.

"So you thought of me, too," he said, well aware that he was seducing her with the tone of voice he was using. "Were you up all day, twisting and turning in those fancy sheets, imagining me on you . . . in you."

As she gasped, he leaned forward. "I'll pretend all you want. If that's what it takes for us to work together. I'll never talk about this . . ." He motioned between them. ". . . thing between us again. I'll be a good boy who keeps his hands to himself—his fantasies, too. But in this moment, honest is as honest does—and in my head, I'm making love to you. Right on that table over there, right in front of him to prove I can."

Axe deliberately raked her body with his eyes, and he left nothing out of his expression: The gnawing hunger, the bottomless pit of need, the rabid, animal lust—he let it all show.

And God help them both, she was supposed to run.

She was supposed to give him another highly logical speech, that intellectual equivalent of a "fuck off" of hers that was so much classier than he deserved.

She was supposed to fire him.

Then storm off.

Elise didn't do any of that.

Instead . . . she bloomed right before him, her body responding in a rush that magnified her natural scent into a bouquet that made him hard as a fucking rock under the table.

In a low growl, he said, "Go back to him. When you're done, I'll meet you outside."

Her lips, the ones he had tasted in his dreams, parted so she could pant.

"Yes," she breathed. "Outside."

As she turned away, he said her name. And when she looked back at him, he said, "Take your time. I like how much the anticipation hurts."

NINETEEN

istorically, back in the Old Country, it had been part of the normal functioning of life for the King to hold audiences with his subjects, ruling on everything from property disputes and petitions for *sehclusion* to noble matings, *rythes,* and even murders and other crimes.

However, when Wrath had refused to ascend to the throne for, oh, a couple of centuries, the practice fell by the wayside. All that had changed recently, though, and now the tradition was back in full swing, the audiences being conducted out of the Federal-style mansion Darius had lived in before he'd been blown up in his BMW by the enemy: Every night, Monday through Friday, members of the race came to the great Blind King and sought his advice, counsel, declarations, and blessings.

And tonight's docket was full, Rhage thought as he opened the double doors to the dining room yet again and let out a *hellren* with his *shellan* and new baby son. The couple were commoners, dressed in clean but unfancy clothes, their miracle wrapped up in a humble swaddling blanket. Ordinarily, Rhage would have nodded and just let them go, but now he really looked at the family, and even rushed forward to open the heavy main door for them.

"You take care of them," he said to the male.

The guy seemed flustered to be spoken to at all by a brother, and as he stammered, Rhage put a hand on the guy's shoulder. "I know you will."

"Yes, my Lord, yes," he said with a bow. "I shall lay down my life for them both."

Rhage smiled at the female and the young, but he made no move to touch them—certainly not the female, definitely not the baby. That would have broken protocol: Even though he was at the top of the food chain socially and accorded all kinds of honor and respect, it would have been inconceivable in the Old Country for a newborn and its mother to have contact with a male, even in a formal setting, during the first year of life.

It was funny, ever since they had started up with the audiences again, Rhage and the brothers had fallen into the Old Ways again. It just felt right.

Especially in this case, now that Rhage knew firsthand what it was like to be a dad.

"Congratulations again," he said to the couple as he stood to the side and watched them go off into the cold.

The female's father was waiting for them in the driveway in a ten-year-old Honda Accord, and the way the guy jumped out and beamed at the young family, you'd have sworn he was driving a Rolls-Royce.

Rhage gave the grandfather a wave, which floored the male and caused him to bow so fast he nearly fell over—and then Hollywood shut the door to keep the winter breeze from sucking all the warmth out of the foyer.

"Last night's good weather was just a chimera, huh," he said to the receptionist.

Paradise's second cousin, Beline, looked up from her computer. "I know, right? Don't tell anyone, but under my desk, I've taken my heels off and put fleece socks on."

Rhage nodded to the fire, which had gone down a lot since he'd stoked it an hour ago. "You want me to throw some more wood on?"

"No, thanks." She smiled and pushed up her glasses. "It's just my feet."

There were two people in the waiting room, but there was another wave coming in.

On a lot of levels, he'd rather be in the field, or beating the crap out of the trainees, but he never was at full capacity right after the beast made an appearance, and it was better for him to pull this admin shift now.

After all, every brother had to put in time here, fulfilling their duty as personal guard to Wrath. Between humans, *lessers*, and members of the *glymera* linking up with the Band of Bastards, they didn't take any chances with the King's life: There were always a minimum of two members of the Brotherhood on site with Wrath. Tonight, it was he and Vishous, which was always fun.

Mostly because the pair of them could do good cop/bad cop. Or rather, V could sit there with his icy eyes and his hands rolled, making the civilians shit themselves in their pants, and Rhage could be a yo-ho-ho, Steve Harvey–on–*Family Feud* grin-and-greeter.

Striding back to what had been the dining room, Rhage stood in between the carved jambs and waited as Saxton reviewed a couple of documents with Wrath down at the far end by the flap door into the kitchen. Saxton was frickin' amazing, keeping all the paperwork and documentation straight as well as making sure that the Old Laws were consulted when appropriate.

The set-up for the private meetings was simple and very non-thronal: just two armchairs facing each other in front of the fire, one for the King and one for his subjects—although there were other seats off to the side to be pulled in as needed. Whichever brothers were on stayed at a discreet distance, with Saxton at a desk that was halfway in between. There was a rolling cart of coffee, tea, and sodas, along with cookies and other kinds of snacks—

A blast of cold air whipped into the foyer behind him, and Rhage turned with a smile at whoever . . . it . . .

. . . was . . .

Rhage's heart didn't so much stop . . . as die in his chest.

The male who had come in was young and healthy, heavily muscled, but not obviously weaponed, as if he were a manual laborer of some kind as opposed to a fighter. His clothes were so well washed that his jeans fell from his hips like drapes, and his jacket was way too light for December. Construction boots were well worn. No jewelry. Nothing in his hands. No strange scents on him.

All of that was incidental to what had driven a stake right through Rhage's sternum.

The face . . . was Bitty's.

The male's face had the same nose and cheeks, the same jaw and mouth, the features simply passed through a filter of masculinity and age. And then there was the hair—his hair was the exact shade of brown and the precise thickness even though it was shorter.

The eyes were a carbon copy, too.

The male didn't look Rhage's way, but instead, went to the reception desk, one hand lifting up to his temples as if he usually wore a hat and was reflexively trying to take it off.

Fast footsteps approached from behind Rhage, but he didn't pay them any mind, at least not until V appeared with a gun out.

"What the fuck's wrong?" the brother demanded.

Rhage tried to answer. Well, he guessed he did. Something was coming out of his mouth.

"What?" V demanded, looking all around and seeing nothing wrong. "Are you okay?"

It was at that moment that the male, who was clearly a relative of Bitty's, glanced up from the reception desk, as if he had heard Vishous's voice. And the second V saw what he was doing, the brother cursed long and low.

Rhage's phone began to ring, but he didn't even think of answering it.

In slow motion, he took step after step toward the male.

Whoever the guy was, he had refocused on the receptionist and was speaking in a quiet voice with a commoner's accent—but then he stopped and turned as Rhage halted in front of him.

Rhage said nothing as he stared into those eyes.

"I'm sorry," the male said. "I don't have an appointment. I wasn't sure where to go. I can leave. I'll just leave—I gave her my number. I'm not looking for any trouble."

The male lifted his fists up as if he were ready to defend himself, even against a brother—but it was clear he would prefer not to have to: His stare was level without being aggressive, his affect calm and watchful as his stance widened, and he settled his weight.

It was the classic preparation of someone used to fighting, who was also not an instigator.

"What is your name?" Rhage asked, grimly aware that people were coming around them. V, Saxton . . . even Wrath himself.

Don't say it, Rhage prayed. *Don't say it, dontsayit—*

"Ruhn. My name is Ruhn. My sister died about two months ago. I'm here for my niece, Lizabitte."

Mary put her phone down again and lifted her hands to her face. As she stared at the computer screen, reading and rereading the short PM, she was screaming in her head even as she remained silent.

"Rhage . . . ," she moaned. "Oh, God . . ."

Back with the phone. Calling him again. Voice mail for the fourth time.

He had to be in with the King, but God! why now—

"Calm down," she said aloud. "Breathe and relax."

This could be anything. Someone who was playing a practical joke—who just happened to have the name that Bitty had used. Somebody who had heard Mary was mated to a Brother and wanted to take advantage of that by posing as Bitty's uncle—even though . . . well, she hadn't identified herself as a foster parent.

Or maybe it was a total mistake, a message for somebody else entirely.

Yeah, 'cuz that was likely.

"Damn it, Rhage."

Her hands were shaking so badly that she fumbled the cell phone, and had to bend over and fish around the dark foot-well of the desk to find the thing.

The downward repositioning was kind of handy, really, considering she was seriously thinking about throwing up.

Righting herself, she looked—

Marissa was in the open doorway of her office and her boss seemed like she had seen a ghost. Great. Did the universe have a BOGO on potentially life-shattering events tonight?

"Mary."

The instant she heard the grim tone of voice, Mary clamped her molars together and thought, Nope, not a two-for-one. This was about her. This was about the private message.

Or that Rhage had been hurt or killed.

Mary got to her feet. "Tell me."

"You have to get to the Audience House right now. A young male has shown up and—"

"He says he's Bitty's uncle."

Marissa came in. "Did Rhage call you?"

"No. I . . . it doesn't matter."

Mary reached for her coat. Dropped it as she had the phone. Took two tries to pick the thing up. Then couldn't get her arm through the sleeve.

"Zsadist is outside." Marissa helped her with the sleeves and then pulled the lapels to order as if Mary were a child. "He's going to drive you."

"I'll be fine."

"No." Marissa handed Mary her purse. Her phone. Put her red scarf around her neck and tied it in a loose knot. "He's going to take you."

Marissa stepped back so Mary could go out first.

But Mary didn't move. Somehow, the messages from her brain to her feet were getting lost in the pathways of her gray matter, the command to left-and-right it out of her office, to the stairs, and down to the front door scattering like autumn leaves in a cold north wind.

Her family. Her precious little family.

Her and Rhage, now with Bitty.

Or maybe . . . not with Bitty.

"I just want to go back," she heard herself whisper through sudden tears. "I want to run the night back, I want a reverse lever, a way to back up. I want to be at home during the day, watching movies and sleeping with them both."

It was emotions, not logic, speaking, of course. Because even if there were a magic remote that could rewind time, the private message would still have been sent . . . and the collision would still be occurring.

Even more to the point, if by some horrible fate the male actually was Bitty's uncle? Mary had no right to rob the little girl of her blood relatives.

"I can't do this." She covered her mouth with her hand. "I can't do this. . . ."

Marissa hugged her close and she clung to her friend. There were no words spoken, because what could be said? This might be a fraud.

Or this might be a rightful, totally legal parental figure coming to claim Bitty.

"Rhage is there," she said suddenly as she jerked back. "Oh, God . . . Rhage . . . is at the Audience House."

That's why he wasn't answering the phone. The uncle or whatever had shown up at the Audience House.

Mary broke into a run for the stairs, her formerly paralyzed legs putting a rush to the descent.

As she hit the front door with Marissa now racing behind her, her tears were flowing fast, streaking off her face. She didn't pay them any mind. She tore across the lawn, feeling nothing of the cold, or the fact that her purse was slapping against her hip, or that she had her phone locked in a death grip in her other hand.

Z was right by Rhage's GTO, his skull-trimmed hair and his scarred face glowing in the darkness like a destination.

He opened the passenger door for her, and when she jumped in and couldn't work the seat belt, he reached inside, even though he hated being close to people, and clicked the tab into place. A split second later, he was behind the wheel and roaring the engine to life.

The tires skidded out on the pavement as he floored the accelerator, the powerful engine fishtailing the rear end before rubber tread found purchase and they exploded forward.

As they sped off, Mary was panting, panting so hard, panting—until she was dizzy and had to lean forward and brace her hands against the dashboard.

Even though they had had Bitty for such a short time, the girl was like a part of Mary's body, and not an arm or a leg. More like an organ you couldn't live without. The heart. The brain. The soul. Only in this case, no transplants.

God, she couldn't do this—

Zsadist covered her hand with one of his, and stayed like that, relinquishing his hold only when he had to shift. And the sense of his strength was the only thing that kept her from screaming out loud until she shattered the windshield in front of her.

She was going to remember this car ride for the rest of her life.

Tragically.

TWENTY

"Z's bringing her in," someone said.

Rhage wasn't tracking much. He was vaguely aware that he was in Darius's kitchen, sitting at a table that was big enough to handle eight or maybe ten people, but had only one at it.

One rocked and shocked, braced-for-disaster, sorry son of a bitch.

"Mary," he said in a cracked voice. "She was calling me. . . ."

Wrath's face got right up in his as the King sat down next to him. Through those wraparounds, Rhage could feel the power and the support of his brother and his ruler. "Z has her in your car. They're gonna be here very soon."

"Where is . . ." What had he meant to say?

The back door to the kitchen opened, another blast of cold air rushing in—just as it had out front some twenty minutes ago.

The instant he caught his Mary's scent, he burst up out of his chair and wrenched around. "Mary—"

"Rhage—"

They met somewhere by the stove, and he held her so hard, he didn't think she could breathe.

"It's all right," he murmured as he scented her tears. "It's okay. . . ."

Bullshit. He didn't know that at all. But as she shivered against him, he doubted she was hearing much.

Damn it, life was in a hurricane again, the pillars of his pathetic existence bending so far from the winds and lashing rain, they were bound to snap, the structures on his beach slapping their doors as their roofs disintegrated shingle by shingle, the windows shattering—

Not that he was being dramatic or anything.

"Come on," he said roughly. "Sit down."

He drew Mary over to the table and eased her into the seat next to the King.

"Where is the . . . where is he?" Mary asked.

"V. V is talking to him." Rhage rubbed his temples, aware that he had a thumper of a headache. "They, ah, they went into the library behind the—it doesn't matter. You know where the room is."

Why the fuck was he babbling about the floor plan?

Wrath spoke up. "Vishous is taking down the male's information and will verify it with Saxton's help. I think it's better that the two of you sit tight and don't meet or speak with him until we've got that shit sorted."

As kindly as the words were spoken, it wasn't a request. But Rhage wasn't going to fight the edict. Separate was better in this case.

"That's right," Mary said in a hollow voice. "We have a conflict of . . ."

"Interest," Rhage filled in.

Sitting down as well, he took Mary's hand and felt her squeeze in return . . . and then no one said a thing.

From time to time, he looked around at the sparkling countertops, the Viking stove with its eight gas burners, the refrigerator. As it was night, the windows over the sink . . . by the table they were at . . . across the way . . . were nothing but black panes separated by bright white slats.

"How long do you think this will take?" Rhage asked no one in particular.

"We just have to wait," Mary whispered. "The answer is already written, we just have to find out what it is."

Glancing over at her, he hated the pain that had sucked the color out of her face and dilated her pupils and was making her hands shake.

He would have taken a bullet for her.

In fact, he felt as though he had. Too bad they'd both ended up getting shot.

Rhage checked the watch he'd recently bought for himself, the one that was a match to the Rolex President he'd given her when they had first gotten together.

Shit, he didn't know whether he wanted Vishous to come right away or hours from now.

"What did he look like?" Mary whispered. When he didn't reply, she cleared her throat. "Be honest. What did he look like."

It was a while before Rhage could reply, and when he did, it was just one word.

"Her. He looked . . . exactly like Bitty."

TWENTY-ONE

*A*xe was in hell. And he ate up the pain.

As he sat in his far-off corner of the restaurant, he watched Elise smile at the human man. Tilt her head as if her professor were saying something that particularly interested her. Motion with her hands. Laugh.

She looked into the other man's eyes. Clinked her wineglass with his. Took a piece of food from his plate to try.

And the whole time, she was so exquisitely beautiful, the flickering candle on the table playing over her face and throat, her shoulders and her hair.

He hated that she was with someone else. Detested that they were sharing a meal—which felt more intimate than the sex he had on a regular basis. Was downright violent about the thoughts that man was undoubtedly having in his head.

But he loved to hurt. The jealousy was an agony that left him deliciously crippled, and he opened himself up to the pain of being on the outside looking in.

Even though he barely knew her, he loved her in this moment. She was the conduit to the vein of torture, and as physically attractive as he found her, the power she had over him turned her into a goddess.

"Would you care for anything else?" the waiter asked him.

Axe shook his head. "Just the check."

"Here."

The leather folio was put at his elbow and the guy marched off. Not that Axe blamed the human. All Axe had had was water and dinner rolls—before rocking the house by ordering a coffee.

The total was five dollars. He left the only ten-dollar bill he had and thought, Hey, fifty percent tip. Check him out, a high-rolling mother-fucker.

As he took another sip from his water glass, he enjoyed an unchar-acteristic, unwelcomed moment of introspection: while Elise laughed again, he was vaguely aware that where he was at was really bad juju.

In her own, almost innocent, way, she was rocking his world. Bringing him to his knees. Demanding all his attention without even being aware that she was asking anything of him.

And in response, he was going to be making a demand of her. The second he got her alone.

She was not going to deny him, either.

Over at Elise's table, the check arrived, and after it was paid, the pair of them got up—which was Axe's cue to sneak out the fire escape behind him. As he pushed the bar, no alarm sounded, and the fresh air made him realize how much the place smelled like steak.

His body was humming, so the cold didn't register at all, and he stayed in the shadows of the single-story building as he walked around to the front, his boots crunching over the frosted ground. The entrance to the restaurant had an awning with no side panels, a thick mat run-ning down the pavement underneath it like the poor relation of a movie premiere's red carpet.

The happy fucking couple came out a moment later, and Troy put his arm around Elise's waist as they went down the three shallow steps to the runner.

And didn't that make his fangs descend in a rush. But he stayed right where he was.

A gust of wind caught Elise's hair, sweeping it in the professor's direction, the ends of the tendrils feathering across his shoulder.

She laughed as she regathered the errant strands, put the length in a twist, and tucked it into the collar of her coat. And then they kept chatting. It was easy to get the gist. The human motioned to the parking lot as if to offer to take her home. She shook her head. He motioned to the cars once more. She put her hand on his forearm and shook her head again.

She was telling him an artful lie about why he couldn't drive her home.

Axe smiled, flashing all his teeth in the dark. Nah, she wasn't going anywhere with good ol', man-bunned Troy. And she knew right where Axe was, his position upwind of her carrying the scent of his arousal right into her nose even as the human remained clueless of his presence.

Those rats without tails were so easy.

But they didn't get a first-date kiss. Nope.

It was pretty clear when Troy was thinking about going in for one. But Elise stepped back and put her hands in the pockets of her coat. And the man respected the boundary, lifting his hand in goodbye.

Which saved his fucking life.

Elise stood under the awning in the wind as the guy got into a perfectly respectful Subaru and backed out of his spot. Then he pulled up to the awning, put the window down, and tossed something off with a grin. She laughed. Waved.

Buh-bye, human.

Elise waited until the taillights made a left out of the parking lot and headed down the main road beyond.

Then she turned to him.

She came to him.

And Axe let her do the walking, staying where he'd planted his boots.

When she was standing in front of him, he purred deep in his throat. "How was dinner," he asked in a growl. "Did you like it?"

Her lips parted, her breath coming hard. "He was good company."

"I wasn't asking about him. How was the steak."

With that, he reached out and locked his hand on the back of her neck. Pulling her up against him, he arched his hips into her so she felt exactly what he was about.

Elise gasped, her eyes closing as she went limp.

He pushed her against the building and held her there with his body as he freed her hair, the gusts whipping it around him. Planting his palms on the cold stone on either side of her head, he leaned in and put his mouth right at her ear.

"So how was he . . . ," he drawled.

Before she could answer, he took her earlobe between his lips and sucked on it, ending with a nip from his fang.

"Hmm?" He extended his tongue and licked at her. "How was he?"

Her reply was her hands coming up to his shoulders and latching on so hard he could feel her nails through the leather of his jacket. Oh . . . *fuck,* he wanted to be naked and have her do that, so that she left little half-moons of blood in his flesh. And then he wanted her to bite him hard at his throat and take from his vein.

Axe ran his lips over her jawline and then hovered a millimeter from her mouth. "You're not answering the question, Elise."

She was panting as hard as he was, her body his for the taking, her sex fully aroused for him. And you want to talk about satisfaction? That Mr. Perfect human in his precious little Merrells and his scarf, who'd gotten to sit across from her at dinner, and charm her with his wit and his intellectual savvy, was never going to get this kind of reaction out of her.

Never. Fucking. Ever.

"Are you going to see him again?" he drawled. "Because I think you should."

She recoiled at that, pulling away. "What . . . ?"

"I like to watch you with him."

"Why?"

"Because it hurts. Now, give me what I want," he growled as he closed the distance between their mouths and kissed her hard.

The bar counter in the club was long, crowded and noisy, and a total waste of time—except for the alcohol. And as Novo motioned for the bartender to bring her another Scotch, she looked down the stretch of men and women, the lot of them crowding in like they were cows at a trough.

She would have been seriously disdainful of them.

But for the fact that she was one of the herd.

"Here," the server said. "On the house."

The guy was tall, on the thin side for what she liked in males, but the shaved head, tattoos across his chest, and gauges in his ears were right up her alley.

"Thanks." She saluted him with the squat glass. "What time do you get off?"

"Four."

"Good to know."

She walked off, heading back for a place she didn't want to be and couldn't get away from.

As usual, Peyton had engineered the meet-up at Ice Blue, a techno club he couldn't seem to live without. And also as usual, he'd gotten them a seating pit in the VIP section, behind a velvet rope that kept out the riffraff.

As she came up to the bouncer, he let her in. "Back so soon?"

"Got my drink. I'm good."

He gave her a confused look, but she left him to chew on the reasons why she might have gone independent, when there was top-shelf bottle service in Peyton's velvet-seated sunken sex pit.

Not that there was any sex going on.

Boone was nursing the same Grey Goose and cranberry he'd started the night off with, his eyes scanning the human crowd with a detachment akin to an entomologist in his lab. Paradise and Craeg were relaxed and not in big hurry to come or go—which was what happened when two people were free to bang anytime they wanted. And Peyton? He was hanging with a couple versions of himself, the defensively heterosexual males dressed in expensive, tight-legged suits.

That collection of arched brows, laconic hand motions, and airs of entitlement were denser than their saturated colognes.

Definitely not her kind.

Resettling next to Boone, she crossed her legs and leaned back in the slick, padded wraparound. Why in the hell anyone would put greased-pig fabric on something drunk people were supposed to sit on was a mystery. Then again, like Peyton, this particular club was more about appearances than anything else. The wait line had been like try-outs for *The Bachelor*—not that they'd had to bother with it thanks to Peyton—and there had been a Manhattan dealership's worth of Mercedes in the lot out back, and if she saw one more Scott Disick wannabe hitting on a fake tan with DDs, she was going to—

Holy shit.

She was boring herself with her own internal conversation. So why didn't she leave?

The answer to that was just across the shallow, carpeted pit. And of course, Peyton wasn't looking at her.

No, Peyton was leaning forward, and looking around one of his silk-suited buddies—and in spite of the fact that he was wearing his blue-tinted glasses, and even with the laser beams spearing through the fogged-out air, it was obvious who he was staring at.

Obvious what he wanted.

Paradise.

And the longer Novo watched the male look at their fellow trainee, the more Novo had to own up to the fact that that obsession was part of the fucker's appeal. After all, he was everything she didn't find attractive, and yet she always ended up knowing when he came into a room and when he left it. Knew what clothes he was wearing. How he was fighting. What mood he was in, and whether he was eating or drinking, and anytime he was on his phone. She noticed when he'd had his hair cut and when it was getting shaggy. When he was injured, tired, or hadn't slept.

Knew when he banged human women in the bathroom at the end of a club night.

It was like he was some kind of homing beacon—except the damn thing kept calling her to a house she didn't want to even enter, much less move in to.

So, yeah, with him rocking his full-scale addiction to Paradise, his elusiveness had to be the explanation for the attraction.

Had to be—

Paradise sat forward and said something to Peyton . . . and he fucking loved whatever it was, throwing his head back, laughing like the female was a cross between Louis C.K. and a resurrected George Carlin.

Novo drank half of her Scotch.

When she brought her head back to level, Peyton was standing in front of her. "Hey, we're gonna go. See you in class tomorrow night."

He clapped her on the shoulder and walked right by, the three look-alike friends in his wake like water-skiers behind a flashy boat.

Boone got up and stretched. "I better head, too. Have a good night."

"We're going as well." Paradise smiled as she took Craeg's hand. "Enjoy yourself."

Annnnnd then there was one.

One advantage to being totally self-sufficient and independent was you didn't care if you were left alone. But for some reason, tonight, it dawned on her that none of them would have done a toilet flush like that to Paradise.

Not that Novo resented the female or thought the object of Peyton's affection was weak. It just seemed . . . weird. Or something.

Whatever.

Novo stared past all the empty seats to the humans that mingled on the far side of the sunken area. There were probably three hundred guys she could fuck if she wanted, including Mr. Four A.M., the bartender. Just as many women if she were in that kind of mood, too.

Too bad not one of them seemed appealing—

Peyton popped into her line of sight from out of nowhere—to the point where she wondered if he wasn't a hologram created by her brain.

"Forgot my phone."

Oh, so this was real—because a hologram wouldn't have to justify its existence.

But instead of going over to the sofa where he'd been, he stayed where he was.

"Yes?" Novo drawled.

"What are you doing?"

"Taking a load off." She indicated the seating area. "I would think that's self-evident."

When his stare drifted down her body, she narrowed her eyes. "The question more is . . . what are you doing here, Peyton?"

TWENTY-TWO

Elise had the hard building at her back and Axwelle's even harder body at her front, and there was no place she'd rather be.

Especially as he started to kiss her.

He was just as hungry and demanding as she'd fantasized, his mouth crushing hers, his hands rough, his erotic greed the kind of thing she knew would make a meal out of her—and oh, God, she went with it, arching her breasts into his chest, holding on to his shoulders, giving herself up to him.

The kiss was everything that she'd thought it would be and more, the cold December night disappearing, consumed by the heat between them.

But what the hell had he said to her? About wanting her to see Troy again?

She pushed at him until the contact was broken. "I don't understand. . . ."

Axe cupped her face in his big palms and rolled his hips against her, his massive erection stroking at her belly because he was so much taller than she was. "Why are we stopping to talk here?"

Good question. If slightly offensive.

"Why would you want me to go out with Troy again?"

She had spent the meal forcing herself to focus on the human, follow his conversation, ask the right questions at appropriate moments, laugh when she was supposed to. But the entire time, she had been completely distracted by Axe sitting down in the far corner of the mostly empty steakhouse, his looming presence like the most beautiful thundercloud she'd ever seen off in the distance.

Heading for her.

"Why?" she prompted him. "If it pains you so much—"

"Because it turns me on."

Axe dropped his head and kissed her again, his lips soft as velvet, his tongue bold and demanding. And holy crap did she want him, her breasts aching for his hands, that mouth of his, her sex lighting up between her legs, her—

Elise forced herself out of his hold. And walked around a little to clear her head. "No. I'm not going to see him again, I'm not going to use him. I want you to want me for myself. If I'm not enough without some kinky, subversive game involved, that's fine—I'm certainly not going to try to entice you by playing hard to get right under your nose."

As Axe smiled, his fangs were fully descended. "Okay. I'll take you any way you come."

Well. If that wasn't a double entendre. And dearest Virgin Scribe, the way he was staring at her with those yellow eyes of his.

She might as well be naked already.

So how 'bout finishing the job, she decided.

"Where can we go," she said hoarsely.

"I have a house not far from here. It's safe and very private."

As a cell phone started to ring somewhere on him, she cursed at the interruption. Yet when he made no move to do anything, she nodded to his body. "Don't you want to answer that?"

"No."

"What if it's an emergency?"

"I have no one who would call me for one." His eyes locked on her mouth. "So are you coming to my house?"

"Yes," she whispered. "Except how will I know where it is?"

"I can take care of that."

She went for her purse. "I know this sounds weird, but I have a little laminated map of Caldwell in here and I—"

"Elise." When she looked up, he smiled again with those huge fangs of his. "Watch me."

With that, he pulled up the sleeve of his black leather jacket, exposing the inside of his wrist. And then he lifted his forearm to his mouth . . . with a hiss, he bit himself, driving his sharp canines deep into his flesh.

Elise parted her lips on a shocked gasp . . . and then licked at them as the heady, wine-like scent of his blood rose between them.

When he extended his arm toward her, he said in a low voice, "This should help you find me—wherever I am. Take from me, Elise. Let me watch you drink. Now."

Her own fangs tingled as they dropped down, and she didn't even think for a second about the twelve different protocols she was breaking if she did this: *commoner!, out in public!, unwitnessed!, arousal on both sides!*

Fuck it. She refused to be derailed as she grabbed his muscled forearm and dragged his wrist right to her mouth. Forming a seal with her lips, she sucked on him, his taste the strongest intoxicant she'd ever known, the rush going through her making her dizzy.

"Oh . . . yeah," he groaned. "Shit . . . *yeah.*"

Abruptly, there was an unexpected shift in the power dynamic— him collapsing against the building, his knees seeming to buckle, as she became the aggressor and he her prey.

And the entire time she took from him, she stared at the straining length behind his fly.

That was what she wanted, she decided as she looked at his erection.

And he was not going to deny her.

"I came back for my phone."

As Peyton repeated the very words he'd spoken to her, Novo smiled a little. "You said that already. So why aren't you looking for it."

He made a show of patting his suit jacket. "Oh. It's here after all. Go figure."

"Yeah." She nursed what was left of her Scotch. "Where are your three friends?"

"I don't know. I don't care."

"Selfish." She deliberately recrossed her leather-clad legs and rubbed her thighs, one atop the other. She hated the way her core warmed for him. "You're a real shit, Peyton, you know that."

"Yes, I do."

"So?" she prompted.

"You want to get a drink?"

"I have one."

"How about going to my place."

Novo cocked a brow. "Your father's mansion, you mean."

"No, I gotta place. It's a suite at the Sterling. I crash there sometimes."

"I should have known," she said dryly. "No Super Eight for the likes of you. And tell me, if I go back to this suite with you, what are we going to do there?"

His eyes went from her mouth to her breasts to her thighs . . . and then took their sweet time returning to her face. "Whatever we want."

"Are you fucking me right now in your mind, Peyton?"

"Yes," he growled.

"Back in that fancy hotel room of yours?"

"It's a suite, not a room. And no. I'm picturing you bent over that sofa right now, your leathers off, my tongue in your sex as you come against my face. Then I fuck you with my cock."

The bolt of electricity that went through her was the good news and the bad news: The last thing she wanted was to feel that way anywhere around someone like him.

Nature didn't care about that shit, though, did it.

"Does that turn you on," he drawled.

"Maybe." She finished her Scotch, put it aside, and slowly got to her feet. Meeting him right in the eye, because she was as tall as he was, she said, "But I have an even better idea."

"What's that."

Tilting toward him, she put her hand between his legs and relished the way he sucked in a hard breath as if she'd surprised the fuck out of him. Stroking him through his fine, perfectly tailored slacks, she was of half a mind to make him come for her in the midst of the crowd.

But no, he didn't deserve the release. Not after he'd spent all night staring at someone else. Wanting someone else. Wishing he were with . . . somebody else.

Running a fang up the side of his neck, she whispered in his ear, "I think you should go to that suite of yours, take off all your clothes . . . and imagine Paradise like that as you squeeze a couple off." She dropped her hold on him and stepped back, narrowing her eyes. "I'll be damned if I ever play substitute for another female. You want that, there's two hundred human women in here who'll take your sperm donation."

With that, she walked away. And didn't look back.

Part of that was because she didn't want to give him the satisfaction. But mostly it was because she would die before she let him know how much he'd hurt her just now.

No one, male or female, was going to see that.

Ever.

TWENTY-THREE

"Oh . . . my God . . . how exquisite is this?"

As Axe shut the back door of the cottage, he gritted his teeth. He should have brought Elise in through the front door so she didn't see the kitchen in the moonlight.

Too late. And clearly she wasn't going to be satisfied with a quick walk-through.

Nope. Instead of following his lead directly to the archway, she went across to the carved patterns of leaves around the windows and trailed her fingertips over the wood that his father had spent hours and hours whittling and smoothing and finishing.

"Who did this?" she breathed. "This is incredible. . . . I've never seen anything like it."

In the silvery blue illumination, her hair shimmered like an aura as if she were an angel fallen to earth.

Too bad all the things he wanted to do to her body were right out of a demon's playbook.

And shit, he could sense his blood in her—and he fucking *loved* it.

As she linked her arms and shivered, he said gruffly, "The furnace is broken. I'm getting it fixed next week. Come this way to the fireplace."

She still didn't follow him. "Seriously, who did all this woodworking?"

She went over to the wooden table with its pine-backed chairs that had ivy leaves for slats.

"My father."

"Really? Your sire did this? Oh, my God, he was an artist."

"Come this way."

She pivoted and went to the cabinetry. "How long did it take him?"

"You're cold. I'm going to go build a fire for us."

Walking out of the kitchen, he yanked his leather jacket off and tossed it on a random chair. And yeah, the dilapidated state of everything weighed on him—that and the fact that there was no heat, no lighting, no food in the place. Where he lived wasn't just a far cry from the palace she crashed in—this hovel wasn't even on the level of an ordinary house for your average commoner.

Crouching down by the fireplace, he grabbed the poker that he'd propped up on the brick and shoved the ashes out of the way. Then he crushed up some newspaper, put some sticks that he'd collected from the yard the night before over it, and laid a single hardwood log on top.

He'd sold one of his father's carved figurines on eBay for four hundred bucks back in the fall, and he'd used the money to buy a cord of mixed hardwood that was enough to get him well into the winter. And yeah, maybe he could have pawned a couple more of the woodland animals and birds in the cellar to get the lights on, but he couldn't bring himself to part with any of them.

Even though he despised each and every one.

The box of matches was kept in a metal container, and he popped the lid, snagged a stick, and flicked the head into flame with his thumbnail.

The newspaper curled away from the heat before allowing itself to be consumed, and then snapping and cracking escorted waves of chalky smoke up the flue.

He knew the instant she appeared in the room.

"This is—"

"A dump. I know."

"No, I was going to say it's homey." As he barked out a laugh, she walked around, touching the stuffed chair and the padded sofa, the faded material on both making him cringe. "Maybe it could use a brooming, but this is a perfect little nest of a house. It's kind of a surprise."

He turned back to the fire, nursing it, encouraging it.

Just like he was going to do to her sex in a matter of minutes.

"I hate the place."

Axe got to his feet, his knees cracking, the erection raging in his pants getting squeezed. He didn't rearrange the thing. He wanted her to be the one to do that.

Oh, yeah . . . the firelight on her was even better than the moonlight had been.

She frowned as she looked at the pallet in front of the flames.

"No," he said. "I didn't think you were coming here. This is where I have to sleep to keep warm."

Her face relaxed. "You better get that furnace fixed so you can go back to your bed."

"Yeah." Axe pointed to the floor right at his feet. "Come here."

She moved across the shallow, glowing space like a dream, the flickering orange light making her beauty mysterious and inaccessible even as she got so close he could count her eyelashes.

Reaching out, he brushed her hair back, tilted her head . . . and covered her mouth with his. Licking into her, he swept a palm down her shoulder and onto the small of her back—before bringing her into him with a hard jerk.

Greedy, he was so goddamn greedy . . . and he'd intended to start slow.

But that went out the fucking window quick.

Next thing he knew, he was shedding her coat for her, yanking her blouse out of the skirt, getting to the warm skin at her waist. Images of her with that human male made him rough, but she didn't seem to care.

She was just as hard on him, dragging her hands through his hair, straining against his body, scoring his nape.

"Lie down," he groaned. "You lie down, female. . . ."

Lifting her into his arms, he knelt and put her on what little softness he had to offer.

Too damn bad it was bedding and nothing else.

With an undulation of her body that nearly made him come, she brought her arms over her head and arched as he straddled her thighs. One by one, he freed the fancy buttons of her blouse.

It seemed like a crime to rip everything apart.

"What are these made of?" he said in a voice so low it was nearly inaudible.

"Mother-of-pearl," she gasped.

They had nothing on her luminous skin.

As he slowly parted the two halves of silk, everything came to a crashing halt, all that hurry, hurry pulling up short as he hissed at the sight of her and clamped his teeth together. Her breasts were hidden behind lacy white cups, and the innocence and sexuality that combined together so perfectly was hotter than all the anonymous, extreme fucking he'd been doing for years.

"May I?" he heard himself ask.

Which was weird. But he felt close to a religious experience here as he loomed over her: it seemed unforgivable to enter any part of the temple without her express permission.

"Allow me," she said.

With hands that only shook a little, she arched up again and reached behind her back . . . and then the cups went loose, her hardened nipples tenting them.

"Oh . . . fuck." Was that him talking? He didn't know. He was out of his goddamn mind. "Elise . . ."

You want to talk about torture. Watching her remove one strap and then the other while keeping the bra in place made the heartbeat in his cock go triple time.

And then she cast the barrier aside.

She was perfect. Just . . . perfect.

Dipping his head, he led with his tongue and licked at her nipples before sucking her in, one after another. It felt so fucking right to be crouched over her like this, worshiping her with his mouth, his body on the knife-edge of losing control, his blood pounding in his veins.

He felt so alive, but not in that manic way he usually did when he was in the middle of fucking.

As he nuzzled at her breasts, he had to rearrange his erection in his pants—it was either that or start singing the high notes. And then he went for the fastening at the back of her skirt, and she helped him by rolling her hips to the side. Yes, he wanted to tear the thing off her pelvis, preferably with his teeth, but again, he wasn't going to . . . and not just because she needed something to go home in.

Patience had its rewards.

As he suckled on her and made her moan, he took off her skirt, hose, and panties at the same time, sweeping them down her long, long legs.

Then he sat back.

Under his hot gaze, she brought her arms up over her head once more and moved for him, stretching, twisting, the firelight bathing her skin with illumination that was like a hundred of his hands over her flesh. And oh, how the reality of her flesh was better than his dream: Her breasts with their straining nipples, and the flat plane of her stomach, and her bare sex, and her creamy thighs, were all blowing the doors off the hypothetical version his subconscious had coughed up the other day.

Moving his hands down her from collarbone to hip, he caressed her body . . . and then followed the path with his mouth—stopping at her belly button.

Looking up her body, past her spectacular breasts, he found her lips parted as she panted and stared down at him, her eyes wide and wondrous as if she had never felt like this before.

Peyton's voice came into his head: *Because you're going to fuck her and leave her ruined.*

Axe shoved the words and the tone out of his head, intending to go down on her until she knew exactly how beautiful he thought she was. And then he would . . .

No. Actually, he wasn't. He wasn't going to complete this act. He wasn't going to end with him inside of her.

He was just going to pleasure her with his mouth and his tongue and then he was going to . . .

Fuck.

Fuck.

Axe sat back, even though pulling away from her was like peeling off layers of his own skin with his fangs.

"What is it?" she whispered. And then she smiled. "Do I get to see you now?"

When he didn't answer her, she frowned and sat up.

God, the way her breasts hung, so full and ready for him—it nearly distracted him enough that he could keep going.

Nearly.

"Axwelle?"

He rubbed his face. "Can you do me a favor?"

"Of course."

"Can you, ah . . . can you not call me Axwelle ever again."

"All right."

"Only my mother ever called me Axwelle. And I hate that name."

"Well, I can understand why you wouldn't want to be thinking about your *mahmen* during a time like this."

The lift to her lips faded as he didn't say anything more. And then she pulled her blouse over her breasts.

"I think I know what you're worried about," she said abruptly.

"Do you."

Her eyes met his and held steady. "Don't worry. I'm not a virgin."

TWENTY-FOUR

*W*ell, guess that was what gob-smacked looked like on Axe.

As Elise waited for him to put into words whatever he was thinking, she found herself shaking her head. "You know . . . it actually feels really good to just tell someone that."

He rubbed his face and then looked away, to the fire. In the flickering light, the tattoos up that one side of his neck seemed to move over his skin. He seemed . . . dangerous. Sexy. And very removed from her, all of a sudden.

"I thought you would be relieved." Elise frowned. "And I mean, come on, it's not like you wouldn't have found out if we did have sex."

"I don't think anything less of you, if that's what you're wondering."

"You don't? Then you have a strange way of showing it."

He shook his head decisively. "Nah, not at all."

"So what's the matter?"

"You want honesty, huh."

"Yes." She pulled one of the two loose blankets across her lower body and crossed her arms over her shirt-draped breasts. "Whatever it is, I want to know."

He muttered something under his breath. Then spoke quickly. "I want to know who the male was . . . so I can go and kill him."

Elise blinked. And then connected the dots. "Oh, my God, it wasn't like that. At all. I wanted it to happen—"

"Fuck, now I *really* feel like murdering the motherfucker."

Elise broke out in a laugh, and when he glared at her, she put her palms up. "I'm not making fun of you, honest. I'm just . . . I'm giddy with relief that you don't think less of me."

"I don't. At all. I'm jealous as shit, but I don't judge you." There was a pause. "So who was he?"

Shifting her gaze to the fire, Elise opened up her memory banks. "He was a male who I fed from. It was all witnessed, of course. But one night—I'm not even sure why—I decided I just wanted to know what it was like. The whole . . . experience."

Axe started to growl. And then cleared his throat to cut off the noise. "Sorry."

She had to smile. "It's all right. I'm complimented." For that, she got a grunt. "Anyway, I went to find him, at his penthouse apartment downtown. I made an excuse and snuck out of the house. He was in the *glymera*, of course, and a friend of my father's."

Now she frowned. "He was surprised, but he didn't tell me no. I was very young, my mother had recently passed after a failed birthing. There was . . . so much sadness in my house, I think I just wanted to escape it. We had sex, I wouldn't even call it making love. To me, it was only a lot of body parts interacting, I can't say as I really enjoyed it."

As she fell silent, she could feel his burning eyes on her.

"Finish the story," he said in a low voice. "It's not over, is it."

"No." Elise took a deep breath. "I've always been a little different from other high-born females, you know? I mean, nothing like my cousin Allishon—I'm not reckless or anything. I just wasn't into festivals and dances and events. One evening, no more than a week or so later, my father asked me to join him at a dance and the male was there . . .

with his *shellan*. I never thought he was mated, you know? It never dawned on me to ask. I mean, in the aristocracy, there are so few males to go around for feedings, and as long as there are witnesses when you take a vein, there is no sex to worry about. But I felt awful as I looked her in the eye. And he clearly hadn't told her. He ignored me the whole night, which was appropriate, and the whole thing left a bad taste in my mouth. Not because I was emotionally attached to him, but because I had used him, and he had let me . . . and together, we betrayed her." She exhaled long and slow. "He was killed in the raids . . . so was she. They were childless. My regrets live on, though, and always will."

"He was a fucking letch."

"I was pretty sure he had done the same thing with other females he was feeding. Otherwise . . . why the penthouse? It wasn't where he lived or stayed with her during the day, you know? It was all just so messy—and the reason I started to focus on psychology. I wanted to understand how people's emotions work, and we vampires are not so different from humans in that regard. For example . . . like, you know what was really nasty of me?"

"What."

She couldn't believe she was speaking so freely, but Axe's silent, non-judgmental listening was unheard of in her world. "After I met his *shellan,* there was a part of me that was relieved he was mated—because then he wouldn't say anything. I had kind of worried about that. After just losing my *mahmen,* I didn't want to lose my father, too, on account of my not being mateable. Can you imagine how selfish that is?"

"Sounds more like self-preservation to me. And you know . . . whoever you mate is going to be the luckiest male on the planet."

For some reason, the way he said that hurt—probably because he was clearly indicating her future *hellren* wasn't going to be him. But that was crazy on so many levels.

"Actually, I'm never getting hitched." When he frowned at her, she shook her head. "I don't want anyone telling me what I can and can't do. I've had enough of that from my father—I mean, everything in the house is his way, his preference, what he can handle within his rigid system of social expectations. Which isn't much. I want to be on my own, and I'm going to figure out a way to do it. I'm going to finish my degree and find a place in the world—no clue what it's going to be, but I'm going to get my own money so I can move out and then . . ." She laughed in an awkward burst. "And yes, my father is going to disinherit me, and I'll be dead to the *glymera* and my bloodline. But it's going to be worth it. . . ."

Wow, she'd never even articulated the plan to herself, much less someone else.

"Anyway," she went on, "some dream, huh? Nothing like a little self-destruction to spice things up."

"I don't think it's self-destructive." Axe stared into her eyes. "I think it's awesome."

"You do?"

"Yeah." He splayed his hands out and then curled them into fists. Then cracked the knuckles one by one. "This is going to sound stupid."

She waited. "What will?"

"The fact that you want to be on your own even if it costs you every-thing? It makes me trust you." He shrugged as if he were trying to down-play what he was saying. "It makes me believe what you said, that you aren't like the rich people who killed my father. Because those types? Never would have walked away from their lifestyle—and before you say that I'm generalizing, maybe I am, but if you can't find it in yourself to extend decency to commoners in a life-and-death situation? You sure as shit ain't leaving your fur coats and your diamonds and your big-ass house on the hill behind, ever."

Elise exhaled sadly. "I'm really sorry about what happened to your father. I hope you know that."

Now it was his time to laugh in a short burst. "The really sad thing? What they did to him, how he died, isn't the half of it."

She wasn't surprised as he hand-and-footed it over to the fire and put more logs on the flames.

"I think I should probably go," Elise murmured as he spent an excessive amount of time nursing the hearth.

"Yeah." Abruptly, he looked over his shoulder. "It's not because I don't want you."

"Good."

But the mood had shifted and there was no going back to where they had been. She believed him, though, when he said he still—

"Can I see you tomorrow night?" he asked without looking at her.

"Yes. Where?"

"Here." He poked at the burning logs, a shower of sparks raining down on his bare forearm, not that he seemed to care. "I have a long training session tomorrow. I won't get off until late, but you said you weren't going into the library or anything, right?"

"That's right. What time?"

"I'll let you know. Probably four? We'll still have some time."

"I'll be here then. I can just wait for you? If you trust me here alone—"

"I'd trust you with my life."

The fact that he said that absently really made her believe that he meant it. And that warmed her through and through, more than the fire did.

"Then we have a date."

"Is that what it is," he drawled.

"What else would you call it?" She started to get dressed, stumbling when it came to getting her bra hooked. "And I'm going to be the first to say, I can't wait to see you again."

When she was finally back in what she'd been wearing, she stood up with her coat. "Good day, Axe. If you think of me, you can text me, you know. No pressure. I just want to put that out there because I think you might not even if you wanted to."

He got to his feet, and as he stretched his back, there were a series of snaps and pops—and yes, she admired his muscles under the tight T-shirt he had on. "Let me walk you out."

They were silent as they left the room—but he caught her and redirected her to the front door, not the one off the kitchen.

"You're going to be cold," she said as she stepped out into the night and he followed.

"It doesn't matter."

And indeed, he stood strong against the frigid wind, unbending, magnificent.

"Be careful," she told him. "You know, in the training. I imagine it can be hard."

He made a noise in the back of his throat that could have been anything from a *Yup* to a *Whatever.*

"Okay, then . . . ," she murmured.

For some reason, the darkened windows of the little cottage made the homey place seem as cold and empty as space itself.

She didn't want to leave him there all by himself.

But what choice did she have?

"Well, good day—"

Before she stepped off the stoop, he grabbed for her and brought her in against him. But he didn't kiss her. He just cradled her close to his chest, holding her tightly. And oh, she held him back.

She got the impression it had been a very long time since he had hugged anyone. She also knew that he didn't want to let her go.

The embrace was, she would reflect later, even better than any promise of mind-blowing sex.

And then she was gone.

Axe stood on the front steps of his father's cottage for the longest time after Elise dematerialized. Under his skull, his brain was bucking like a bronco, what he and Elise had shared so outside of the norm of where he usually went with females—hell, with anyone—that he felt rattled down to his marrow.

It had been so long since he'd connected with another person.

And yeah, he didn't like what he was feeling now—the things she'd told him about herself sticking around in his thoughts, processing and re-reprocessing, calling up all kinds of emotions he could really fuck-ing do without. It was so bad that the only thing he could think of to do was go and find a fight somewhere. He knew how to fight. Knew what to do, how to strike, how to avoid getting hit—hell, he'd known that before he'd gone into the training program.

Whatever had happened in front of his fire back there?

No fucking clue how to handle it. Or its aftermath.

It was easier when he'd just seen Elise as a becky to fuck. Now? She was a person.

When he finally headed back inside, his stomach rumbled with hunger, but there was nothing to eat, and besides, he was used to an empty gut. As he shut the door, he intended to go take a shower and then crash, but he didn't get that far. For some insane reason, he was drawn to the kitchen, to the door in the far corner, to the creaky old stairs that took him down into the basement.

He fucking hated the basement.

When he got to the bottom of the steep steps, he put his hand out into the pitch-darkness for the lantern on the hook. Cranking up the glowing kerosene wick, he almost hoped it wouldn't come alive—

The illumination was yellow like the fire, fixed like the moonlight.

And the ghosts of the past came alive as he looked at his father's workshop.

Breathing deep, he could still smell the wood chips and the sawdust that carpeted the dirt floor like honey-colored snow.

Even though nothing new had been made down here in over two years.

Holding the lantern out, he went over to the tall table with its scarred top and its countless tools and the drawings that had been tacked to the bare wall studs behind it. There were blocks of wood that would never see an artistic form and then figurines that were half-whittled, the rabbits, birds, squirrels, and flowers looking as if they were struggling to pull free of their squares.

There was also an extensive shelving system across the way, where his father had lined up his finished products. It was like a woodland scene, the winsome creatures frolicking together in a miniature forest, the fauna crouching, rolling over, running, climbing, sitting pretty, among tiny, intricate trees and perfectly carved rocks.

Axe hated to see what his father had been able to do.

The skill was that of a master, the end results the kind of thing that belonged in museums or under the protective, nurturing care of collectors.

And yet they were sitting here in the basement.

He wanted to light it all on fire. Just burn it all.

It was too fucking pathetic that the male had stayed down here all day, every day, making this shit because he was hoping a female who had left him for a better offer might be impressed when she came back.

But see, Axe had always wanted to say, *she ain't coming back.*

And he'd been right.

His father had been such a gentle male—an uneducated one, but a gentle soul for sure. And commensurate with his nature, he hadn't dealt with the betrayal by drinking and getting violent, by turning into a man-whore, by abusing the little boy who had been left behind with him. Instead, he had simply faded away, becoming a ghost that drifted in and out of the rooms and ended up haunting this space down here.

Axe had hated him for the weakness.

And yeah, a part of him still did.

But the tragedy that night of the raids had fucked all that righteous anger up—adding a watershed of self-hatred and guilt on top of the psychotic sundae he'd already been carrying around with him 24/7.

God, why the hell was he down here?

Well, that was a no-duh if he'd ever seen one.

Axe ignored the fact that he stumbled a little as he headed back for the stairs, and he took the lantern up with him, leaving it at the top by the door into the kitchen.

Needing something, anything, to focus on aside from his precious little fucking feelings, he went back to his leather jacket and got out his phone. Except he wasn't sure exactly who he was going to call or text.

Not Elise, that much he knew.

He didn't get to his nearly empty contact list, though.

Somebody had left him a voice mail, and it wasn't a number he recognized.

As he played the message, he frowned—but two words in, and he knew who it was.

Good evening, Axwelle. This is Elise's sire. There is an additional service you could provide me, and I would be most grateful if you would call upon me tomorrow eve, an hour after sundown. I shall look forward to your presence. Thank you.

What the hell was this about?

From out of nowhere, the hum of his addiction started to vibrate, that thing he had always thought of as part cancer, part dragon, standing up on its hindquarters and starting to roar.

The good news? At least he wasn't thinking about Elise. The bad news?

Once that hum started talking to him? It would rise and rise until he had to deal with it . . . and there was only one way that had worked for him now that he'd quit heroin—

The phone went off in his hand, the electronic pattern of sound loud as the *pop!* of a gun in the quiet house.

He answered before the second ring was over. "Novo."

"Hey."

As background noise made her hard to hear, he frowned and turned up the volume with his thumb. "Where are you?"

"At a club. You know that Euro-trash one Peyton goes to all the time."

"Yeah."

He took the phone away from his ear and checked what time it was. Also noted that he was running out of battery life. Shit, he'd forgotten to charge the damn thing in the restaurant—when you lived without electricity, you learned to vampire volts when you could and recharge your stuff everywhere.

When his fellow trainee didn't say anything further, he frowned. "You drunk and need a pickup? 'Cuz you know I don't have wheels."

"No, I need to ask you something."

"What."

"You want to fuck?"

Axe popped his brows. And for a split second, he entertained the idea of the female coming over and the pair of them hardcoring it all over the fucking house, breaking furniture, slamming into walls, letting the fire die because their body heat was more than enough to keep them warm.

"Is that a yes," she drawled in a low, sexy voice that should have been better than an actual hand down his pants.

Keeping the phone to his ear, he walked over to the fireplace, bent down, and picked up the blanket Elise had wrapped around herself. As he put it to his nose, he breathed deep.

And missed her so much he dropped the damn thing like he'd been burned by it.

"I don't shit where I eat, Novo," he heard himself say.

The come-on went out of her voice immediately. "Thanks for suggesting sex with me would be excrementally awesome."

"You know what I mean."

"I won't get emotionally attached," she muttered dryly. "Trust me."

"I know." He thought of the asshole Peyton and the dumb-ass's little Paradise obsession. "We got enough fucked-up dynamics in the group already, though, and someone would find out. That shit's hard to hide even if you do it vanilla."

"Fine. See you at class—"

"I'll take you to The Keys, though."

"When?" she demanded.

"Night after tomorrow." He closed his eyes and rushed through the rest: "We'll go together. It's guest night. You'll find what you're looking for there. I know I always do."

TWENTY-FIVE

It was five hours before Vishous came back into the Audience House's kitchen. And Rhage couldn't decide whether he was glad the initial interview of the uncle was over . . . or shit terrified to find out the results.

As V sat down at the table with all of them, he was clearly tired, his hair plastered back off his forehead like he'd been pulling his hands through it, the tattoos at his temple glowing in contrast to skin that was too pale, his gloved hand shaking a little as he lit a hand-rolled and took a deep drag.

Rhage took the teacup he'd been drinking hot chocolate out of off its saucer and pushed the little porcelain plate in his brother's direction. So the guy had an ashtray.

Then he sat back, took Mary's hand, and waited some more.

It wasn't a surprise that Vishous took his time before he spoke, and even Z came over and sat down.

"So here's what we got." V tapped his cig over the saucer even though there was no ash at the end. Then he pointed to the thing. "Thank you for this."

"You're welcome," Rhage murmured.

Fucking hell, he almost didn't want to hear it. Mary, on the other hand, was leaning forward, obviously prepared to deal with whatever the news was.

He drew from her fighting spirit. 'Cuz at the moment, he was feeling pretty fucking ball-less.

"So Ruhn gave me all the details he knows about Bitty's mother. The names of their sire and *mahmen*. When and where she was born. Where she lived and who with before she came to Caldwell. How she met that asshole she mated. What he knew of what happened after she came here." The brother took another inhale and released more of that Turkish smoke. "He also told me about where he's been living, what he's been doing, who he's been associating with."

"What does he do?" Mary asked roughly.

"He's a manual laborer. He lives in South Carolina. He works on a big estate down there."

"What's the bloodline?" Wrath demanded. Like the King was prepared to go and seize the estate as if they were back in the Old Country. "And did the stories make sense?"

V put his palm up even though Wrath couldn't see it. "Look, I'm not going to tell you your royal business—"

"But you're going to anyway," Wrath muttered.

V focused on Mary, as if he recognized that she was the one who was going to care most about the process. "The most reasonable and responsible thing for me to do is go down there myself and verify everything. I have addresses, contacts—including the family he's worked for. I have all the details of his life up until now—"

"I'm coming with you," Rhage said, and started to get to his feet.

Except now he was the one getting palmed. "No, you're not."

"The fuck I'm going to let someone else get to the bottom of this shit—"

"No," Mary said. "You have a conflict of interest. So do I. This needs to be done by a disinterested third party."

Rhage eased back down into the seat. The idea of sidelining an investigation like that made him want to pound his forehead into the table until the thing splintered and then powdered into sawdust—

"This is bullshit," Wrath announced. "Let me talk to him. I'll know whether he's telling the truth."

V shook his head. "With regard to the facts as the guy sees them, sure. But it's not that simple."

"Yes, it is." Rhage was aware of the beast surging under skin, the stress juicing him up. "If he's a lying piece of shit—"

"The issue is his fitness," Mary cut in. "Fitness to be a parent—"

Rhage released his *shellan*'s hand, curled up a double's worth of fists, and slammed them into the table, splitting the heavy oak boards down the center. "We're her parents! *We're* her fucking parents!"

As he leaped up, Mary went with him, catching one of his arms and hanging all her weight off it. "Rhage, you need to relax—"

"I'm her father! You're her mother—"

Mary lost her hold on him and then he was pulling a *RHONJ* and flipping the table, sending his brothers and the King jumping back as china and glassware went airborne and then shattered all over the place.

"This is fucking *bullshit*!"

Immediately, his brothers were on him, Z catching him from behind and cranking him into a neck hold, Butch coming from out of nowhere—when had he gotten to the house?—and grabbing him around the waist from the side, Mary trying to get in his face so he would focus on her.

The only thing that kept the beast still inside him was the fact that it had gotten out the night before. If that shit hadn't gone down at the clinic, he would have trashed the whole back wing of Darius's old mansion.

"He can't take her away!" he screamed at no one and everybody. "We just got her! He can't take her—he's a fucking stranger—"

"Rhage," Mary got directly in front of him, jumping up to catch his eye. "Rhage, we have to—"

Latching onto her wide, sad stare, he moaned, "She's ours . . . she's ours . . . this stranger can't take her away—she's ours. . . ."

He was babbling, he knew he was babbling, but it was like someone had uncorked the bottom of his brain and every boogeyman fear he'd had about Bitty's future was funneling down and out his mouth.

Mary let him go for a time, but then she took the reins. "Rhage. The reality is that we knew we had to get through this six-month waiting period. And Bitty . . . she talked about an uncle. We need . . . as hard as this is, we have to see this through. It's what's fair . . . it's what's legal."

"She's *my* daughter. She's *your* daughter."

"In our hearts, yes. But legally—"

"Fuck the law!"

"It doesn't work like that and it shouldn't. Think about it—if we'd made it through to the final adoption, we wouldn't want anyone showing up at some point in the future with rights. This is the reason why we give notice and wait to see if anybody responds."

"I can't believe you're being so logical—"

"I'm breaking in half right with you, Rhage. Just because I'm trying to keep it together doesn't mean I'm not bleeding on the inside."

As he went limp, his brothers loosened their holds and he pulled Mary against him. Looking over her head, he watched V stab out his hand-rolled in the sink and immediately light another one.

After a long silence, Rhage said to Vishous, "You'll be the one? To go down there and . . ."

"Yeah." V sucked so hard on the end of that cig, he nearly consumed the entire thing on a oner. "And I'm the right fucker to do it. Not only did I conduct the interview, but out of all of us, I'm the one most likely to remain neutral."

True, Rhage thought. V was the smartest among them. The most logical. The most unlikely to be affected by emotion.

Goddamn it, how the *fuck* were they in this situation.

In a brutal series of mental snapshots, he saw Bitty in the movie theater with him and Mary, her arms and legs in those casts. Then he remembered teaching her to drive around the courtyard and up and down the hill . . . and helping her make her bed in the early evenings . . . and their ice cream breaks and the bad dreams that he'd woken her up from . . . and Mary smiling at their little girl. . . .

"How long?" he asked as Butch and Z started to pick up chairs and debris. "It will take how long?"

"At least two nights, maybe three. But everyone will see me when I'm down there. Either because of my status or because I'll put a gun to their head."

"No coercion," Mary warned grimly. "I can't—we can't have that."

"Take Phury with you," Wrath announced. "He has a way about him. He's a good foil for you."

"All right." V nodded once. "As you wish, my Lord."

"You'll leave tomorrow?" Rhage demanded.

"No, right after I finish this cigarette. I already spoke to Jane, and I have a place to stay."

"My brother—" Rhage started.

"No," V cut in. "Don't you dare thank me. This is a fucking nightmare and I hate it. I hate everything about this. But goddamn it, I'm going to do this right, no matter the outcome."

There was a long pause and Rhage watched V's eyes focus on some point about two feet in front of his face. It was clear the brother was already prioritizing things, making lists, thinking of what he had to accomplish.

Then Rhage looked around at the mess he'd made in the kitchen.

"Where is the uncle now?" he said roughly.

V talked through an exhale. "I put him up in a bolt-hole here in Caldie. He didn't want to accept the digs, but I told him it was non-negotiable. I can't disclose where he is—there really can't be any contact between the three of you right now. Lot of emotion."

Rhage went over and righted the mangled table with Z's help. The thing no longer sat square on the floor, one leg twisted and bent at an angle, the top cracked, one plank missing from where he'd punched it. He wanted to move the heavy expanse back into position, to have them all sit around it again, to return things to normal, but there was no future in that.

"Did you tell him . . ." Mary cleared her throat. "Did you tell him about us?"

V leaned against the wall and ran his black-gloved hand over his goatee. "I told him that Bitty was with a well-qualified and well-vetted foster family who was keeping her safe. I did not share any identifying information or mention the formal adoption. Unless he's got a legal claim, there's no reason to go into your private information."

"What's . . ." Mary rubbed her face. "What's he like?"

Rhage got quiet, freezing in the process of picking up the chair he'd been in from where it had ended up across the room.

V just shrugged. "I'm going to find that out."

Mary and Rhage took the GTO back to the mansion, the two of them quiet for most of the ride, their hands nonetheless linked except for when he had to shift. During the last leg of the journey, Mary stared out her window, the trees on the shoulder of the rural road a blur in the night, the moon overhead so bright that the headlights were unnecessary.

"I don't know how to be when we see her," Rhage said. "I mean, you know, how to be normal."

"I don't either."

They'd decided it made no sense to tell her about the male showing up. What if he turned out to be a faker? How cruel would that be? And yet . . . how were they going to pretend to Bitty that everything was fine and nothing unusual was going on?

That was going to require acting skills far out of her league.

Mary's stomach ache, which had begun riiiiiight after she had read that private message back in her office, got even worse as they started up the mansion's drive, the ascent seeming to compress the unprocessed omelet and bagel, which she'd had at First Meal hours before, into a cement block.

As the great gray manse came into view, with its gargoyles and its countless windows and its towering, monolithic mass, she felt like she couldn't breathe.

"Take your time parking," she muttered as Rhage slowed to go around the winterized fountain in the center of the courtyard. "God . . ."

He eased in between Qhuinn's second Hummer and V's new R8. Turned off the engine and the lights. Even undid his seat belt. But neither of them made a move to get out. They just stared ahead, at the rolling, snow-dusted lawn that dipped down to the edge of the forest . . . at the drop to the valley below . . . at the show of stars above.

There was so much ugliness that she felt prepared to deal with. And by that, she didn't mean that she was excited to see tragedy or disease or loss up close and personal. But she at least had frames of reference for all of that.

This?

Well, life was just full of surprises, wasn't it.

And all things considered, she would have rather learned what winning the lottery was like. Or maybe try going around the world. Or becoming president of the United States.

But not this bungee cord of learning she wasn't ever going to be a mom. And then finding out she was. And then having all of that taken away.

Potentially taken away, she reminded herself.

Plus on top of that, Bitty was in a damn wheelchair, still recovering from what they'd had to do to her at Havers's.

"Come on," she said. "Let's go see her."

They got out together and reunited at the trunk of the muscle car, Rhage putting his arm around her shoulders. As they came up to the fountain, she was sad that it had been all drained and tarped up: The gentle fall of the sparkling water was something she had come to associate with home. But winter in upstate New York did not offer the kind of climate where you wanted exposed exterior pipes to be full of H_2O, even if the system was running.

The main entrance to the Brotherhood mansion looked like a cathedral's front door, a pile of broad stone steps leading up to a portal made all the more regal because of the carvings that graced its jambs. Rhage led the way into the vestibule, and then they put their faces in front of the camera and waited for someone, likely Fritz, to allow them entrance.

The whole time, an inner voice was screaming that she couldn't do this, she couldn't meet Bitty's eyes without being honest, she couldn't lie by omission, she couldn't—

"Good evening, master and mistress," the ancient butler said with a smile as he pulled the heavy door wide. "How fare thee?"

Like I've been shot through the heart, Fritz, thank you. . . .

Mary stepped over the threshold. Frowned. Looked around.

At first, she didn't understand the sound she was hearing. Laughter, yes. And it was Bitty—but why was it accompanied by—

A water balloon flew right in front of Mary's face, and it was a case of duck or get soaked. And then Bitty was right on its tail, running full tilt out of the dining room, her hair streaming behind her, her shirt wet, one red and one blue water balloon in her hands.

"What the hell!" Rhage barked as he marched inside.

"Hi, Mom! Hello, Father!"

The little girl kept right on going into the billiards room. And yup, what do you know, Lassiter was on her, a yellow balloon high over his shoulder—at least until he threw it at the girl, catching her solidly in the back. The squealing sound was all delight—and then Bitty twisted around without missing a beat and nailed Lassiter full in the face.

Perfect aim.

Splash!

But that wasn't the point.

As the wet bomb went off, drenching the angel's face and all of his blond-and-black hair, Rhage grabbed on to the male and ripped him right off his feet, landing him back-flat on the ground—and then he double-palmed him by the neck like he was prepared to choke the life out of the immortal.

Or . . . something like that. Whatever.

Mary rushed over. "Rhage—"

"What the hell did you do to her! Where are her casts!"

But then the mom in her made Mary switch gears. "Yeah, what the hell! She's not supposed to be out of them for six weeks! And not even walking!"

Lassiter tried to answer, but his crushed windpipe wouldn't let any air out. Bitty was the one who solved the mystery.

"He healed my arms and legs! Don't hurt him! He made them better—honest! Don't hurt him, Father."

Instantly, Rhage released Lassiter and then fell back on his butt as if he realized the show of violence might have triggered memories.

But Bitty didn't seem worried about that. "See?" She hopped from one foot to another. Spun around with her arms out. Laughed in a happy giggle. "All better!"

As Mary watched the show and then looked at the angel, she had a passing thought that she was kind of done with surprises for the night. "What . . . what did you do to her?"

Bitty spoke up for her buddy again. On account of the coughing and the gasping. "He just sent sunshine to my arms and legs. He put his hand over the casts, without even touching them, and there was this heat . . . and then, I don't know, nothing hurt at all. We sawed off the fiberglass in the garage. That was the coolest part."

Okay, now Mary was light-headed—and she had to take a load off on the floor. "You did what with a saw?"

When Lassiter finally lifted his head, he was red-faced, but no longer doing an impression of a rescued swimmer. "I didn't like her suffering."

"See?" Bitty said. "So don't be mad at him."

Mary shook her head. "I don't understand—"

"Why the fuck did you let them break her bones," Rhage snapped. "If you could do something like this, why the *hell* did you stand by while she was tortured in that exam room."

Lassiter sat all the way up, his oddly colored, pupil-less eyes not shying from Rhage's hard stare in the slightest. "It is not my job to affect destiny. That I cannot change without exacting proper balance, and sometimes the cost for the gift is worse than not giving it in the first place."

Mary thought of the bargain that Rhage had made for her to live, before the Scribe Virgin had learned she couldn't have children; the one where, for her cancer to have been cured, he would have had to never, ever see her or talk to her again, in spite of the fact that they were in love.

Balance was the way of the universe.

"But"—the fallen angel held up his forefinger—"that doesn't mean I can't cushion the fall of fate's dominoes. If you get what I mean. Easing the pain without changing the course? That I can do."

Bitty smiled. "And I'd much rather be running around now as opposed to six weeks from now. Besides, those casts were itchy already. And bathing? Ugh."

Mary found herself blinking back tears as she squeezed Lassiter's forearm. "Thank you."

"Shit," Rhage breathed. "I'm sorry. And shit, I shouldn't have said 'shit.' Fuck. I mean . . . damn it."

As her *hellren* skidded to a halt with the cursing, Mary felt like breaking down—and Bitty clearly sensed it, bending low with a hug.

"I'm okay. I know you guys worry." Bitty smiled as she tugged Rhage to his feet. "Come on, let's go have Last Meal—and before you tell me to clean up the mess, Fritz doesn't let us."

Right on cue, a whirring started to fill the foyer.

"He loves his wet vac," Lassiter said. "Don't that sound dirty?"

"Not in front of my kid it doesn't," Rhage muttered.

Everybody turned to the butler, who, sure enough, had fired up the canister-and-vacuum combination and was cheerfully sucking up the splashes on the mosaic floor in his formal black and white uniform. He paused and looked concerned.

Turning the wand off, he inquired, "Does anyone require aught? Last Meal is going to be served in ten minutes. Perhaps a libation?"

"We're good, Fritz," Rhage said, sounding exhausted. "But thanks, man."

The *doggen* bowed deeply and then resumed his sucking. Which, Lassiter was right, did sound dirty.

"Come on, Father, you've got to be hungry." Bitty pulled at Rhage's arm. "Right, Mom?"

God, that hurt. Those names . . . were like broken glass in her heart.

"Yes," she said slowly. "I imagine he should be eating something right now."

That didn't mean he wanted to, however. And yet Rhage could not deny the little girl, and the two of them went off for the dining room, a tiny sprite who had her mobility back skipping next to a mountain of a male who was walking like he was half dead.

Mary jumped when a hand to help her off the floor appeared in front of her face. Lassiter was back up on his Nikes and staring down at her from his great height with a somber expression.

Abruptly, the fact that the butler was wet-vac'ing up the remnants of a water balloon fight became crystal clear, largely because the grand and colorful foyer—with its malachite and red marble columns and its three-story-high painted ceiling and its grand fireplace and great stairway—was exactly where you didn't ever want to have one.

Meeting the eyes of the angel, she said, "You knew, didn't you."

"That Fritz was going to love the wet vac?"

"That her uncle was going to show up and that Rhage and I were coming home a mess. You knew the distraction was going to help."

"Oh," he made a pshaw motion with the hand she had yet to take. "I'm not that smart."

"And you couldn't stand to see her in pain any more than the rest of us could."

After a moment, Lassiter sank down onto his haunches next to her. Reaching out to her face, he brushed one side of it with his right hand and the other with his left.

Then he made a pair of fists and squeezed hard enough to make all the veins pop up in his heavy forearms. A second later, he unfurled his hands. In the center of both his palms, there was a faceted diamond, the two gemstones reflecting the light around them with rainbow flashes.

"A mother's tears," he whispered. "So hard . . . so beautiful."

"I'm not her mother," Mary choked out. "Oh, God . . . I'm not really her mother."

"Yes, you are. And I'll keep these so that I can give them back to you when this is over."

"He's going to be real. I can feel it. The uncle . . . is real."

"Maybe so." Lassiter stood up again. "But why don't I keep these just in case, 'kay?"

He strolled off, hair dripping, clothes a mess, all that gold jewelry he wore like part of the sun stuck with him even when he was indoors.

Mary looked at the archway through which Rhage and Bitty had disappeared.

When she felt like she could walk that far . . . she got up . . . and did.

TWENTY-SIX

The following evening, Elise was in her bathroom, blow-drying her hair, when her phone started shimmying across the marble counter.

She went for the thing so fast, she nearly fumbled her Conair right onto the floor.

But it wasn't Axe.

"Finally," she said as she turned off the dryer.

"What kind of hello is that?" the male voice demanded over the connection.

"The kind you give somebody who takes this long to call back."

Peyton, son of Peythone, cursed softly. "I'm sorry. I've been busy. But I'm all yours now. You okay?"

She turned away from the mirror and leaned her butt against the counter. It was hot in her fuzzy pink bathrobe, but she was keeping the thing on: Even though they weren't FaceTiming, it didn't seem right to be naked while she talked to her cousin.

"Why did you try and buy off Axe?"

There was a silence. "So this is about your new bodyguard, huh."

"That was really insulting to him."

"Lemme ask you a question, here. Exactly who do you think is guarding you? Do you know anything about him?"

"Is that a leading question? If it is, just answer it already, will you. I don't want to play games."

"Elise, your family has already lost so much—"

"Spare me. I'm living in this house, okay? Like I don't know how much people are hurting?"

"Yeah, and I was the one who had to look Allishon's parents in the eye when I told them she was dead."

"Are we really competing over my cousin's death here? Really?"

"Elise . . ." There was a long muttering. "Look, I'm not going to argue with you."

"Good, because I feel safe around Axe. He's been nothing but a gentlemale to me. And I don't appreciate you disrespecting him by trying to bribe him over something that is none of your business."

"You are my business."

"No, I'm not. I'm your third cousin. That's it." As silence stretched out, she was beyond frustrated. "Maybe I shouldn't have called."

"Maybe." He cursed. "I gotta go. I have to get ready for class—you want me to tell your boy you said hello?"

"Why are you being like this? And he's not my boy."

"Good luck with him. You're going to need it—"

"No, you don't get to do this. You either tell me what you're really worried about or you cop to being an ass because you're being overprotective. Those are your two options, Peyton. What you do not get to do is play this smoke-and-mirrors game, and then huff off like you're being offended by my behavior."

There was a pause. And then the laughter was rueful. "And this is why I could never date you. Cousin thing aside."

"Well, I'm not asking you to, so there's also that."

"Fine, I'm being overprotective and I have no right to be. There."

Elise exhaled and smiled a little. "You're a pain in the ass, you know that?"

"So I am told." Peyton exhaled. "Look, I know people like us don't talk about these things, but that shit with Allishon is still with me. I can't . . . I can't get it out of my mind. And yes, I realize it's making me a little psychotic. I just . . . I'm not sleeping, I'm—my head's all fucked. It's been rough."

Elise dropped her voice to a whisper. "I'm so sorry."

"It's not your fault. God, not at all."

"What happened to her? No one will tell me. Nobody will say anything other than she died out in the human world. They haven't even done a Fade ceremony for her. It's like she was here—and then she was gone, as if she never existed. And meanwhile, my aunt never leaves her room, and my uncle wanders around aimlessly. . . . I would love to help or understand or . . . just finally know what happened."

There was a long pause. "Peyton? You still there? Hello?"

"I saw what was done to her. I saw . . . the violence that killed her."

"Oh, my God, Peyton . . ."

"I wasn't the one who found her. But I was the one who found out . . . what was done to her."

"No wonder you're struggling." Elise covered her mouth with her palm. "I had no idea."

"She wasn't killed by a human. It was one of us."

"Who?" she breathed.

Peyton cleared his throat. "Okay, I'm not being a dick right now, and I don't want to end this all abruptly, but I really do have to get ready. Can we meet up and talk in person sometime?"

She thought of her date with Axe. "Tomorrow night?"

"I have it off. I'll come to you."

"Better that I go to your place. Especially if we're going to be talking about her. I don't want anybody to overhear anything."

"Fine. And Elise, I'm sorry."

"For what?"

"I don't know. I'll see you tomorrow. Come when you can, I'll just be hanging in my room."

"See you then."

Just as she hung up, a strange tremor went through her body—and at first, she assumed it was from what she and Peyton had been discussing. But then . . . no, that wasn't it.

Putting the phone down, she looked around, but come on. It wasn't like someone was lurking in a darkened corner—in her all-white marble bathroom that had all its overhead lights on.

Leaving her phone behind, she went out into her bedroom. Glanced in all the corners, of which none were dark because she had all the lights on in there as well.

Except she wasn't exactly scared.

More like pricklingly aware—

"Axe?" she said out loud.

Even though Elise was in her pink bathrobe, she padded out into the hall. Followed the instinct down to the main staircase. Proceeded to the first floor—

Fresh air. Someone had just come into the house.

And . . . Axe's scent. It had been he who had been let in. Moreover, thanks to the blood she'd taken from him the night before, she knew precisely where he was.

Snapping her head to the left, she saw that her father's study was closed up.

Making no sound at all, she whispered over the marble floor to the parlor that was located behind his private work space. Inside, the peach-and-silver loveliness of the wallpaper and the drapes was lost on her as she went to a built-in shelving expanse that had a scalloped top and Herend figurines of roosters and waterfowl and other birds of all kinds on its levels.

The release was hidden on the right at shoulder height, the kind of thing you couldn't see and wouldn't guess at—and when she toggled it, the entire unit, built some hundred and fifty years before, unhinged from the wall and slid soundlessly to the side.

Stepping into the hidden passageway, she pulled an old-fashioned metal cord with a wooden handle on the end . . . and back the shelves went, moving so seamlessly that the priceless porcelain collection wasn't disturbed in the slightest.

The space was cramped and dank, but not cold, and there was enough light from the seams of the molding high above that she made her way forward about five feet . . . to a set of wooden steps that led up the back of a wall.

She was careful as put her slippers on the slatted wood. She didn't weigh a ton, but she was worried about creaking sounds giving her away. Once on the highest step, she reached up to a slide that was roughly at eye level.

When she moved it aside, she could see out into her father's study, visualizing the fire across the way, the desk, her father's figure . . . and Axe, who was sitting across the desk from her sire.

Yes, she was staring out of the "eyes" of a portrait. Just like in the movies.

Her mother had cut the holes in the painting herself—and her father had nearly fainted. But oh, her *mahmen* had been able to get away with things like that with him.

She'd been the only one who could.

If Elise was careful not to breathe heavily, and if she concentrated on drowning out the sounds in the ductwork and the soft whistle of a breeze in the rafters, she could hear them speaking.

Her father was just sitting down, which would make sense. Clearly she had become aware of Axe's presence the instant he'd entered her home.

And by extrapolation, he would soon guess where she was—

Sure enough, he frowned and looked across directly at her. His expression was one of almost annoyance, as if he couldn't figure out why the hell he'd been distracted by a two-hundred-year-old portrait of some old vampire in formal dress.

"Thank you for coming," her father said as he pulled his cuff links into proper position under the sleeves of his navy blue suit jacket. "I gather that your first evening with my daughter went satisfactorily."

Cue a quick image of her naked, stretched out in front of Axe's fire, his mouth and hands—

Okay, that needed to stop right now.

Axe glanced at her father. Looked back at the portrait. Refocused. "She came home safely."

"For that I am most grateful." Her father smiled, and seemed sincere. "She is my heart. She reminds me so much of her mother. A fiery spirit, a fierce intellect, afraid of so little. That is also why I worry."

"And why you hired me."

"Indeed." Felixe cleared his throat. "On that note, I should like to expand your duties."

"How so."

"I will never put her under *sehclusion*. She would not do well with that. And I am aware that she must leave the house for other reasons than her studies from time to time. Mayhap for a festival or a get-together of females of her station."

Yeah, right . . . because she was really looking to go out and have her nails done with a bunch of get-mated-obsessed Barbies?

She'd much rather save the money, keep her toenails to herself, and read through her dissertation paper one more time.

"I should like her to find a suitor."

Elise frowned. Oh, *hell* no.

"Do you have one in mind?" Axe asked.

"There are a number of appropriate males whose families are looking for them to settle down. She is of age and then some. It is time, but I am certain if I state that I support the prospect in any way, she shall rebel. So I am in a very difficult situation."

"What do you want to do about it?"

"I am aware that she left the house last night. I do not know where she went. She did not arrange for you to escort her to school—or you would have sent me your hours as we agreed and you did the evening before."

"You want me to follow her. Even when she's not in school."

"And tell me where she goes. I will pay you, of course."

Axe shifted in the chair, crossing his legs, ankle on knee. He glanced over to the painting again. Looked back. "I have training. I can't be with her twenty-four/seven."

"I had a GPS program installed in her phone. My butler is rather electronically adept. He can monitor where she goes and provide you with coordinates."

"But again, what if I'm in class."

"You could investigate where she goes afterward. On your time off."

"Let me get this straight. You don't want her under *sehclusion*, but you want to know where she goes, and if I can't be there, you want me to pretend to be a P.I. and figure out what she was doing and with who?"

"Yes." Felixe smiled with relief. "Exactly."

Damn it, Father, she thought. And of course Axe was going to do it. He'd maintained he needed the job, and more money was always better—

Axe got to his feet. "Sorry. That's not for me."

"What?" her father said.

What? she thought.

"Look, I'm good with being her bodyguard. But sneaking around behind her back and reporting to you what she does, just so you can use it against her, isn't my thing. If you're so concerned with what she's doing and who she's seeing, you need to ask her yourself. Your daughter is one of the most up-front people I've ever met. She'll tell you. She's honest like that, even if it's a hard discussion."

"But . . . I'll pay you more. I can pay you double."

"Wow. You people . . ." Axe glanced in Elise's direction one last time. "I have to go. Training starts in an hour and I have to eat."

"I wish you'd reconsider." Felixe seemed deflated. "I need your help."

"You really don't. You need to talk with your daughter, not treat her like she's the enemy."

"I only want what's best for her."

"If there's anyone who's going to know what that is, though, it's her."

As Axe let himself out, Elise shut the slide and hopped off the steps. Gathering her robe, she raced for the hidden shelving.

Back at the Brotherhood mansion, in his and Mary's new bathroom, Rhage checked his pair of forties and made sure the clips were full. Then he put both of his black daggers into his holster, handles down, and verified his backup ammo.

"Merry Christmas," he said to the reflection in the mirror over the sinks.

Funny, that this human holiday was about the birth of a savior, and yet here he was, going out into the field, on the search for death.

And yeah, he looked like a killer, especially as he pulled on a leather duster and covered up his blond hair with a black skullcap.

Then again, he could have been in a pink bathrobe and fuzzy slippers and his eyes would have given him away.

Turning from himself, he went out into the bedroom beyond.

When they had moved up to the third floor only two months ago, it had felt like home immediately because Bitty had been with them. Now the suite seemed like a hotel room, something that was lovely, but transitory.

If the girl left them, they were not staying here.

In fact, he would never again go up to the third floor.

Leaving their room, he went next door, and stopped in between the jambs. Mary and Bitty were sitting on the girl's bed, the pair of them in sweats, Bitty's hair still damp from the shower. Mary was brushing the long lengths, starting at the ends and working her way up, as Bitty chatted along about the Christmas party that Beth and Butch were organizing for the end of the evening.

"And so this big fat guy in a red velvet suit comes down the chimney?" the girl said.

"Yes. He leaves presents under the tree, and in the morning, everyone opens their stockings and packages. You eat too much at four in the afternoon. Watch football and fall asleep. Wake up at nine o'clock. Feel peckish. Eat more. Go to bed and pass out."

"Oh, that is Father's kind of holiday! But we should have done it at dawn this morning, then."

"We had to fit the schedule to what worked for the most people."

Yeah, there had been plans in place for weeks now, but with that male showing up at the Audience House? No one had been in the mood for celebrating. Rhage and Mary had insisted the gathering go forward, though.

Maybe it would be another good distraction along the lines of Lassiter's little miracle/balloon fight/perfectly timed show of excitement for the little girl.

Bitty went on to ask questions about Mary growing up, and Mary answered everything in the same way she was brushing that hair . . . slowly, gently . . . as if she were never going to have a chance to do it again.

"Oh, Father! Hi!"

As Bitty turned to him, her face was so open, her smile so genuine . . . that he wanted to lose it all over again. But he didn't. He walked in, as if it were any other night, and murmured something, smiled, patted Bitty's shoulder, kissed Mary on the mouth, said his goodbyes.

Bitty seemed worried.

Mary was resigned and sad.

He wanted to stay with them. He needed to go.

The beast may have stayed in its cage of flesh last night, but that wasn't going to last with all the high-flying tension—so he had to find a fight to burn the edge off. It was going to be his only salvation.

"Be careful," Bitty said as he took his leave.

"Always," he whispered over his shoulder.

Instead of going to the prearranged meeting spot and joining Z and Butch and the trainees for orientation, Rhage went straight to the alleys west of Caldie's financial district, proceeding directly into the heart of the field, to the pavement and shadows he had stalked for how long now?

The night was as cold as the previous one, but there was a humidity in the air that spoke of coming snow. The humans would like that. They would find it "seasonal" for their holiday.

There was no one wandering the stretch of deserted buildings he chose to hunt, nothing to mark the street but the burnt-out shell of an old sedan, a rotting couch, and a series of scrawny dead trees in the cracked sidewalk.

No Christmas trees twinkling in the windows. No ho-ho-ho's from partygoers. No carols, no sleigh bells, no reindeer, no presents.

Breathing in deep, he felt a great burn inside his chest . . . and it was as if he were back to square one.

Ever since Mary had come into his life for good, he had enjoyed the killing because thanks to the Scribe Virgin's good old breeding program, he had been designed since conception to protect and defend his race. But there had been none of this old-school desperation, this twitchy unhappiness, this . . . sad sense . . . that he was not a master of his destiny but subjugated to it because of his curse—

Cranking around, he tilted his nose up. Inhaled again.

Let out a growl.

Lessers were fewer and farther between now than ever, and there had been sightings, by others in the Brotherhood, of a very different kind of foe.

They were trying to determine who and what it was. Sea changes like that in the war were rarely good news—and clear evidence that the Omega was thinking again.

But the stench of baby powder that rushed up to greet him now?

It was like the one wish he'd needed to come true had been granted.

Well, the one other than Bitty staying where she belonged.

Baring his fangs, Rhage went on the hunt.

TWENTY-SEVEN

The only way that meeting could have been more offensive, Axe decided, was if Elise's father had suggested his daughter was dealing drugs on the side. Into prostitution after dark. Leading a second life taking candy from babies and kicking puppies.

Unbelievable, he thought as he let himself out the big fancy-ass door and strode away from the mansion—

About twenty feet off to the left, standing in the freezing cold wind in—wait, was that a pink fuzzy bathrobe?—Elise was like an apparition. Except she was oh, so very much alive, her hair swirling in the gusts, her scent filling his nose, her presence warming the night to tropical temperatures.

"What are you d—"

He didn't get any further than that. She ran up to him and threw herself into his arms, holding him around the neck and squeezing for all she was worth.

"Wait, what are you doing?" Or something like that. "Elise, you can't be seen like this."

Holding her up off the ground, he strode behind a big maple tree so that the trunk would give them some privacy.

"What are you doing out here?" he demanded as he lowered her down. "You'll end up getting pneumonia—"

"I just needed to thank you."

"For what—" He stopped. "It was you. You were behind that painting."

"I knew you were in the house. I just didn't know why. I heard what you told my father . . . thank you."

Axe wanted to say the right thing. Or hell, say anything. But the way she was staring up at him with those shining eyes, her hair all clean and fragrant, her body under that robe something that he could remember every single inch of . . .

He cupped her face and rubbed her cheek with his thumb. "I dreamed about you. All day long."

Elise smiled more widely. "Did you?"

"Mmm-hmm."

"What did you dream of?"

"This."

Tilting his head, he bent down and kissed her, working her lips with his own, wrapping his arms around her, pulling her close. The winter wind danced around them, snowflakes starting to fall, the dark velvet heavens above seeming to encourage lovers everywhere.

When he finally edged back, he massaged her shoulders. "I can't wait for this night to be over."

"Me, too."

She put her hands on the pads of his chest, massaging. "I wish you didn't have to go."

"I couldn't stay here anyway."

"You could—"

"I don't want to cause trouble for you."

"Never."

God, he couldn't get enough of her face, her throat, the feel of her waist under his palms. She was like a drug he needed another hit from, and the fact that that made him want to run in the opposite direction was ironic, given how he'd embraced heroin and cocaine. Sex. Violence.

But the screaming voice telling him to get the hell away from her and never look back was countered, punch for punch, by an even stronger need to be close and stay close.

From out of nowhere, an image of those figurines of his father's came to mind.

Axe stepped away abruptly. Missed the contact immediately.

Felt his head get even more scrambled.

"I'm sorry. I got to go."

"Be safe out there?" she whispered as she tucked her arms around herself.

Nodding, he took one last look at her . . . and then dematerialized to the meeting place west and south of where her family's estate was.

As he re-formed, a gust that made his sinuses hum hit him right in the face and he breathed deeply. All his life, he had had great success pushing emotions down deep and putting a cap on them. And he did the same now, banishing any feelings or thoughts about Elise.

Too bad he could still taste her.

Peyton was the next to show up, and as they faced off, Axe was ready for a fight, prepared to start shit if he had to to get things going.

But Craeg and Paradise arrived and stepped between them.

"Nope," Craeg said. "Not doing this. Waste of time, waste of effort— and out here in the real world, a dangerous goddamn distraction. What the hell is wrong with you two?"

"Nothing," Axe said without looking away. "Absolutely fucking nothing."

"Good." Craeg didn't move. "And you, Peyton?"

"I've got no problems."

Paradise hooked an arm through Pey-pey's elbow and pivoted him around. "So you were going to tell me about that female you went back to in the club last night, remember? Was she hot?"

Classic reroute move, and pretty fucking pathetic that it was required. But Mr. and Mrs. Training Program were right. The group of them were headed back out into the field tonight. None of that classroom work. No sparring in the gym.

Real guns and fun, as the Brothers called it.

Last thing anyone needed was interpersonal drama that got somebody dropped.

Into a grave.

Elise was floating on air as she went up the back staff stairs. The last thing she wanted was to be caught in her bathrobe, smelling of the night air and the male she had just kissed out in the front yard.

Funny, she had wanted exactly this tingling enticement when she had thought about being with Troy only nights ago. She had wanted this exact blossoming, even though she hadn't really known what it was. She had been searching, and she had been found. And it was beautiful.

Her bubble of happiness did not persist.

She reached the second floor and was padding quietly down the carpeted hall, going past the closed doors of the guest suites and her father's quarters, when she neared an open portal into a black room.

The voice of her uncle was distant, even though he had to be standing just inside the darkness. ". . . this eve? Mayhap I shall have a meal set upon a quiet table for the two of us?"

The response from her aunt was so quiet, Elise couldn't hear the words.

"Well . . . ," her uncle murmured. "Yes, I shall come back then.

Mayhap at some other, later time. I think there is—what? . . . Yes. I know you do not sleep. . . ."

Elise crossed her arms around herself and walked quickly past him with her head down and her eyes on the carpet. But her uncle must have heard her or sensed her because just as she came up to their room, he wheeled around into the light.

His face was that of a skull, his skin gray from stress and suffering, his eyes hollow. "Elise," he said in a dead tone. *"How fare thee this eve?"*

She bowed and likewise used the Old Language. *"I am well, mine uncle. And you?"*

It was the customary response to the customary question that did not, in fact, request an honest reckoning of her state, but was more a polite gesture, as someone would utter "Bless you" after a sneeze.

"I am well. Thank you."

And then the door was closed.

She hadn't really seen her aunt since the tragedy, and could only guess the shape the female must be in.

Elise continued on to her own room, where she changed into comfy yoga pants and a fleece pullover her father did not approve of. A quick check of the clock suggested she had waaaaay too many hours before she was going to sneak out.

Leaving her phone behind, of course.

Thank you, Father.

Taking a seat at her French desk, there were scholarly articles to read and that draft lesson plan Troy had sent over early in the afternoon for the January seminar. But her mind was scattered and inefficient, snippets of Axe's conversation with her sire, her phone call with Peyton—and then the kiss on the lawn . . . as well as what she had just witnessed down the hall—jamming up her thought processes.

For some reason, she found herself back out in the hall . . . in front of Allishon's room.

This time, she went right in, but then she stalled out, unsure what she was doing, what she was looking for. After a moment, she proceeded over to the walk-in closet because there was nowhere else to go, really.

Shutting herself in, she looked around as the motion-activated lights came on. The lineup of hanging clothes was messy and there were piles of discarded things all over the floor.

God, it still smelled like Allishon and her signature perfume.

And the wardrobe of shirts and skirts and jeans and boots and high heels was nothing Elise would ever have worn, everything tight, short, leathered, studded, ripped on purpose. Where Elise followed the rules, Allishon had entirely resisted any kind of social expectation.

The classic good girl/bad girl dichotomy.

Clinically speaking, it wasn't a mystery why nobody was talking about the death. Her father felt guilty and maybe a little superior that his young, the "conservative" female, had been the one to survive; his brother was distraught and bitter that his daughter, the one who had been so resistant and hard to deal with, had come to the very end everybody had tried to scare her away from; and her aunt was likely suicidal.

Meanwhile, Elise was trying to live her own life in the morass, trapped between sorrow and a yearning for independence.

What a mess.

On that note . . .

She picked up a black blouse that was held together by safety pins and not much else and put it on a vacant hanger. And then she did the same with a flannel shirt that was mostly shredded. And a bodysuit that was black and had a blood-splatter pattern on the front like its wearer had been shot in the chest.

She wasn't sure why she was cleaning up—actually, that was bullcrap, she knew precisely why. She wanted to help her family and she could think of no other way to make even a marginal improvement.

Her father couldn't stand her even offering him a hug. Her uncle would not look at her. Her aunt wasn't getting out of that bed of hers . . . not unless it was into her early grave.

This was all she had.

At some point—later this year, maybe next year, maybe a decade from now—someone was going to come in and box up these things, relegating them perhaps to the basement or the attic, as, in aristocratic families, nothing was ever given away or resold. It was considered bad luck.

Maybe they would burn it all somewhere on the property.

But at least if she did this, whoever it was wasn't going to see the mess.

Thinking back to what Peyton had said, she could only shake her head. Her father had always made it seem as if a human had killed Allishon. But to find out it was another vampire?

What the hell had happened?

TWENTY-EIGHT

With Novo's and Boone's arrivals in the fairly well-lit alley, the training class was complete—and shortly thereafter, a vehicle the size of a bank turned in at the far end. It was the Brotherhood's mobile surgical unit, and as it came to a stop, Axe assumed that this was it. Playtime was over.

The Brother Butch, a.k.a. the *Dhestroyer*, stepped out from the front passenger side. "No more training runs."

Yup.

"This is not a trial or a test." The Brother reached back in and brought out a duffel that was nearly the size of a bodyguard. "I'm going to be swapping out your ammo. These are hollow-tipped bullets with a little extra kick to them."

Boone, the class hand popper, naturally couldn't let that go. "What is it?"

"Water from the Scribe Virgin's Sanctuary. Or what had been her Sanctuary." Butch shut the door, banged his fist into the RV, and the thing trundled off. When it was out of sight, he dropped the bag and unzipped it. "Come on, move it."

Boone was first in line, kicking both clips out of the butts of his forties and exchanging them for new slides.

"Gimme what's on your belt, too," Butch demanded.

More swapping. And then Craeg, Paradise, Novo . . . Axe was the last one to do it, getting his new bullets and falling in line with the others. There were no humans around, not walking, stumbling, or even driving by in cars; whether that was on account of that holiday with the holly and the candy canes or the frigid temperatures, Axe didn't know. Didn't care.

But that didn't mean they were alone.

Zsadist was standing about ten feet away, his scarred face and pit-black eyes the kind of thing that made even Axe's bowels get a little loose. Tohrment was beside the Brother. And so were John Matthew, Blaylock, and Qhuinn.

Holy shit, Axe thought. They weren't fucking kidding about this.

Butch spoke up again. "We're getting close to the end of the war. That means *lessers* are becoming hard to find and easier to kill because the only ones left are brand-new recruits. Last field session for you all, things went tits up, so we are pairing you up with a Brother or a fighter. In concert with your mentor, you will go out in a grid pattern running west to east. Do not vary unless you engage, and then only as necessary. You and your mentor will both signal everyone else upon engagement. When a signal is received, we all will converge, returning to our search patterns only after an assessment of the engaged situation occurs. Do not go rogue. Do not think on your own. Do not get dead. Any questions? And may I remind you bunch of idiots that this is not a drill. Now is the time to back off and get the fuck out if you're going to. Any moment after this will be considered desertion and reason for dismissal from the program. I'd rather you bail now, not fuck us in the middle of a mission."

No one flaked. No one wasted any time with dumb-ass questions.

They were as prepared as much as any bunch of newbs could be.

And each one of them had known this night was coming.

"Axe," Butch said, "you're with me. Paradise, you go with Tohr. Z gets Boone. Craeg is with John Matthew. Peyton, you're with Qhuinn. Blay is functioning as a scout for this mission, going out on the rooftops ahead of us all. Keep your guns up, your eyes peeled, and your phones live."

Nobody said anything as the pairs linked up, with him falling in line with Butch as each team got assigned a street. The plan was for everyone to proceed through their given territory until the neighborhood started to improve, approximately thirty blocks up. Then the entire system would move six streets to the north, away from downtown—because the war tended to steer clear from the skyscrapers due to the exterior security cameras and internal security teams in all that expensive real estate.

Security shit meant humans potentially all over the fuck, and nobody needed that.

It was the only rule of engagement that both the Brotherhood and the Lessening Society adhered to: no human interaction, if at all possible. And if you did interact? You cleaned that up quick.

Axe and Butch were the farthest out of the pairings, the two of them setting off at a jog because Butch, as a half-breed, was not able to dematerialize—not that that really mattered. As the Brother was of the King's own bloodline, he was bulldog strong, his shitkickers covering the pavement at a fast run that Axe had to keep up with.

When they came to Fifth Street, Butch palmed both his guns. Axe did the same.

"We go down this side, son," the Brother said in his Boston accent. "Be wicked fuckin' careful."

Together, they strode forward in a flanking position, sticking to the fronts of the brick buildings—which was to say they were pretty much sitting ducks. But Axe kept his eyes on the windows across the street, covering Butch as the Brother provided the same service for him: Both of them were looking for any flashes or figures moving around in the windows of the law offices, social service agencies, philanthropic organizations. . . .

This was the nicest of the real estate they were going to see.

And yup, the denigration and depression of monetary values started up pretty damn quick. Soon, the five- and six-story walk-ups were displaying signs of age and decomposition, front stoops exhibiting cracked steps like teeth that were on the verge of falling out, paint jobs flaking off, and, even farther on, missing windows beginning to make appearances.

Now, he was tromping across a slushy debris field of trash, hubcaps, random beer cans and booze bottles, parts of engines, fuck only knew what else. But he didn't give a shit. He had good treads on his combat boots, sure footing, and razor-sharp instincts that were firing like cannons. In fact, his whole body was humming, his blood crackling through his veins, his trigger fingers ready to party.

And all the time, his eyes scanned the buildings across the way and then flicked to what was ahead of him and then returned to those fucking rooflines and dirty glass panes.

To say he fell into a rhythm was not accurate. There was no rhythm to be had when you were aware that you might have to start either shooting or bleeding at any fucking moment. But he was definitely in a zone—

He caught the scent first.

Just as he was crossing a thin alley opening, a gust brought something that smelled like three-day-old roadkill topped with fake vanilla icing and baby powder.

He knew better than to stop, even though his feet faltered. Instead, he jumped across the opening and back-flatted it against the far corner of the next abandoned building. With a short whistle, he got Butch's attention—and he didn't need to explain what it was.

The Brother was already on it, reversing so that he was on the far side of the urban aperture.

Axe was aware of his heart pounding, but he kept his breathing slow and steady. If he started panting, it was going to decrease the accuracy of his hearing and that was not going to help.

Finally, he was going to engage with the enemy—

Shit, he thought as he caught another scent on the breeze.

Blood.

There was vampire blood down there.

At that very moment, his phone went off in his sleeve and he popped his elbow up, reading the screen that showed through the clear pocket retrofitted onto his combat jacket.

Fuck, Qhuinn and Peyton had engaged.

Almost immediately, another text came through. So had Tohr and Paradise. And John Matthew and Craeg.

It was a cluster-fuck.

And as he realized that Rhage wasn't among them, he thought . . . fucking hell, what if the Brother was down there fighting alone?

Deep in Allishon's closet, Elise had worked herself all the way around the space, and what she left in her wake was Macy's display-worthy, the garments tidy and orderly on the rods, even if some were wrinkled or so deliberately tattered that they barely had enough to hold themselves together on the hangers. She'd also sorted the things on the carpet, putting the bags and shoes in a lineup according to type and color.

As she stepped back to measure her success, she frowned. There seemed to be a wad of something in the far corner, so she got on her knees and pulled the . . . it was a bundle of cloth, like a large, loose bag, or a—no, it was a black cloak. That smelled like—

Oh, yeah, no. Cigarettes, alcohol, other things.

Elise folded the thing on the floor and was about to put it back when she leaned down and looked into the corner again.

There was something else there.

Reaching forward, she really had to stretch her arm back—

"What the hell?" she muttered.

A box. Metal, by the cool feel of it.

She tried to pull the thing out, but it weighed a great deal. Two hands. She needed two hands, and she grunted.

It turned out to be one of those lockbox, mini-safe things, the kind with the heavy reinforced sides and top. There was a keyed entry to it, and when she tried the latch on a whim, she didn't expect—

Except it did open: With enough pressure, the top half cracked and then started to come fully up. She stopped her hands from following through, however.

Falling back on her butt, she moved the lockbox between her legs and thought about what she was doing. This was maybe private . . . something that Allishon's parents should see first. Yet as she tried to picture bringing anything of their daughter's to them, she knew that was never going to go well—and though she had mixed feelings, she did peek inside.

Just a bunch of folded-up papers, legal-size. That was it.

Taking them out, she flattened the bundle. It was a real estate contract. For the lease of . . . what looked like a condo. That was downtown, going by the address of a numbered street?

Was that where Allishon had gone all those nights and days she hadn't come home—

"We rented that for her."

With a gasp, Elise wrenched around.

Her aunt was standing in the closet's archway, and dear Lord . . . the female looked as if she had been in a car accident—or maybe one involving a motorcycle with her as the cyclist: her hair, once always coiffed and sprayed into a beautiful fall onto her shoulders, was a ragged mess, with roots showing that were two shades darker than the streaky California blond so popular in the *glymera*. And instead of a fashionable little Escada suit or St. John knit, with plenty of pearls at her throat and on her ears, she was in a stained, wrinkled nightgown that once had been made of silk but now seemed to have more in common with a crumpled paper napkin.

Her eyes were wide and crazy.

She wasn't looking at Elise, however. She was staring at the order of the hangers.

"Did you do this?" the female asked in a wobbly voice.

And as she came in a little farther, her steps were equally unsteady.

"I'm sorry." Elise fumbled with the paperwork to get it back in the box and shut the lid. "I just . . . I didn't know what I could do to help."

And yeah, eavesdropping had been so frickin' laudable.

"Her things . . ." A frail hand reached out and brushed the clothing Elise had put to rights. "God, how I hated these clothes of hers."

Elise pushed the safe back where it had been and got to her feet. "I shouldn't have come in here—"

"No, it's all right. You've done . . . a better job than I have."

"It wasn't my business to—"

"We leased her that apartment because we couldn't stand to have her coming and going here all hours of the night. Disheveled. Drunk. Drugged up. The stench of sex on her."

An inner *Mayday, Mayday, Mayday*, started to go off in Elise's head. As did a refrain of *Be careful what you wish for*.

This was not what she had imagined when it came to talking.

Her aunt's gnarled hand gripped and twisted one of the short skirts. "Her father felt certain that the banishment would be the corrective action for all her disobedience. That she would get out there, realize her folly, and snap out of the behavior." The laugh was madness personified. "Instead, she lived more on her own terms than ever before. I couldn't reach her. He barely tried. And all the time she got worse. She enjoyed torturing us."

"Auntie, perhaps you should speak with Uncle—"

"I hated her." The female snapped the skirt free of its clips and threw it to the carpet. "And I hate her even more in her death."

"I'm sure you don't mean that—"

"Oh, but I do. She was a filthy whore, then and always. She got what she deserved—"

"You're her mother," Elise blurted. "How can you say that?"

Her aunt moved down and made a fist out of one of the safety-pinned blouses. Ripping it off the rod, the hanger popped free and ricocheted right into her face. Not that she seemed to notice.

"Look what she's done to us! After we lost our son, we now have a murdered daughter! Who was found bloodied and half-dead in front of a domestic abuse house! How could she have embarrassed us like that!"

All Elise could do was stare into that ashen, emaciated face as her aunt began to tear the closet apart.

She was the reason for the disorder—not Allishon. She was the one who had trashed the clothes—and she was going to do it again, right here and right now.

Abruptly, Elise wanted to cry. The idea that social expectations had so completely ruined any even biological connection between mother and daughter was just . . . unfathomable.

And yet she never would have guessed at the splintering. Before the death, everything had been kept under wraps, her aunt and uncle showing up dressed beautifully and smiling at events, ever the perfect couple . . . as their daughter had self-destructed after her brother's death, first by inches, and then by yards . . . until the fracturing of the family unit had become obvious to the other people in this house.

The others in society.

"We are not welcomed anymore," her aunt gritted out as she pulled more and more off the rods, throwing the clothes down, trampling over them with her bare feet. "We are invited nowhere! We are outcasts and it is her fault!"

Elise swallowed hard and eyed the escape.

She was fairly certain she was going to throw up.

"Have I shocked you with my honesty," her aunt sneered. "You look like you've seen a ghost."

"No," Elise whispered. "Not a ghost. I'm looking at a version of evil that I never expected to see in my own family."

Stumbling by, she shoved her corpse of an aunt out of the way and ran not just out of Allishon's room, but the mansion itself.

Out on the front lawn, she braced her hands on her knees, leaned over . . . and dry-heaved in the bushes.

And then she kept running down the drive, not even caring she had nowhere to go.

TWENTY-NINE

As Butch signaled for go-time, Axe and the Brother entered a cramped service lane behind the abandoned buildings, Axe falling in tight behind and sticking with the warrior as they efficiently progressed down toward God only knew what.

Fucking hell, it was darker than he'd thought, although Axe recognized that this was because he had no goddamn clue what was going to happen and it was reflexive to think that illumination would put him in a better defensive position.

The sounds of fighting soon echoed in the distance and got more intense, as did the scents of spilled blood . . . both of vampire and slayer.

The first of the writhing *lessers* showed up about eight blocks from where they'd rerouted, and Butch barely paused as they went by the damn thing. He merely unsheathed a black dagger, lifted it over his head, and stabbed the undead right in the chest, the *pop!*-and-smoke show the first time Axe had ever seen it done.

No dwelling on the shit, though: the reality that he could get shot in the head at any second kept Axe focused on what was living and not what was being sent back to the Omega.

Farther down, black stains that gleamed like spilled oil showed up on the worn pavement . . . and then came the red splatters on the brick walls of the walkups—

Gunshots went off.

Pop! Pop! Rat-a-tat-ata-ta—

With a burst forward, they redoubled their speed until they got to yet another alley-artery, skidding around the corner and dropping into shooting position, Butch facing forward, Axe facing the other direction at the guy's six.

Axe shot a quick glance over his shoulder—oh, hell, he was never going to forget the image of the cluster-fuck going down about fifty feet away.

Rhage was in the center of three *lessers*, all of which had knives—and the Brother was fighting them without weapons in his hands, in spite of the fact that he had daggers strapped right to his chest.

There was also the clear indication, if that red waterfall down his left arm was anything to go by, that he had been shot at least once, probably more.

It was as if he'd had red paint poured all over him—

A *lesser* came running around the same corner Axe and Butch had just ridden hard, and thank fuck for training. Instead of wasting a crucial nanosecond thinking *Holy fuck!*, Axe went beast with his guns, hitting those triggers—

Jammed. Both of them.

"Fuck!"

Butch started shooting in the direction of the fight, trying to pick off the slayers without hitting Rhage—which was proving impossible because the Brother was still trying to fight even while bleeding out.

"Dagger!" Axe shouted. "Now!"

Again, the training worked. Butch glanced behind for a second, knew there was no choice but for Axe to engage in tight quarters, and the Brother took out an actual black dagger.

"Don't showboat! Get the fucking job done!"

With that, he flipped the weapon back and Axe caught it on the down arc, leaping forward and going right for the slayer's chest.

He didn't miss.

That fucking black blade went right where it needed to, like there was a homing device in the forged steel.

There was no celebrating, though.

A stray bullet, either on a ricochet from Butch's gun or from one of the two new slayers who'd suddenly shown up in the alley, caught Axe in the thigh, the blaze of pain as if someone had taken a red-hot fireplace poker and jammed it into his upper leg.

And then yet another slayer came around the corner.

No time to think.

Axe leaped on the fucker, taking the soulless human down to the pavement and rolling him over. But the bastard was smart, or really into survival, because he managed to grab on to Axe's fresh wound and squeeze.

Axe's vision went in and out, his switchboard momentarily overrun with so much electrical impulse that it went on the fritz.

But then he got pissed. Clamping a hand on the *lesser*'s throat, he had a snapshot of bared human teeth with those weird flat-tipped canines of theirs, and the tattoo of a tear under one brown eye, and shaggy hair that looked like it hadn't been cut in a month.

And then he lifted that dagger over his shoulder, just as Butch had done, and stabbed it right through the frontal lobe, driving the blade through the skull and into the cake of gray matter behind the bone.

Seizures. The slayer went full-tilt boogie, that grip on Axe's thigh flipping free, the arms slapping against the asphalt like he was clapping for a show, the legs kicking as if he were swimming.

Axe rolled off and retched from the pain. But then he went to get the dagger back from where it was flag-poling right above the slayer's eyebrow—

It was stuck. There was no getting the weapon out.

He'd driven it so hard, he'd crushed the skull and buried the tip in fucking pavement.

Jumping to his feet, he staggered, and figured, Fuck it, at least the slayer wasn't going anywhere.

There was no more conscious thought.

His eyes provided him with an instant assessment of the state of the battle: Butch was now involved in hand-to-hand maneuvers, fighting for control of the gun he had been using with a slayer who looked like a defensive end for the New England Patriots . . . while Rhage was sinking to his knees in the center of the alley, the fighting not so much going out of him as leaking out, his blood pooling under him to such an extent that there were puddles getting splashed.

With a battle cry, Axe lunged forward, taking three running leaps even with his gunshot wound.

He attacked the first *lesser* he came to, jumping on its back, going bullrider-squeeze with his thighs and locking hold on its ears with his hands. Then he snapped that head so far to the right, the ligaments and tendons on the left side broke free of the neck skin.

On to the next.

Leaving the body to fall where it did, he burst forward—just as a slayer coiled up a chain and went to get Rhage around the throat. Yeah, fuck that shit. With a quick jerk, Axe outed his smaller hunting knife, and tackled the *lesser* to the side.

Talk about your fucking Jason-maneuvers. He stabbed so fast and so hard and so many times, he didn't just incapacitate the bastard, he tenderized it.

Then he scrambled to get to the last one. Scrambled so hard.

It had a knife. A long, serrated blade that could do a lot of damage, especially to a Brother who was clearly on the verge of losing consciousness: Rhage's hands were flopping and slapping instead of strategically hitting, his balance all wonky, his skin as white as the snow.

Axe slipped and fell. Went down hard. Landed badly.

As he snowplowed, his leathers protected him from dermabra-
sion . . . but did nothing to save him from another gunshot wound—
which arrived in a now-familiar strip of pain on one of his shoulders.
And something stabbed him, too, maybe?

But then Rhage collapsed and nothing else mattered. The mighty
Brother went down first on one palm, then the next, and the math was
tragic as Axe made the assessment that the slayer with the knife was
going to hop around, come at Rhage from behind, and slit his throat,
finishing the job.

No roar this time. Axe was losing strength of his own.

Instead, Axe just got the fuck up, even though his vision flickered
again, and he bolted forward, not so much running as falling and
scrambling—

Something was buzzing around his head—why were there flies out
at the end of December? What the fuck?

And God, his body suddenly weighed twice as much.

Fuck, he smelled so much blood.

He didn't care. Reaching Rhage, he grabbed the Brother's hair, and
put every ounce of power left in him into wrenching Rhage out of the
way of the arc of that swinging *lesser* blade—

Axe was the one who took the knife.

And it went deep into him. Right between his ribs on the side.

He gasped, his eyes lifting to the sky. And then suddenly everything
went slo-mo and numb. The world was falling—no, it was probably
him, wasn't it?

What was with the flies?

Boom! He landed hard again—not that he felt it through the numb-
blanket he was wrapped in; he just assumed he did because he bounced,
the buildings around him going up and down until gravity won against
the laws of basketballs and falling bodies that offered no resistance.

Exhale.

He tasted copper. Gurgling. He heard a horrible gurgling . . . and figured it meant he was drowning in his own blood.

The last thing he saw as he passed out was Rhage rolling over and staring at him, as if the Brother was as surprised as Axe was.

Rhage opened his mouth and said something, his bloodied hand reaching out for Axe as if offering him something to hold on to.

Axe tried to move his arm in response.

But it was too late.

He was gone.

THIRTY

𝒯he heart of a warrior.

Rhage had never seen anything like it. Or certainly never expected it out of a trainee. He himself had been going down, the reality of war reminding him that battles were like Mother Nature: No matter how strong and well-trained and well-equipped you were, every once in a while, the tide could turn against you, and if it did, you could get in over your head in a heartbeat.

And that was what had happened.

Too much blood loss. Too many opponents. Too arrogant in assuming he could handle his shit when half of his mind was back home with Bitty and Mary, and the entirety of his soul was in pain.

And he should have used his fucking weapons.

The tide had turned so quick, too. His legs had started to go jelly, and then he'd realized he was going to go to ground—and soon thereafter it was over, a father's promise of safety to his daughter turned into a lie: He was going to get swarmed and they were going to kill him—and even the beast couldn't help him. He'd expected the great dragon to come out, and it nearly did—but just as the transformation was about to happen, he'd gotten the arterial wound and his blood pressure had started to tank, and all bets had been off.

Still, the beast had saved him once in that condition, though . . . not tonight, however.

Not tonight.

But then Axe had come from out of nowhere, attacking the first of too many *lessers* by daggering it in the chest. The trainee had then gone for the next, stabbing its skull into the asphalt—only to get counter-attacked from behind, a huge slayer leaping onto his back and lashing Axe's face and shoulders with a length of chain.

There had been no stopping the trainee, though. Hell, Axe hadn't seemed to even notice what was on top of him: Even bleeding, stabbed in places, shot in the leg, and with a *lesser* riding him like a horse, the male had been unrelenting, lurching to Rhage and ultimately taking the knife that had been meant for Rhage's throat in his own side.

Down the male had gone, like a great oak in the forest.

And now Rhage was reaching for the trainee, extending a hand across the pavement as the snow started to fall on both of their bleeding bodies.

So brave.

Axe's unfocused eyes shifted in his direction, their stares meeting. Blood was coming out of Axe's mouth and was all over his chest.

Thank you, son . . . , Rhage mouthed. *Thank you* . . .

All at once, people came running, all kinds of Brothers and then Manny with the surgical RV and still other folks. There was immediate surgical intervention, right on the ground, for both him and Axe, and Rhage refused to lose consciousness. Just wasn't going to.

In spite of the fact that his body was cold and numb and his eyesight was blurry and his heart was square dancing behind his sternum, he refused to let go of reality.

He was afraid he wasn't going to come back.

The view of what they were doing to Axe got blocked as Manny started to work on the bleed on Rhage's shoulder, and Rhage looked up to the sky. The snow that was coming down from the heavens landed on his lashes and melted, and he pictured Mary and Bitty, their heads together, the pair of them smiling at him as if they were in a snow globe.

Two Chosen arrived, and when a wrist was slit and placed against his mouth, he did what he had to in order to survive.

He hoped Axe was doing the same.

He didn't want that kid's death on his conscience. . . .

Sometime later, he was loaded onto a gurney. Axe was, too—with no shroud over his face. So the male must still be alive, right?

"Let me see him," Rhage demanded. Okay, "asked" was more like it, given how weak his voice was.

He was rolled over to the guy. Axe was naked and patchworked with bandages, an IV running into his arm, tubes coming out of his ribs, a heart monitor beeping like a metronome that wasn't working right.

"Is he going to die?" Rhage asked.

Manny put his face within Rhage's sight. "Not if I have anything to do with it. That goes for you, too." The surgeon turned away and barked, "Get him in the unit."

Rhage hissed as a bumpy ride started, and then he got a great view of the brightly lit ceiling of Manny's RV. Axe was loaded in behind him.

"Don't tell Mary," Rhage said to anyone who might have been listening.

Manny's face came back. "Really. You really think that's an option? I just field-treated you with about a hundred and fifty stitches—and I'm going to have to fine-tune that back at the training center. You think that shit isn't going to come up in conversation?"

"I don't want her to worry."

Butch's puss entered the picture, too—and the Brother was furious.

"Then maybe you shouldn't have gone rogue, asshole. Jesus fucking Christ, did you want to die out there—"

Manny put his palm over the cop's ENT. "Enough. He's my patient right now. He can transition to being your punching bag when he isn't catheterized and can stand up on his own two feet to take a piss."

"Axe saved my life. . . ."

That was the last thing Rhage said before he went nighty-night.

There was something magical about Christmas trees.

As Mary sat in the library at the mansion, her feet up on the coffee table in front of a crackling fire, a mug of hot chocolate in her hand, a candy cane between her lips, she stared across at a perfect Douglas fir. Decorated with red velvet swaths and gold balls and red and gold lights that twinkled in silence, it was the tradition that she, Beth, John Matthew, Butch, and Manny had all grown up with, a reminder of things past, a centering and grounding that helped her connect the two parts of her life story, the before and the after.

"There are so many presents under there," Bitty said as she came in with a refill on her cocoa. "I have extra marshmallows, by the way? I'll share?"

"Oh, thanks, but mine are still holding up."

Mary patted the cushion next to her and it seemed like the most natural thing in the world for Bitty to come over and snuggle close, the girl tucking those Lassiter-healed legs under her bottom.

"I better hit the songs again," Mary said as she reached for the remote to the surround sound. "I love Bing Crosby."

"Ohhhhh . . . 'Winter Wonderland,'" Bitty murmured, "I think this is my favorite."

"Mine too."

"Do you think Father will watch *Home Alone* again when he gets off work?"

"I think you can take that to the bank."

There was a period of quiet between them, the soft chatter of the fire and the old-fashioned Christmas music the only sounds that filled the cozy room.

"Mom?"

"Hmmm?" Mary took a sip of her hot chocolate and marveled how, even with so much being wrong, the warm drink was still delicious. "Is there something you need?"

"What's going on?"

Annnnnd now what was in her mug tasted like dishwater. "What do you mean?"

"I know there's something wrong. You and Father are not acting right. Did I do something bad? Do you not want to adopt me?"

Mary sat up so fast she nearly cocoa'd the couch. "God, no, never, we want you always and forever."

The girl stared across at the tree. "Are you sure?"

"One hundred percent. Bitty, look at me. Please." Those beautiful eyes swung up. "Don't ever doubt how much we love you. No matter what happens, that is one thing you will never have to worry about."

"So what's wrong?"

Mary hesitated. She didn't want to lie, but at the same time, the stuff about that male was not the kind of news that she wanted to share without Rhage being with them—and even more to the point, she still didn't know what to say about the "uncle" who'd turned up out of nowhere.

"Ah—"

The sound of fast footsteps made the hair on the back of her neck stand up: In the mansion, that noise coming in your direction was not something you ever wanted to hear when your *hellren* was out in the field.

When John Matthew appeared in the doorway, she got to her feet as she saw his ashen face. "How bad?"

"What's going on?" Bitty said with alarm. "Father—what happened to my father?"

John Matthew started signing, and Bitty just got more agitated. "What is it? What's wrong!"

"Okay, okay . . ." Mary reached out for the little girl. "It's all right. He just got injured, but they're bringing him in and I'm going to go see him—"

"I'm coming, too—"

"I don't think that's a good idea, sweetheart."

Bitty crossed her arms over her chest. "Am I a member of this family or not?"

Mary swallowed an abrupt lump in her throat. "You may not like what you see."

"He was with me when I was at Havers's. I will be there the same for him."

John Matthew whistled softly and then signed as Mary looked over. She nodded, and made up her mind.

"Okay, come with me. But here's the deal, it's up to the medical professionals. They may only let one of us in at a time—or maybe not at all."

"Whatever Doc Jane and Dr. Manny say, I'll do."

Mary held out her arm and Bitty came in close again for a quick, frantic hug. Then together, they hustled to follow John Matthew out into the foyer, around the base of the grand staircase, and down into the underground tunnel to the training center.

As they rushed along, passing beneath the blocks of fluorescent lights in the ceiling, she and Bitty stayed linked, their strides falling into the same gait because Mary shortened her stride a little and Bitty lengthened hers.

"Don't cry, Mom," the girl said softly.

"I didn't know I was," Mary whispered as she wiped her cheeks. "I'm just so glad you're with me."

THIRTY-ONE

"No, I'm *not* staying here."

Axe made a move to sit up in the hospital bed, and the chorus of *whatthefuckdoyouthinkyouredoing* from just about every single bone, sinew, stretch of skin, and muscle was so loud, he couldn't hear Dr. Manello's no doubt highly reasonable explanation as to why he had to chill.

"Nope." Axe started to go for the IV in his arm. "I'm out."

Dr. Manello snapped a hard grip on Axe's wrist. "What the hell do you think you're doing?"

"I'm taking this out if you won't."

"Listen, kid, I want to remind you that I operated on you, in a fucking alley, about an hour ago."

"I feel fine."

"Your lips are blue."

"My body, my choice."

As they bickered back and forth, the stark decor of the hospital room and the reclinable bed he was in irritated the hell out of him. As did the johnny he was wearing. The fact that his feet were bare. And also the idea that he might get trapped here during the day.

Actually, pretty much everything irritated him.

"Really." At least the surgeon let go of his arm as the guy spoke. "That's your comeback. Your body, your choice?"

Wait, was that what he had said? He couldn't remember.

Whatever.

"I thought it was a good one." Axe shook his head. "And come on, I fed from a Chosen back there. Within six hours, everything will be healed up. Inside and out. I have no broken bones, you yourself said I didn't have a concussion, and I saved the life of a member of the Black Dagger Brotherhood."

"And you believe that gives you carte blanche to AMA yourself?"

"Okay, I don't know what AMA is—"

"Against. Medical. Advice. Asshole."

"Actually, that would be AMAA, wouldn't it?"

"You're making me want to hit you in the thigh, FYI."

"That rhymes, and isn't there a hypothetical oath or something you human doctors take?"

"Hippocratic. And hypothetically, you could leave here and have a complication in the next three hours where you could need to be opened up again, but there you'll be, at home with your thumb up your ass, bleeding out for no good reason."

"My thumb has never been near that area."

"Maybe you should try it. It might stimulate your brain to work right."

Axe couldn't help it. He started to laugh, and then Dr. Manello followed along—at least until Axe ended up coughing and grabbing for his side where he'd been stabbed.

"See?" Dr. Manello said grimly.

"Just sore." Axe took a deep breath and mostly hid his wince. "Look, Doc, just let me go. I'll catch the shuttle out and—"

"You won't be able to dematerialize."

Shit. The guy was probably right.

"What the hell you got at home?" Dr. Manello demanded. "A cat? Some kind of house-eating dog?"

"I just want my own bed." Even though he slept on the floor. "It's that simple."

As Dr. Manello leaned back against the wall, the guy frowned as if someone who spoke a different language than he did was about to drop an anvil on his foot—and he had to figure out how to tell them no, please don't do that.

"You're really going to leave," the surgeon muttered.

"Even if I have to walk all the way home."

There was a long pause. And then Dr. Manello said, "Fine, I'll drive you in the surgical unit."

"What? Oh, shit, Doc, I can't ask you to do that—"

"What's my other option, you hardheaded pain in the ass. You're just going to limp out of here, hide on that fucking bus if you have to, and then get out somewhere in Caldie—only to discover when you've been left there that you can't walk much at all and you die an over-cooked pancake from sun exposure. After I wasted seven feet of my best suturing thread and twelve gray hairs Humpty Dumptying your goat fuck back into place."

"Wait, didn't Humpty Dumpty fall and break? I think the meta-phor you're shooting for is more along the lines of Elmer's glue? Duct tape?"

Dr. Manello smiled and pointed at the IV bag. "Do you have annnnnnnny idea the kind of shit I can put in your bag?"

"That sounds dirty. And I like females recently, so you're not my type."

The surgeon was laughing as he headed for the door. "Gimme ten minutes to get organized. Ehlena will be here to unplug you—and if you touch that line into your vein? I'm not letting you go. We do this right, on my terms, clear?"

"Clear."

Just as the human opened the door, Axe said gruffly, "Can I see Rhage. You know, before I leave."

Dr. Manello looked over his shoulder. "Yeah, he's been asking for you. And you can take your time in there—you're going in in a wheelchair. Oh, and shut the fuck up with the complaining on that, will you."

"I haven't bitched about it."

"Yet."

As the door eased shut, Axe thought, Well, at least the guy seemed to get him.

And what do you know, after he was "unplugged" and had shifted his bare feet to the floor, standing up turned out to be realllllly tricky.

Turned out that surgeon had had a point about him not being able to go far.

Ehlena, his nurse, was patient as he grunted and shifted himself from the bed down to the wheelchair, and then she pushed him two doors closer to the exit and knocked.

"Come in," a female voice said.

The nurse opened things up and Axe rolled himself in. The tableau over at the hospital bed was totally Norman Rockwell, Rhage on his back looking like death warmed over, his loving *shellan* and his dark-haired daughter by his side.

And it was funny, even though Axe didn't believe in the nuclear anything, unless it was a bomb . . . the three of them together made him a little sentimental. After all, it was the kind of thing anyone would want—because he could tell the family was close, Rhage holding the little girl's hand, and Mary, who Axe had met in passing once or twice, with her arm around their daughter.

"Don't mean to interrupt private time," Axe muttered.

"No"—Rhage motioned forward—"come here. . . ."

Axe wheeled over as close as he could and thought, Fuck it. He put the brake on, struggled to get out of the chair, and used the handrails of the bed to hold himself up.

Wow. Nauseous.

"Thank you, son," Rhage said hoarsely. "You saved my life."

Man, those eyes were so blue, they almost looked fake. And they shone with tears unshed.

"Nah, it's good. I'm just glad, you know. . . ." Fuck, wait, what the hell, was he tearing up, too? "Look, I got to go—"

Rhage caught his arm in a shockingly tight grip, and repeated, "Thank you. For saving my life. And do us both a favor and don't try to pretend you didn't. You're the only reason I'm alive right now."

Axe just stood there like a planker. He had no idea what the hell to do.

Mary broke the silence, speaking up from the other side, her voice wavering. "I don't know how to repay you."

"Nothing. I don't want anything, ma'am." Axe looked up, way up, in an attempt to create more surface area for his welling eyeballs. "I better go. I'm going home."

"They're releasing you?" Rhage asked. "No offense, son, but you don't look well enough to be breathing on your own, much less going home unsupervised."

"I'll be fine."

The Brother laughed. "You sound just like one of us."

There was another moment of quiet, during which Axe desperately tried to keep from leaking.

"Come here, son."

Rhage grunted as he sat up, and for some stupid, insane, inane reason . . . Axe leaned down with a groan. As the two embraced, Axe heard himself say, "What if I hadn't gotten there on time? That's what I . . . that's what I keep replaying in my head."

"But you did."

"What if I hadn't, though? You'd have died and it would have been my fault."

Rhage let go and collapsed back against the raised half of the bed. "No, it would have been mine. We'll go into it later, but trust me, as someone who knows that pattern of thought well? It's the definition of stupidity to beat yourself up over something that fate decided was going to happen or not."

"Yeah."

"You know," the Brother exhaled roughly, "I'd like to tell you war gets easier. It doesn't. But you do get used to how awful it is. That much I can promise you. And hey, check it. You're starting out on a win. Better than having your ass—" He glanced in the direction of his daughter. "You know. With a broomstick. Plunger. Hockey stick. Tent pole. Tent pole. Tent pole."

Axe laughed and eased back down into the wheelchair . . . which was both a relief and as painful as Rhage's pain-in-the-ass point— literally.

And damn it, you'd think his thigh would appreciate not having to carry any weight? Why was it doing that heartbeat thing again?

"No class tomorrow night," Rhage said.

"Yeah, listen, is it true no one else got hurt, just you and me?"

"There were some other brief engagements, but no one saw real action. The other slayers just ran off? It was as if they were afraid of getting sent home. I think the Omega's in some kind of flux. I don't know."

Axe nodded like he had something to contribute to any kind of discussion about the Omega, the Lessening Society, or the ins and outs of the war. He really didn't. He'd just happened to be at the right place at the right time tonight and hadn't fucked everything up.

He felt like people were making him out to be some kind of hero— and he was anything but.

He alone knew exactly what a lie that was.

"So, ah, I'm going to take off now. Dr. Manello's driving me back home."

"You sure that's a good idea, son?"

Axe glanced at Rhage's family. "I, um . . . I got someone waiting for me."

Rhage's smile was slow and knowing. "Well, good for you, son."

"Too good for me, is more like it."

"Oh, I know that one. Again, I'll say, trust me."

Axe nodded at the two females and then started rolling himself back from the bed so he could K-turn and—

The little girl came around and stood in front of him. She was so tiny and frail looking, with wrists that seemed no bigger than one of his fingers and shoulders that were barely wider than the span of his palm. But her lovely brown eyes were bright and intelligent and her hair was thick and shiny. In her leggings and her cozy red Christmas sweater with its snowflake pattern . . .

. . . she was more terrifying than a pack of *lessers*.

What if he broke her? And not that anyone was asking him to pick her up. But what if, like, he breathed the wrong way, and she shattered like glass?

Well . . . for one thing, half dead or not, Rhage would get out of that bed and turn him into floor polish.

"Ahhh . . ." Axe glanced to the parents in a panic. "Ahhh . . ."

"Can I give you a hug? For saving my father?" the little one said.

Axe immediately looked at Rhage again. And yeah, Axe might possibly have shaken his head back and forth real tight. Kind of like you would if someone said, Hey, how'd you like to hold this snapping turtle? Or . . . How about you volunteer for malaria? Or the all-popular, How about you jump into this alligator-infested cesspool?

With pork chops tied around your neck and a rib roast shoved down your—

Axe frowned. Mary and Rhage both seemed like somebody had died all of a sudden. What the hell?

Jeez, he didn't want to offend them.

He glanced back at the tiny female. "Ah . . . um, yeah. Sure—"

The kid was on him the next moment, her surprisingly strong hold taking his breath away. Reaching up, he patted her bird-like shoulder blades.

And then froze as she whispered in his ear, "He saved my life. I wish I could do what you did for him someday."

She broke away from him just as quickly as she'd come at him, and it was weird. In the center of his chest, he felt this bizarre kernel of . . . he didn't know what it was. But it was warm and seemed like the complete opposite of the freezing-cold self-hatred he usually carried around behind his sternum.

The kid went back to her parents. And before shit got even more too-much-emotion than it already was, Axe gave the family one last wave—and then the little girl had to come over again and open the door for him because he had no idea how to get out of the room without help.

Dr. Manello was outside in the corridor. "You ready?"

"Yeah."

"Let's do this."

The pair of them ambulated together, the good doctor on his feet in some kind of fancy loafers, him in his ass cruiser that had wheels that squeaked on the polished floor.

For the trip to the cottage, Dr. Manello made him ride in the back of the RV, in the surgical bay, because the front of the thing didn't have tinted windows.

And Axe was more than fine without knowing the precise location of the training center.

It gave him time to think.

For some reason, that shit Rhage said was sticking in his head.

It's the definition of stupidity to beat yourself up over something that fate decided was going to happen or not.

Axe groaned and rubbed his eyes. God, he was tired—

"Hey, we're here."

Axe jumped—and promptly cursed as his body lit up with agony, all of his pain receptors simultaneously firing.

Dr. Manello was in the back of the RV, standing over the wheelchair. "You want me to help get you out?"

"No." Axe gritted his teeth and put his palms on the padded armrests. "I'll do it."

The surgeon stepped back, those keen, miss-nothing eyes of his checking for all kinds of organ and structural failures as Axe managed to haul himself up onto his two feet.

"You can keep the johnny and the slippers. Hell, take the wheelchair—please."

Axe grunted as he shuffled to the rear doors. "Like they're door prizes? And yeah, I'm leaving the chair."

As the surgeon hopped around with admirable ease and opened the rear doors, Axe felt like he was a hundred and eighty thousand years old. But he managed to get himself to the ground with only a little help . . . and then he was doing the old man over to—

Why was there smoke coming out of the cottage's chimney?

It was only three in the morning?

Shoving all of his owies aside, he focused on who was in his house—yup, it was his Elise.

Not that she was his.

Guess she had decided to come early—

"You got this?" the surgeon asked, puffs of white breath leaving his mouth in the cold. "You want me to help you get settled in there?"

"No, thanks, Doc." Axe looked at the human and put out his palm. "I owe you a lot."

"Yup, you do. But the service with a smile is free. Just make sure you come see me first thing at nightfall, 'kay? I know there isn't class, but we've got to take those stitches out."

"Deal."

After they clapped hands, the surgeon shut his mobile unit back up, and took off while Axe headed for the front door.

Crap. He could have used a minute to brush his hair and his teeth before he saw Elise. And then there were all the bandages. . . .

Ha, and she thought that cut by his eye had been a thing.

At least she couldn't accuse him of not keeping things between them spicy. Or at the very least . . . surprising.

THIRTY-TWO

Emotions were tricky little devils.

A lot of the time, Elise knew, when you had something happen that was upsetting, shocking, or disorienting, you got through whatever it was—the confrontation, the abuse, the bad news, the accident that was your fault or maybe someone else's—and came out the other side feeling relieved it was over.

But then the stewing started.

As she sat in front of the fire that she had set hours ago in Axe's hearth, she stared at the yellow and orange flames and replayed her aunt's "maternal" monologue over and over again. God . . . it was as if her brain had grooves in it and her thoughts were the stuck needle on the record.

Even after having broken-and-entered into this house that was not hers—granted, the front door had not been locked—and in spite of sitting here, in the very place Axe and she had nearly made love the night before, all she could see and hear was what had happened in that closet—

The sound of an engine outside the little house had her leaping to her feet, and for a moment, she panicked, thinking her father had somehow found out where she was—but then she sensed Axe's presence, the blood he had given her once again a homing beacon she was so glad to have.

Except what if he were angry that she'd come so early? It must be three? Three-thirty? Which was less of a problem than the fact that she'd arrived here just before midnight.

Hopefully, he wouldn't be—

The door swung wide, and as Axe lurched in, she clapped a palm over her mouth so she wouldn't scream. Throwing out a hand blindly, she caught herself against the hearth's warm face.

Axe was dressed in a hospital johnny, his bare legs plugged into a pair of slippers. He was walking as if he were in great pain, and there were bandages visible on his biceps and his shoulder—undoubtedly in other places, too.

But that wasn't the worst of it. His face was lashed with scars, as if he had gotten too close to a series of knives or maybe barbed wire.

He stopped as he saw her reaction. "That bad, huh?"

"Oh, God . . ." She ran to him with her arms out, and then pulled up short. "Where aren't you hurt? What happened!"

Before he could stop her, she stepped to his side and put a supporting arm around his waist. "Lean on me."

She was surprised when he did. And that scared her almost as much as the sight of his face did.

"Come by the fire." She said this even though she was heading in that direction. "Did you break out of the hospital? How did they let you leave?"

Over at the pallet, she helped him ease down, the firelight licking over him, hopefully giving him warmth. And as soon as he was even partially settled, she jumped up and rushed over to close the door.

"May I bring you anything?" she said as she returned and crouched beside him.

All he did was look up at her, his eyes softening, the strain in his face relaxing. "I have everything I need right here."

As he reached up to stroke her cheek, she met him more than half-way so he wouldn't have to work for the contact.

"What happened, Axe?"

"It doesn't matter." His fingertips drifted over her jaw, her throat. "And nothing hurts anymore."

She looked down his body and cursed. The johnny's hem had risen up, and there was a thick bandage around his thigh. Also, a bulge under his opposite arm, right where his ribs were. And oh, dear Lord, that face.

"Am I that ugly?" he whispered.

"Never. Not to me."

"It's okay, you can say it. You like the truth, remember?"

All Elise could do was shake her head, because her eyes were water-ing and her hands had started to tremble and everything seemed to crash down on her at once.

"I'm all right," he murmured. "Come here, lie beside me."

Elise stretched out and propped herself up on her elbow. "You're not going to tell me what happened, are you."

"It's just not important."

"Yes, it is."

But he clammed up. And simply stared at her.

"I wish there was something I could do," she said.

"There is."

"What?"

"Get my toothbrush, toothpaste, and a cup of water from upstairs? I'd love to brush my teeth."

For a second, she thought he was kidding. And then she smiled because it did make her feel useful.

"Anything else?" she said as she sat up.

"Yes, but I'll tell you after I floss."

Elise blinked. And then shook her head. "You're not . . . you're not coming on to me, are you?"

"Does it offend you?"

She laughed in a burst. "No, not at all. It's just, in case you haven't noticed, you're half dead."

Axe started to smile, and it was a beautiful thing to see. "Not even close, female. Not even close."

It was amazing how a change in scenery could perk a male up.

When Elise came back downstairs and knelt by him with the requested minty-fresh delivery system and a glass of rinse-out, you want to talk about a morphine drip? Only without the opiate and no tubing? He felt absolutely no pain whatsoever.

"Why don't I get this set for you?" she said, holding up the brush and the tube.

When he nodded, she got to work, her head angling down, her hair, which had been pulled back in a ponytail, slipping off her shoulder and hanging forward as she concentrated on getting a line of Crest on his bristles.

Okay, that sounded dirty.

Then again, in his current mood, he could take anything as innocent as popping the top on the tube or rolling from the bottom or even her taking his brush firmly in hand, and turn it into full-tilt XXX—

"How are we going to do this?" she asked.

Axe looked down his body, and answered in his head, *Lift up my gown and straddle me after you get naked. Then ride me like the bull I am.*

Wow. The romance.

"I'll hold my head up. And—" He hissed and let the deadweight at the top of his spine fall back to the ground. "Damn it—"

Elise's smile appeared right over him. "Open wide."

As he complied, the cool, refreshing flavor was completely over-shadowed by her scent, her beauty, his need. She ended up rinsing the toothbrush out in the water over and over, getting the paste from his mouth that way—and if the end result was a little gritty, at least he didn't taste old blood.

And neither would she.

Elise moved the glass and the brush to the side and pulled the sleeve of her simple fleece down over the heel of her palm so she could wipe his mouth.

"How's that?"

"Am I too banged up to kiss?"

"No," she breathed.

She leaned back over him, but he stopped her. "Will you free your hair?"

Something about that memory of it whipping around the human male outside the steakhouse was still with him, and he wanted to own that stretch of wonder and magic that some other chump had had with her, take it away from the human, stamp it as his.

Plus he loved the smell of her shampoo.

As she pulled the band free and returned to him, soft waves framed his face . . . and then her lips were brushing his and he was using all his strength to rest his hands on her upper arms.

"You can lay on me," he said into her mouth.

"Where are you hurt?"

"Just stabbed in the side, no big deal—"

She jerked up. "*What*—"

Axe waved his hand back and forth. "It's not a problem."

"Let me see."

Hmmmmmm. If she stripped him, she'd get a really good picture of how bad it had been. On the other hand, hello. Nakey.

His conscience spoke up. "Ah, I'm not wearing anything under this. I mean, like . . . nothing."

Her eyes grew hooded. "That's all right with me."

Axe's hips rolled at that sexy tone of hers. "Then cut the damn thing off me. There are scissors in the kitchen. By the stove."

The sound of her walking through the little house, just as when she'd gone upstairs, made him realize how empty it usually was—and also how quiet everything was here in the sticks: Out in this rural part of Caldwell, there was no ambient noise from late-night city traffic, no extra light from buildings or streetlights, no neighbors too close.

Funny, he had never had much of an opinion about the property before . . . but he liked the solitude.

Especially with her around.

"I'll be careful," she said as she came back in and got down on her knees next to him. "I think I'm going to have to start at the bottom."

His breath caught and then started to pump. "Elise?"

"What?" she asked as she moved down to the hem with the blades. "You realize I'm . . ."

It was funny that a male like him, who'd done just about every sexual thing that was physically possible, often in front of crowds of people, was suddenly pulling the shy-guy routine. But the difference was, he wanted Elise to like the way he looked. In the other situations, he hadn't given a shit.

"You're what," she whispered. "I want to hear you say it."

"I'm hard," he moaned. "For you."

Yes, it was the least sexy thing in the world to have a hospital patient say that to a female . . . to have some battered, bunged-up, stitched-together Frankenstein of a guy tell you that the one part of him that wasn't bruised was ready and rearing to go.

But for whatever reason, she didn't care about all the oh-so-uglies.

Her smile was one for the ages.

"Well, then I'm going to have to do something about that, aren't I," she murmured.

His cock twitched like it was doing sit-ups as she went to work, the silver scissors shiny and reflecting the firelight, the blades flashing as she started to cut. Right at the center of the gown.

The slicing sound of those two sharp halves coming together over and over again so close to his erection made him nearly orgasm. And then she was right where the action was.

She ran those scissors directly up the length of his erection.

Grabbing on to the blankets, fisting them hard, Axe kicked his head back, gritted his teeth, and groaned, "I'm coming—oh, *fuck . . .*"

The release was stronger than any he had been having down at that sex club, the sensations so crisp and clean, they were just like those blades, slicing through his body.

But he was worried what she would think of him. He didn't want to go too far, too fast—

Nope, he shouldn't have worried. Elise was enthralled, her white fangs biting into her lower lip as if she were holding in her own groans of pleasure, her eyes rapt on his cock and his ejaculations, her body poised to mount him.

Except when it was over, she just kept right on cutting, the head of his cock doing a desperate dance as she went up over his six-pack. Higher still to the pads of his pecs. All the way to his neck.

Axe couldn't have moved if he'd wanted to. Especially as she finished the job, moved all the material out of the way, and sat back.

"I want to touch you," she said with an awe that made him flush.

"Anywhere." God, his voice was rough. "Fuck, do anything you want to me."

She kissed him first, and holy hell, he loved being under her control, her mastery. He was naked, vulnerable from the injuries, and so fucking hot for her that she could violate him twelve different ways to Sunday and he would have begged her for more, *harder, again, again, again, oh, please, Elise, take me again. . . .*

Her hands were like water passing over his skin as her tongue licked at his mouth and penetrated him, taking him while she gave of herself. And then she was kissing down his throat.

"What are these tattoos?" she asked as her lips brushed over his jugular. His collarbone. "Only one side? Your earrings and piercings as well."

"Two halves," he mumbled as he arched his lower body, his erection heavy and hot as it lay on his lower abdomen.

"Of you?"

He nodded and tried to answer. "Who I am . . . who I wish I were."

She paused. "Who do you wish you were?"

For a second, the mood was threatened, cracks appearing in the heat and lust. He couldn't afford to have it shatter, though. This was too good, too rare. . . .

"Axe?"

"I want to be good. I really do." Fuck, he sounded like a child. "I want to be a good son, not a broken one."

"Well, I think you're good."

You don't really know me, he thought with a sudden fear.

Shit, what if she found out he was a dirty whore . . . and a former drug addict who had let his father down when the male had needed him most?

And it was sad, but as misplaced as her faith was, he needed it: Her belief in him was almost a form of forgiveness, something he desperately wanted, but had never expected to find.

"I want to be good for you," he said, meaning every word. In every way possible.

Except there was no dwelling on that—Elise proceeded to be reallllllly good to him, her mouth traveling down his torso, until it lingered at the head of his cock. Oh, fuck, her eyes were staring up his chest at him, and then she extended her tongue and tasted his tip. As he cursed out loud and jerked, she sucked him in—

A blaze of pain, in a place males generally didn't tolerate discomfort well, made him jump and make things worse.

"Ouch!" he barked as her teeth caught him again. "No, no—don't stop—"

"I'm sorry!" She sat up in a panic, his arousal still wrapped by her palm. "I've never done this before—I forgot I had fangs—"

"Keep going—"

"I don't want to hurt you—"

"I like it—"

All at once, the absurdity in the sexual situation hit them both, and he wasn't sure who started laughing first, but soon, they were both roaring.

It was so good to be free of pain and emptiness, to feel instead not only pleasure . . . but happiness.

It had been so very long for him.

Not since his mother had left and not looked back.

THIRTY-THREE

lise couldn't believe how crazy it was that she was acting like some kind of seductress—when in reality, she'd only had sex once, it hadn't been very good, and she'd certainly never tried to give anyone a . . . you know.

God, she was so repressed, she couldn't even say the words in her head.

Blow. Job.

"Yes. Please."

As Axe answered, she realized she'd spoken out loud. "Oh, jeez— guess I'm not very smooth, am I?"

He reached down and brushed her cheek. "You are . . . amazing. You make me feel things I never have before. You're perfect just exactly the way you are and with precisely what you are doing."

"But I just bit you on your—" And P.S., holy crap, she couldn't believe she was just sitting here with his sex in her hand like the thing was nothing more unusual than the receiver on a desk phone.

"Say it," he commanded.

"Um . . ."

"Love handle. Dumb handle, little head, dick, cock . . ."

More laughing with him, the two of them smiling together—and then she wanted to get back to business.

"Any suggestions?" she asked in a husky way. "What do you like?"

His hips rolled, and she was momentarily aware of the big white bandages on his thigh and the one on his ribs. But then his eyes flashed and he breathed hard and his voice dropped an octave—and suddenly she wasn't thinking about anything other than his taste.

"Run your tongue . . . up me . . . and around my head. . . ."

Keeping her stare locked on his, she extended her tongue . . . and leaned back down to follow instruction.

"Elise . . ."

Yup, she knew without question she'd gotten it right this time, his erection kicking in her hand, his pelvis pumping, his expression of total heat and wonder.

"You are so beautiful . . ." he gasped as he watched her.

Lapping at the tip of him, she opened wide and tried to keep her teeth out of the way—and she must have succeeded, because although he went stiff all over, there were no yelps. Instead, he arched his spine and worked with her as she found a rhythm: Up and down, sucking him, stroking him on the bottom with her palm. Faster . . . faster . . .

"I'm going to come—" He groaned and went rigid—but also tried to push her away.

No, she was going to see this through.

As he barked out a curse, she took all of his orgasm, which seemed to drive him mad with passion, his convulsions and the response in her mouth as erotic an experience as she could ever imagine.

When it was all over, he went limp—to such a degree, his limbs banged into the floor.

"I love the way you taste," she said as she licked her lips.

And that made his erection flare in her hand.

"Climb up on me," he said gruffly. "I want to be inside you—climb up."

For a split second, Elise wondered, was she really going to do this?

The extent of his injuries scared her. If that was what could happen when he went out to fight, every single night, how long before he did not come home?

On that logic, though, she should do this because she could lose him at any moment.

And then she thought of herself, of the years she had spent on the sidelines of life, of her behaving according to values that had been imposed on her, rather than ones she had generated from her own core beliefs.

Right now? A beautiful male who had been nothing but kind and understanding—and supportive of her even against her father—wanted to be with her. And she was unattached, attracted to him, and in the privacy of a sacred space.

It simply didn't make sense to say no. Especially because she wanted him so badly.

Elise stripped off her fleece and the long-sleeved shirt she had on underneath. Ditched her bra and stood up.

And then she moved slower, because Axe was watching her with those rapt eyes of his, clearly memorizing every nuance of her body. Down went her yoga pants, past her thighs, her knees, and then she was kicking them free . . . and standing over him wearing only a pair of white panties.

"Turn for me?" Axe said in a tone that was so close to a begging.

Rising up on the balls of her feet, she pivoted around, showing him her backside. That was when she hooked her thumbs into her underwear and took it to the floor, bending her body while keeping her legs locked so she showed him exactly what she knew he wanted to see.

He didn't have to say a word of approval. His pumping purr and those volcanic eyes told her everything she wanted to know.

Elise stepped over him, straddling his hips. The firelight on her skin, the heaviness in her breasts, the curling urge between her legs, made her feel powerful and commanding—and she was glad it was happening like this.

This was going to be incredible.

Because she and Axe were going to make it that way.

Kneeling down, she put her hands on either side of his head and kissed him, over and over again, aware of how open her core was above his sex, how ready she was, how perfect this felt. And as they continued to move their mouths against each other, the warmth of his body rose up to her, and his palms stroked her thighs, her waist, cupped her breasts. When she couldn't stand the anticipation a moment longer, she was the one who stood his erection up and she was the one in control as she brushed him against her sex, stroking herself with the head she'd sucked.

They both cursed.

And then she gingerly angled him into the right place, and lowered herself onto him. The sensation of stretching and filling wasn't painful at all—and she was glad she had lost her virginity before so that the discomfort was out of the way and she could enjoy all parts of this.

Friction.

Using the small of her back and her hips, she began to ride him, and he helped her, countering her thrusts with those of his own, a momentum getting started. Her breasts swayed and her breath caught and the firelight turned everything into slow motion—or maybe that was her brain.

The oncoming release was like a train inside her body, gathering speed, the pleasure compounding on itself, radiating from her sex. And all the time they kissed and locked eyes and—

Her orgasm came first and unexpectedly, like a rubber band snapping, only there was no sting of pain, just a bursting and a welling and round after round of pleasuring contractions that she wanted to get lost in forever. And then Axe was thrusting up hard, going even deeper, a kicking taking over just as it had in her mouth.

After that? After it was all finished?

After the heat started to fade?

He started it up all over again.

It was the best sex of his life.

Absolutely mind blowing, Axe decided much, much later, when Elise was finally stretched out on his chest, their bodies sated, their erotic needs on the back-off, at least for the next hour or so.

Running his fingertips up and down her spine, he loved the smooth feel of her skin, and the weight of her body, and the scent of her sex. He could have stayed right where they were for the rest of his sorry-ass life.

But he knew it was getting close to dawn.

"Elise? You awake?"

"Mmmm?"

He stroked her hair. "As much as this kills me, it's got to be almost six a.m. You better go home."

She lifted her head off his pec. Her eyes were sleepy in the dying firelight, her lips swollen from his kisses, her cheeks still flushed.

"I want to stay here," she said.

"I want you to stay here, too. But do you think that'll help your situation? It's up to you."

She frowned and became very quiet for a while. "I'm sorry I came early, by the way."

"Not by much. Besides, you're welcome anytime, all the time. I never lock up. Just come in."

"I got here before midnight."

"Why?" He passed his palm up and over her shoulder. "And again, I don't give a shit. Move in if you want."

Holy fuck, did he just say that?

"I was upset. And I had nowhere else to go."

All at once, his protective male instincts fired up, his fangs descending, his body going back on the alert in spite of its injuries. "What happened? And who do I need to kill."

Yeah, he was only partially kidding on that last one.

At least she smiled a little. But it didn't last. "I, ah . . . well, I told you that my cousin was killed? You remember?"

"Yeah. Of course."

"Well, I went into her room. After you left? I didn't really plan on it, it just kinda . . . it was where I ended up. And I went into her closet—I was cleaning things up in there. It was such a mess. Such a mess . . . clothes everywhere, shoes . . ."

When she didn't say anything further, he stroked her shoulder. "Talk to me, Elise. And know it goes in the vault."

"Oh, I trust you. It's just . . . so ugly."

"I know from ugly. I'm not scared of it."

Her breath left her on a shudder. "My cousin, Allishon, and I? We weren't alike at all. I mean . . . the polite word for her was *promiscuous*. Her clothes weren't like mine. She didn't think like me. She didn't behave as I did—and she reveled in being the wild one. She was beautiful and out of control, and I always had the feeling that she enjoyed sticking it to her parents."

"I've walked that road," he said remotely. "It's good for nobody."

"Maybe if there had been more time? I don't know. Maybe she would have changed." Elise exhaled in a rush. "Anyway, I was in her closet—and I was cleaning up the mess. My aunt came in and surprised me—I mean, I haven't seen her since the night Peyton came to tell them about the murder. She looked . . . so bad. Sickly. Horrific. As if she had aged a thousand years, been starved and beaten."

Axe repositioned them, rolling over onto his side and cradling her face-to-face. "Was she grateful for what you were doing?"

"No. Not at all." Elise's eyes got a faraway look to them. "She said . . . the most hateful things about her daughter. It was all about image and the family's position in the *glymera*. She was angry and bitter about the fact that there was shame upon her. She was upset that she wasn't getting invited . . . to parties. It was the most extraordinarily selfish display I'd ever seen—and I just keep thinking, Well, of course Allishon acted the way she did. With a *mahmen* like that?"

Axe ground his molars as anger choked him. "Selfish mothers are the worst. That shit'll do a number on you."

Like, oh, say, a female who would desert her *hellren* and child for the money of the *glymera*. Yup. Read that book, saw the movie, bought the T-shirt, the insulated coffee mug, and the Blu-ray. Poster over his bed, too.

But he kept quiet about all that. They were focusing on Elise, and damn him, he really wanted to listen to what she was saying.

Elise shook her head. "I was so upset after I left her that I ran downstairs and out of the house . . . and I threw up on the front lawn. And then I just kept going, down to the bottom of the hill, out onto the road."

He imagined her careening through the night, her heart breaking, no one in her family understanding where she was at or really even caring.

"I'm glad you came here. And I wish I had known."

"Thank you for not being mad."

"Never."

"I asked Peyton to tell me what happened to Allishon. I'm meeting him tomorrow."

Axe had to regulate a spike of unease. Because that bastard had better STFU on the subject of bodyguards.

"I have to find out the truth." She looked away. "I need to know and I'm not sure I understand why that's so important. The death isn't reversible, nothing will change by my knowing what transpired. But my brain can't let it go and I'm not going to fight it."

"Maybe you're just going after the series of events because you can't get the real answers you want."

"I'm sorry?"

"Like . . ." Axe cleared his throat. "Maybe you can't ask your father what he really feels about the death. Maybe there are other things you'd like to know about him. What he thinks about your mother's passing. What he worries about night to night. Maybe he's unreachable." Axe thought about his own father down in the cellar with those blocks of wood. "Maybe you want to know what he actually feels about you. But you know that's never going to happen. You're never going to be close. He's always going to be focused elsewhere. And the shitty thing is, though . . . that just because you're aware of all that, doesn't mean the searching goes away. And you can only sit with that for so long before you go crazy." He shifted his eyes from Elise . . . but then refocused on her and shrugged. "So you're looking for facts as a way to get close to him, because that's what people do. They go to the wrong places for things they can't get in the right ones."

When she just stared at him, he felt like a royal idiot.

She was getting her Ph.D. in psychology for fuck's sake. What did he know?

"Or not," he muttered. "I don't know what I'm talking about—"

Elise cut him off by kissing him. "God . . . you are so smart."

"I am? I mean . . . yeah, I'm an Einstein. Whatevs."

She laughed. "No, really, you're spot-on. I've just never thought of it like that."

For a long moment, he stared at her. Until she prompted, "Why are you looking at me like that?"

Axe kissed her, but then moved back. "You probably should go."

"I think you're right. If I'm going to spend the night with you, I want it to be on honest terms. And that is not going to happen over the phone with my father—and not just because I left that GPS-riddled cell of mine at home."

"If he kicks you out, you can stay here with me. And I'm only half joking about that."

"You are very sweet."

The snort he let out was an ugly sound, the kind of thing that he tried to keep down, but couldn't catch. And yes, she laughed at him— which made him resent the noise less.

But then Elise sat up and, tragically, began putting her clothes on. When she was back in order, she knelt down and pulled one of the blankets over his nakedness.

"Are you sure you're going to be okay here alone? I'm worried."

"If what we just did together didn't kill me, I guarantee you I'll make it to sunset."

"I'm serious."

"I'll be fine."

She kissed him and then went over to the fire, restoking it for him.

"You don't need to do that," he said.

"Too late." She smiled at him over her shoulder as she poked at the logs she'd added. "You know what I'm doing right now?"

"Looking hotter than what's going on in that hearth?"

"I'm trying not to ask when I'm going to see you again."

"I got an easy answer for that. Four a.m. tomorrow."

"Is that a date?"

"You better believe it." He wadded an old sofa pillow up under his head. "Call me when you're home safe?"

"Always. Where's your phone?"

"Oh . . . shit. I have no idea. Probably back at the training center with what was left of my clothes. And I don't have a landline."

"Well . . . I'll be fine. I can take care of myself."

There was a long, long pause.

"Go," he told her. "So I know you're safe before the sun comes up."

Elise nodded and then she was gone, the front door closing behind her quietly.

In the wake of her departure, he thought, God . . . the house was so empty.

THIRTY-FOUR

The following evening, as Elise got dressed to go to see Peyton, her thoughts were on Axe, not either of her cousins. She was worried about him having been okay through the day. How his wounds were doing. Whether he'd let the fire go out and turned himself into a Popsicle.

He had to get that heating system at the cottage fixed. The weather was going to get a whole lot worse before it improved. In, like, May.

The problem was, it felt a little too stalkerish for her to just show up at his house and be all, *Hey!, just wanted to see if you're still breathing!* Besides, in the middle of their sexual marathon, he'd mentioned that he had to get his stitches out at the clinic, and surely if he failed to turn up there, someone would go looking for him.

Right?

"Damn it," she said as she left her room—with her phone and its GPS tracker going strong.

She had skipped First Meal. There was just no way she could sit between her father and her uncle and make small talk, not only considering what she had done with Axe, but also in light of what she'd seen in her aunt the night before: Even with all her schooling and self-actualization, she wasn't capable of shelving that much emotion.

Maybe she was her sire's daughter after all, not wanting to share.

Down on the first floor, she knocked on the closed door to her father's study. When she heard his greeting, she opened it and went in. He was at his desk, in one of his suits, looking like a posed Dunhill model.

For an ad in *Life* magazine, circa 1942.

"Good evening, Father."

He looked up from his paperwork. "Oh, hello, dearest."

"Father, I'm going over to see Peyton, son of Peythone? His sire and his *mahmen* will both be there. The purpose is to discuss Paradise's birthday party? It is coming up and he and I will be planning a small event, at his home, in her honor?"

For the first time in so long, Felixe actually smiled. Really, truly smiled. To the point where he even had to put his gold pen down on the blotter. "Oh, darling, I think that is marvelous. I think that is just splendid."

"I thought you would be pleased." With effort, she kept the judgment out of her voice. "I'm not sure how long it will take."

"Oh, do enjoy yourself. I shall see you at dawn, then."

"Yes, Father."

With a brief bow, she exited, the center of her chest aching because she would have loved to have had that reaction from him to her studies, her work, her real plans. But no, he was happy she was throwing a party.

She told herself it was just his way, his generation, all he knew.

But it hurt to be minimized.

Outside, she realized she forgot a coat, but it didn't matter. Closing her eyes, she coasted off the estate, riding a surge of relief across the cold air.

Peyton's mansion was not far away, and every bit as grand as the one she lived in, just of a different style. His family's manse was a Tudor, with all kinds of cupolas and angles and fun rooms inside—not that she was all that familiar with the place.

As she approached the front door, it was opened by a butler who wore the same uniform as the head *doggen* at her house.

"Mistress, welcome. Master Peyton is up in his room. He requests that you wait in the library for his arrival."

"But of course," she said as she followed along into a huge room filled with leather-bound volumes, heavy, medieval furniture, and enormous brass chandeliers.

With all the tapestries and the oil paintings and the way footsteps echoed on the gray slate floor, it was like something out of Harry Potter, just sans the owls and the wizard wands.

How anyone felt at home in it was a mystery, but then, the *glymera* cared more about impressions than comfort. And it was impressive.

"Would you care for something to drink?" the butler asked her.

"No, thank you."

"My pleasure." The butler bowed low and backed out of the room. "He shan't be long."

Before she could even pick a spot to sit, her phone went off, and she answered it on the first ring with a frown. "Peyton? I'm downstairs. What? Ah . . . yeah, no, it's fine. I don't care. . . . Sure. Where . . . ? Okay, right."

Ending the call, Elise went across to a second set of oak doors and slipped out. Tracking the hallways through the back of the house, she found the pantry, got the bag of Doritos her cousin had asked for, and hurried up the staff stairs to the second floor. After ducking into a laundry room for a maid to pass, she jogged down—

Peyton was hanging out his door, one arm locked on the jamb, the other swinging free as he waved at her. "Hey, girl!"

He had no shirt on, satin PJ bottoms, and the mental functioning of a microwave oven.

Great. Just what she'd had in mind, damn it.

"Peyton," she muttered as she came up to him. "How drunk are you?"

"Very. And stoned. And wait . . . I think I did some cocaine about two hours ago? But the buzz has mostly worn off."

"Well, here is your sodium delivery system." She handed the bag over and glared at him. "And I'm going home."

"No, you're not. We're going to talk."

"And how's that going to happen. You're slurring your speech so much, I'm pretty sure you're speaking French. Or is it Italian?"

"I'm more likely to spill if I'm drunk."

"What you're drinking, you mean. As in out of your glass."

"Come on, Elise. Gimme a break, will you. You think this is going to be easy for me?"

Shaking her head, she crossed her arms. But then cursed and stepped around him, entering his suite. "You shouldn't need to be intoxicated to talk about things."

"That and a bag of chips will get you lunch."

"What the hell is that supposed to mean?"

"I don't know," he muttered as he shut his door.

His room was the size of a football stadium, it seemed, with a sitting area kitted out with sofas and chairs like a living room, a TV with a screen as big as a movie theater's, and a bed that, naturally, was king-size but round. The decor was done by Grey Goose—as in bottles of vodka. Which were empty—oh, no, wait, over there by the open bathroom, there were eight fresh, unopened ones.

And of course, you could do laps in his Jacuzzi, she thought as she looked into the marble expanse. Who knew those kinds of tubs came in Olympic-swimming-pool?

"Will you do me a favor and put a shirt on?" she said as she turned back to him.

Peyton had stretched out on his bed, and crossed his feet at the ankles, his hooded eyes the kind of thing that might have set a female's pulse racing a little—if they didn't know Axe.

Hadn't been with Axe.

Weren't going to be with Axe again soon.

Nothing compared to her tattooed male.

"Want to join me?" Peyton drawled, running his hand in a circle on the monogrammed duvet. His pillows were monogrammed, too, as was the great canopy of cloth that hung from a gold crown on the high ceiling.

But the grandeur made sense. He was the equivalent of a prince, the high-bred son of a Founding Family, the heir to great wealth, one of the race's most eligible bachelors.

And he was also a looker, what with that blond hair and those blue eyes that were the stuff of fantasies.

"Are you telling me no?" he said. "I'm not used to no."

"I believe that."

There was a pause. "So did your bodyguard call you up and brag about what he did last night?"

"He did not—and I'm going to do you a favor right now and tell you to shut up about him. If you don't have anything nice to say, then I don't want to hear it."

"He didn't mention anything? I find that hard to believe."

Elise frowned. She was not interested in playing hide-and-seek with a drunk for information, but if it was about Axe? "So what did he do?"

"He saved the life of a Brother."

"*What?*"

"Single-handedly." Peyton's eyes drifted to the TV screen across the way and the football game that was on it. "Real live hero stuff. The

Brother Rhage, literally, would not be alive tonight if it weren't for the fact that Axe, even after having been shot himself, managed to put his own body in the way of a knife—while a *lesser* was on his back, beating him with a steel whip."

The world spun around and Elise threw out a hand to steady herself. When there was nothing to catch her fall, she stumbled over to the foot of that palace bed of his and sat down.

"It was amazing," Peyton said softly, his eyes getting a faraway look to them. "I saw it happen. We were stationed on different streets, but there were suddenly slayers everywhere. I followed mine right to the alley Axe was fighting in—just as he got himself stabbed. I thought . . . I really thought Axe was dead, you know?"

"He didn't say a thing," she whispered.

Peyton reached over to the bedside table and picked up a tumbler that was full of ice and something fizzy. He took a long drink, emptying a good quarter of the thing.

"I've never done anything close to that." Peyton took another drink. "Maybe he is the right male for your job, you know?"

"He has been . . ." She cleared her throat. "Perfectly professional. Were you hurt last night?"

"No. No one else was seriously, either. It was like Axe took all of our injuries at once."

Peyton fell silent and so did she . . . while across the way, that football game played on, humans in the stands dressed in blue-and-orange and red-and-white.

"What is this?" she asked numbly. "On the screen?"

"It's the Iron Bowl from 'thirteen. Auburn–'Bama. Auburn wins with a one-hundred-and-nine-yard kick back run. War Damn Eagle."

"What does that mean?"

"Not a clue. It's the Auburn fight song. Our vet, who is human, went to school there? So that's how I started rooting for them about twenty years ago. Habits, you know."

Peyton finished his drink, then added, "I can't believe Axe didn't tell you."

"I don't think he cares about showing off."

Peyton laughed. "Yeah, he doesn't give a shit about much." Abruptly, the male grew serious. "So you want to know about Allishon, huh."

"Yes, I do."

"Okay," he said after a long moment. "I'll tell you."

It really wasn't rocket science.

As Axe leaned into the mirror over the sink in his bathroom, he wiped the condensation from the shower off the glass with his forearm and then picked up the pair of fingernail scissors he'd found in the cabinet. Twisting around, he got his torso at the right angle and went to work.

Pushing the small, sharp-tipped blades under each one of the shit ton of sutures, he went snip, snip, snip . . . then he used a pair of tweezers to get the knots of thread out. Repeated on his thigh. Checked to make sure he didn't have any others anywhere. Nope. Clean. And everything had healed so well, the scars were nearly invisible. By dawn, no one would ever know he'd been hurt.

His body wasn't stiff, either. Eyesight and hearing were perfect. No headaches, muscle pulls, joint discomfort.

That Chosen blood was a thing.

Well, that and the fact that after Elise had left, he'd passed out—and shit, had he dreamed of her, vivid, erotic fantasies playing in his mind to the point where, when he finally woke up, he reached out as if she were beside him.

And what do you know, for the first time in recorded history, he had no interest in going to The Keys. What he was actually into was getting back home in time to see Elise at four a.m. But he'd promised to take Novo out—and while they were at the sex club, he was going to put her up for membership so that she didn't have to ask him any-more.

She was a female who could really use a place like that.

And who knows. Maybe he was transitioning out of that phase in his life—

Axe stopped himself, a low-level anxiety threatening to break through and ruin his fantasy of what the night was going to be like.

God, for some reason, he saw those figurines of his father's, those impotent little exercises in mourning.

With how much he was becoming attached to Elise already, was he just going to end up like his pops? In ruins when the relationship ended . . . likely because Elise recognized where she properly belonged.

In the *glymera*, with her kind.

Shit, he'd known her for how long? Fuck . . . five nights? And he'd seen her for the first time six nights ago?

Refusing to meet his own eyes in the mirror, he double-checked that the now-sutureless wound on his thigh wasn't bleeding. Inspected the stabbing area. And got in the shower.

Ten minutes later, he was dressed in black with his cloak and his skull mask on. Dematerializing to the west, he re-formed in a vacant parking lot that was about a three-minute walk from the club. Novo was already where they'd agreed to meet.

And holy fuck.

That just about covered it: The female was in a black latex bodysuit that fit every curve and straightaway she had, a fringe belt hanging off her tight hips, her breasts looking like a million bucks, her legs long as highways. Her black hair was braided and her thigh-high boots were spiked, and she looked like exactly the kind of badass she was.

Her mask was not on, however, and her eyes went on a travel up and down his body. Not sexually, though. "I can't believe you're alive."

Axe walked up to her. "You ready?"

"Are you all right? To do this—"

"Let's go."

"Axe."

"What."

Novo's arms shot out and she gave him a stiff, hard hug that ended almost as soon as it began. And as he cleared his throat from some kind of non-sexual feeling, he thought, Well, what do you know. Poor folks have something in common with rich ones: He had absolutely no interest in talking with Novo about the night before, and not because he didn't like her.

"I'm glad you survived," she said, as gruffly as if she were a male. "And I'm impressed as hell at what you did."

"Thanks. Now let's drop it. You're clearly good to go tonight, not that I expected anything less."

"Yeah, let's do this."

Novo put her own mask over her face, the featureless panels for her eyes and the black mesh for her mouth leaving her with an alien vibe.

Axe walked off, his black combat boots eating up the pavement, Novo moving beside him with the same deadly grace she always did. As they went along, an ambulance rushed by with its lights bubbling, its driver pumping a siren as the vehicle came up to an intersection with a light. Then there was a snowplow, one of the ginormous muni ones that were orange and had a dump truck's worth of salt in the back. And then they saw two humans, a pair of males, hustling down the opposite side of the street like they'd just scored drugs and were in a hurry to get their fixes.

The Keys, from the outside, was nothing but an urban garage, its front building flat, uninteresting, and seemingly not that big. Bullshit. The club was actually a series of connected facilities, all engineered to flow one into another through a series of covered passways.

There was only one entrance, but there were multiple exits, always before the next section.

Shit got more hardcore the further you went in.

No wait line for him. As he approached the guards—who were dressed as if they were patrons, just with something red on somewhere—he flashed his superior key, and they nodded him and Novo right in.

Moody music. Smoke machines. Purple lasers shooting through the darkness.

A crowd of mostly humans with masks and latex and leather clothes milling around. Women in Lucite boxes, their poses contorted so their sexes were offered to whoever wanted them in whatever way they chose. Men strapped facedown, ass-up, to the floor. Glory holes. Pits of naked bodies twisting and turning, limbs upon limbs. Suspensions. Lashing and lickings.

And this was only the beginning.

Axe just kept walking forward slowly, the crowd parting for him, getting out of his way. Which suggested that humans had better senses than vampires gave them credit for: These rats without tails may not have known exactly why he was different and not to be fucked with, but they were careful around him.

As they entered the next building, the beat of the music changed, the bass line becoming all-pervasive, like hot steam being pumped into a cold room.

The men liked Novo. So did the women.

Novo, on the other hand, was hard to judge. She seemed to float above it all, that faceless mask of hers panning left and right.

"What are you looking for?" he asked over that heavy bass.

With any other female, and also most males, Axe would have cautioned them that what was coming was going to make these introductory rooms seem tame. But he didn't worry about her.

"Anything that isn't blond and male," she replied in a voice that was synthesized.

Axe smiled. "Really, you don't say."

When she didn't go any further with it, he just shrugged and continued onward. As he progressed, there were a couple of regulars he

recognized, either from their masks or their bodies—and he was looking for one in particular.

"I want you to meet somebody," he said as they transitioned into
another dim room that had more moans than music.

Bodies were writhing in a pit in the center, a naked woman getting
covered by men, her cries of ecstasy triumphant even though she was
the one being consumed.

"I want to meet somebody, too," Novo said in that electronic voice
of hers.

"Not for sex. You're going to apply for membership."

"You're prepared to vouch for me—" With lightning-quick reflexes,
Novo spun around, caught a masked male by the throat, and pile-
drove him back against the wall.

"I'm not the woman in the pit, asshole," she bit out. "You touch my
ass one more time and I'm going to rip your hand off and feed it to
you. Are we clear?"

As the idiot nodded like a bobblehead, Axe hung around and
waited to see if she was going to castrate the SOB on principle.

And when one of the staff closed in, Axe cut the intervention off.
"Non-consensual, repeated. And she's with me."

Axe had watched that human male ride up on Novo a couple of
times as they'd gone along, but it hadn't been for him to have an opinion. The main rule of the club was, Everything Goes. Although the
second rule was just as important: Consent Required.

Axe would have gotten involved if he'd known she hadn't been into it.

The staff nodded. "Roger that."

"And I want to put her up for membership. Her name's Novo."

All humans who worked for the owner were called Staff. No first or
last names, ever. And the only reason you knew who they were was the
way they approached you and the fact that they always had something
red on. Well, and he recognized their scents after having been a member for the last couple of years.

"Gimme ten," the staff said. "Keep going and I'll find you."

By this time, Novo was letting the aggressor resume breathing, dropping her arm and falling back in.

"You done here?" Axe asked.

"Yup."

They kept going, entering the next room, and the one after that . . . until they eventually got to the Cathedral. With its tall ceiling and mounted, altar-like formation high above the floor, this was where the public displays happened—and where he had fucked that human woman almost a week ago.

There was an event happening now, a male suspended up high, two other males taking turns with him—

"You were better six nights ago," a Scottish accent said.

Axe turned to the male who had addressed him. The human was six-six, maybe six-eight, wearing leathers and not much else, his pierced nipples glinting in the low light, the tattoos running down his arms and across his chest representing classic album covers, everything from the Sex Pistols to G N' R to the Ramones and MCR. His mask was classic Grim Reaper stuff and he was wearing a pair of New Rocks that were the biggest Axe had ever seen.

"And you lasted longer, too, mate."

With that, the human moved on, which was kind of a bummer. Axe had liked the guy's vibe.

"So you went up there?" Novo asked. "Tied up?"

"I wasn't the one on the rack."

She laughed softly. "Figures. I don't see you as the submissive type."

Neither did he. Which was why he found being powerless with Elise—and getting off on it like he did—such a surprise.

"Why don't you want a blond," he asked to change the subject.

"I hate rich blond assholes."

Axe stopped and looked at her. "Peyton?"

"Yeah, not a fan."

"Well, you're not his type anyway."

"Whatever, he's not mine."

Novo resumed her stride, her shoulders tense, her back ramrod straight, her affect one where she seemed to be grabbing someone by the balls—at least in her head.

Axe fell in step with her. "I didn't know you wanted him—"

She spun around, and in spite of the covers over her eyes, he could feel the burn coming right at him. "I do not."

"Yeah, you do. Come on, like I give a fuck?"

Novo got up in his face. "I'm glad you brought me here. But don't try to be my shrink, k? It's not going to work for you."

"Why be so defensive? You think I'm going to go second grade on you and start skipping around the class, singing the kissing song or some shit?"

"I mean it, Axe. Back off."

"So you know about him and Paradise, huh."

"Who wouldn't. If he were any more into that female, he'd be inside her."

"And then Craeg would slaughter him."

"At least Peyton counts as grass-fed organic meat with the way he smokes up." She looked away. "And I'm not into him—so there's that."

"Whatever." Axe put his palms out. "I'm not going to say anything."

Novo looked up at the sex that was going on at the altar. "So you did that, huh? I was unaware you were into public displays."

"That wasn't the point."

"What was, then."

He knew exactly what she was doing, demanding inside his head because he had momentarily gotten into hers. "Just burning off energy. That's all."

"You made an impression on the crowd, obvi."

A member of the staff came up to them, a different guy from the one he'd spoken to. "You Novo?"

Novo squared her jaw and met the human male straight in the eye through her mask. "Yeah."

"If you want in, you and your sponsor come with me now."

Novo glanced at Axe. "You're seriously putting me up?" When he nodded, she shrugged. "Good, and thanks."

The two of them fell in line behind Staff, and as they moved through the crowd, Novo said under her breath, "And you know the management. Impressive."

Axe just shrugged again. "I aim to please."

THIRTY-FIVE

As Rhage and Mary sat in front of the Christmas tree in the library, with all its twinkle and glimmer and unopened gifts, Rhage was mourning the loss of what he had hoped would become of his *shellan's* favorite human holiday. He had had such a wonderful time planned for their little family, all those presents they'd been collecting ever since Bitty had come to stay with them finally being unwrapped by the girl and enjoyed.

There was so much that Bit needed, and more than that, so much Rhage had wanted to give her.

And he'd also put some surprises under there for his Mary. Not that she would approve.

His *shellan* was a minimalist—or maybe it was a necess-isist. She didn't like fancy jewelry or cars or clothes. She liked her Kindle and the books she got on it . . . all of which had no pictures and little tiny writing and words he had never heard before in them. She didn't collect anything, she preferred to wear her shoes until they fell apart, and her handbags were functional, not a fashion expression.

Guess that was what happened when you became fully actualized as a person: You didn't have to worry about being defined by anything other than exactly who and what you were. No binge eating or drinking or gambling. No sexual dysfunction. No credit card debt for things you couldn't afford but were determined to have.

It was beautiful—and frustrating if you wanted to shower your mate with presents.

With Bitty's arrival, though? He had been looking forward to a new receptacle for his gifty exuberance.

Nothing had been touched under the tree, however.

Even though Christmas night had come and gone, the presents remained unopened, not just his and Mary's and Bitty's, but the whole household's. The gifts were just sitting there, a visible representation of joy that had been rerouted into fear and sadness.

Hell, if those precisely wrapped boxes and their sloppy, gloriously misshapen compatriots had been fruit, they would have been decayed and fly-ridden, their previously perfect paper skins and satin bows eroded into rot.

"She loves Nalla," Mary commented.

There was only one "she" between them. No need for a proper noun.

"She does."

"Bella appreciates the help."

"And Bitty is earning a little money."

They were each speaking in flat tones, not because they didn't care, but because they desperately wished they were free to care—

The scent of Turkish tobacco was the first clue. The heavy falls of shitkickers heading their way was the second.

Both he and his Mary jerked off the cushions. And Rhage knew that for the rest of his life, he was going to remember that paneled door swinging open and the birthed son of the Scribe Virgin striding in.

Vishous was back from South Carolina early.

And what do you know, it was impossible to read that goateed, tattooed face. Mostly because the brother was drinking Grey Goose right
out of a bottle.

V kicked the door shut behind him and came right over. As he sat
across from them, he replaced the vodka at his lips with a hand-
rolled—which at least gave Rhage a little more surface area to try and
tea-leaf the Brother's expression.

No luck, but given that those diamond eyes were sharp as knives
and not meeting his?

Yeah, he knew where this was going before V opened his piehole.

"He checks out," the Brother said. "His whole story."

It seemed kind of symbolic that Vishous was blocking the view of
the presents under the tree, the Brother's big body a physical manifes-
tation of the reality that the gift of Bitty in their lives was being seriously road-blocked.

V continued after another swig from the bottle. "Who he says he is.
Where he's from. Who his parents were—Bitty's grandparents—and
the fact that they're both dead. I also met with people at his household
of employment—he's worked there for decades, reliable, good em-
ployee, never a slacker. Lives alone on the estate, keeps to himself.
Widely known in the community that his sister, Bitty's mom, disappeared up North with a bad guy against the wishes of her family." He
glanced at Mary. "Nobody knew about Bitty's existence until you
posted what you did on Facebook, and it took time for word to filter
to him because he's not online at all."

Rhage could feel the tension in Mary's body increase with each
sentence, sure as if she were being pounded on by fists. On his side, he
wanted to roar, but who exactly was he going to yell at? V, the messenger? Bitty's uncle?

Who had done nothing wrong except come forward when he
learned his niece was out in the world alone as an orphan?

The Christmas tree?

Yeah, 'cuz all that tinsel was really going to give a shit.

"Fuck," he breathed.

V sat forward and tapped his ash, his black-gloved hand a badass contrast to the delicate and lovely Hermès ashtray. "I asked Ruhn to come down to South Carolina and meet me late last night. He did. He took me personally to his house, even though his employer had already let me in. He was willing to introduce me to anybody and everyone. He's well liked, if, again, a loner."

"But is he ready to take care of her?" Mary blurted. "A child is . . ."

As she trailed off, she put her head in her hands. "Oh, what am I saying. Blood trumps everything."

"I don't know the answer to the fitness thing," V said. "That's way above my pay grade. So Marissa is—"

A knock on the library door made Rhage jump, but it was just Marissa coming in, the female walking over, hugging Mary, sitting with V, talking about some kind of plan for assessing something or another and deciding . . . whatever the fuck.

In Rhage's mind, he retreated far, far away, his eyes shifting back over to the Christmas tree and lingering on the way the lights twinkled in the deep green branches, and how the shiny foil of some of the presents reflected the golden flicker of the fire.

". . . Rhage?" Mary prompted.

He shook himself. "I'm sorry, what?"

"Are you okay with everything? That we go to the Audience House and meet him there?"

"Yeah. Sure."

Everybody stared at him.

"Do you have any questions?" Mary said gently.

Rhage refocused on the gifts. "Can I still give Bit what I got her for Christmas before she goes?"

•   •   •

One hour later, Mary and Rhage pulled into the Audience House's driveway and eased on around to the back garages. As Mary tried to collect her thoughts, Rhage parked the GTO, turned off the powerful engine and the headlights . . . and then together they sat there, staring at the row of hedges that he had nosed the muscle car into.

I have no idea how to do this, Mary decided.

For the entire trip from the Brotherhood's mountain to town, she had been searching for some emotional footing, some perspective, some . . . anything . . . to carry herself through looking Bitty's rightful next of kin in the eye and not completely breaking down.

So far she had come up with nothing.

"Are you ready?" Rhage said.

There was the temptation to try to be strong for him because she knew he was hurting as much as she was. But honesty won out over a lie.

"No." She looked across at him. "I'm not."

"Me neither."

"I love you."

"I love you, too."

And that was the best and only foot forward there was, wasn't it: The simple words they shared were a vow on both their parts to get through this together, a reaffirmation that just as they had been side by side going into the joy of having Bitty in their lives, they would likewise go through the pain of losing her side by side.

Together, they got out and shut the doors, and Mary lifted up the fleece she was wearing and retucked her turtleneck into her waistband. As if somehow having a smooth presentation would impact anything at all.

Hell, Ruhn didn't have to like them or approve of them. The male wasn't vetting them in any way.

No, he was just going to take their daughter away—

Mary stopped herself right there on that one.

As Rhage held open the back kitchen door, she walked in and reminded herself that Bitty only felt like their daughter. Legally, that was simply not the case. And in a classic head-wins-over-the-heart situation, reality wasn't going to vote with emotion.

V had already dematerialized over and was waiting for them at the table Rhage had done such a number on. "Marissa's in there with him right now."

"Okay," Mary said.

When Rhage faltered, she took his big hand. "We're ready when he is."

Vishous nodded and got to his feet. "I'll come back when it's time."

Cue an awkward period of waiting . . . which Rhage spent prowling around from cupboard to cupboard, taking out bags of potato chips, boxes of cookies, loaves of bread, jars of pickles. He always ended up putting whatever it was back after an inspection, as if he wanted to nervous-eat, but his stomach wasn't finding anything appealing.

Or even tolerable.

After God only knew how long, V put his head in through the flap door across the way. "They're ready."

Talk about the longest walk of her life. As she and Rhage went past the pantry, and out into the foyer, and then around the base of the stairs and down a little hall, it seemed to take forever—and Mary was good with that.

They were entering the new reality as soon as they saw that other male.

As they came up to the library doors, both sides were closed and V knocked once. When Marissa answered, the Brother opened things up . . . and Mary found herself blinking a lot and staring at the floor.

And then somehow, she was in the room.

As with the Brotherhood house, there was a fire crackling and first editions on the shelves . . . and nicely arranged furniture . . . even a plate of cookies and some tea sitting on a low coffee table. No Christmas tree, though. No hand-wrapped presents. No Bing Crosby playing.

And there he was.

Her first impression of Bitty's uncle was that he was just as nervous as they were. His foot was tapping and his arms were crossed over his chest and his eyes bounced back and forth between her and Rhage.

Her second thought was that he was big. Much bigger than she would have imagined, given Bitty's size and Annalye's relatively delicate build. In his clean blue jeans and red and blue flannel shirt, he took up almost all of the sofa he was on, and not because he was fat. He was covered in muscle, clearly a field worker of some kind.

His hair was dark, just like Bitty's. His eyes were some flavor of pale brown. Skin was the tone of Rhage's. Face was . . . yes, there were clear echoes of Bitty's features there.

Marissa stood up from the chair next to the male. "I'm going to make introductions."

Ruhn got to his feet, and yup, he was very tall. And he wiped his palms on his thighs repeatedly as names were traded.

He offered his hand only to Rhage—which was a measure of respect and showed an awareness of vampire etiquette. Given that she and Rhage were mated, it would have been entirely inappropriate for Ruhn to touch her without express invitation by either her or her *hellren*.

"Sire," he said in a low, soft voice.

Rhage reached out, and as they shook, Ruhn bowed deeply.

Then he turned to her and did the same, just without the palm-to-palm contact.

Mary glanced at Rhage. His face was remote, but his eyes were not so much narrowed with aggression . . . as sad with unhappiness.

"Perhaps we should all sit down and get comfortable?" Marissa said, indicating various chairs and sofas. "Tea, anyone?"

The female was obviously falling back on her finely bred manners, and it was helpful, filling the silence as Mary nodded about the offer of Earl Grey because she needed something to do with her hands.

Vishous stayed standing in the far corner, a menacing presence that was a reminder that the rest of the house was empty, all the appointments with the King rescheduled just so they could have this neutral space. He alone was here on guard.

But you know, he was more than enough to feel safe—

Except abruptly Mary noticed a figure outside on the back terrace. Z, going by the skull trim. And . . . wait, was that—yes, that was Butch at another window on the other side.

Undoubtedly, other members of the Brotherhood were elsewhere, remaining unseen—and she drew strength from having family with her and Rhage.

"So we all know why we're here." Marissa leaned forward with an admirably steady hand, passing a full teacup to Mary. "Perhaps someone would like to say what's on their mind."

Everybody looked at her, including the uncle. Which gave her an idea that maybe Ruhn was not unfamiliar with what she did for a living.

Mary cleared her throat and decided to cut through the bullshit. "Bitty is our primary concern. Her health, well-being, and happiness is the only thing we care about—but of course, we respect your bloodline tie."

Ruhn looked down at his hands. They were heavily callused, the forearms exposed by those rolled-up sleeves, veined and thick with muscle.

"I'd like to meet her." His voice was soft, quiet . . . totally unaggressive. "My sister . . . it's hard for me to believe she's gone. And seeing Lizabitte would be . . ."

As he trailed off, Mary frowned. It was a surprise to feel compassion for the male.

"I feel like I let my sister down." He shook his head. "Living with that is a curse . . . I mean, I tried to find her when she came up here. But I didn't have many resources—I still don't, and she disappeared with that male. I knew he was going to kill her. We all did." He cleared his throat, and his tone deepened, grew stronger. "Lizabitte is the only part of my sister left—and doing right by that young is fulfilling the duty I failed at to Annalye."

Mary swallowed hard as Ruhn met her straight in the eye, and concluded, "There is nothing I wouldn't do for that young."

THIRTY-SIX

Peyton didn't stop talking. And as Elise sat at the foot of his bed and listened, the picture that emerged of her cousin's alternate life was both overwhelming and not a surprise.

"Wait, so what is this club?" Elise asked.

"It's downtown, it's called The Keys. I've never been to it. The shit that goes on there is not my thing."

"But Allishon was a member of it?"

"Yeah. She used to go there when she, you know."

"She what? When did she go?"

Peyton's baby blues gave her a don't-be-daft stare, but when he saw that she honestly didn't get what he was saying, he shook his head.

"She should have been more like you."

Elise winced, thinking that, given where she was headed at the end of the evening, she doubted she was half the paragon of virtue Peyton was giving her credit for.

"Why did she go there?" she prompted.

"Look, Allishon was always on the hunt for something new." Peyton reached for yet another Grey Goose bottle and poured some more into his tall glass. The ice cubes had melted long ago, but he hadn't seemed to notice—or maybe he just didn't care. "She was always searching. And a lot of the time, she found it there."

"So she was drinking and doing drugs."

"And having sex." He cursed as if he didn't want to go into it all. "She was fucking in public. With lots of different humans in lots of different ways. It was what she got off on—the real hardcore shit. And that club is where it happens in Caldie. She went there a lot."

Elise couldn't help but recoil at the thought of a place like that. Nothing she could handle, that was for sure.

No, she was into monogamy. With Axe, specifically.

But she didn't judge, and again, she'd known that Allishon had different tastes than she did: "So . . . she went there, and someone found her and hurt her."

"Anslam found her and killed her, you mean."

Elise covered her mouth, her eyes popping wide. "Wait, Anslam—as in, hold on, *our* Anslam?" She'd known the male all her life. "But he was in the training program, wasn't he? I heard he died during a mission. That's what my father told me."

"Not what happened." Peyton stared across at the football game. "Not even close. You sure you want me to go into this?"

"Yes. I need to know."

"Anslam was . . . hurting women and females . . . and taking their photographs while doing it. He hooked up with Allishon at some point, I don't know when, exactly—neither of them said anything to me. And you know, clearly, something went down between them. . . ." Peyton trailed off, his head lowering, his voice going so soft, she could barely hear what he was saying. "I went to her apartment downtown after no one had heard from her for several nights. That's when I found . . . how badly she'd been hurt. What had been done to her."

At that point, he choked up, and Elise had to force herself to give him space to get control of his emotions—she had the sense that if she tried to console him or hug him, he was going to pull out of whatever he was remembering.

Peyton cleared his throat. "There was a lot of blood. On the sheets—I mean, the bed was stained with it. There were footprints of the stuff across the carpet, and the red smudges of handprints on the sliding glass door to the terrace. She didn't die in the apartment, however. Somehow, she was able to dematerialize out of there. She was found on the lawn of Safe Place, that domestic violence shelter? She was in bad shape. They didn't know who she was—took her to Havers. She passed there. But again . . . until I went to her apartment nights later, they didn't know who she was."

"I'm so sorry," she whispered.

"Me, too. She must have been in so much pain."

Elise closed her eyes. "And it must have been very hard for you to find all that."

"I'll be fine," he clipped out.

Of course, he said this as he was pouring more liquor down his throat.

"And then," Peyton continued, "see, one of those photographs fell out of Anslam's pack on the bus to the training center and Paradise found it. She was the one who put the whole thing together—and Anslam tweaked to the fact that she knew too much. He went to her house and attacked her—nearly killed her, too. But she and Craeg took care of business. He died in her foyer. When they found even more photographs on him, it all . . . came together."

Elise rubbed her eyes. "My father . . . when you came over that night, what did you tell him and my aunt and uncle?"

"It was fucking painful. Her parents were . . . frozen. I'll never forget it—they didn't show any . . . they were just emotionless. It was the shock. Clearly. Your father was the one who cried. Later, the Brotherhood visited them, after the rest of what happened came out. 'Cuz when I told them she had died, we didn't know who had done it yet."

Elise's eyes teared up, as she pictured her father emotional.

"I think her parents blamed Allishon," Peyton muttered. "Like it was her fault for getting herself killed. And you know . . . I felt like she was murdered all over again, with that attitude of theirs. I mean, someone offed her because they didn't recognize her rights and humanity, but then putting it all on her? You do that all over again. And Christ, it's her own parents."

As they both fell silent, it was as if a pall settled in the suite.

"I told you it was better not to speak of this," Peyton muttered.

"And I disagree completely." She got to her feet and stalked around until she was right in front of the huge screen. Different teams were playing football now, the uniforms red and black and blue and white. "I think we need to talk about it. Not just as a family, but as a community."

"When is the Fade ceremony?"

"I don't think there is going to be one."

"She has to be buried."

"She was cremated. But I think that's as far as it's going to go."

"Well, I still pray for her," Peyton murmured, holding his glass up. "Blessings upon her soul, may she rest unto the Fade, that kind of shit. Usually when I'm drunk, which has been most of the time lately."

"Have you thought about speaking to a therapist?" Elise said as she turned back to him. "This is a lot to hold in."

"NFW—I'm going into the business of war. If I can't handle blood and death, I might as well get out now—and I'm not going to do that."

"But we're talking about a family member's death here. It wasn't the enemy."

Peyton just shrugged. "I'll be fine."

"Well, if you need someone, I'm always here."

He smiled in an absent way. "You know . . . I'm proud of you, Dr. Elise."

"You are?" She blushed. "And by the way, I don't have my doctorate yet."

"You don't need one. Actually a friend of mine recently taught me that females are just as good as males."

As that smile of his faded, she got the impression he was sad. "Who was that?"

"No one special."

That's a lie, Elise thought. But she respected the boundary.

"I'm worried about you," she said softly.

"Like I told you . . . I'll be fine."

For the first time since he joined The Keys, Axe sat back and watched the action from the sidelines.

Novo was still in with Staff: Axe had left her alone in the interview room after giving the boys in red a synopsis of the human story she had concocted as a cover. Which made him think . . . he didn't even know how old she was, who her people were, what her background actually was. He had his suspicions that a lot of it hadn't been great.

And that wasn't because she liked the same kind of sex he did.

Or the sex he'd *used* to be into.

The truth was, though, you could be perfectly well-adjusted and still like the fucking that happened here. That was what people outside of this lifestyle or whatever you wanted to call it didn't understand. Yeah, there were folks running from shit. And folks who were fucked in the head. And maybe a couple of sociopaths. But the vast majority of members were good to go.

Hell, Tinder wasn't any different. eHarmony. Blind dates, office set-ups, bar-crawl meetings. You name it, you were going to find a mix of good and bad—

A woman with bared breasts and a long leather skirt swanned by, her white hair piled up high on her head, her steampunk headgear making her look like the twenty-first century had gotten into a cage match with Victorian England—and the remnants of the conflict had fallen all over her face.

She paused in front of him. Her nipples were covered thanks to two metal disks that were held in place by piercings, a delicate chain running between the tips.

Axe had been with her a number of times, once at the altar, then in other situations. He didn't know her name or her number. But he was well familiar with her sex.

On any other night, he would have gone somewhere with her.

But now, he was just counting down the minutes until he was meeting Elise—and no one here, or anywhere else on the planet, was going to come close to what was waiting for him at the end of the evening.

He shook his head and she nodded and moved on.

"Not your type?" Novo drawled.

Axe looked over. The female had emerged from the back, and he hadn't even known she'd returned. "You want to go hang for a while? Or call it a night and come back?"

If he remembered the way new membership worked, you had to wait awhile before you were approved. But you could come as a guest of the club until that happened.

"You really weren't into her?" Novo stared after the female as if maybe she liked what she saw. "No?"

"Not tonight."

"Well, I know you're not saving yourself for me." This was said without bitterness. Which Axe appreciated. "You sure you don't want to get something off your chest—waaaaaaaaaaaaaaaaaait a minute."

"Let's go," he said, moving away.

But she kept after it and him. "Peyton's little cousin. The one who showed up at the cigar bar. You're getting her, aren't you."

"Nope."

"Yeah, you are—"

Axe stopped. Turned around. Met Novo right in the eye. "Why in the hell would a nice female like that have anything to do with me? Think about it."

He could imagine the frown on Novo's face behind her mask.

"Well," she said, "when you put it like that . . . I can't argue with you."

Just his luck, he thought as they resumed their stroll through the sex rooms: He won that argument because he was a piece of shit.

It was like getting a trophy because everyone else forfeited the race.

'Cuz they didn't want to be on the track with the likes of you.

But whatever . . . this thing with Elise was not going to last; he knew it down to his soul. The question was when and how badly it ended.

Until then—he was in, though. Totally fucking in.

THIRTY-SEVEN

Rhage almost would have preferred to hate the guy.

He'd come into the Audience House ready to protect his *shellan* and defend his family. It was a war of sorts, with the field of battle being nature over nurture: Were two fit, non-biological adoptive parents better than a not-as-fit, but biologically related, potential parent? After all, even if Ruhn had had money, there was no way he lived in as safe a house or environment as Rhage and Mary did.

Because, hello, the two of them bunked in with the First Family.

And Ruhn was single, not very educated, and had no experience with kids of any age.

So, yeah, Rhage had come into this library ready to fight.

But instead . . . he found himself sitting across from what appeared to be a tragically calm, respectful, and reasonable male. And wishing the entire time that he could find fault with something—anything—about Bitty's uncle.

"Well," Marissa said gently—there had been a lot of gentle prompts from the likes of her. "I think the next step . . . is for you, Ruhn, to meet Bitty."

Rhage bared his fangs and then quickly hid the flash of dental art.

Mary spoke up. "How do you suggest we proceed with that?"

"I think it should be supervised, but not by either of you," Marissa murmured. "I just believe it's best for the two of them to have an introduction where Bitty's allegiances are not divided. She's going to want to align with you and Rhage out of loyalty."

"How long has she been with you?" Ruhn asked.

"Two months," Mary said.

Rhage opened his mouth and spoke up before he could think. "But it feels like a lifetime. We love her like she's our own, and she feels the same about us and—"

Mary elbowed him in the side.

And helllllo, sound of crickets.

"No one is doubting your love," Marissa said. Again, gently.

Rhage burst up and marched around. "Well, good. Because it's there and it's going nowhere." He glared at Ruhn. "And even if you take her away from us, we're still going to love her. She's still going to be in our hearts and our heads. Just so we're clear, you leave with her and go back to wherever the fuck you're from? There is not going to be a night that she"—he pointed to Mary—"and I aren't going to think about her, wonder how she's doing, worry about her—"

"Rhage," Mary said. "Rhage, calm down—"

He stopped in front of the guy. "And I want you to remember this. If you ever hurt her—"

V closed in, grabbing Rhage's biceps. "Okay, let's roll back—"

"—I will field-dress you while you're still alive and eat your heart out of your chest—"

There was a sharp whistle, and all of a sudden, Z and Butch were both in the room, coming in through the French doors. As they got in front of and behind him, he realized he'd been wrong. He'd assumed they were there to prevent an outside attack.

With those doors unlocked as they had been? Clearly, folks had been a little more concerned with an inside killing, with him as the aggressor.

And Rhage had to give Ruhn some credit. Instead of shrinking back in the sofa like a pussy . . . or going on a preemptive strike . . .

The male simply rose to his full height and sank into a defensive stance.

Just as he had two nights ago.

"It's okay," the goddamn fucking uncle said as Rhage felt himself being moved out of range. "He can hit me if he wants."

That stopped everyone in the room.

V looked at the guy. "You didn't mention you had a fucking death wish."

"I don't."

"Then I want it in his file that he has very poor risk assessment," Vishous muttered dryly.

"Let me go," Rhage demanded. "I'm not going to light him up. I'm just telling it like it is."

Clearly, that was not very persuasive, as his brother-bodysuit stuck with him.

"And I'm glad you feel that way," Ruhn said, "because it means you've treated her well while you've had her. Which is more than her sire ever did."

Damn it, why did the SOB always say the right thing?

Mary cleared her throat. "I think I would like Rhage and I to be the ones to tell Bitty. I want to make sure this is framed correctly. I don't want her to feel as though she is being wrong or bad if she wants to see him, be with him . . . go with him." She focused on Ruhn. "You, I mean."

Ruhn's eyes didn't shift from Rhage. "That's kind of you."

"It's really what's good for her." Mary pushed her hair back behind her ears. "And that's all that matters. On that note, we should probably get going. Rhage and I should go tell her in person and then . . . first thing tomorrow night? And this is neutral but safe territory—if we can put off the King's appointments for another evening?"

"Consider it done," V declared.

"Okay," Ruhn said as he reached into his pocket. "But, um, can you give her this for me? You can read it first, of course. It's just . . . I wanted to introduce myself. I can't read or write, so I dictated it."

Something must have changed in Rhage's body, because suddenly he was on his own again, the holds on him released—not that his brothers went very far.

Mary's hand shook as she took what turned out to be a couple of pages of lined paper that had been ripped out of a spiral notebook, the frayed edges fluffing up one side of the otherwise neat square.

"I'd be happy to give this to her," his *shellan* murmured.

"Like I said, you can read it. There's nothing much to it. It's not, like, well written or anything. I just wanted her to know who I am."

"All right."

"And the last page is, just, you know, nothing special."

"Okay."

Things kind of petered out at that point, Ruhn sitting back down and staring into the fire. Mary coming to stand next to Rhage, her arm linking through his.

"There's one other thing," V announced as he addressed the uncle. "The King wants to meet you. Before you can see Bitty, you will be required to sit in his presence."

Ruhn nodded slowly. "All right. Whatever it takes."

But the guy was obviously not looking forward to it. Because he had something to hide? Rhage wondered.

"I'm going to be in on that," Rhage said. "I will be in on that audience."

"Wrath wants it private." V shook his head. "And by that, he meant without you or Mary."

"It really should be just between the two of them." Mary stroked his arm. "When will that meeting occur? We should wait to speak to her until it happens—"

"He can sit in if he wants." Ruhn shrugged as all eyes swung back his way. "I have nothing to hide. I mean, I'm just a nobody, and I'm used to my lack of status. No reason to have airs if you've got nothing to back them up with, and if all you've done is live a simple, honest life? That's the kind of thing you can explain even to a King, with a straight back and a level eye—no matter who else is in the room with you."

Rhage blinked. And then had a horrible thought.

Fuck, under other circumstances, he might have liked the guy.

"We appreciate that, Ruhn." Again, Marissa with her gentle way was easing things. "But it is better if it's just you and Wrath. And a guard."

"Wrath said he could come here now," somebody interjected.

"Then we should go." Mary looked at Rhage. "Let's just go, all right? And we'll hang out somewhere and wait for word about the meeting with Wrath before we head home."

Someone said something—Marissa. And then Mary was talking. After that, people started nodding like there was some kind of consensus happening.

Then it was time to leave—and Rhage put his arm around Mary's waist as they walked to the double doors. They paused as Z did the duty of letting them out.

Just as Rhage was stepping from the room, he glanced over his shoulder. Ruhn was still sitting on that sofa in front of the fire, the mostly untouched tea service in front of him, his hands lying on his thighs, his eyes unfocused.

He was nervous. But he wasn't backing away.

"Come on," Mary said.

Next thing Rhage knew, he was behind the wheel of the GTO, the engine was on, and the heater was going.

"You want to get something to eat?" he asked, even though he wasn't hungry.

"Sure. Let's go to that twenty-four-hour diner you like. The one with all the different kinds of pie."

"Sounds good."

Annnnnd so, some ten minutes later, he was parking between a heavy-duty pickup truck and a BMW. Snow was swirling in the air again, but not heavily—as if maybe the clouds above had separation anxiety and were reluctant to let their flakes fly.

The All-Nighter, as the place was called, was your standard diner, with a blinking sign outside and a row of bar stools at the counter inside. There was an annex that had tables, and waitresses who were bored and hostile, and a loyal clientele of which he was a member. On the menu? Free coffee, pie that was to die for, and breakfast around the clock—as well as a Reuben that could make you see God every time you bit down.

His normal table was in the back by the emergency exit, and the waitress who worked the night shift jerked her head in that direction.

Which was her way of saying, *Hey, good to see you again. Your favorite spot's open, and I'll bring you your coffee ASAP. Oh, and glad you brought the wife with you this time.*

Given everything that was going on, the lack of cheerful interaction was a serious bene.

He and Mary took their seats. Coffee was served in heavy mugs. Rhage got the banana cream, Boston cream, and a slice of apple. Mary got a second fork for sampling.

Before he dug in, he put his phone right out on the Formica tabletop. Just in case, you know, reception was bad in the pocket of his leather jacket.

They sat in silence, that cell with its unlit screen between them like a fucking black hole in space, sucking all matter and energy into it.

Mary sipped her coffee. Left that fork where it was on the folded-up paper napkin. From time to time, she looked around at the mostly empty tables.

"You know what I like about this place?" she murmured.

"The pie?" he said between bites. Which were all texture, no taste tonight.

"Well, yes. But it's so bright in here. Usually, at night, everything is dim. I never really noticed this until I came to live with you and started doing the night-is-day, day-is-night thing. Like, for some reason, humans tend to make the insides of all restaurants dim after sundown. Here, though, it reminds me of what it's like to be out during the day."

"Do you resent the changes?" he asked, wiping his mouth. "You know . . . in your life?"

"Not at all." Her eyes swung over to his. "I have you, and that makes everything better."

"Not in this situation with Bitty, it doesn't."

"Nothing could make that any better."

"Too right."

He pushed the banana cream plate away with half the slice still on it. He didn't know why he'd ordered the damn thing. He wasn't a big fan of bananas, and even with the crunch of the graham cracker crust, there was a uniformity of texture between the custard and the cream that kind of made him gag.

It was the reason he couldn't do key lime. Or chocolate mousse . . .

God, he was really hurting, wasn't he. If he was debating desserts in his head.

"You didn't like that?" Mary remarked.

"Not really. But I thought I'd try something new."

Yeah, 'cuz this was a night to expand your horizons. Or maybe try out the theory that there was a keep-your-daughter god who required you to override your gag reflex as tribute.

"I've been here to eat so many times," he said as he pulled the apple in for a landing. "For years and years. And I never thought it was going to be part of our story, you know?"

Because sure as hell, he was going to remember exactly where they were sitting now and what he was eating and how Mary looked until he was dead.

"I know exactly how you feel," she murmured.

As he set to work on his number two, he looked around at the other people, the two over there by the window, the three spaced out evenly on stools at the counter.

Who the fuck knew what was going on in their lives, good or bad. After all, there was a tendency to assume that the anonymity of strangers translated into calm, clear slates for their lives, but that was just bullshit. Everyone had drama. You just didn't know what it was if you didn't know them.

"What do they say about life?" he muttered. "Nobody gets out of this alive?"

Bing!

They both jumped, him dropping his fork on his plate, her splashing coffee out of her mug.

He leaned into his phone, entered his code, which was Mary's birthday, and waited for the cell to cough up the text. "Wrath says it's a go. We can proceed."

They both straightened and sat there for a moment.

Then, without words, he took two twenties out of his wallet, she mopped up what she'd spilled, and then they were making their way to the exit.

I don't know how to do this, he thought as they stepped outside.

I don't know how to look that little girl in the eye and tell her to go meet her uncle.

I don't know how to ever let her go.

In the GTO, he turned to Mary. "I love you. I don't know what else to say."

"I keep thinking I'm going to wake up, and take a shuddering breath . . . and become crazy-relieved that this was all a bad dream."

Rhage paused to give reality a chance to hop on that train.

When nothing changed, no alarm went off, no elbow from Mary nudged him awake . . . he cursed, started the engine, and headed out.

To have an impossible, lose-lose conversation with his daughter.

THIRTY-EIGHT

"So where are you going?" Peyton asked from his reclining pose on his bed.

As Elise felt a flush hit her face, she hoped he was too drunk to notice.

"I just want to clear my head." She took her phone out of her pocket. "So you'll answer this if my father calls?"

"Are you seeing Axe?"

"Not right now." It was the closest she could get to any truth. "I'm not going into the university tonight. I really need to get my head straight and that is not going to happen if I go back home."

"So I'll ask again. Where are you off to?"

"I'm really not sure. But I'll be safe, promise."

Peyton raised a forefinger. "Don't you think if you don't know where you're going that it's especially important to have your phone?"

"Not if it has a GPS tracking program in it that your father had installed. Not if you don't want to get peppered with questions the instant you get home. Not when you simply want to take a deep breath and not get in trouble for it."

Peyton sat up off his pillows and then got to his feet. As he walked over to a table that ran along the back of the sofa, he weaved like there was a stiff breeze blowing around him.

"Take mine, then. The code is oh-four-one-one. It's only so you have something on you—and I'm not naive. I won't push you, but you're obvi not going home at dawn. Just be safe, okay? I don't want to find another body—and this time feel even worse because I enabled you."

"I'm going to be fine."

"That's my lie—I mean *line*." He came over and held out his iPhone. "And whereas you looked at me with pity as I said those words, I'm staring at you with something else. It's called warning."

"I'll be careful. I swear to you."

"Don't make me regret this," he muttered as he opened a window for her.

"I won't."

Elise gave him her own code and put his phone in the pocket of her coat. Then, with a quick hug and a final wave, she ghosted out of his suite, leaving him to his human football games and his bird vodka . . . and the shadows that haunted him.

Talk about not going far. She rematerialized out in the gardens of his estate, just so she could do what she had said and breathe a little. Snow was swirling around, not really getting organized into a proper fall, and the wind was bitter. As she looked over her shoulder at the Tudor mansion, she could see Peyton moving around in his bathroom, his blond hair catching the lights, his bare torso so powerful, she thought for a moment that he didn't look like an aristocrat anymore. He looked like a soldier.

Burrowing into her coat, she knew it was too early to go to Axe's. He'd told her the door was always open, but . . .

When the idea came to her, she didn't immediately dematerialize. After thinking things through, however, she ghosted out . . .

. . . and re-formed downtown, at the foot of a fancy high-rise.

Stepping back so that she was in the middle of the empty street, she counted the floors. The address on those papers she'd found in Allishon's closet had listed an apartment number of 1403.

"Did you forget your key?"

Elise glanced to the left. A human female with an open face and an easy manner was on the sidewalk in front of the entrance.

"I'm here to see my cousin," Elise said. "She isn't answering the buzzer. She's on the fourteenth floor?"

Yeah, she was into honesty—but technically it was true: Allishon wasn't going to be answering anything, ever again.

"Come on in." The woman started for the door. "You can ride my coattails."

"Thank you."

Elise followed her into the lobby and made small talk by the elevator, and then on the ascent. The female got off on the fifth floor and Elise made the rest of the trip by herself. When the *ding!* announced she was on the right level, she got off and looked both ways. A little placard with apartment numbers on it pointed her to the left and she walked down the carpeted hall, passing countless doors.

When she got to the right one, she raised her hand to knock, but then dropped her arm—because, really? Reaching out, she tried the doorknob, and of course, it was locked.

Well, this was a great plan.

Placing her hand on the painted panels, she just stood there, replaying what Peyton had told her. In a sad way, she felt closer to her murdered cousin than ever before—even though it was too late for them to have a relationship.

God . . . she really wanted to get into this apartment, she thought.

And yes, Axe was correct. She was looking for a connection to her father, to her family, in the only avenues that were open to her. It was an imperfect quest, to be sure. But she wasn't going to stop.

Not until she had gone down every path—

As Peyton's phone went off in her pocket, she frowned and took it out. It was Peyton from her own cell.

"Hello?" she said as she accepted the call.

"Your boyfriend called." Peyton exhaled like he was smoking up. "You could have just told me."

Axe had called? "I'm sorry?"

"Troy. Your boyfriend? I told him you were out, that I was your cousin, and I asked if I could take a message. He wants you to call him. Guess he's been trying to get ahold of you. Elise, what the hell are you doing . . . that is not a vampire name."

She frowned. "He didn't say we were dating, though, did he. Because we're not. He's my professor and I'm his teaching assistant. I have no intention of ever getting involved with him. He's the reason I need Axe."

Well, one of them. And the only one she could bring up in mixed company.

Hell, to anybody.

"Just be careful," Peyton said after a moment.

"Always. Now, will you please stop smoking and drinking and start sobering up? At this point, you're going to need a month to get back to normal."

"Too right. Have a good night—but call me if you need me."

"I will."

As she hung up, her surroundings suddenly became clear to her. She was alone, in the human world, in a place where her cousin had been murdered.

The hall with all of the doors had seemed perfectly safe, but as the elevator dinged and a human male stepped free, Elise suddenly felt unsure of herself. If he decided to attack her with a weapon? Would anyone help her? And no one knew where she was other than Peyton— and going by the way he'd slurred his words, he was about two puffs away from passing out.

Elise put the phone up to her ear and made like she was speaking to someone. "Oh, really? And then what happened?"

Walking onward, she kept her eyes on the carpet and the human who was approaching her in her peripheral vision. He didn't seem particularly interested in her presence.

One benefit to wearing jeans and a long, puffy coat was that her body was totally hidden.

Still, she tensed up as they passed . . . but he simply kept about his way and so did she.

And then she was on the elevator, going down.

She couldn't wait to get to Axe's place.

Rhage was not in a big hurry to get home. But the distance from the diner to the Brotherhood mansion didn't change, and he was, as always, a very efficient driver.

Too soon, he and Mary were walking into the foyer.

Going by the laughter, they knew where Bitty was . . . and they found her in the billiards room. Bella was on the sofa, and their girl was playing hide-and-seek with Nalla among the pool tables.

Bit was so carefree, darting from one place to another, moving quickly, but not so fast that Nalla couldn't catch her and feel the triumph of winning from time to time. For clothes, the toddler was wearing a jumper with a big strawberry on it, her yellow eyes sparkling like sunshine, and Bitty had on one of Mary's blue fleeces, the thing so big, it flopped around her arms and torso.

As he and Mary watched the playing, the scent of their sorrow was so thick, his nose filled with the acrid burn of it—and Bella must have caught the stinging smell, because she looked around sharply.

Her face went from hopeful to resigned.

"Girls," the female said as she got to her feet. "I, ah, I think it's time for Nalla's bath. And Bitty, your parents need to talk to—ah . . ."

"Hey!" the girl said as she saw them. "How are—"

She frowned. Straightened from her tickling crouch. "What's wrong? I don't have to go back to Havers's, do I?"

"No, honey." Mary walked forward and gave Bella a brief hug. "But we need to speak to you."

"Did I do something wrong?"

"No." Rhage nodded at Z's *shellan* as Bella scooped up her young and disappeared with sadness. "Not at all. You want to sit down with us, please?"

"All right."

And then the three of them were on the leather sofa that faced the big TV, Bitty in the middle. On the screen over the fireplace, an episode of *Seinfeld* was muted. It was the one with Kramer's Junior Mint ending up in the surgical patient. One of Rhage's favorites.

He felt like smashing the television to pieces.

"What is going on? You're scaring me."

Rhage cleared his throat and looked at Bit. When he came up with a big, fat nothing, he had to get to his feet and pace around. It was either that or find a baseball bat for that redeco job.

Mary picked up the slack, like she always did, and he hated the way he let her down. But her voice was admirably steady.

"Honey, do you remember . . . when you were talking about your uncle?" his *shellan* said. "You know, right after your *mahmen* went unto the Fade. You told me he was coming for you?"

"Yes, but I didn't really think he would." The girl's beautiful brown eyes went back and forth from Mary, who was beside her, to Rhage, who was making a lap around the nearest pool table. "I'd never met him. I was just . . . hoping someone wanted me. And then you two did and everything is okay now. I have my home."

Mary took a deep breath.

And when she stalled, Rhage knew he needed to man up; he

couldn't leave this all for Mary to handle. Walking over, he knelt down in front of the girl.

"Well, actually, he contacted us. See, Mary tried to find him for you before you came to live with us, because it was the right thing to do. When there were no responses, we were sad for you, but happy for us."

Bitty frowned and edged back from him. "Wait . . . he's here. He's alive?"

Mary nodded. "He is and we just met him. He seems very nice and very sincere. And he's really interested in meeting you."

That frown on the girl's face became deeper and she crossed her arms over her chest. "Well, I'm not going to. I want to live here with you guys, and the Brothers and Lassiter. Nalla, L.W., and Boo and George. This is my home."

Rhage rubbed his face. "He's your family, sweetheart."

"You're my family."

"Bitty," Mary started. "He's your mother's brother—"

Bitty burst up from the sofa and wheeled around on the both of them. "This is because of my arms and legs, isn't it. You guys don't want to deal with a kid who might be a cripple after their transition. You don't want me anymore because I'm broken—"

"Bitty!"

"Not at all!"

But the girl wasn't hearing either one of them. "You want me to go away! Fine! Just throw me out!"

With that, Bitty ran out of the room. And damn it, he and Mary were right on her tail, scrambling in her wake as she hit the foyer and kept on going.

"Bitty, stop!" Mary said as they all headed for the grand staircase and started a frantic ascent. "Bitty, that's not what's going on—"

The girl stopped halfway up and turned around again. "You don't love me—you never loved me! You don't care—"

Rhage's voice thundered out of him, exploding so loudly, it nearly shook the house: "Lizabitte! You will *not* address your *mahmen* in that tone of voice!"

Helllllllllllllllo, inner father, he thought numbly.

And yup, that shut everyone up. Froze the females where they were, too.

Even made some poor *doggen* outside of Wrath's study drop her duster and duck for cover.

And apparently, he wasn't done laying down the hammer.

He took the steps two at a time until he was on Bitty's stair, and leaned down so that they were eye to eye. "I understand you're upset. We're upset, too. This was not part of the plan we had for any of our lives—but this is where all four of us are at. He seems like a nice male and he is your blood and you should meet him. I don't blame you for being emotional, and Mary and I are going to support you through all of this. But I will *not* have you ever thinking that we don't love you like you were our own. You are *not* defective. You are perfect and smart and a blessing to everyone who knows you. And we will love you forever."

There were so many other things he could say: *You're the only child we'll ever have. I am dying on these steps just like my Mary is. We are going to be nothing without you.*

But that was grown-up stuff. Things that he and Mary were going to have to work through.

They were not Bitty's problem and he was not going to make them her concern.

Abruptly, the little girl burst into tears. "I don't want to leave you guys. . . ."

Mary wrapped her arms around Bitty. And Rhage wrapped his arms around both of his females.

As a unit, they sat down in the middle of the grand staircase . . . and cried.

THIRTY-NINE

Axe ended up leaving Novo at The Keys after she found a likely candidate—in fact, it was that human woman Axe had been with a number of times, the one with the nipple piercings and the Cruella de Vil hair. Knowing that his fellow trainee was in good hands—namely, her own—he nodded at her, pointed to the exit, and got a nod in return.

For the first time in recorded history, it was a relief to get home—and damn, he was in a hurry to get clean. The second he walked in the front door, he dumped his black cloak on the back of a chair, and went directly to the shower.

Even though he hadn't had sex or even touched anyone, he wanted to scrub every inch of his body before he saw Elise.

The hot water and all the soap was a godsend, and he spent a lot of time with his head back under the spray, the delicious rush pouring down over his face and his chest. He was just about to step out when he sensed he was no longer alone in the cottage. Sure enough, a soft knock sounded out.

He started to smile. "You're early."

"I'm sorry," she said through the closed panels. "I'll wait for you downstairs—"

"I can't reach my back." He pushed the shower curtain aside. "Can you help me?"

The door opened little by little, and then there she was, her lovely face peeking around the corner, her blond hair down, her cheeks flushed from the cold . . . or maybe she was thinking about the same kinds of things he was.

Axe's erection was instantaneous, and he kept himself facing her as it rose.

Even though there was hardly any light, he could tell where her eyes went—and stayed.

"Do you like what you see?" he growled.

"Yes. . . ."

"Then come in here. The water is warm."

Elise stepped in and shut things closed behind herself. In the cramped, steamy space, she took off her sweater and her shirt. Peeled those jeans down her long legs. Lost her bra . . . then her panties.

As he moved back for her to join him, she lifted her lips so he could kiss them at the same time she put her hands on him.

And not as in on his shoulders or his biceps, his stomach or even his ass.

Axe arched so hard, he threw his head into the back wall of the shower. "Fuck—"

"Oh, God, I'm sorry—"

"Like I care?"

With a guttural sound, he kissed her, his hips jerking as her grip restrengthened, the sex surging between them, going from a low-level burn to a solar flare in a split second. And he was not gentle with her. Desperation made his hands rough as he yanked her against him, and his mouth was brutal on hers, and his need went out of control.

But dearest Virgin Scribe, she matched his desperation with a starvation of her own.

"I want you so bad," he groaned against her lips.

"So take me now."

Even though her thighs were slick from the warm water, he grabbed them and popped her up, fitting her around his hips. Then he found her core with his fingers—she was so ready for him—and oh, yeah, she took charge, reaching between their bodies, taking his erection and—

He cursed again as he found home. She gasped his name.

And then he pumped furiously into her, banging her against the shower wall, going in deep. She took everything he had to give her, holding on to his shoulders and squeezing her legs around his pelvis as tightly as she could.

Axe gritted his teeth as the smooth, hot hold of her got to him on all his levels. But he wasn't orgasming first. He wasn't going to go before she did, because how she felt was more important than what was going on for him. And soon enough, she started bucking against him, her head kicking back, her arms clenching.

Her sex tightening against him.

Holy hell, she was milking him so well that he let himself go flying, too, releasing into her, filling her up, her wet hair whipping him in the face, his body feeling like she was surrounding him all over even though they were connected in only one place.

A really fucking important place, granted.

When the first wave was over, Axe eased her down from him until her feet caught her weight and she was standing on her own.

Smoothing her wet hair back, he cradled her face in his palms. "Hey," he whispered as he kissed her in a much more civilized way. "So I'm glad you came—I mean . . . you know . . . are here to . . . shit. I'm just happy to see you."

"Me, too."

Her smile was a little shy, and he loved the contrast between how hot she was and how demure she could be.

As he went after her again, he took his time with the kisses, lingering at her mouth, plying her with his lips, licking at her with his tongue. The steam boiling up around them was like a soft summer breeze, the winter's cold breath—like any other reality aside from the two of them—locked out of this sacred space.

Her breasts were just as perfect as he remembered, and as he lowered himself to his knees, he came up right at her nipples, sucking at them as he kneaded her ass . . . and then dipped his hands between her legs.

She cried out his name as he touched her, her fingers dragging through his wet hair as that warm spray continued to fall all around them.

When he put one of her legs up onto his shoulder, she fell back into the corner of the shower, gasping and going on a shiver as he nuzzled his way into her sex. With a pumping growl, he lapped at her, teasing her, penetrating her with his tongue, and she ended up bracing her palms against the walls, holding herself upright thanks to the tension he was creating in her.

Axe was in heaven.

And he didn't intend to return to earth anytime soon.

As Elise looked down past her breasts and her stomach, it was an erotic shock to see the huge male crammed into the bottom of the shower stall, his hot eyes staring up at her, his tongue licking free of her core, flashing pink before he went back in again—

Another orgasm racked her body and she ground down on his mouth, working herself against him.

In response, he came at her with even greater intensity.

He was possessed and possessing her . . . and the erotic pleasure was almost too much for her to handle, the sensations ricocheting through her body, her brain sizzling, her senses on fire.

She didn't want him to stop.

And he didn't.

Sometime later, much later, after he put her up on his hips again and they had more crazy, wild sex, the water started to go cold and that was when they got out together. Axe only had one towel and he attended to her first, drying her off with gentle hands—and as he cared for her body, his face showed a tenderness that all those tattoos and piercings seemed to suggest he would never show to anyone.

"Come on," he said, "let's go down by the fire before you have to leave. We need to make sure your hair is dry so you don't get pneumonia."

He made a quick pass over his own body with the totally damp terry cloth and then he told her to wait and left her in the bath. A moment later, he came back with a clean blanket and wrapped her up.

Scooping her into his heavy arms, Axe carried her down the stairs as if she weighed nothing, and as he set her before the fire, she saw that he had restocked it first so that she would be warm.

"I wish you didn't have to go," he said as he stretched out next to her on the blankets.

Okay, wow . . . he was so very naked. Really, very naked . . . and even though they had just hooked up in twelve hundred different ways, all she wanted to do was ogle the way his sex lay on his thick thigh muscle.

"I'm not," she heard herself say.

"Excuse me?"

Shifting her eyes to his, Elise shook her head. "I left my phone at Peyton's. He's going to take care of it if my father calls me—and my sire is thrilled about where I supposedly am and what I'm doing, trust me. He thinks we're planning Paradise's birthday party."

When Axe grew silent, unease rippled through her. "Unless you want me to—"

Axe kissed her into silence. "I don't want you ever to go."

Well . . . didn't that warm her even more than the fire did. Too bad the admission didn't seem to strike the same chord in him.

As his eyes went to the fire and his jaw got hard, she touched his face. Ran her fingertips down the tattoos on his neck. Traced over his shoulder.

Trying to recapture the mood, she whispered, "I can't believe I met someone like you."

"A degenerate?"

"Hardly."

His face got a faraway look to it. "Don't try to make a hero out of me, Elise. I'm anything but."

"You've always been good to me."

He sat up, and disappeared even as he stayed right where he was.

"Axe, why do you find it so hard to believe the good in yourself? I mean . . . Peyton told me what you did for the Brother Rhage. You saved his—"

"Don't go there." He put his face in his hands. "Elise. Please stop."

As she laid her hand on his shoulder, he flinched away, and that hurt. But she gave him his space.

"Help me understand why, Axe. And I'll leave it alone."

He was quiet for so long, she became convinced he was going to ask her to leave. But then he cleared his throat.

"So you know that my father was working at an aristocrat's house on the night of the raids. I told you that." He paused. "Actually, let me go back earlier. You remember that kitchen you liked so much when you came in here?"

"Yes. It's incredible."

"It's a memorial to my mother."

"I'm so sorry that she passed, too—I had wondered—"

"Oh, she's still alive. Living in a rich gentlemale's mansion, earning her keep on her back like any other prostitute." His brows sank so low, his eyes all but disappeared. "So yeah, my father actually died long before he was killed."

"He loved her that much," she said sadly. "Oh, Axe . . ."

"I hate that kitchen. I hate every one of those fucking leaves and the dumb-ass roses he carved for a female who didn't want him—and Christ, you should see what's in the basement. My father spent his daylight hours down below, working on all these figurines after my mother left." The firelight played over features that were harsh with anger. "That male was fucking pathetic, the way he mourned her. She leaves him and her kid behind, just walks out one night—so disgusted with their life as a family that she didn't even bother to take any of her clothes or her things. And what does he do? Collapses in mourning. I mean, whatever, he should have just fucked her off and gone about his life."

Elise shook her head. "How old were you?"

"It was before my transition. I must have been ten or so. She upgraded us like we were stereo equipment. An eight-track tape player when she wanted to be with an iPod. She never looked back—and my father never looked forward again. He got stuck, always convinced she was going to walk through that door at any moment, say she was sorry, and fall right back into place by his side and mine. He was so fucking deluded, though. Come on. We lived in this shitty little house, with a beater for a car and his rough workman's hands on her. Her son? I was this scrawny little shit." He shook his head. "But I grew up fast after she pissed us away. I wasn't going to miss her, fuck no. I hated her and I was glad she stayed away. I don't know where she is and I don't fucking care—shit, I wish they'd killed her in the raids."

Elise took a deep breath. "I can imagine how betrayed you must have felt. Both for her leaving and your father for deserting you as well."

Axe shrugged. "He didn't leave, though. He fed me. Kept a roof over my head. But he was too wrapped up in his fantasy of her and her divine return—" He frowned and focused on her properly. "I can't believe I'm talking about this."

Taking a risk, she reached out and stroked his arm. "I will never judge you, Axe. You've got to believe me."

"You sure about that?"

"Keep talking and I'll prove it."

One by one, Axe cracked his knuckles, the huge muscles of his shoulders bunching and releasing as he did. "I took a lot of drugs. After my transition, you know. I just couldn't stand being here with my father. I hated him, I really did, even though none of it was his fault. He was a good male, a little on the soft side, maybe, but he deserved more than what he got for a *shellan*. More than what he got for a son."

"You were a child. As children, we have to survive, so we contort ourselves into whatever family of origin we grow up in. We are forced to cope and sometimes it's in ways that harm us."

Axe shook his head. "I wasn't a child when I started going on benders. When I'd disappear for nights at a time. When I froze him out. I ended up breaking his heart as much as she did at the end." He ground his jaw. "The, ah . . . the night he died? I was out in the city, I'd been high for . . . shit, for three, four days at that point, bouncing between cocaine and heroin like the two were a circus ride."

"You couldn't have saved him," she whispered. "I don't even need to know the particulars. But you couldn't have saved him, Axe. You've got to forgive yourself—"

"He called me. When the attack happened. He left me a fucking message on my cell phone—right when it happened. You want to know how I know what time it was? Because I bumped him to voice mail. And when I saw he'd left me a message? I erased it. I fucking . . ."

Axe looked away, hiding his eyes.

"Axe, you were not responsible for your mother leaving him. And you were not responsible for his death, either—"

"Is that what they teach in all those psych classes you took?" He sniffed up hard and rubbed his face into the crook of his elbow. "To placate everyone even though they were wrong and bad? You know, give 'em participation trophies just for breathing, even though in reality they're fucking shitheads who let people down?"

Elise looked at him steadily and wished he would meet her eyes. "No, they teach us that self-hatred is a self-fulfilling prophecy."

"What's that supposed to mean."

"Until you learn to let go of the responsibility for your parents' relationship and choices, you are going to see everything through a prism of blame. And you're going to eat yourself alive."

"But I erased his message." He scrubbed his face with a hard hand. "The last thing he said on the planet, I let it go like it was worthless. I'm no different than she was. I left him when he needed me."

"Is that why you nearly killed yourself last night to save Rhage? You just had to be there for someone and you weren't going to let anything stop you?"

He was quiet. "Maybe."

"We find ways of repeating things until we get them right. But that can be dangerous. Especially if we're trying to fix things we never should have owned in the first place."

Thinking of herself in front of the door to Allishon's apartment, Elise wondered if maybe she shouldn't heed her own advice.

"Axe, you might just want to consider the radical idea that your mother didn't leave because of you or your father. She left because of herself. She deserted both of you because of some failing she had. Or maybe it was that she and your father weren't compatible. Or . . . maybe she fell in love with someone else. There are a whole host of reasons why relationships fail. But one thing I know for sure? No child, no matter how they behave, is responsible for keeping their parents together or in a healthy relationship. That's up to the grown-ups. That's their job."

He was quiet for a long time. Then he got up, wrapped a blanket around his waist, and stood over her.

Shit, she thought.

She should have known better than to try and act like his therapist. It wasn't what anyone needed in a personal relationship, for one thing. For another, she wasn't trained as a shrink.

Just because you took psych classes, as he'd said, didn't mean you were qualified to tell people how to frame their lives.

"I'm sorry," she said sadly as she, too, stood up. "I'll go—I shouldn't have let my mouth get ahead of me. I'll just grab my clothes from up-stairs in the bathroom."

FORTY

As Elise got to her feet, still wrapped in the blanket Axe had given her, he couldn't find the words he wanted to say.

"God, I'm so pissed at myself," she muttered as she turned away. "And I'm leaving before—"

He caught her arm. "I don't want you to go."

Looking over her shoulder, she seemed dumbfounded. "But—"

"I want to . . ." He cleared his throat. "I want to show you something."

Taking her hand, he led her past the stairs, into the kitchen, and over to the cellar door. On so many levels, he couldn't believe what he was doing. Couldn't believe what he'd said. Really, totally couldn't believe that she didn't seem horrified in the slightest.

She also didn't seem to judge him at all.

And all of that made him want to go deeper into his past with her. Even though that made no sense.

Opening the cellar door, he kindled the lantern he'd left at the head of the stairs and then led her on a descent down the wooden steps. As the yellow glow fanned out at the bottom, she gasped.

"He did all this? Your father?"

She let go of his hand and walked forward to the shelves of finished figurines. "These are . . . incredible."

Axe hung back, aware that, as she inspected the woodland creatures his father had excised—or maybe exacerbated—his grief with, Axe was showing her a part of himself.

"He was an artist," he heard himself say. "A master. And yet he wasted it all just pining away for her."

"Is that why you never got mated?" she murmured as her slender hand cradled a rabbit that was up on its haunches with ears pricked. "Are you always worried that the female will leave you and you'll do what he did?"

"I don't . . ." Axe shrugged even though she wasn't looking at him. "I don't think about it a lot."

Coward, he said to himself. And what a liar he was.

That was exactly the reason. Well, that . . . and he'd never met the likes of her before.

Putting the woodland rabbit back next to a deer and a raccoon, Elise came over to him, moving in that lovely way she did. As she put her hands on his upper arms, he jumped at the contact, but didn't step away.

"I'm not going to try to fix you, Axe. That's not my business. But if I think you're off base, I'm going to tell you and then you can do with it what you will. No judgment."

"Well, you know all my dark secrets now."

"And I'm still here, aren't I."

He reached up to brush her cheek and wasn't surprised that his hand was shaking. "You scare the shit out of me, female."

He'd rather face a thousand *lessers* than her in a blanket, standing in front of his father's wall of misery. And yet he wasn't leaving. And he sure as fuck wasn't going to tell her to go.

"Intimacy is scary," she said as she stroked down his arms, soothing him. "If you let people in, they can hurt you. In fact, in your case, that's what you grew up believing was a natural consequence of loving someone. They fail you. You fail them. And everything falls apart. But it doesn't have to be like that."

Axe put his hands on her waist and brought her up against his body. As he stared into her blue eyes, he whispered, "I lied."

"About what?"

"I'm flat-out terrified of you."

She shook her head. "You can trust me. I'm not going to desert you."

Axe kissed her mouth. Because he wanted to. And because he desperately wanted to stop the conversation. "Come on, let's get out of here. It's cold."

More to the point, he had this superstitious fear that maybe his parents' bad road was something the two of them could catch. A relationship virus or something.

Back upstairs, he hurried her into the living room. The sun was coming up soon, and the heaviest drapes were in there.

Damn, he'd never given it much thought before, but he didn't feel safe with her here during the day. He wanted them behind steel doors, so sheltered underground from the sun that it was as if that big, glowing death orb didn't exist.

As they resettled in front of the fire, lying together, he said, "I haven't done any drugs since the night I found out he was killed. I stopped using them then. I still drink every once in a while, but not like I used to."

"So that was your bottom point," she commented.

"Guess so."

The fact that he didn't tell her about the sex stuff wasn't something that sat well with him. But he wasn't going to do that anymore, either. Going back to The Keys tonight had been a revelation in how much he did not need that now that he had the real deal—

The sound of a phone ringing across the room made him frown.

It was his cell. Which Craeg had dropped off for him earlier.

The thing went silent. Only to ring again.

"Goddamn it," he muttered as he got up.

Fishing through the pockets of his cloak, he took the cell out and frowned. Answering it, he said, "Novo? You okay? . . . Yeah, I'm fine. . . . Nah, I'm home. Where are you? . . . Are you leaving now? . . . Novo, seriously, it's right before fucking dawn. What the fuck are you doing—huh? . . . Yeah, I lose track of time there, too, but Christ, come on. Don't make me regret getting you in. . . . Fine. Will you get off the phone and call me when you're home? Dumb-ass."

He hung up and kept the phone with him as he went back over to Elise and lay down again.

"Sorry. That's one of my fellow trainees. A real hardheaded hard-ass who's just about as stupid as I am. I just—you know, I don't want anyone hurt."

Elise nodded. "Of course. Do you want to go see if he's okay or something?"

Axe just rolled his eyes. "Novo will be just fine, as long as—"

The phone rang again and he answered before the ring-a-linging stopped. "Where are you." He exhaled. "Good. Don't stay that late again, okay? You can always go back, just not if you're fucking dead. See you tomorrow night, asshole."

He was laughing a little as he hung up. "What a psychopath."

Elise smiled, but it was a remote kind of thing. "It takes a special breed to do what you all and the Brothers are doing."

As Axe recognized that her mood had changed, he wanted to ease her. "Don't worry. I know where you've gone in your head, but I'm safe. I'm careful—"

"Axe . . . I think I'm falling in love with you."

• • •

Riiiiiiiiiiiiiiiight, Elise thought. Not what she'd expected to come out of her mouth. Like, not even close.

And as that bomb landed between them, Axe blinked like she'd spoken a foreign language. Which, yup, was precisely the kind of reaction you were looking for when you told a male you loved him.

"Oh, God." She put her face in her hands. "I can't believe I just said that."

With subtle pressure, he made her drop her arms down. And his expression was . . .

Well, he was smiling.

It was a slight kind of thing, not a big flash of the fangs or anything. But it was definitely a small, secret smile, meant only for her—and created, she suspected, only by her.

Now, that's what she was talking about, she thought as she smiled back at him.

"Say it again," he whispered. "Send some more sunshine my way just so I'm sure I heard you right."

Elise was very aware that she had two paths to choose from. She could deny the words, downplay them, be safe. Or she could let herself fly.

She picked glorious flight over fright. "I'm falling in love with you."

Axe smiled a little bigger and then he was kissing her, his heavy body easing her back on the pallet. With sure hands, he disappeared the blanket between them, and then he rolled on top of her, his hot, hard erection going in between her legs.

It was the most natural thing in the world to kiss him back and welcome him inside. And there was no frantic pumping this time, just a gentle rolling motion that warmed her first before it lit her on fire.

As they made love in front of the hearth, she felt like her world was complete: Yes, it was early in the relationship, but with honesty and trust, all things were possible.

Especially as Axe dropped his head and whispered into her ear, "I'm falling in love with you, too."

Elise giggled.

Yup, she let out a girlie giggle that was more fitting for the kind of female who got her nails done and had streaks in her hair and wore high heels and flirty skirts.

At the sound, Axe stopped and eased back. "Was that what I think it was?"

"No, not at all."

"Did my psychology Ph.D. candidate actually—"

She clamped her palm over his mouth. "I did not."

"Did too."

"Did not."

"Did—"

As he thrust fully into her, Elise arched under his body, pleasure flooding her veins. "Axe . . ."

"Admit it."

"What?" she mumbled.

He rolled his hips twice. And then stopped. "You giggled."

"Not fair—" He thrust again and this time she went for his butt with her nails. "Finish what you started!"

"Admit you giggled!"

"Why!"

They were laughing so hard, it didn't matter what they were saying. A buoyant bubble of happiness had engulfed them both, and they were bouncing in the center of the joyful space, free of anything on the outside.

"Fine, I giggled—"

In response to her capitulation, Axe got down to business, thrusting into her . . . before reaching down, grabbing one of her legs, and stretching it all the way up so she was cocked to the side and he could get in still further.

Even through her pleasure, she managed to keep her eyes on him. He was magnificent in the firelight, his warrior's body dominating her, his muscles standing out in sharp relief, the massive veins that ran down his neck and into his arms showing starkly against his tan skin.

When he bared his fangs, she knew he was going to go for her jugular, and she wanted him there. Turning her head to the side, she bared herself to him—

The strike was brutal, his fangs going in so deep, she screamed— but not in pain, even though it hurt in a delicious way.

This was the marking she had heard about.

This was the owning of the female by the male, the staking of the claim. And sure enough, he held her in place at the throat with his teeth as he marked her from the inside out by coming into her sex.

But he wasn't done with her.

Before she could catch her breath, he pulled out, flipped her over, and yanked her onto all fours. Rearing up behind her, he bit her again, on the other side, and then he was in her once more, taking her from the rear, one hand running up between her slapping breasts and locking on the base of her throat, the other planted on the floor, holding them both up.

She was facing the fire, and her vision swung wildly with each of his pounding thrusts—the flames jumping this way and that, her hair flying around until some lashed into her open mouth.

At some point, her upper body just collapsed onto the blanket, her sex up in the air, his for the taking as he drilled her over and over again, coming so many times, he coated her with his marking scent.

Elise forgot how many orgasms she had.

All she cared about was that he never, ever stop.

FORTY-ONE

*T*he following evening, when the sun was safely below the horizon, and the temperature was dropping from the twenties into the teens, Rhage found himself once again exercising great self-control.

He was down in the mansion's foyer, standing in front of the double doors of the vestibule. No, that wasn't quite right. He was actually off to one side of them, staring out of the bubbly, antique glass framers that faced the courtyard beyond. Which meant he couldn't see much.

Kind of apt, really, considering he had no idea how this was going to go.

He sensed, rather than heard or scented, his females upon the great staircase, and he turned around and watched them descend. Bitty was in a red velvet dress he and Mary had bought her in preparation for the human holiday, and the girl had white tights underneath, patent leather black shoes, and a black felt coat that had been made in the Victorian period and passed down through Bella's family.

She and Rehv had wanted Bitty to have it, and with its gorgeous satin lining and black velvet collar and cuffs, the thing was certainly made better than anything available at any store today.

Indeed, Bitty's outfit was so proper and festive . . . but in spite of her pretty clothes, she looked like she was going to the gallows.

And Mary didn't appear any better.

As for him? Personally, he felt like someone had cut off both of his legs and left him to bleed out on the floor.

But hey, who was comparing?

As his females hit the mosaic floor and crossed over its depiction of an apple tree in full bloom, he took a deep breath. "You ready, Bitty?"

Dumb fucking question, he thought as she stopped before him.

"Please," she said in a shaky voice. "Come with me? Don't make me go alone?"

His hand was trembling as he brushed her cheek. "You won't be alone. Fritz is going to drive you in, and Vishous and Zsadist are going to be there waiting for you."

Actually, V and Z and were going to track the Mercedes all the way into town, the pair of them dematerializing at regular intervals along the route until she arrived safely at the Audience House. And they would have ridden with her, but the concern was that the girl might feel as if her uncle were dangerous if she made the trip in with two heavily armed Brothers sitting on either side of her.

"I can't do this." Bitty looked frantically at Mary. "Please, don't make me go. What if he takes me?"

"He won't." Mary stepped in and smoothed the little girl's hair. "And we'll be right here, waiting for you—in fact, as soon as it's done, Rhage will dematerialize right there and he'll ride home with you, okay?"

"You will?" Bitty asked him. "You promise."

"I absolutely promise—"

"How about I go with you and stay with you the entire time."

All three of them wheeled around at the disembodied, synthesized voice. But no one was there, even though it sounded like—

"Lassiter?" Rhage said, as he glanced at all the thin air in the foyer. "Where the hell are you?"

"Bitty," came that voice. "Put your hand out."

The little girl did as she was told—and from out of nowhere, a tiny pool of golden light formed in her palm.

"It's warm," she said with wonder.

The light spot traveled up her arm to her shoulder and stayed there, as a bird might have. And then the odd, phantom voice said, "I'll be with you the whole time. No one else needs to know, okay? Only you'll know, and your parents will know—"

Rhage and Mary both winced at that word.

"—and most importantly, you won't be alone. 'Kay?"

Bitty took a long, slow inhale. "Okay. That's good. Thank you."

A set of headlights flared in those old, narrow-paned windows by the exit . . . and sure as shit, Rhage wanted to bust out of the house and scream at Fritz to go away.

"All right," Mary said in a strained voice. "Big hugs."

As the two embraced, Rhage stared at that little sun spot on Bitty's shoulder. It had gotten even smaller, so that it was nearly invisible, the sort of thing that was easily missed.

He was going to owe the angel big-time for this one.

"You're so brave," Mary said over Bitty's head. "I'm so proud of you."

"I'm not brave, I'm scared."

"And you're doing this anyway—which is the very definition of brave."

Mary stepped free and brushed her own hair back. She was glancing away a lot, her eyes shimmering with tears that she was clearly determined not to shed.

Bitty came over to stand in front of Rhage. Looking up, up, way up at him, she said, "You promise you'll come."

He sank down on his haunches, both knees cracking like tree branches from a trunk. "I promise. V will let me know and I have my phone right here."

As he showed her his cell, Bitty threw her arms around his neck and he pulled her in close, shutting his eyes and sending a prayer up that this would all somehow magically be okay.

And then he and Mary walked the girl out through the vestibule, across the stone pavers of the mansion's entrance, down the steps, and to the black Mercedes. Fritz helped the little girl by opening the door for her, and then the butler shut things up and bowed deeply to Rhage and Mary.

Those taillights going down the hill were the most tragic thing Rhage had ever seen.

He and Mary stayed where they were, standing side by side in the cold, well after the pair of red eyes were long gone.

"Let's go inside," his *shellan* said dully.

"Okay."

"There's nothing we can really do but wait."

"Yeah."

She turned away and started back for the vestibule. But for some reason, he couldn't move. Rhage just stood there, immobile, staring out at the moon, which was full or pretty damn close to it.

His heart was in that fucking Mercedes. His heart was heading away from him, leaving his body and traveling in that car to someone else, to some other construct of family, to a future that didn't include him or Mary—

"Rhage?"

Pivoting on his shitkicker, he looked toward the mansion. Mary was standing just inside the vestibule and holding the door wide for him.

He wanted to go over to her, but his body seemed to be ignoring the signals from his brain. And then he decided he should say something . . . but speech didn't seem to be coming.

"I'm sorry," he mumbled.

There was a pause. And then Mary exploded forward, racing across the distance, throwing herself in his arms. As he caught her against him, he really couldn't believe it was all happening.

"You always tell me," she groaned, "that I know what to say. But I don't know what to say, I don't know what to do, I can't help you, I can't help her, I can't change anything. . . ."

Rhage smoothed his palm up and down her back, and felt so powerless.

"I've got to stop this," she babbled. "I've got to stop . . . this from happening. . . . oh, God, she's leaving. . . . Rhage, my baby is leaving me, my child. . . ."

He ended up scooping her into his arms and holding her off the ground, cradling her as she wept.

Eventually, the emotional burn-off eased up, and she took some shuddering inhales. "Oh, God, I'm so sorry—"

"Why?" He shifted his hold and brushed her hair back. "Why would you ever apologize?"

"Because I need to be there for you. I need to support you."

For a long moment, he stared down into her face, tracing the features he knew so well with his eyes. And then he smiled a little. "My Mary Madonna, by letting me take care of you? You make me strong. You give me strength by relying on me to take care of you."

"That's not fair, though. What about you—"

Rhage shook his head. "Do I have to explain male bonded vampires to you again? You are . . . my reason for being. And I've never loved you more than I do right now."

"Even if Bitty leaves."

His eyes went to the moon overhead. The bright shining moon. "If she leaves, nothing will be the same again for me. Nothing will be quite as bright or funny or free. I was forever changed the minute she came into our lives—and I guess I didn't really understand how fully until now. It happened in an instant . . . and it will take a lifetime to get over." He refocused on his *shellan*. "There is only one thing that will remain unchanged. And that is my feelings for you. In fact, my love for you is the one thing that will keep me standing at the end of this."

Mary teared up all over again, especially as he kissed her.

"Our strength must be tested," he whispered, "for us to know it's still there. And I will always be your warrior, Mary mine. Always and forever."

Mary reached up to his face and stroked his cheek.

"I love you," she breathed.

He nodded. "We're going to get through this, Mary. Even if we're limping and bloodied at the end. We will go on because . . . maybe she'll come and see us someday, after she's grown. Maybe she'll remember us. Who knows. But even if she doesn't, we have to still be a family together, you and I. Otherwise . . . God, the alternative doesn't bear thinking about."

FORTY-TWO

"Wait, so you don't have class?"

As Elise asked the question, she was pulling on her jeans in Axe's bathroom upstairs, her damp, fresh-out-of-the-shower skin making it the kind of job she had to do sitting on the toilet with the seat down.

Axe shook his head as he put shaving cream on his face and picked up his razor. "We were supposed to, but I don't know what's going on. The text said that the Brotherhood is 'otherwise engaged,' whatever that means."

"So do you think we can go have First Meal together?"

"Sure, where?"

Okay, it was totally sexy, watching your male shave. And Axe was tragically efficient about the job, running those blades down his jaw, across his chin, over his upper lip. There was no light on above the mirror, but she could see well enough thanks to a candle he'd lit and put on the side of the porcelain sink.

"I love all the candlelight here," she remarked.

Loved even more what it was flowing over: the great pads of Axe's pecs, and his six-pack that was so sharp it threw shadows, and his long, low-hanging sex, and his heavy thighs.

He glanced at her. "You keep looking at me like that and we're not going to make it out of this house before sundown tomorrow."

Elise smiled. "Well, if you weren't so good to look at, I wouldn't stare so much. Anyway, I need to head over to Peyton's and get my phone first."

Axe frowned. "I'll go with you."

"You don't have to."

"Worried about being seen with me?"

Elise recoiled and then stared up at him. "No, not at all. Why would you say that?"

"Because I'm jealous."

Okay, that was hot. But then she did the math. "Wait, of Peyton?"

Axe rinsed his razor under the water, knocked it twice on the edge of the sink, and then resumed the de-bearding on the other side of his face. "Yeah."

She put both her hands up. "Let me tell you right now, you have nothing to worry about. First of all, I saw him shirtless last night—"

Axe turned his head so fast, he cut himself. "What—"

"—and he doesn't hold a candle to you. At all."

His eyes narrowed at her. "Did he come on to you?"

"No, and he wouldn't ever." She got to her feet and eased into Axe's body; extending her tongue, she lapped up the bright red blood— which caused an immediate physical response in her male. "He knows better."

Before Axe could say anything else, she sank down onto her knees, opened her mouth . . . and slid his erection home, sucking him deep as she cupped his heavy sac.

"Oh, fuuuuck—" There was a bang and a crash as Axe fell back against the wall. "Oh, *shit* . . ."

Popping his erection out of her mouth, she ran her tongue up the underside of him, and then circled his head. "Still jealous of him?"

"Evkaeeio jgo eo faiofkal flla."

Or something to that effect.

With a smile, she went back to work, stroking him, sucking him, twisting his balls, teasing him with the sharp points of her fangs. Soon, he was panting and straining, and then coming in her mouth—and she was relentless, milking him dry until he sagged, all his power gone and inside of her.

And oh, the way his eyes clung to her, as if she were the most sexually exciting and satisfying female on the planet.

"I owe you," he said with a speech impediment she'd never heard come out of him before.

"And I look forward to collecting. I think I'm going to go downstairs now, though—or we'll never get out of here."

Axe mumbled something, and then she was leaving him be . . . with the biggest smile on her face.

There was a serious rush to turning a male like that into putty. Go fig.

Down by the dwindling fire, she got Peyton's phone and called her own cell.

Her cousin picked up on the first ring. "Yelllllo."

"Thank God you're alive."

"You, too. Where are you? And no, your pops didn't call—you want to know why?"

"Why?" She switched the phone to her other ear so she could tuck in her shirt. "And please tell me it's not because he drove over to your house the second the sun set to look everywhere for me."

"He didn't call because I reset the GPS locator."

"You did what?" She shook her head. "I'm sorry, what?"

"I made the GPS locator report that you've been in your room all night. Well, as of three a.m., which is a perfectly respectable time to come home."

"Peyton, no offense. You aren't that smart."

"Screw that—I'm in school. The Brother Vishous himself taught us how to do it. So as long as your sire didn't check your room, you're good to go. Did no one call me?"

"I don't know. You've got some texts, I didn't read them. They're not my business."

"Well, nobody came looking for you in my room at my house. So I must have done something right. You can kiss my ass when I give you your phone back."

"Excuse me?"

"Meet me in a half hour at the cigar bar—I'll bring it to you then. And boooonus, I'm going to get off hearing you tell me how wonderful I am in your stupid bodyguard's presence, because he'll be there with the rest of us. He always shows up if there's free food."

Elise rolled her eyes to herself. But she did owe Peyton. Unfortunately. "You are such an egoist."

"Ha! If I'm the reason you got to be out all day without getting in trouble? I'd call that accuracy, not ego, when it comes to me being a god."

"I'll see you soon."

"I bet you can't wait, either. Buh-bye."

First stop actually turned out to be Elise's family's mansion, and Axe let her go into her father's house alone. As he waited on her frozen front lawn, he wondered what it would be like to live in a place like that. With servants, and a museum's worth of stuff, and money, money, everywhere.

He thought of his unheated, dingy cottage.

Had his mother made it happen? he wondered. Had she made it to where she had told his father she wanted to go? Mistress of a house just like this one?

Was she happy—assuming she was alive? Hell . . . did she ever think of him? Wonder what had happened to the son she had left behind?

As Elise emerged out of the front door, he could tell by the skip in her step that all was well. Her father hadn't caught on.

"Are you ready?" she asked as she came up to him.

"Always. Everything okay with your father?"

"No problems—and I told him I was meeting Peyton out, with you as an accompaniment, and he was fine with that."

Axe almost kissed her. But then he remembered that there were probably security cameras all over the outside of the mansion and around the property. Shit, he was still worried whether anyone had seen their little clinch behind the old oak tree the other night.

"Let's go." She smiled so widely, he couldn't help but return the grin a little. "And brace yourself, Peyton thinks he's a god because he re-wired the GPS system on my phone."

"Oh, yeah. V taught us that—should have thought of it myself. And if that cousin of yours is a god, it's only because his bong is telling him lies again."

Axe dematerialized downtown first and checked the alleyway. Then he texted Peyton's phone, which Elise still had, and told her to come along ahead.

"This feels like a date," she said as they walked around to the front of the cigar club. "Don't you think?"

As she took his hand and kept holding it, he frowned. "Are you sure you want to come out of the closet with me, so to speak?"

"I'm all about honesty, right? I have nothing to hide."

"Once Pandora's box is opened, you can't shut it back up."

"I'm not afraid. Are you?"

He cleared his throat. "Fuck no."

As they came up to the entrance, Axe held the door open for her. And he had to admit, he wanted Peyton to know that Elise was his and his alone.

"I'm going to take my cues from you," he muttered after he followed her in.

"Good." She linked an arm through his. "Let's do this."

As they walked back to Peyton's regular table, Axe was aware that he was blushing like a motherfucker—but hopefully, the dim lighting and the ambient smoke in the air hid the shit well enough. Funny . . . for as many people as he'd fucked, he'd never been . . . claimed . . . before. Never wanted to be, either. And the realization made him like something else about Elise: She always knew where she stood. There was no waffling, no inconsistency, nothing hidden or misrepresented about her.

She was solid as a rock.

And given that he'd had a void for a mother and a ghost for a father?

Okay, wow. Enough with the psychoanalyzing.

Peyton was already at the seating arrangement, holding court with some other vampire males, his casual, Rich Guy suit and open-collar shirt making him seem like exactly what he was: a son of privilege who always got the girl, had the car, led the pack.

And that male's eyes snapped to where Axe and Elise were linked.

Axe was ready for anything. But what he got, at least in the short term, was nothing much: Peyton just stared over at them and then smiled remotely as Elise broke free and approached him.

The bastard didn't get up, but made her come to him—which made Axe want to leave the guy spitting teeth and shitting out his lower intestines.

"How great am I?" Peyton said, like he was the fucking Pope or something. "G'on, tell me. Don't hold back."

Elise just cocked a brow, took out his phone, and swapped it for her own. "You are amazing. Incredible. And a total blowhard—which, considering how young you are, is really saying something."

"I'll just focus on the first two, thank you very much." Peyton looked at Axe, his tone hardening. "And if it isn't the man of the hour. The big hero. Sit down and have a drink. Or as you're working, maybe you should stand in a corner and just watch her, bodyguard."

Elise froze, but Axe didn't.

He simply parked it across from the guy and kept his hands out and ready. He didn't think Peyton would make a direct move, but there clearly had been a lot of alcohol consumed already, and the male was giving off territorial hormones like he had Elise's certificate of title in his back pocket.

Fucking asshat cocksucker.

Elise crossed her arms over her chest. "I can't believe you just said that."

Peyton shrugged. "It's the truth. He works for your father, doesn't he. He's supposed to keep you safe, isn't he. What exactly do I have wrong here?"

"Your tone of voice, for one thing."

"Ah. Interesting. So you're coming to his rescue." Peyton lifted his Scotch. "See, I thought it was supposed to be the other way around."

"We're leaving." Elise shook her head. "This is ridiculous. And you're being totally inappropriate."

"Am I? Funny, does your judge of character only kick in when you're not fucking someone?"

Annnnnnnnnnnnnnnd it was go time.

Axe exploded up out of his chair and was on the son of a bitch a blink later, picking the male up by the throat, knocking his leather armchair over, and forcing him backward until they hit the emergency exit and burst outside.

Axe spun Peyton around and hung him up on the outside of the building. "Time for you to back off."

"You asshole," Peyton hissed. "You fucking got her, didn't you."

Elise came rushing out of the cigar bar—but Axe stopped her with an order and a palm in her face. "Go back inside."

"Axe, don't hurt him—"

"Let me handle this—"

"Let him go—"

Peyton's fancy loafers were dangling above the ground, and he was turning blue, but he was so furious, he didn't seem to care.

"Why do you"—Peyton gasped—"want her to leave?"

Axe snarled, baring his fangs. "Because there's no reason for her to see what I'm going to do to you."

"Axe, please—"

That was when Novo materialized on the scene, sauntering over from across the street, the female more amused than surprised as the emergency exit clicked shut.

"Peyton," she drawled, "you always find the fun, don't you."

"Al—" He choked and coughed. "—ways."

It was hard to say when exactly Axe tweaked to the fact that they were in trouble. But one minute, he was focused on getting Elise to go back inside so he could kill Peyton, and the next . . .

Novo caught the scent at the same time he did, the female's head turning to the direction the wind was coming from.

"Oh, shit," she said under her breath.

Axe dropped Peyton and let the guy find his feet and his oxygen. If he did. "Elise, back inside. Now."

"No, I'm not leaving until—"

Axe took her arm and airlifted her to the door. "That's a *lesser*. That smell—it's not old garbage, that's a fucking *lesser*."

Elise's look of alarm was the good news and the bad news: bad because he never wanted to see her scared; good because she didn't argue with him anymore.

He grabbed for the handle on the door they'd come out of and—locked. The emergency exit was locked. Duh.

"Goddamn it," he hissed.

Axe only had one gun on him, but as he glanced at Novo, she was already taking her forty out. Peyton was the same, palming up—except he was coming toward Elise.

"I'll take care of her," the male announced.

"No, she's my responsibility—"

"She's my cousin—"

"Will you two cut it out—"

The three of them escalated to yelling, which was exactly the wrong fucking thing to do, because down at the end of the alley, the *lesser,* who had previously had no concrete direction, glanced their way.

And then started coming at them.

"I'm going to do this—"

Axe's bonded male ended Peyton's op-ed right goddamn there with a roar to rival Godzilla's—proof positive that whatever civilized veneer vampires sported as they went about their nightly biz, at their heart, they were animals, unconstrained by logic when pushed.

Especially the males.

Peyton's shock was obvious, but there was no time to go into the how-did-bonding-happen thing. The slayer, previously on the approach to tease out whether they were human or vampire, now had its answer—and it whistled, calling others in for backup.

Axe put Elise behind him. "Stay with me. Use me as a shield."

And then he raised his gun. There were three slayers now, and—

"One at six," Novo barked.

Snapping his head around, Axe cursed. "Peyton—"

"Yeah, I'm covering her, too."

Elise's cousin fell in tight, closing ranks around her, as Axe got his phone out and tried to text—

"Go into Contacts," he said as he thrust his phone back at his female. "Text the Brothers."

A trio of *lessers*. Humans everywhere. Elise in the middle.

This was the definition of a cluster-fuck.

FORTY-THREE

Rhage was losing his mind.

His ever-loving mind.

As he and Mary sat in the billiards room, the mansion was empty except for *doggen*: Wrath and Beth were taking a breather with L.W. down in Manhattan; Phury was up at Rehv's Great Camp in the Adirondacks with the Chosen; V, Z, Tohr, and Butch were at the Audience House with Bitty and that uncle of hers along with Marissa—and Lassiter was riding sunshine shotgun on the little girl's shoulder. Meanwhile, iAm, Trez, and Rehv were in town at shAdoWs and Sal's, with Rehv helping the Shadows optimize their revenue. The other females were out on a girls' night. And he hadn't seen any of the young bucks since First Meal.

It was as if the community knew they needed some space to self-destruct.

Rhage checked his Rolie again. "How much longer can it take?"

"I don't know. I mean, it could be hours." Mary looked at her phone by tilting the screen. "Marissa said she'd shoot me an update when she was able to."

"Goddamn it. I feel like I'm waiting to hear if I have cancer."

"As somebody who's gone through that one? Yup, it's pretty close."

"I just—"

"Shit!" Mary jumped up. "I forgot!"

"Forgot what?"

She put her hands up to her face. "The letter he wrote. I never gave it to Bitty. Oh, God, I don't want Ruhn to think I'm obstructing anything!"

Justlikethat, she was out of the billiards room, her feet carrying her fast up the grand staircase. Moments later, she came back down breathing heavily, with the folded papers in her hand.

"What does it say?" Rhage asked. "I mean, he told us we could read it."

It seemed like the closest they could get to what Bitty was experiencing with the guy.

"I really hope . . . well, there's nothing to be done now." Mary sat down and opened the pages. "I will apologize. It was an oversight . . . it's all just been so emotional."

As she read what had been written in pencil, she was silent for a while, her brows moving up and down as her eyes went back and forth.

"What's in there?"

"Sorry. Ah, he works on the estate as a handyman, fixing fences and tending the lawns and buildings. He . . . takes care of the barn cats and the two security dogs. Lives by himself. Says . . . well, this is too bad."

"What, that he molests farm animals?"

Mary shot him a look. "No, he seems apologetic he wasn't schooled." She went to the second page. "Oh . . . this is about Bitty's mom."

"What?" he prompted.

When she didn't reply, he let her go and waited, drumming his fingers on his knee. Checking his fucking watch. Letting his leg bounce against the sofa.

Her eyes finally lifted. "It's so sad. It's . . . heartbreaking. He talks about all the things he used to do with Annalye when they were kids.

Sounds like a pretty perfect upbringing on that estate. Their parents worked for the landowners—it's been generations of the two families together. Everything changed, though, when Annalye met the male who was Bitty's father. Ruhn's respectful about it and doesn't give many details. But he says he never stopped thinking about his sister and he tried to find her numerous times. He didn't know for a while that they had even come up here to Caldwell."

Rhage rubbed his face. "You know, this would be so much easier if I could hate him."

"Would it . . . ?" Mary murmured. "I'm not so sure."

"He can't take care of her like we can."

Mary went to the last page. "Oh . . . my God . . ."

"What?" Okay, now he felt like going for his dagger. "What—"

"Look at this."

She turned the final sheet to him. And "Oh, my God" was right. Covering the white paper, there were incredibly detailed and beautiful pen-and-ink drawings of a big house, and fields . . . a little cabin . . . a close-up of a dog . . . a cat napping all curled in a ball.

"He's an artist," Mary breathed.

As Rhage let his eyes travel over the pictures, he wanted to hate everything about the letter and the dumb-ass fucking drawings. He wanted to take a shit all over those pages, rip them to shreds—hell, nail them to a tree trunk and put bullets into them until there was nothing but shreds left.

Except he couldn't.

Both his logic and his instincts were telling him that Ruhn was a good guy, a simple guy—which was not to say there was anything stupid happening with her uncle . . . just that there was an honest life of hard work being lived on his part. And yeah, the tragedy of that dead sister of his was only going to be eased if Ruhn could do right by his niece.

Mary's phone went off with a *bing!* and the two of them both reached for it on the sofa cushion—Mary won the race and didn't waste time opening whatever it was up.

"It's Marissa. They're still talking, Ruhn and Bitty. She says that . . . Bitty was really shy in the beginning, but is now asking questions. They're going to eat."

Yeah, 'cuz First Meal had been a no-go, even for him.

"It's going to be a long while," Mary concluded. "And it should be."

Rhage scrubbed his eyes. It was so weird. When Ruhn had turned up and turned out to be real, there had been a tearing in him, a ripping apart, a searing pain. And now, with each new piece of information, Rhage felt like Bitty was a ship going out to sea, disappearing first by feet and then by yards and soon by miles as she floated off, leaving him on the shore.

Now the emotions were settling into more of a pervasive sadness.

"Well, do you want to—"

His phone went off next, and as he looked at it, he frowned. "Fuck."

"What is it?"

As Mary glanced over at him, he jumped up. "Shit. There's an emergency downtown—listen, tell Marissa to call me when Bitty's ready—I've got to go, but I can break free."

Or at least he hoped he could.

"What is it?" Mary asked.

"Trainees trapped with slayers—and I want the brothers to stay with Bit and the uncle, she's more important."

"Be careful," his *shellan* said.

"Always." He bent down and kissed her. "You know it."

He hated leaving his mate there all alone, her eyes wide and scared. But there was no time to waste. He went upstairs, geared up, and then popped a window, dematerializing to the location that Axe had sent the SOS out from.

He'd been looking for a distraction.

Saving three recruits wasn't exactly what he'd been after, but he would take what he got.

Elise's heart was thundering against her sternum, beating so hard, it was a wonder the muscle didn't explode.

From behind Axe's huge shoulders, she could see the three *lessers* approaching, their bodies moving with deadly-smooth strides, their expressions cold and flat, utterly emotionless.

They had guns.

The female trainee—Elise couldn't remember her name, but she recognized her from the night she'd first met Axe—stepped into their paths with a gun up and a murderous expression on her face.

Elise couldn't imagine being that calm or that aggresive in a situation like this.

"Stop where you are," the female said. "Or I'll shoot you."

A fourth *lesser,* who seemed to come out of nowhere, just laughed. "Really, bitch. Do you actually know how to use that—"

Elise's entire body jumped as there was a *pop!* and the slayer fell to the ground.

That female had put a bullet right between its eyes.

"Holy shit," Elise breathed.

But that was the last time she had a chance to track anything. All at once, the drama went into overdrive—the three slayers rushed in, bullets flying everywhere and ricocheting around as she was spun to the left and shoved behind something big and metal.

Car? Dumpster?

No, it was a discarded meat locker the size of an SUV.

A split second later, Elise felt a lash on her shoulder, like someone had put a curling iron on her skin—but she couldn't worry about it as Axe jumped in front of her again, and Peyton pressed into her from the side—

"He's on top!" Peyton said.

What? she thought.

"Motherfucker!"

As Axe cursed, he angled his gun up to the heavens and pumped off more rounds—and then a body was falling on them, a body that leaked black blood and smelled like baby powder and spoiled milk.

"I'm out!" Axe said. And she took that to mean he had no more ammunition.

Someone cursed. More gunshots. Her ankle hurt now, too.

And then Peyton fell away. Just dropped off like a blanket falling from the side of a bed.

"Peyton!" she screamed as she turned.

Just as she was reaching out for him, that female soldier grabbed her by the back of her coat and hauled her to her feet.

"Can you shoot?"

Elise blinked, her vision going fuzzy. More bullets were whizzing by. God, where were the bullets coming from? And then she focused on the female. "You're bleeding! Y-y-y-you're—"

The slap came from the left and made a cracking impact on Elise's face. But it was like throwing a window open in a smoke-filled kitchen. She was suddenly able to concentrate on the soldier.

"Do you know how to shoot?" she was asked again.

"P-p-point and pull the trigger," Elise blurted.

"That's right."

Suddenly there was a heavy piece of metal in her palm. "Two hands. And only if you need to."

And then Elise was picked up and thrown.

As she was airborne, her hair whipping her face, her body totally numb, she had the absurd thought, How the fuck was this happening right now? How the holy fuck was she—

Bam!

She landed on her ass, her body slamming back against something else—it was a Dumpster this time. She'd been thrown behind the bar's Dumpster.

As she fought for her breath, her hands were shaking so badly they were a blur, but she was not going to drop the gun.

Looking out into the alley, she saw Axe going hand to hand with a slayer as the female stood over Peyton, who—oh, dear Lord—looked like he'd been hit in the head. So much blood—too much blood!

And the human police were coming—she could hear the sirens.

Except then the tide turned. From out of nowhere, the biggest vampire she had ever seen in her life materialized right in the middle of the alley. He was blond and dressed in black and he attacked like a demon, grabbing on to the slayer that Axe was trading punches with and pitching the enemy against the side of the building like it was a doll.

Axe moved on to the next, and so did what had to be a Brother.

More *lessers* showed up, having obviously been called, but between Axe and the Brother and that female trainee, heads were snapped, and black blood that stank flowed, and bodies lined the pavement—

Right as things were winding down, just before the cops arrived . . . something caught her eye.

A subtle flash.

That *lesser* who had been shot in the head, the one behind the meat locker where they had started out, was still moving, and it had raised its gun up, pointing the muzzle at the Brother.

"He's going to shoot!" Elise screamed.

Everything went into a slow crawl, and Elise watched in horror as the Brother turned his upper body in her direction—which put him directly in line with the shooter.

And the *lesser* pulled its trigger, emptying bullets into that huge chest. *Pop! Pop! Pop!*

Someone screamed—probably her—as the blond-haired Brother

threw up both of his hands and fell back onto the pavement. And still the slayer discharged its weapon.

Fuck this shit, Elise decided.

Without thinking, spurred by an aggression that was as uncharacteristic as it was manic, Elise jumped out from behind her cover, ran across the alley, and got as close as she could to the *lesser*.

Then she pointed . . . and fucking shot.

Blam! Blam! Blam!

Two hands, arms outstretched, eyes and body steady, she let the gun do the talking, black blood splattering back on her as she kept closing in and shooting and closing in and . . .

She didn't know when to stop.

Wait, she couldn't stop.

Even when the gun was no longer talking, when the clip or whatever you called it was empty, even when the slayer was so bullet-ridden it was a sieve, she stayed where she was, standing over it, that gun muzzle pointed at her target, her body trembling so badly her teeth were chattering, her knees knocking in their sockets, her breath sawing up and down her throat.

And her forefinger squeezing the trigger—

"Elise?" Axe said from a distance so far off she could barely hear him. "Elise . . . sweetheart . . . I'm right behind you."

"Wh-wh-what—"

"I'm just going to take the gun, 'kay? Let me have the gun—no, don't turn toward me. Stay where you are."

His hands traveled gently down her arms and carefully released the weapon from her cramped fingers.

As soon as it was out of her grip, she turned to him and burst into tears. "I tried to save him, the Brother, I tried to—"

"We've got to go—"

Elise looked past his biceps at the dead body of the Brother: The blond-haired fighter was lying flat on his back, his arms out straight in a T formation, his heavy boots lolling to the sides.

"I was trying to save him, oh, God—"

"Elise, we need to go before the humans get here—"

Across the way, the female soldier picked Peyton up in her arms. "He's not doing well. Where do we go—"

Human police cars screeched to a halt at the head of the block, humans swarming free of the vehicles and pointing down to where they were in the shadows.

"We can't leave him—"

"Put down your weapons," came out from a speaker system. "Put down your weapons now or we will shoot to kill—"

And then things got truly surreal. Like something out of a movie, the Brother's torso rose up from the pavement. And he looked down his chest, cursed, and said something that sounded like, "I just had Fritz buy this fucking thing."

Then he reached into what seemed to be his own flesh, picked out a bullet, and flicked it across the alley.

That was when he seemed to notice what was happening with the police cars.

"Fucking humans, not again." He got to his feet and winced, but seemed otherwise fine. "You two, take the wounded and the female and go that way." He pointed to the far end of the alley. "Manny should be coming—there he is."

At that precise moment, a large, boxy vehicle pulled across the other end of the lane, where the humans were not.

"Go now!"

At the barking command, Axe grabbed her hand and started running. And the female with Peyton did the same, the four of them hightailing it down the slushy way to what turned out to be some kind of fancy van.

Just as its wide door slid open and she was about to jump in, Elise looked back. Flashes were flooding the sides of the buildings, and there were popping noises, but not from bullets being discharged.

The Brother was stabbing the slayers back to the Omega, she thought with awe. Holy crap, was she actually seeing this?

"Get in," Axe said as he gave her a shove into a well-lit interior.

He followed and then dragged the door to a close.

"Hang on, folks!" somebody yelled from up front. "This ride is going to be bumpy—stay on the floor."

There was a roar and a lurch, and then they were moving. And Elise collapsed back against Axe. How had . . . what had . . .

So fast. Her mind couldn't comprehend how fast it had all gone down. It was like . . . one minute they were walking up to Peyton inside the cigar bar, and the next she was in an action movie, except it wasn't a film set at all. It was real.

Looking across the way, Elise blinked away tears. The female fighter had Peyton in her lap, and had braced herself against a mounted table in the center of the space—this was an ambulance, Elise realized. A massive ambulance with all kinds of supplies tacked to its walls or packed in glass-fronted cabinets mounted on the sides.

"Is he alive?" Elise said.

The female didn't look up. "Yeah. At the moment."

There was so much blood. Oh, dearest Virgin Scribe . . . the blood . . .

But at least they seemed to be going even faster—hopefully to someone who could operate in here, Elise thought. And as they banged and crashed, things rattling all around them, Axe kept her from bowling-balling it, his powerful arms locked around her waist, one of his legs braced against the stand of that operating platform.

"How did he do that?" Elise mumbled. "How did the Brother . . . survive?"

"Bulletproof vest," Axe said grimly. "He must have been wearing a bulletproof vest—and the damn thing saved his life."

FORTY-FOUR

xe's adrenaline didn't stop flowing until Dr. Manello's mobile surgical unit pulled into some kind of downtown garage and the surgeon opened the sliding door.

And even then, Axe was on a hair trigger. Natch.

As he got out, he looked around at a dim, industrial interior that smelled like oil, gas, and old metal—and tried to pretend he wasn't losing his fucking mind.

He couldn't believe that not only had Elise gotten ambushed with the rest of them, but that she had discharged about a pound and a half of lead into a *lesser* who had a gun—and worse, it was all his own fucking fault. If he and Peyton hadn't been going at it, playing dick toss in that bar, the three of them, and then Novo, and then Rhage, never would have ended up outside, exposed, and wrong-place-wrong-timing it with all those slayers.

And yeah, then her fucking cousin, Peyton the Golden Boy, never would have gotten popped in the head. Plus, what if Rhage didn't get out of that human cluster-fuck okay? What if the cops got him or another *lesser* or—

That open-ended nightmare was solved when a side door got thrown wide and the stench of vampire blood and *lesser* death wafted in.

"How is Peyton?" the Brother Rhage said as he came into the light thrown by the surgical unit. "And what do I need to do to help."

As Rhage passed by, he clapped Axe on the shoulder in acknowledgment, but focused on Dr. Manello, who had laid Peyton out on the operating table and was hooking up all kinds of shit to him. Before there were any answers, Doc Jane came in through that same door. She was in surgical scrubs, just like Manello, and she was not interested in anyone other than her patient.

Inside the van, Novo was standing against the far wall with her arms crossed over her chest and her head down. Blood was dripping off her chin. She'd been cut there. Also on the forearm.

Someone's phone started to ring.

"That's me," Elise said next to him.

Snapping to attention, Axe put his arm around her as she fumbled with the thing and put it up to her ear.

"Troy? No, I'm so sorry, I can't talk right now. Tomorrow? Sure. What? Well . . . I've got . . . a friend who's in trouble. We're at the ER right now. No, it'll be fine. I'll call you tomorrow. Bye."

She hung up and leaned against him as if the interruption had never happened. Which made it less likely he'd stalk across Caldwell to find her professor and black-eye him on principle.

Okay, fine. He wouldn't do that. At least not in a world outside of his jealous streak.

And why the fuck was he thinking like this right now?

"Is he going to be all right?" Elise asked nobody in particular.

"We just have to wait," Axe heard himself reply. "We just have to pray."

After all, he didn't particularly like Peyton, but that didn't mean he wanted the bastard to go brain dead or into an early grave. Especially if Elise was even tangentially involved.

After a little while, Rhage ducked his head out of the SUV. "Listen, I want you two to head home. There's nothing you can do here. We'll let you know what happens with him, okay?"

"Is he . . ." Elise just let the sentence drift as if she recognized its futility.

"We'll do everything we can for him." Rhage looked over at Axe. "You were a huge asset again, son."

"It's my fault."

"How you figure that? You send up a flare or some shit? Put an ad in Craigslist for your buddy to get shot in the head? Don't think so. G'on now, get her home and you do the same." Rhage then met Elise's eyes. "And you were amazing. You really showed up when you had to."

"I don't know how to shoot a gun," she mumbled. "I've never shot one before."

"Well, you have now. And I'm sorry you had to learn the skill."

With his head thumping, Axe led her over to the door and opened the way out. He stepped through first, and as he glanced around, he saw that they were close to the river under the bridges, the highway elevated up on pylons, the sound of the occasional car and truck above echoing around.

"You go now," he said to her. "And I'm right behind you. To your house."

She nodded in a way that broke his heart. And then she closed her eyes.

It took her at least a minute, maybe two, to ghost out.

And then he was on her tail, traveling through the cold night in a loose collection of molecules that seemed to represent better who he was as opposed to the more organized, corporeal version of himself.

Scattered was his very definition.

When he re-formed, it was right beside her, something made pos-sible because of the blood they'd shared.

As she took his hand and started for the front door, he pulled her to a stop. "You have blood on your clothes. Is there a back way we can use?"

Elise looked down at herself like she had forgotten what clothes were at all, much less what she was currently wearing and what condi-tion it was in.

"Funny," she whispered. "This was how it all started."

"I'm sorry?"

She looked up at him. "With you. I walked into the house through the front door by mistake and that's how my father saw me. And if I hadn't done that . . . I never would have met you."

Yeah, and how's it working for you, he thought grimly. *You shot a lesser, nearly got killed yourself, and you're covered with the stains of war.*

"Tell me where the back door is," he said in a grim voice. "And I'll take us in."

There was nothing Rhage could do.

As Doc Jane and Manny went to work on Peyton, stitching up the streak by his temple, assessing his concussion, trying to fix his too-low blood pressure, Rhage was pretty fucking tired of being in situations where he couldn't do shit.

He glanced at Novo. The female trainee hadn't moved the whole time. It was as if she had turned to stone. "You want to go?"

"No."

In other circumstances, he might have argued, but she was tough. No matter what happened, she could handle it—

His phone went off and he grabbed for it. "Oh, shit . . . I gotta go," he said as he read the text. "It's Mary."

"We're safe," Manny said.

"I'll send some people over."

"That'd be good."

Rhage was out the side door and dematerializing a split second later. As he re-formed in front of the Audience House, he didn't think twice about running up the front walkway and shoving open the door—

Lot of people in the foyer and everyone turned to him—

Complete. Fucking. Chaos.

Mary gasped. Bitty yelled. Somebody started cursing—V, by the sound of it. And then his females were coming at him, talking a mile a minute, pointing, gesturing to his chest.

He couldn't fathom what they were going on about.

"Hold up," he said, putting his palms out. "How was it with Ruhn—are you okay, Bitty?"

"You're shot! You're bleeding!"

"Huh?"

Except then he looked down at himself. Sure enough, there were bullet holes through the front of his shirt and his leather jacket; there was bright red blood on his hands and all over his clothes . . . and black *lesser* blood dripping off his daggers, which he'd restrapped.

Oh. Right. That whole, you know, fighting thing.

"I'm fine," he said. "I'm—"

"I'm calling Doc Jane now!" Mary said as she went for her phone.

"No!" He put his hand out again. "They're operating. And I'm not hurt—"

"I just lived through you getting shot in the chest! Why are you still standing! Rhage—"

He stepped in front of his mate and ripped his shirt clean down the middle.

As buttons went flying and then skipped across the marble floor, he exposed what used to be his shiny new bulletproof vest. But that now had more in common with Swiss cheese.

Rhage pounded on his chest. "Kevlar." He picked another bullet out and let the thing fall to the floor—where it obligingly bounced along to play with all those buttons. "I've been wearing them since I got shot, you know, the last time. I mean, yes, we agreed you'd stay with her after I die, but there's no reason to rush that."

All at once, he became aware of Ruhn standing in the far corner, his eyes missing nothing.

Rhage cleared his throat. "Or, you know, there *was* no reason to rush that."

There was a pause. And then Mary and Bitty were on him, his females hugging him and talking a mile a minute, nervous energy being burned off, the fact that he was sweaty and bloodstained not seeming to matter to them in the slightest.

"Z," he said over Bitty's head as she poked her fingers into the holes. "You need to get down to the garage. They're unprotected and operating on Peyton. And V, I'm pretty sure they could use another set of hands."

There was conversation at that point, and someone suggested Ruhn head off to wherever he was staying.

And that totally changed the vibe. Bitty turned to her uncle and so did Mary.

"When do I see you again?" Bitty asked with her customary directness.

"Tomorrow night?" Ruhn said in his quiet way.

"Okay."

At least they didn't hug, Rhage thought uncharitably as the male bowed, murmured a few words to Marissa and Mary, and then walked to the door—

"Wait," the little girl said.

Without warning, she burst forward . . . and embraced Ruhn.

It was just the way she had done it when she had been getting to know Rhage and Mary: Fast as a blink, but the first sign she was opening her heart.

Rhage felt tears spear into his eyes. More than any detail of the meeting, more than any he said/she said, this-was-discussed, that-was-explained, Bitty's actions told him exactly how her time with Ruhn had gone.

Funny, when he and Mary had been in the process of adopting the girl, Rhage had gotten flashes of insight that things were happening between the three of them, were changing, were going in a certain direction. Like his showing her the GTO and her liking the way it smelled . . . he and Mary taking her to T.G.I. Friday's in Lucas Square and him explaining that it was okay if they had to leave if it was too much for her to handle . . . that trip to the ice cream parlor . . .

He was getting exactly one of those flashes now.

Except instead of it showing him an open road . . .

. . . it was all about a brick wall.

FORTY-FIVE

Peyton woke up with the worst headache he'd ever had.

But he didn't give a shit about the pain.

There was a wrist at his lips, and the most amazing blood he'd ever had was filling his mouth, blazing down his throat, pooling in his gut. And the more he took, the more some instinct for survival ordered him to drink and drink and then keep on going.

It wasn't until he opened his eyes that he found out whose it was.

Novo was standing over him, her face drawn and pale, her shoulders and arms bare, whatever jacket she had been wearing gone.

Were they moving? he thought as something bumped and he felt it throughout his body—

All at once, the argument in the cigar bar came back to him, he and Axe going at it hardcore, Elise running out after them, Novo showing up . . . the *lessers*—

Releasing the seal of his lips, he mumbled, "Dead? God . . . Rhage dead?"

"Only *lessers*," she said, before forcing her wrist back at him.

He exhaled and returned to the drinking. And after what could have been years or at least hours, but was probably only ten minutes or so, he went lax, the floating, blissful feeling of satiation working to calm him better than any amount of morphine.

It was the most perfect high.

But he couldn't get lost in the delicious sensation. Not with that female standing over him as she was.

"I'm gonna be fine." Or at least, that was what he meant to say. It didn't seem to come out right. Either that or his hearing was going.

"What?" she asked, leaning in as if proximity might work as well as a Google translator set to stupid.

He cleared his throat and forced his brain to come back online. "Elise okay? Axe?"

"Both fine."

"You?"

She held her arms out and moved around in a circle . . . and not for the first time, he noticed she was a damn fine female, if a little intimidating. She was just so tough, that body filed down to all its hard, muscular edges.

As Peyton started to become aroused, he took that as a good sign.

"I'm glad nothing hurt you," he said roughly.

"Are you getting emotional on me?"

"No, you're turning me on."

She seemed nonplussed for a second. Then she started to glare at him—which for them was probably progress. As in, things getting back to normal.

"Are you kidding me?"

He shrugged. "You're an attractive female. Surely I'm not the first male to tell you that. And what can I say, I've always had a healthy regard for the fairer sex."

She threw her head back and laughed. But it was not a happy sound. "Let me get this straight. You and I are in the Brotherhood's mobile surgical van, on our way to the training center because you

were shot and now have a tube in your head to reduce brain swelling . . . and you're coming on to me?"

"My gray matter isn't the only thing getting bigger."

"You're like the indestructible slut, aren't you."

"You know, to most people, *slut* is an insult." He tried to lift his
hand to make the point. And failed. "I personally take it as a compli-
ment. Shows commitment to my work."

"Your work?"

Considering everything that had happened tonight, they might as
well spend the trip to the training center arguing: He was rattling
around inside his skin, and that energy needed an outlet—and shit
knew she could give as good as she got.

"Sure," he said. "I work at being with the females. Practice makes
perfect and all."

When she just re-crossed her arms over her chest and leaned back
against the wall again, he frowned. "If we're moving, shouldn't you be
sitting down?"

"Yes, but I don't want to."

"Far be it from me to suggest reasonable behavior."

"That's the first intelligent thing you've said."

"Since I've regained consciousness?"

"Since I've known you."

He started laughing, but it made his head hurt, so he stopped. "Tell
me something . . . where were you last night?"

"I'm sorry?"

"Do I need to speak more slowly? I'm the one with the cracked
skull."

"What the hell are you talking about?"

For a moment, Peyton entertained the possibility that he'd had a
stroke and he had slipped into aphasia. But no, he was speaking correctly.

"I called you last night."

"No, you didn't."

"Mmm-hmm." He went to nod his head, but the stinging pain stopped him. "I sure did."

"Not from your phone, you didn't."

Oh, right. "Shit, it was on Elise's. She had to leave it with me so she could go fuck Axe."

Yes, he sounded bitter. Which was a little rich, considering the guy had probably helped save his life tonight.

Take out the *probably.*

Novo frowned. "Axe was with me."

Now Peyton was the one pulling a blank. "I'm sorry, what?"

"Axe took me to The Keys."

Peyton actually tried to sit up. And as he gasped, Novo put a hand on his chest and forced him back down.

"Will you stop moving?" she ordered.

"What the hell is he doing taking you to The Keys? No female should be going there."

A bump in the road made everything hurt on him, as if the asphalt itself was taking her side.

Oh, and you want to talk about a death stare? If he hadn't already been flat on his back, her glare would have blown him out of his loafers.

"I asked Axe to take me there, for one thing. And I had sex with a woman, so yes, there are females at that club."

Peyton blinked a couple of times. Then pulled his laconic mask into place. "I didn't know that was your thing."

"I like women, females, men, and males."

"And Axe."

"Yeah, and Axe."

The tips of Peyton's fangs started to tingle. "Well, I bet you two had a great time. Before he went home to my cousin." He lifted his hand to rub his face, but the IV in his arm prevented him from moving as freely as he'd like. "I told him not to go near her—and before you start lecturing me, no, it's not because he's just a civilian and she's an aristocrat. Elise isn't like us. She's . . . clean. She's better than we are. She deserves respect—like Paradise does."

"Oh, riiiiiight. Your progressive paradigm of females. And I keep forgetting which of the two buckets you've put me in."

"Spare me, Novo, okay? You know what I mean. Paradise and Elise wouldn't be caught dead in a place like that, much less banging randoms and fellow trainees for shits and giggles."

"I'd like to remind you, Paradise is, currently, banging a fellow trainee."

"Yeah, but that's a relationship. Paradise was a virgin. Elise was, too. Goddamn it—how's she ever going to get mated now?"

Novo stared at him for a long time. "You know what I find fascinating?"

"What? And if it's the color of my eyes, I feel the same about yours—"

"How you can be such a sexist, judgmental pig. You have fucked twenty or thirty females since I've known you—and don't deny it, I've been out in the clubs and watched you go off with them. And yet you're saying a female shouldn't, or even can't, do it, too. Tell me, does that double standard you're sporting not bother you at all? Like, not even a little?"

"Females are different." He shrugged. "That's just the way it is."

Novo stared off somewhere over his head—and he had the distinct impression that in her mind, she was finishing off the job that slayer had started on him.

"No," she muttered, "actually, assholes are just assholes, no matter what's going on between their legs."

Across town, in a totally different zip code of Caldwell, Elise invited Axe into her bedroom and closed the door quietly behind them both.

"We made it," she said as she went directly to her bathroom. "Without anyone . . ."

The moment she saw her reflection in the mirror, she stopped and put her hands up to her cheeks. God . . . the blood.

Axe stepped in beside her and shook his head. "I didn't want you ever to see anything like that. Much less get stuck in the middle of it."

"Is that what your life is like? Going out there . . . every night . . . getting almost killed until some *lesser* finishes the job?"

"Don't think like that. You can't."

"How can I not?" She turned to him and found herself wanting to touch him all over, as if there were bullet holes and other injuries that had somehow been missed on him. "How can I forget?"

As if Axe knew what she needed from him, he put his mouth to hers and kissed her deeply. And all at once, she was consumed by the need to have him, her hands rough as she stripped his clothes and her own, the stained pile on the floor left where it landed as they went to her shower.

Whereas his was a simple stall with a tub bottom, hers was an entire enclosure you walked into, six shower heads raining down water that could be programmed to specific temperature preferences. And there was also almost no waiting at all for the warmth.

But she didn't need the luxury. Not to be with him, now or ever.

After they soaped each other up and down, and rinsed away the gruesome souvenirs of the night, they left the bathroom and she turned off all the lights except one in the far corner. Lying down in her big bed, under her soft sheets, they made love quietly with him on top of her, their eyes meeting as their bodies were joined together. She found her release first, scoring his back with her nails—and he soon followed, his hips jerking and bucking against her, his powerful orgasm filling her up and teeing off another for her.

There was no lingering closeness afterward, though.

"I need to go," he whispered. "I can't stay here."

"Sure you can. My father never comes in my room."

"I don't want to take even a small risk of getting you in trouble. I already nearly got you killed tonight."

As he got out of the warm nest their bodies' exertions had created, she stood up and pulled on her pink bathrobe—and thought it was a shame to have the stained things he'd worn during the fight put on over his now-clean skin. But he didn't seem to care.

All too soon, he was standing in front of her, rubbing her shoulders. "I can't believe how brave you were tonight."

"Brave? Are you kidding me? To use a vernacular expression, I was crapping in my pants."

"You walked right up to a *lesser*, shooting the whole time. If I hadn't been fucking terrified for you, I would have been totally aroused."

She smiled a little, but it was hard to hold on to. "When can I see you again?"

"Tomorrow night. And before you ask, yeah, definitely. I'll let you know the second I hear anything about Peyton."

"Please." She frowned, thinking back to the cigar bar. "I'm sorry he was so disrespectful to you. He can be . . . old-fashioned and difficult sometimes, but he's not a bad person."

"I don't want him to die. And I don't want trouble from him. He just needs to stay out of my way and I'll stay out of his."

Elise nodded and then went into a kind of stasis. She didn't want him to go, but knew he didn't feel comfortable staying—and she couldn't blame him.

"Shit," Axe breathed. "Come here."

Safe in his arms, she relaxed and held him close, feeling his warmth and strength.

"I wish there was something I could do to help you," he whispered as he rubbed her back. "I feel like I'm bad for you."

"No, you're not."

After a while, she said, "Actually . . ." Pulling away from him, she took a deep breath. "There is something you could do for me."

"Name it," he replied. "And it's yours."

FORTY-SIX

The following evening, Rhage and Mary let Bitty go to the Audience House again to see her uncle.

It wasn't any easier, Mary decided. Nope. Not something you got used to—especially not after Rhage's getting shot.

And as the Mercedes took off down the hill once more, she and Rhage went back into the house and stalled out in the foyer. The mansion was largely quiet, First Meal being cleaned up, the Brothers going on about their nights, the *shellans*, too.

"I kind of feel left behind," she said as she went over and sat on the lower step of the staircase. "You know, our lives are ending in a way. Everyone else is going on. I mean, I realize that's sadness talking, but it's how I feel."

Rhage came across and joined her. "I'm with you."

She glanced at him. "I'm so glad you were wearing that vest last night. But why didn't you tell me?"

"It's just an addition in gear. You know, after that last chest wound—that was too close a call, even for me. And with Bitty around . . ." He cleared his throat. "So, yeah, I asked Fritz to get me some. I tried a number of them out. And the one I had on last night is my favorite. Worked like a charm, too."

"Are you going to order another one?"

He shrugged. "Guess so."

Mary put her arm around his shoulders—well, not all the way around because of his size. "Bitty was so glad you're okay."

"She's a sweet kid."

As Rhage looked at his hands and pretend-picked at his clipped nails, Mary felt a now-familiar mourning that she recognized she was going to have to live with for the rest of her life. There would be times when it wouldn't be this acute, she told herself. Times when it was even worse. But it was now her companion, a scar on her insides that was always going to be there.

She didn't have to ask Rhage to know that it would be the same for him.

"Do you have any regrets?" she asked softly.

"About taking her in?"

"Yes."

He was quiet for a long time, and she studied his handsome profile. His blond hair needed a trim. His cheeks seemed hollower than usual. And the grim light in those beautiful blue eyes made him look so much older.

As she rubbed his back, she felt the beast following her touch as she passed over his muscle shirt, the tattooed representation shifting to stay with her.

"I don't know," he said. "This is pretty rough. This is really hard. But no, I would still have wanted to take her in. If all I'm supposed to get is two months of being her father to tide her over to her rightful home? Then I'll be grateful for what I was given. I'd rather me suffer for the next thousand years over not having her than for her to have been alone in the world, getting those arms and legs fixed, wondering where she was going to end up. That trade-off's worth it to me."

Mary laid her head on his biceps. "That's how I feel, too."

"I owe you an apology, by the way."

"About what?"

"I should have told you about what they were going to do to Bitty's limbs. I didn't want to concern you, and I was hoping it was all going to be okay."

"Oh, God . . . not to worry. Water under the bridge."

"Yeah."

They sat there for oh, so long, the sounds of conversation in the kitchen and a distant vacuum and Wrath up in his study talking to someone trickling down.

Eventually, Boo, the black cat, padded by, the animal curling into a sit right in front of them.

"Have you got something to tell us, Boo?" Mary murmured. "We could use some good news."

A couple of meows were released, but they were hard to translate. And then Boo kept on going, attending to very important feline business, clearly.

"Did you talk to Marissa about how it was going to work?" Rhage asked. "You know . . . and when?"

Mary took a deep breath. "A social worker went down tonight to check Ruhn's cottage again. There will have to be regular welfare visits there, but V did all the due diligence brilliantly. Oh—and it turns out Ruhn's employer has access to schooling for Bitty. They're totally willing to help Ruhn get her into a program. That would be fantastic."

"She won't know anyone."

"She didn't know anyone when she came into this house. But she adapted."

"They won't know what she likes to eat. Her ice cream—she's in a mint chocolate chip phase now."

"She'll tell them." Mary rubbed her eyes. "I'll help her pack up her things. I think it's best that we don't draw it out longer than we have to. The transition is going to be hard enough on her without her having to stay in limbo."

"I'm not staying on that third floor. The second she leaves, I'm moving us back down to our old room."

"I think that's a good idea." Mary cracked her neck. "Poor Trez. He's going to be yo-yoed again."

"He doesn't seem to care about much right now."

"No."

And indeed, Mary found herself struggling not to fall into a similar despondency.

"I'm going to go in to work tonight," she forced herself to say. "I don't feel like it, but I'm going to do it."

"Me, too. There's a meeting at twelve midnight to talk to the class about what went down last night."

"Did Peyton survive?"

"Yeah, Manny sent out a text to all of us—that bastard is a brilliant surgeon. The brain swelling is down, stats are fine. The kid's not cleared to work out or fight for a couple more nights, but he'll be good to go soon enough. Novo saved his life."

"I'm so glad everyone came through."

"It was a close call."

Even though it was time for Mary to leave, she didn't move. She just sat next to her male—and when he reached out and took her hand, she went back to resting her head against his shoulder.

Being left behind was a special kind of loss.

• • •

After Elise drew on her coat and wrapped a scarf around her throat, she opened a window in her bathroom by the tub and dematerialized to where Axe was waiting for her downtown, their blood tie helping her triangulate him in an instant, even though they had agreed on the address.

As she re-formed, he was staring up at the condominium building like he was assessing its structural integrity.

"Allishon was on the fourteenth floor," Elise explained after they kissed hello. "The front door to the apartment is locked, but maybe the terrace is open?"

"Do you have any idea which side of the building she faced out of? This place has hundreds of units."

She thought about where the elevator had emptied out in the hall. The direction the hallway had run. Which way she had gone.

"Facing the Hudson. On that side."

"Let's go around."

The two of them walked to the far edge of the high-rise, squeezed through some evergreen bushes, and whispered down its flank until they reached the river-view side.

Craning her neck, she had to hold her hair out of her face as gusts blew against her back. "Almost all the lights are on in the units." She counted floors. "But see? There are two that are out on the fourteenth level—assuming they started the count with the lobby being the ground floor. One of them has to be it."

"I don't care if we have to try fifty of the damn things. If we attract any human attention, I'll just scrub their memories."

Elise nodded. "You first?"

"No, you. I want to guard you when you're on the ground."

With a nod, she closed her eyes . . . and went flying in her molecular form, coalescing herself on the terrace of the darkened apartment that was three units in from the end. Axe followed right along, materializing by her side.

There was a sliding glass door and she went over and grasped the handle. Bracing herself to be denied, she—

Yup. "It's locked."

Axe cupped his hands and looked inside. "Seems pretty average human stuff. Not a place for a vampire to hide out."

"Next door?"

"Next door."

They proceeded over to the other unit, and her first thought as she leaned into the slider was, No way was this a vampire apartment. Even with the darkness inside, she had the impression the drapery was white and diaphanous—nothing that would keep out the sun.

"There's a bloody handprint here," Axe said in a grim voice. "On the outside jamb."

As she glanced across to where he was pointing, Elise's heart started to hammer—and then she closed her eyes. After a moment, she reached out, took hold of the handle—

The slider pulled free without any problem at all, as if the glass were almost relieved to be getting out of the way.

"I can smell blood," Elise said roughly. "It's faint . . . and it's Allishon's."

Stepping over the threshold, that first impression of white everything gained traction. Even the carpet was the color of a sheet of paper. And as her eyes adjusted, she focused on the bed across the way. The sheets were gone. So were the pillows. There was nothing but a headboard and a mattress.

"You want me to turn a light on?" Axe asked.

"Yes, please."

Still, she jumped when illumination flooded the bedroom.

Oh . . . blessed Virgin Scribe. There were stains on that mattress, most of them at the top of it, by the headboard. And there were footprints that were brown on the carpet. Another brown smudge on the doorjamb.

It was as if the violence had been filtered through the passage of time, drained of most, but not all, of its characteristics.

The remnants were more than enough.

Wrapping her arms around herself even though it wasn't cold, Elise walked out of the bedroom and down a short hall. The living room was also done in white with those same filmy drapes and a set of all-white furniture. The galley kitchen was unremarkable, the counters clean, nothing really in the cabinets. The refrigerator was empty.

No blood to be seen. But that was no relief, really.

"She came here to do drugs," Elise said to Axe as he loomed in the hall. "This was her party house, apparently. And one night . . . she brought back someone. . . ."

Not just someone, she reminded herself. Anslam. One of their own, and not only because he was a vampire, but because he was a high-bred member of the aristocracy.

Had been, at any rate.

And now they were both dead.

Elise took her time going around and around, pacing through the limited floor plan, even though she didn't know exactly what she was trying to make sense of. It was, she supposed, yet another example of how having all the education in the world about emotions didn't necessarily help when your own were raw and damaged.

Heading back into the bedroom, she went for the closet. She had to. It was almost like closing the loop, her stepping into the walk-in and looking at . . . emptiness.

There was nothing but a couple of jackets hanging off the rods and a formal gown pooling on the floor.

Allishon must have come here after one of the *glymera*'s grand events. Stripped her mask of civilization off. And proceeded to . . .

"So sad," Elise murmured as she went over and picked up the red swath of satin.

It wasn't a fancy dress, though. It turned out to be a cloak, one that had beautiful trim and buttons of mother-of-pearl—

As she went to hang it up on a hanger, something knocked her in the leg.

"Ow." She looked through the folds, wondering what was hanging off the cloak—or perhaps in a hidden pocket. "Okay, that hurt—"

Elise frowned as she took out a large piece of black metal from the lining. It was oddly shaped and heavy . . . kind of like a key, but not really.

"Did you find something?" Axe asked from behind her.

"I don't know." She held the thing out. "What do you think this is?"

When he didn't answer, she glanced at him and then rolled the object over in her palm. "Is it some kind of self-defense weapon? It isn't like there's a blade in here or . . . maybe it's a key, except not to any door I've ever seen."

"I don't know. But I think we should go."

"Yes."

She was tempted to take whatever it was with her. But she didn't want to have to explain, if she was found with the object, why she had gone to Allishon's and nosed around.

Putting the weight back in the pocket of that cloak, she stepped out of the closet and shut the walk-in's door.

Going over to a stuffed chair, she sat down and stared at the bed. "Thank you for coming with me."

She was acutely aware of Axe standing by the sliding glass door they'd come in through, his big body taking up nearly all of the slider's expanse.

"I really appreciate it." She shook her head as she imagined what had happened in the room. "I guess . . . you know, I had to come here."

"Yeah."

"I think I can let her go now. I've taken this as far as I can—this is the dead end that means stop for me. I just have to mourn her in my own way. Maybe I'll even do some version of a Fade ceremony for her." She took a deep breath. "It's funny, I feel closer to her now than I did when she was alive—and all mourning is private, isn't it. We all do it in our own ways for our dead. And she was mine. Close or not, she was my blood and nothing will change that."

Axe stayed quiet, but that was probably because he didn't know the right thing to say—and she could understand that. Except then he gave her something more important than words.

He came over to her, kneeling down and reaching out his arms.

As she went into him, up against him, she sighed with gratitude.

Sometimes, you didn't need the right syllables.

You just needed the right person.

FORTY-SEVEN

"So you don't mind if I go to your house?" Elise asked a little while later.

She and Axe were back down on the street, the apartment shut up again, the memories of having walked through those rooms stained on Elise's brain forever—even as a fragile peace began taking root in her heart.

"Axe?" she prompted into the bitterly cold wind.

Her male shook his head like he was trying to clear his own thoughts of where they'd been. "I'm sorry. What?"

"Are you sure you're okay with my going back to your place? I promise I'm just going to sit in front of the fire and probably fall asleep."

"I want you there," he said, tucking a strand of hair behind her ear. "I like the idea of you in front of my fire. And my meeting shouldn't last too long."

"I'm so glad Peyton's okay and resting at home."

"Me, too."

"Thanks again for coming with me."

"Anything for you."

Axe kissed her, and took his time about it. Then he stepped back. "Let me get you to the cottage safe, and then I'll take off. I've got to be at the meeting point in five minutes."

She hurried away, and so did he, and then he was escorting her into the house—and insisting that he get the fire going for her even though it meant he was going to be late.

"It's going to get down to zero tonight," he said as he started stacking hardwood on the lit kindling. "All that Canada air coming south and turning us into Popsicles."

She put her hands up to her wind-burned cheeks. "It was really windy downtown, too. Hey, listen, I can do that."

"I know."

Soon enough, the flames were snap-crackle-and-popping and he was disappearing into the rear of the cottage.

"I'm locking this back door," he yelled out from the kitchen. "And I want you to lock the front one after I leave."

As he returned to the living room, she was already sitting in front of the hearth, but she got up again. "Absolutely."

"And call me if you see anything."

"I will."

"My extra gun is under that sofa cushion, right there. Loaded and the safety's off."

"I'm not shooting anything again. Or at least not for a very long time and only if it's a snake in my car. Now, will you go? You're going to miss the bus—and yes," she drawled, "I'll be naked when you come back."

Axe let out a growl. "Okay, there's an incentive."

A quick kiss and he was out the door—and yelling, "Lock up! Or I'm not leaving!"

She laughed and went over, turning the dead bolt. "Locked! Go!"

Elise went back and sat before the fire, tucking her legs up tight and linking her arms. In the peaceful solitude, she thought about Troy and how much she was looking forward to them starting that seminar after New Year's. He'd been so understanding when she'd told him that as much as she liked him, she had just started to see somebody, so there could be no dating between them. He had almost seemed relieved, explaining that it was probably for the best, given their professional association.

So all was good there.

And Axe was going to get her back and forth to the classes safely. She was even excited to have him see her teach—

A gust of wind hit the side of the cottage, whistling through the shutters and making the eaves moan. When another hit, she turned around and looked behind her. She felt like she was being watched, but . . . no.

There was no one around.

As a third battering gust of wind howled, she could swear she felt the chill inside. But maybe that was because her brain was bouncing between the actual violence she had witnessed the night before in that alley . . . and the representations of violence she had seen at Allishon's.

Even with her coat on, she got cold.

Axe had stoked the fire perfectly, though, and at least the front of her was warm. But she sure could use . . .

Getting up, she went over to the chair by the front door. There was a nice heavy throw draped over the back, and as she picked it up, it smelled like Axe's body. Perfect.

Halfway on the return trip to the fire, something dropped out of its folds, and she bent down to—

At first, Elise couldn't believe what she was looking at.

So much so, that instead of picking the object up, she knelt down next to it.

A piece of metal. Painted black. In an odd shape that was kind of like a key, but not really.

Her heart started pounding and she looked around, which was ridiculous. Like any of the furniture or those banked flames were going to help her reconcile the issue?

Which was the fact that not more than fifteen minutes ago, give or take, she had looked at Axe and asked him what this "key" was—and he had told her he didn't know?

Letting the weight of the fabric fall to the floor, she flattened the expanse out . . . and was entirely unsurprised to find that it was a cloak. Just like Allishon's—

There was a large bulge on one side, and she ran her hands over it, wondering if she wanted to go any further with this. But of course, she had to. Heart pounding, she reached inside and—

With a curse, she dropped the mask of a skull. The thing was evil looking, realistic to the point of nightmare, hinged so that he could talk while wearing it.

Her hands shook as she put the horror back. And then, bending down low, she breathed in deep—and smelled Axe . . . along with some other things.

That made her want to throw up.

Images and memories filtered through her brain: of the two of them together, talking downstairs in that cellar; of him smiling at her for the first time; of him kissing her outside of that steakhouse; of their bodies in front of this very fire.

Maybe there was some kind of confusion or . . . an explanation for why he'd lied to her.

Surely there had to be.

Folding the cloak back together, she stared at the metal object.

Yes, there most certainly was an explanation . . . but she was abruptly scared of what it might be.

∙   ∙   ∙

All in all, Peyton had it good.

He was reclining in his bed, his every need catered to by his family's staff, his pain controlled by some Oxys that were, for once, entirely legal. And what do you know, his head was working fine—i.e., it was running his body and generating reasonable thought processes—like, yes, definitely, he wanted the underdog Louisville Cardinals to beat Kentucky in men's basketball.

He had good money bet in Vegas with his bookie.

But he couldn't say he was happy. Even with the feel-fine opiate in his system.

That shit with Novo was staying with him and not in a good way.

The issue for him was not so much that he cared he was a douche bag. Hell, if that bothered him, he'd have hanged himself in the closet years ago.

It was the idea that *Novo* thought he was a douche bag that was putting a hair across his ass.

Shit, maybe he was more old-fashioned than he thought. He'd certainly flown those same colors with Paradise when she'd told him she was entering the training program—and look at how that had worked out. She had ended up being the *Primus*, the number one trainee during that brutal orientation they'd all been through. So yeah, he'd been wrong about her.

Was he wrong about Novo? About females in general?

Maybe he just needed to have sex with that hard-ass female.

The instant the thought hit him, he started to get hard—and this was not a surprise. He'd been attracted to her since day one.

Paradise, though, was who had his heart—not that she was even a remote possibility with Craeg around. Which sucked. It was just . . . well, they'd developed a real bond during the raids, during all those phone calls when they had both been in their safe houses outside of Caldwell, isolated from everyone but their immediate families.

He trusted her in ways he didn't anyone else.

And he was attached to her in ways he wasn't with anybody else—

The knock that sounded out on his door was quiet, too quiet to be the butler—or that nurse who had forearms like Popeye and seemed to enjoy manhandling him around when she changed the dressing on his head.

"Come in—" He sat up as he saw who it was. "Elise, hey, girl. What are you doing here—what's wrong."

The female didn't answer him. Hell, she didn't seem capable of speech. She just shut the door behind her and stood there, ashen and shaky.

His first thought was that Axe had done something to her.

And his second was that if that fucking asshole had? Head injury or not, Peyton was going to castrate the bastard.

"Come here," he said, patting the bed next to him. "What can I do?"

But she paced around, and it was a while before she spoke. "You told me . . . back in the beginning . . ."

"What did I tell you?" he prompted gently. "Keep talking to me."

"About Axe . . . that I didn't really know him."

Mother*fucker.* "Yes, I did. What's going on?"

She put her hand into the pocket of her coat and took out an object. As soon as he saw it properly, he frowned. "What are you doing with one of those?"

"You know what this is?"

"Yeah, it's a pass to that sex club downtown. The Keys. I'm not a member, but I've seen them every once in a while. Allishon had at least one—I asked her what it was once."

"This is not hers." Elise stared at the thing. "But I went to her apartment tonight. I just had to—Axe was with me. When I found the one that was hers, he said he didn't know what it was."

"So whose is that one?" Peyton had already guessed, but he wanted her to have to say it.

"Axe's."

"So he lied to you."

"Yes." She shook her head. "I found his, by mistake. It was in the pocket of this cloak. I found a mask of a skull, too. They're both his. I could smell his scent on them—and it's fresh."

As she stopped talking and stared across at him, Peyton realized he was at a crossroads with her, and it was funny. After getting slapped with Novo's little asshole label, he wasn't going to enjoy being honest if that was what Elise wanted—

"I want you to be honest with me."

Shit. "Okay."

"Did you disapprove of him because he's a civilian, because he likes hardcore sex, or . . . because of something else?"

Noting her past tense, he fell silent—although things were far from quiet in his head: All he could hear was Novo's voice in his ear, railing on his double standards about males and females. About judging the two sexes differently.

And what do you know, lightning kind of struck Marblehead: If he thought females who slept around were sluts . . . that meant it was the female's fault that he himself was sexually promiscuous and kind of cruel when it came to the opposite sex. After all, if fucking was okay for males, but not females, then no matter how many people he banged without feeling, no matter how many hearts he trampled, nobody could hold him accountable.

'Cuz he was a male.

It was the ultimate unassailable justification for being an asshole.

Peyton closed his eyes and rested his head back against his downy soft pillows. All things considered, given that he had been shot in the noggin the night before, he could have done without that flash of insight.

Mostly because the OxyContin, no matter how good it was at erasing his physical pain, didn't touch the emotional burn in the center of his chest.

The one that informed him he was not a nice guy. In spite of his looks. His money. His breeding.

Novo was right . . . he was an asshole.

"Damn it," he whispered.

"I'm sorry. I shouldn't put you in this position—"

"No, it's fine. I'm fine. You're fine."

Bullshit. She was an emotional wreck and he was starting to feel like he was having an identity crisis.

"I should go—"

"No," he said sharply, and opened his eyes. "Look, I don't want to get in the middle of you two. I did last night and it nearly got us all killed—and even though there aren't any *lessers* around right now and nobody is armed, I just . . . I'm going to try and not be such a judgmental dickhead."

He was going to have to apologize to Axe, too.

"Novo . . . is that female who fought with us last night. Isn't that right?" Elise asked.

Peyton nodded. "Yeah. Why?"

"I'd forgotten her name. But you introduced her that first evening I met everyone at the cigar bar."

"Yeah."

Elise's eyes started to water, except then she sniffed hard and blinked while looking up at the ceiling. "Her scent was on the cloak. I didn't put it together until I was dematerializing over here—but I scented her in the mobile surgical van when she was with us. I remember what she . . ." As Peyton looked away, Elise's voice got steady. "He was with her. And recently. Like within the last night or two."

Peyton just kept his mouth shut. Funny, as early as the night before, he would have jumped at this opportunity to take a shit all over Axe.

And he was jealous—but not when it came to Elise. He was pissed that the fucker had been with Novo.

"Look," he said, "the only piece of advice I can give you is to go with your gut. It's never wrong."

"Well, what it's telling me, then, is that while he and I were to-gether, he was going to a hardcore club and having sex with someone else."

Peyton shook his head. "I knew this was going to come to a bad end for you. I mean, shit, I'm aware that you two are consenting adults and all, but this is exactly why I told him to stay the fuck away from you."

Ordinarily, he loved being right.

But not tonight, he didn't.

Not at all.

FORTY-EIGHT

As Mary sat at her desk at Safe Place, she accomplished absolutely nothing.

Well, that wasn't exactly true. She succeeded, quite admirably if she did say so herself, in moving a pile of paperwork from the right corner to the left—and, in the process, managed to review every page in said pile of case notes, intake forms, and schedules for grammatical errors, typos, and coffee stains.

Real high-level stuff.

Yup. She'd located several *its*-versus-*it's* problems, a *there* instead of a *their*, and, the pièce de résistance, an *orientated* versus the American English *oriented*.

Go. Her.

Sitting back in her squeaky chair, she swiped the mouse pad and checked the time on her computer screen. Holy crap. It was three a.m.

She hadn't heard from Rhage—and guessed that quick meeting about the attack on those trainees from the night before hadn't been all that quick.

Taking a deep breath, she smelled chocolate chip cookie dough cooking in the ovens downstairs, and a wave of sadness hit her. She could remember trying to get Bitty to participate in the community baking right after her mother had died. The little girl had preferred to sit upstairs in the attic room she had shared with her *mahmen*, those battered suitcases all packed with her meager possessions, her stuffed tiger and that doll head beside her on the bed.

They hadn't even known her real age at that point.

God, that seemed like a million years ago—

Her phone went off, and as she checked the text, she hoped it was Rhage. She needed an excuse to leave—

It was not from him.

As her hands began to shake, she got to her feet, tucked her blouse into her slacks, and carefully pulled on her coat. Then she picked up her purse and her phone.

Instead of telling everyone down below that she was going, she just sent a message to the group that she was leaving.

Now was not the time to stand in front of anybody and speak about anything—especially not the compassionate females who worked here and would read her like a book.

Outside, the night was terribly cold and that seemed appropriate. After she got into the Volvo and started the engine, she went miles before any appreciable heat came out of the vents, but it was okay. She was too numb to feel either hot or cold.

The King's Audience House was some distance away and yet her destination arrived too quickly. Then again, her intention had been to use the drive to collect herself—and really, she could have gone to California and back and not felt any different.

Just as she was getting out by the garage, Rhage was materializing.

As she saw him, there was a temptation to rush into his arms and wail again, but she was over that. She didn't have the energy, even if the emotions in her chest remained that big and hard to manage.

"Come on," he said in a dull voice. "Let's get this over with."

They entered through the back door, using the code, and then walked through the kitchen, heading for that library.

When they entered the formal room, Bitty was sitting on the sofa in front of the fire. Next to her uncle.

Damn, the family resemblance was so clear.

Do not cry, Mary said to herself as she forced a smile. *Do not make Bitty feel one ounce of guilt over this.*

You're the adult. She's the victim of domestic abuse, an orphan, and a child.

Do not *make this worse.*

Of course, all that self-talk didn't really change the way she felt. But at least the stern lecturing distracted her from melting down.

Marissa was seated beside the pair of blood relations and she got to her feet with enviable grace. "Thank you for coming."

As if they were outside third parties attending a meeting in a lawyer's office. For, like, a fence dispute.

Except they *were* third parties, Mary reminded herself.

Somehow, she and Rhage managed to sit down on the sofa across from Bitty and Ruhn. Things were said. Who knew what. And Rhage was as quiet as she was.

God, she couldn't meet Bitty in the eye for more than a second or two, and she needed to work on that—

"So, Ruhn? Or Bitty?" Marissa said. "Would you like to speak now?"

There was a long silence, and Mary was the one who broke it. Looking right into Bitty's eyes, she said in a voice that mostly didn't crack, "It's okay, Bitty. It's all right, it's all going to be—"

"So you'll let him move here?" the little girl said. "And live with us?"

Mary blinked. "I'm sorry—what?" She shook her head. "I'm sorry?"

Bitty looked at her uncle. "I want him to come live with the three of us. And he said he would. He doesn't need to be adopted like you guys are doing with me. But he has no family, and we have a big family, and Father always says the more the merrier? And we live in a big house. There is room. Ruhn can help, you know. That's his job."

Mary shook her head again. Opened and closed her mouth. "Wh-what?"

Rhage leaned forward. "I'm sorry, what are you saying?"

Ruhn cleared his throat. "I don't have anything to keep me in South Carolina. Bitty's my only family and I could use a fresh start—I don't have to live with you all—"

"Yes, you do." Bitty looked at him and spoke firmly. "We have a big house. And we have a cat and a dog. You like cats and dogs. You will come and live with us, and my parents will make sure you have work— Mom? What's wrong?"

Mary couldn't answer. Not with the tears streaming down her face and her breath catching in her throat and her whole body feeling like it was going to explode.

Putting her head in her hands, she was so overcome, all she could do was sit there and cry.

Bitty's voice was close to her when the little girl spoke next. "You'll like him, Mom. I promise."

All Mary could do was reach out . . . and pull her daughter in tight. There were no words, no words, no words at all.

Wait. No, there were: "I know I'm going to just love him."

Rhage's first thought was that this was the dream. He was finally in a dream, and of course, his subconscious was kicking out a fantasy world where everything worked out okay. Yup. Any second, the alarm was going to go off and they'd be back in hell.

Except . . . no electronic dinging.

Rhage put a hand out, aware that Bitty and Mary were hugging and talking and Mary was crying.

The fighter side of him, the part that had been honed by countless cluster-fucks in countless engagements in the war, was no more willing to believe this than he would Santa Claus coming down a chimney.

Rhage got to his feet and nodded at Ruhn. "I want to talk to you. Alone."

The uncle didn't hesitate to rise to his full height. "Anywhere you want."

Naturally, nobody was going to let him be alone with the guy: Vishous, who Rhage hadn't even been aware of being in the room, came with them as they stepped out into the rear part of the foyer and closed the doors of the library.

But Rhage wasn't about to, well, rage.

He kept his voice down and his eyes leveled on the guy. "I thought you came here to take her away."

The male nodded. "That's right."

"So what's changed? And think this over carefully. Because my *shellan* is bleeding to death in there. Again. And I'm getting really fucking bored with what's making her cry."

Ruhn stepped off, but didn't back away. Instead, he paced around, his big body clearly unable to contain his emotions.

"Yes, I wanted to take her back to South Carolina with me. I did. And I won't apologize to you or anyone else for wanting to do right by my bloodline. But then I got here . . . and I was only told she was in foster care. I didn't know that you all had started an adoption process until later. I really liked the both of you, and it was clear Bitty was well cared for. But last night . . . when you came through that door and you'd been shot at?" He pointed to the front entrance of the mansion. "You were frantic to get here and help them. And when Bitty saw you, she was terrified and relieved. Then the three of you were together. Right there."

The male went over and stood in the spot. "I was looking at all of you, and I thought . . . that is a family. Right there. That is . . . what I wished for my sister but knew she wasn't going to get with that male of hers. It was what I'd hoped to bring to Bitty's life—but she already has it, see. With you guys. She told me about how you took her in. What you've been teaching her about movies and cars and life. How good Mary is with her. How Mary took care of my sister at that place for the battered females. How you two stayed with her during her procedure for her bones—and about your beast. And by the way, wow, is all I can say about that." Ruhn shook his head. "She talked non-stop about the two of you. She loves you like you're her blood. And my stuff with my sister? That's not enough to justify breaking up a family. It just isn't."

Rhage just stood where he was and blinked like an idiot. "So . . ."

"I'll sign whatever you want. You know, to make it legal." The male put his palms up. "And honest, I don't have to move in or anything. I don't want to impose. That's her idea—but I would like . . . I don't know, if you could see your way clear, to letting me see her maybe once every couple of years—"

Rhage was not aware of moving. But the next thing he knew, he was throwing a bone-crusher around the guy, holding that fucking uncle so tight, the muscles in his shoulders and arms popped hard.

"You will come and you will live at the mansion." He shoved the guy back and then had to catch Ruhn as he tottered on his work boots. "And we'll find a job for you. And you will stay with us. And that is the way it is going to be."

Ruhn seemed nonplussed. "Ah . . ."

Vishous spoke up. "Wrath has to approve this. The security check's done, but the King is going to need to weigh in on it."

"It'll be fine." Rhage jacked up his leathers. "It's gonna be great—"

Ruhn rubbed his forehead like it hurt. "Wait, I'm grateful and all. But why would you do this? I'm nothing to you. I'm a nobody."

"Bullshit," Rhage said. "You're family."

FORTY-NINE

ell, that was fun, Axe thought as he finally got off the bus with Novo, Boone, Paradise, and Craeg. The meeting had gone on forever, new procedures being put in place for them entering the field downtown, new weapons being fitted for and ordered, reviews of defensive practices drilled into their heads until he'd wanted to scream.

But at least the Brothers weren't stepping back from having the trainees engage with the enemy. Not at all.

The good news? Now he got to rush home to Elise.

After a quick goodbye over his shoulder, Axe went ghost and then materialized on his front lawn. Smelling the burning fire and sensing her presence, he smiled.

It was amazing how much someone could bring to your life. Fill you out on the inside. Make you feel stronger and more peaceful at the same time.

He climbed the front steps, knocked on the door, and was so ready to have her answer it . . .

When nothing happened, he frowned. Knocked again. Then took

out a set of keys he hadn't though he'd need to use. Opening the way up, he—

The first thing he noticed was that Elise wasn't sitting in front of the fireplace, on the blankets where they made love.

She was on the sofa, almost out of reach of the heat.

The second thing he tweaked to was . . . that she had the cloak he wore to The Keys in her lap.

Axe closed the door slowly.

As she looked over at him, she met his eyes calmly. But her face was shut down, no emotion showing at all, no life in her eyes or her expression.

"What's up," he said, keeping his voice level.

Crossing his arms, he leaned back against the door. In his head, a litany of *She's leaving you, she knows, she's leaving you, she knows . . . you're going to be just like your father . . .* started up, a bad chorus that was off-key, off-tempo, and the kind of thing that was going to make him mental.

"So I found this," she said, running her hands over the black folds. "And I found what's in it. The mask . . . and the key."

Boom, boom, boom, boom—

For a split second, he looked over his shoulder, thinking that that sound must be someone beating on the kitchen door to get into the cottage.

Nope. It was his heart.

"I, ah, I've been sitting here, thinking, for hours." She scratched the base of her nose. "Running through things to say to you in my head. Questions to ask you—like how could you possibly stand in front of me at Allishon's and pretend you didn't know what I'd found there. How could you lie to me—"

She stopped as her voice got higher and more urgent, and seemed to re-collect herself.

"So I went to Peyton's, right after I found your key . . . found that you'd lied to me."

"Great," he muttered. He could only imagine how the guy had enjoyed fucking him up the ass with all kinds of—

"He wouldn't go into it with me. He didn't really say anything. And I respect him for staying out of this. I shouldn't have put him in that position in the first place. But I didn't know where else to go, and sometimes, when people are emotional, they don't make the best choices."

Axe waited, knowing that the hammer was about to fall—and it did.

"And I guess . . . that's my conclusion." She motioned between the two of them. "The night I met you, I'd decided to date Troy. It was as random a decision as they come. What I realize now is that what happened to Allishon and the stress in my household were eroding parts of me that I was unaware of becoming weak. I was flailing around, looking for an outlet—and then I met you. I threw myself into this—whatever it was—between us, headlong and out of control."

Annnnd there it was, he thought. Past tense.

Was. Not *is*.

"At the end of the day," she concluded, "you don't owe me anything. We're not in a relationship. The fact that you had sex with Novo at that club and then came home and were with me—"

"Wait, say what?" he barked. "When did this happen? If you're going to rewrite history, at least give me a timeline so I can keep up here."

Elise shot him a bored look. "You took her to the club. Two nights ago. And don't pretend you didn't. I was right here when she called and you wanted to make sure she was home safe. At the time, I didn't put two and two together, because I didn't remember the name of the female who was with you the night we met."

"I didn't have sex with her. That night, or any other."

"Maybe that's true. But I can't believe you. I can't believe anything you tell me. You didn't even correct me when I said she was 'he.' You lied to me about knowing what the key was at Allishon's. How will I ever know if you're being truthful?"

Axe laughed in a hard burst. "I told you shit I haven't told anybody."

"Did you? Or was that an act to get my sympathy, falsely gain my trust?"

"Are you fucking kidding me."

She shrugged. "This is the problem with lying, Axe. You do it once, and the other person has no idea what else you've been untruthful about. I come from a family of lies and silence. I can't go into that shadow world with someone I'm intimate with. Moreover, I won't do it. I told you in the beginning, honesty is the most important thing—"

"Honesty? You want to talk about honesty? You've been sneaking out of your father's house for how long? And you only came clean about what you were doing when you got caught. You switched phones with your BFF Peyton so no one knew where you were when you were with me. You broke in to your cousin's fucking apartment." He jabbed a finger across the tense air at her. "You want to make me out to be an asshole, fine. Have at it. But don't pretend for an instant that you're in some holier-than-thou ivory tower. Because that's bullshit, sweetheart. The only difference is, I'm not judging you and I'm not jumping to conclusions."

Elise looked toward the dying fire. After a moment, she nodded. "All of that is fair."

"Thank you for that seal of approval. It means *so* much to me."

She got to her feet and laid the cloak aside, placing that fucking key on the folds. "It doesn't change anything, though. The reality is, I'm not mad at you for sleeping with Novo or going to the club or playing dumb—"

"You sure about that?"

"Yes, I am." She turned to face him. And with the way she was star-ing at him, he knew without a doubt, this was the last time they were going to be in an enclosed space together. "I'm mad at myself. I'm mad that I didn't recognize I was addressing an emotional problem concern-ing my dysfunctional family-of-origin with the distraction of a poorly thought-out physical affair."

"Yeah, looks like you've got it all figured out. You've even tagged it with fancy therapy-speak. Good for you."

Yes, he was being a bitter son of a bitch, but what the fuck else was he supposed to do. Judge, jury, guilty verdict—it was all finished, all wrapped up. And he was going to the death chamber.

Because that's what life was going to be without her.

Death.

Elise shook her head slowly and put on her coat. "I had no business jumping into anything, with anybody. And like I said, I don't blame you. You didn't owe me a thing. It's not like we had some big conversa-tion about monogamy and then you went out and were with other people. I've only known you a week, so . . . there you go. Lesson learned."

Axe narrowed his eyes. "And what exactly did you learn?"

"That the only person you can really trust is yourself. And as long as you remember that, you're going to be okay. No matter what hap-pens."

As Elise finished saying her piece, she stared across the room at Axe . . . and felt like she was looking at a stranger.

Which was actually more accurate than the illusion of closeness and intimacy that had been created thanks to the really good sex they'd had together. But come on. The Scribe Virgin, when She created the race, had set things up right. Because pregnancy could be a result of sex, during a time of needing, and young were deadly to bear and hard to raise, the male and female had to reeealllly want to get it on so that the species survived.

Otherwise no one would take the risk. Ever.

So sexual tension and sexual expression were powerful things—and potentially destructive when what made procreation possible for the species was brought to bear in a casual affair between two people who otherwise had no business being together.

Elise was living proof of it.

And yes, she wanted to go into her feelings of hurt, rejection, and betrayal with Axe. She wanted to yell and scream, throw something. Kick him, maybe. But she knew damn well that was a persuasion thing, a negotiation, in addition to a punishment: By revealing more of herself to him instead of less, she was looking for him to do a complete turnaround and become, once again, who she had believed him to be.

But what was the saying? When somebody showed you who they were, you needed to believe them the first time.

Axe's true colors had come out. But only because he'd slipped up, and gotten caught by a happenstance of facts and circumstance.

Elise had laid Allishon to rest tonight. And now she was putting this . . . thing . . . between her and Axe down along with her cousin.

"So that's all I've got," she told him. "I'm going to go now. I wish you well, and I will not speak of this again to anyone. You do as you wish, however. I don't need you to protect me. I'm a big girl, and if there's fallout, I'll take it."

Because actually, her situation with him wasn't the only thing she'd been mulling over as she'd sat here alone and waited for him to come home.

She'd arrived at some other conclusions, too.

"Goodbye, Axe."

Her body was a little shaky as she approached him, but not because she was afraid of him hurting her or saying something awful: Proximity was just hard . . . even though her mind had changed gears when it came to him, her corporeal form still wanted his.

That was never happening again, though.

"I think you're really going into the right field," he said as he got out of her way.

"I'm sorry, what?"

His eyes shifted over to hers. "You're going to make a great professor. You excel at one-sided conversations and you have all the answers. You've given me an F, kicked me out of the class, and you're ready for the next student. And you feel terrific about it."

"No," she said softly. "Not terrific. But the biggest fallacy people sell themselves is that they should be happy all the time."

"I've never believed that. And you've just proved my position all over again."

He leaned to the side and opened the door; then he walked away without looking back.

Which was fine.

She was going to do the same.

Once outside, Elise dematerialized back to her house, and after she went in through the front door, she proceeded directly to her father's study. Knocking on the closed panels, she waited . . . and then let herself in.

He was, as always, at his desk. Dressed impeccably. Shuffling papers. Working on his investments.

"Well, good evening, daughter mine. How fare thee?"

Elise ditched the preamble and sat down without being invited to do so. "I'm moving out as soon as I find a suitable place to live. I have some money that *mahmen* left me, and I'm also going to be taking on more hours at the university for pay. I'd like to stay here while I apartment hunt, but if that makes you uncomfortable, I'll locate other accommodations."

As her father dropped his pen, and his lower jaw, she nodded. "And yes, my mind's made up. I'm sorry if this causes you any grief or embarrassment, and I would very much like to continue to have a relationship with you. That's your choice, of course, and if you need to distance yourself from me temporarily or even permanently, it will break my heart, but I will understand."

She got back to her feet. "I need to go live my own life, on my own terms—and that's not something that you, or anyone else, can grant me permission to do or withhold permission from me for. It's up to me, and me alone. And actually . . . I'm really good with that."

FIFTY

The following evening at around midnight, Mary stood to the side and watched Bitty walk Ruhn through the vestibule and into the great, colorful foyer of the Black Dagger Brotherhood's mansion.

Bitty's uncle had been interviewed by Wrath, and actually all the males of the household, the night before—and you want to talk about a grilling? The poor guy had been two feet shorter after the interrogations were through, and Mary and Bitty had practically had to pour him into one of the beds down below at Darius's.

And then there had been the trip down South right after sunset, Ruhn, Rhage, and V heading back to where Ruhn stayed, and talking to his employer, who hadn't required notice. There had been so little in terms of personal belongings that the three of them had been able to fill up some backpacks and duffels and dematerialize the stuff up here to Caldwell, traveling at jumps of fifty to a hundred miles.

"Isn't it beautiful!" Bitty exclaimed as she let go of the male's hand and started to jump around. "And don't worry, you get used to it. I promise!"

Ruhn looked like his head was spinning as his eyes bounced around the gold leafing and the crystal and the columns. "It's . . . well, I've worked in a big mansion. But nothing like this."

Bitty grabbed his hand again and dragged him into the billiards room. "Come meet the pool tables!"

As the pair of them went off, Rhage put his arm around Mary and whispered, "His place was spotlessly clean, my Mary, but there was nothing in it. Just a bed and table with one chair. Breaks your fucking heart—he was prepared to make it work, though. His employer told me that Ruhn was going to take on more hours to put Bitty in school on the estate. He was ready to do his best."

At that moment, there was a chiming sound from the vestibule door and Mary glanced at the security screen. "Oh, it's Saxton."

She went over and let the King's attorney in. "Come to join the festivities?"

The blond-haired lawyer was perfectly dressed as always, a cravat at his neck, his dark suit set off with a coral shirt and pocket square. And oh, dear Lord, did he smell good.

And also, oh, dear Lord, did it feel great to be lighthearted enough to notice that kind of thing.

Ever since Ruhn and Bitty had come forward with The Plan, as Mary thought of it, she felt as though her life had been returned to her. It was incredible. Everything was back to normal, almost like the pain and fear and uncertainty had never happened.

And it was funny . . . Although Mary didn't know firsthand what birth was like, she decided that she had been through something at least emotionally similar: She had been out of control, in pain, grinding through hours and days, terrified and in a nightmare that seemed to have no end. Then there had been some tearing, and a vital separation . . . only, in the end, to have her daughter in her arms, safe, the world righted once again, her life more complete than ever because the transition was over and everyone was okay on the other side.

It was a miracle—and the pain, instead of crippling her and Bitty, had just made their bond stronger.

"Actually," Saxton said, "I've brought the paperwork Ruhn requested."

As the attorney took a folded sheaf of papers out of his inside pocket, Mary was very aware that both she and Rhage went totally still.

"Ruhn just has to sign them," Saxton explained gently.

"Sign what?" the male said, as he came back into the foyer with Bitty. "Oh. Yes, please."

As he spoke, Saxton turned—and did a double take.

"You haven't met, have you," Mary said. "Saxton, this is Bitty's uncle, Ruhn. Ruhn, this is Saxton, keeper of all papers, strategist, and all-around great person."

Saxton stared at the other male as Ruhn bowed low. "Sire."

There was a pause. And then Saxton offered his palm. "Please. Just Saxton."

Ruhn stared at what was outstretched in confusion. "My . . . ah, my hands are rough."

"But of course," Saxton murmured as he dropped his arm. "Would you care to review this and give it your signature?"

As things got quiet, Mary stepped up. "Are you sure you want to—"

"Yes," Ruhn said. "There needs to be clarity in the event decisions have to be made or if she is unable to communicate in a medical crisis."

For some reason, Mary got teary again. And then she remembered his limitations. "But you need to know what it says."

"It says you are her parents, right?"

"That's correct," she whispered.

"Then I shall sign."

"It really is prudent," Saxton interjected. "So let us go into the library and you two should come as well."

"This way," Mary said as she started across the depiction of an apple tree in full bloom. "Rhage?"

"Right behind you. Bitty, give the grown-ups two secs, 'kay? Go find Lassiter and kick him in the butt for me, would you?"

"On it!" the girl said as she tore off in search of the angel.

Once inside the library, Mary shut the doors—and saw that Ruhn was staring at the tree. "Oh, that's our Christmas stuff. I'm human—or I was. You know. Ah, long story."

Which made her think of something—

"Would you read the papers to me?" Ruhn asked her. "Please?"

"Oh . . . yes. Yes, of course." She took the document from Saxton and they all sat in front of the fire. "This is . . ." She had to clear her throat as she held the pages out in front of Ruhn. "This is a release of all your . . . parental rights to Bitty." She pointed to places. "See, this is your name. This is her name. This text here states that forevermore, you will not make any claim to any custody of her, physical or otherwise, or claim any benefits that may accrue to her, or be a party or consulted about any decisions that affect her life. Do you know . . . I mean, once you sign this, it's done. It can't be undone."

Ruhn stared at the paper and then pointed to his name. "That's my name, right there."

"Yes."

"Hers . . . is here."

"Yes, that's correct."

He looked at the words for a while. "Funny, this is the only time our names will ever be together."

Mary swallowed a knot in her throat. "Ruhn, you don't have—"

"Does someone have a pen?" the male said.

Saxton, who seemed to be holding in some kind of emotion, put a gold one out. "Here, use mine."

Ruhn took the writing instrument and seemed amazed by it. Then he appeared worried. "I can't . . . I don't really have a signature. I don't know how to write my name."

"Any mark," Saxton said in a soft voice, "will suffice. And I will witness it as your own down below. You want to put it here."

Ruhn nodded as the lawyer pointed out a line three-quarters of the way down the second page. And then Bitty's uncle bent down over the document.

He was there for quite a while. Much longer than the two secs it took for most people to scrawl their name.

When he sat back up again, Mary covered her mouth with her palm.

"That's me," Ruhn said, pointing to the small sketch he'd made of his face. "That is my mark."

It was an absolutely beautiful rendering of his features. And everyone grew silent.

"It's all I know how to do," Ruhn explained.

Saxton pinched the brow of his nose. "No, no . . . it's perfectly lovely. And perfectly sufficient."

Saxton did his thing, notarizing the document, and then the lawyer was standing up. "I shall go file this at the Audience House."

"Come back, though," Mary said. "Please? We're going to have a little welcome party at the end of the night, and you should come if you can."

The attorney looked at Ruhn briefly. "All right. Thank you, I shall."

On the bus ride in to the training center, Axe sat in the rear, far away from the others. Peyton, meanwhile, stayed up front, choosing a seat close to the partition that separated them from the butler driver.

Elise's cousin hadn't looked back as he'd gotten on the bus. Didn't look back as they made the trip north.

But he also didn't get off when they stopped inside the parking area and everybody else went in for class.

"You waiting for me?" Axe said when they were alone.

Now the male turned. "Yes."

"I don't need to attack you from behind, you know. I can do that right in your face."

"I know." Peyton shifted his legs around and put his elbows on his knees. As he stared straight ahead, his mood was hard to read. "I'm guessing you heard Elise came to see me last night."

"Oh, she let me know it, all right."

"I didn't say anything about you and Novo."

"Well, good for you. Elise told me how much she hates liars, and considering I've never fucked Novo, at least you're clean on that one."

"That's your concern, not mine."

"Damn fucking right. And I also haven't been with Novo."

The long silence was a surprise, but Axe didn't really care one way or another. "We done here? FYI, I'm not going to cut you or anything. I don't want anything to fucking do with you, but that hasn't changed since orientation."

"Her father called me. She's moving out of the house. He's re-quested that I keep an eye out for her and I've agreed to do that."

Elise was leaving home? Holy shit.

Except then Axe reminded himself that it wasn't really his business anymore, was it.

"So you got what you want." Axe got to his feet. "Congratulations. Then again, shit always works out for people like you, doesn't it—"

Novo came up the short steps and leaned into the bus. "Are you two killing each other or something?"

Axe shook his head. "Nope. We're good—oh, but he thinks I fucked you three nights ago—or whenever it was we went to the club."

"What?"

"You heard me."

Novo stared at Peyton. "Axe put me up for membership. That's why he took me there. And it was because I asked him to—oh, and Axe shut me down when I asked him if he wanted to be with me. Turned me down flat. Jesus, Peyton, could you be any more of an asshole?"

Axe walked forward, shaking his head. "It doesn't matter. S'all good. Moving on."

Pushing past Novo, he stepped off the bus, went over to the door that had been propped open, and entered the training center.

As he headed for the gym, where they were going to be sparring, he was aware of a whole lot of things: He was exhausted, for one thing, but he had a feeling he needed to get used to that. He was in pain, but yeah, file that along with the former.

And he was terrified.

In his head, he was monitoring each and every thought he had, checking for signs that he was going to crash and burn as his father had. It was like he was searching for cracks in his foundation, waiting for his superstructure to collapse, anticipating the paralysis that he had watched for years.

He was already crippled on the inside. Surely the outside was going to go, too.

Because the truly pathetic thing? He had bonded with Elise.

Yes, as she had pointed out, it had been only a matter of nights, but—as he had so often heard, and never truly believed—when it came to males and their soul mates? It didn't take time; it took the right female.

And Elise was right for him even if he was wrong for her.

So yeah, he was crippled and going to remain that way for the rest of his life.

But what the hell.

He'd already been crippled before. He was used to this.

Just as some people were destined to be happy?

Others simply didn't win that lottery.

FIFTY-ONE

At the end of the evening, as everyone at the Brotherhood mansion came together and took their seats in the dining room, Rhage waited for Mary to give him the cue.

And when she did, just as the feast of Last Meal was being served, he turned to Bitty, who was next to him. "Hey, will you come with me and your mom for a second? Nothing is wrong, we just need to talk to you about something."

"Sure!" The little girl was up and at 'em, ready to go. "Uncle Ruhn, I'm going to be right back. You stay with the BABUs!"

The male blinked in confusion. "I'm sorry?"

Lassiter leaned in. "Buffoons. She has a speech impediment. It's really sad—"

Bitty nailed the angel in the arm. "Bad-Ass Big Uncles. And will you stop."

"Nevaaaaaaaaaaaah!" the angel cackled. Before giving Bitty a playful tug on her hair.

As Bitty skipped out ahead and Rhage drew Mary in against him, he called out, "The library, okay? Bit, we're going in the library."

"Roger that," she said.

"You ready?" he whispered to his *shellan*. As she nodded, he murmured, "It's going to be fine."

When they were all in there together, he shut the doors. Man, it felt like he was back in his own skin, his own life, his own ocean, swimming freely with the current instead of against it. And Mary was the same way—Dearest Virgin Scribe, it was good to see the light back in his *shellan*'s eyes and the smile on her face.

And as for Ruhn? The guy was a gem. Quiet, dignified in himself, not a pansy, either. He had insisted on carrying his things up to the guest room he'd been given down the hall of statues. And was already looking for projects to fix, clean, or improve.

Fritz was going to learn to hate the motherfucker.

"What is it?" Bitty said—before she got distracted by the Christmas tree. "Oh, my—we need to celebrate your holiday, Mom. But not yet. Ruhn needs presents. We need to . . . we need to figure out what he likes and I have an allowance. I can get him some myself—but you guys need to, too."

Mary laughed and drew the girl over to the sofa. "Absolutely, we will."

"Yay! So what's going on—Father, we need to watch *Deadpool* with him. He hasn't seen any movies. Like, ever. Not even *Jaws*. I have a draft list, and I want you to go through it with me. We'll set up a viewing schedule just like we did for me."

Rhage nodded. "Absolutely. That kind of deficit is more important than literacy."

Mary put her head in her hands. "You two are insane."

Rhage put his palm out for a high five and Bit slapped it with her own. "Nailed it," Rhage said. "Now, we need to get serious. Your mom has something she needs to tell you."

Bitty focused on their Mary. "G'head, Mom."

Jeez, it felt good to have that word back in their vocabulary.

In the short silence that followed, Rhage frowned and looked around.

For some reason, he was aware that they were not alone . . . and yet no one else seemed to be in the library with them.

Mary took Bit's hand and smoothed the back of it. "Do you remember when I told you I was sick?"

"The cancer isn't back?" the girl asked with fear. "You aren't—"

"No, no. Absolutely not. And that's kind of what I need to tell you."

"What? . . . I don't understand."

In a steady stream of perfectly chosen words, Mary told the story from start to finish. The cancer. Rhage coming into her life. The Scribe Virgin's intervention . . . and what it meant.

"You mean . . . you're immortal?" Bit breathed. "You're like a god or something?"

"Oh, no. No, no, not a god. Never. That is one job I wouldn't want. But it does mean . . . well, think of it like this. I get to choose when I go into the Fade. Like, you know how everyone ages along a line? They get older every year? And sometimes bad things happen to them and they get sick or hurt or something?"

"Yes. As with Father when he was shot. Before his vests. Or . . . what happened to my *mahmen*."

As Mary reached up and stroked the little girl's face, Rhage thought, Oh, my two females. My two perfect females in the firelight . . .

"Well, it's not like that for me," Mary said.

"So you can live as long as I do?"

"Yes, I can."

Bitty's eyes got watery. And then she threw her arms around Mary. "So you'll never leave me. I'll never lose my mother."

Okaaaaay, time for some throat clearing.

"Never. Ever." Mary held the girl and smiled through beautiful tears. "Not ever. And I didn't want to hide this from you—but I also didn't want it influencing your decision to stay with us?"

"I just feel lucky. I just feel so lucky." Bitty pulled back and looked at Rhage. "But what about you?"

"Bulletproof vests, my girl." He sniffed like he had allergies. 'Cuz it wasn't like he was crying or some shit. Nah. "Training and equipment. It's what I told you before, I go out to do my job and intend to come home to my females every night."

Bitty got quiet for a moment. But then she nodded. "Okay, but you'll be careful—"

Rhage frowned as something caught his eye.

A sun spot. On the carpet. By the tree.

"Lassiter," he called out. "Really?"

The angel appeared all at once, his blond-and-black hair and his gold hoops and necklaces and earrings creating that aura he always had. Or hell, that glow was probably just him.

"What I say?" the angel demanded as he Vanna-White'd the three of them. In zebra-striped leggings that were clearly out of Steven Tyler's wardrobe. "Have faith. Believe. And all will be well. What. Did. I. Say."

Rhage had to laugh. "Fantastic. Another reason for you to be full of it."

"Greatness is as greatness does." The angel pivoted in a circle and then pulled a Michael Jackson, moonwalking backward until he popped up onto the toes of his shoes. "And I am awwwwwwesommmme."

Mary and Bitty started laughing, too, and Rhage just sat back and smiled.

Then he started to think. Okay, so if Ruhn hadn't even seen *Jaws*, where did they start?

Probably not there. Or with Jason. Michael. Freddy. The guy wasn't a pussy by any stretch, but for godsakes, you didn't want to make him crap in his pants, either.

"What's the matter?" Mary asked.

Rhage rubbed his face and looked at Bitty. "You know, your uncle?

We might need to start him off slow with the movies. I don't want to scare the sh—er, crap out of him."

"Die Hard?" his daughter suggested.

"Too much."

"Really, that bad?"

"Really."

There was a pause. And then they both said, at the same time, in the same tone of voice: *"The Goonies."*

You want to talk about fatherly pride? Rhage mused as he held his hand out for another high five and Bit slapped him a good one.

There you had it.

FIFTY-TWO

There was something about New Year's Eve that made you want to start fresh.

Nights later, as Peyton sat on the foot of his bed, in his going-to-get-laid club clothes, he found himself scrolling through his texts. So many invitations, from his boys in the *glymera*, humans who thought they knew him from the Caldie club scene, females, females . . . more females.

And the pings just kept coming through.

Paradise and Craeg were going to be chilling at her house, and she'd invited him to join them—but also tacked on that she knew he'd be busy painting the town red. Boone was going over there. No one knew where Novo was at.

Axe certainly hadn't checked in with any updates.

Peyton put his phone aside and stared across his room. He was uncomfortably sober at the moment, and had every intention of fixing that shit.

Yup.

Any moment, he was going to hit the bottle or one of his bongs, and float away in the inside of his skull—just . . . leave behind the mess that had been stewing in his head for the last while.

He thought back to him and Axe and the others out on the streets the previous evening, working the blocks of abandoned buildings, instincts prickling, weapons up and ready to go, Brothers with them.

It was a new phase.

They were now not trainees, really. More like soldiers in training. If that made sense.

And Axe always kept it on the DL, never giving a hint of emotion away about anything, strung tight as a piano wire around someone's throat. But man, you could tell he was hurting. He'd lost weight. The bags under his eyes were so big you could have packed for overnight in 'em. And the grim mood was a tangible weight he brought with him into every room, every alley, every bus ride to and from.

It didn't take a genius to realize Elise was in no better straits. Peyton had seen what she'd looked like when she'd come to him.

Time and the breakup surely was not improving that.

Shit, he thought as he rubbed his face. Just . . . *shit*.

His phone rang. For like the fiftieth time. Another random calling to get him to come out.

When he finally picked up his phone, he went into his contacts and dialed a number he'd only phoned once before.

One ring. Two rings. Three—

"Hello?"

He cleared his throat. "Novo? Look—don't hang up, okay?" There was a pause. "Hello?"

"What?"

"Listen, I need you to do me a favor."

"Unless it involves hitting you somewhere with a frying pan, I'm not sure I'm interested."

"What are you doing tonight?"

"Nothing with you."

He flexed his LV loafers. "I need your help."

"If you're looking for a personality replacement, try eBay. You won't have to be too picky. Anything but Serial Killer would be an improvement."

Peyton stared at the blank, dark screen of his TV.

"Hello?" she said.

"I need you to help me right a wrong. And I'm not fucking with you, I really . . . I can't do this alone."

Something in his voice or . . . he didn't know what . . . must have gotten through to her. "Are you drunk?"

"No, and I'm not high, either." He shoved a hand through his hair. "Fuck me, maybe it's part of my problem. But I need to fix this first and then . . . yeah, whatever."

"Where are you?"

"My house."

"Go down and open your front door." She sounded annoyed. "I'll be there in a minute."

Peyton left his phone behind. Frankly, he was sick to death of the people in it. And as he went to leave his suite, he passed by a mirror. Checking out his reflection, he saw the same features, same hair, same good looks he had every night of his life.

And yet he didn't recognize himself.

Maybe that bullet had given him brain damage, he thought as he opened the door and stepped out.

'Cuz he hadn't felt right ever since he'd been shot in the head.

Elise was sitting at her computer, combing the "Apartments for Rent" section of the *Caldwell Courier Journal* online, when the house phone rang beside her little Tiffany lamp.

Picking the receiver up, she listened to the butler tell her she had guests and that they were waiting for her in the parlor. "Thank you. I'll be right down."

As she hung up, it dawned on her that she hadn't even asked who they were. But she didn't really care. Could be cousins. Or, hell, an intervention set up by her father to scare her straight.

But she wasn't afraid of even that. If she could get through losing Axe, she could get through anything.

Heading out of her room, she walked down the hall, passing by Allishon's old suite. Nothing had changed. Her uncle was still floating around, trying to find his footing, while his *shellan* self-destructed in their bedroom. Her father still didn't understand why Elise had to go, what she was doing getting her Ph.D., why she insisted on being such an iconoclast.

Everything would be okay, he had maintained, if she would just settle down and stop trying to talk about things that simply didn't need to be discussed.

To his credit, he wasn't telling her he would never see her again.

But he was sad that she was breaking away.

And so was she. She was going to miss the family she had been raised in, even if it was so broken that her only chance of living an authentic, halfway self-aware life was outside of it. You couldn't change others, though. Only yourself.

On that note, she hadn't heard from Axe.

She hadn't expected to.

She was surprised she missed him as much as she did, though. Was frustrated by that, actually. The trouble was, the high points of their . . . whatever it was . . . had been so high that in quiet moments of reflection, it was impossible not to remember them and mourn.

It was a process, though.

Or at least that's what all her fancy schooling had taught her.

And part of what was going to help her through her grief was that her and Troy's seminar started in a couple of days.

She was going to make it.

Because she wasn't going to have it any other way.

Downstairs, Elise crossed the foyer's marble squares and went over to the parlor—but before she entered the pretty room, she halted.

"Peyton? And . . ."

Okay, it was hard to say the female's name. Hard to look at that incredible body that just seemed to ooze sex appeal.

"You have a minute?" Peyton said. "We need to talk to you?"

Elise nodded and made herself walk forward. Peyton was looking great, as usual, his casual suit the kind of thing that had obviously been handmade for him, that open collar and perfect fit making him seem ready for a spectacular New Year's Eve night. Novo, in all her black leather, looked more prepared to fight.

Or have some hardcore sex.

Elise shook her head at herself and closed them all in. "What . . . ah, what can I do for you?"

God, even though she told herself to keep calm, her heart was pounding.

Novo looked at Peyton. Peyton glanced at the female . . . and then stared at Elise.

"You need to know some things. It's about Axe," he said.

Elise put both hands out like she was warding off an attack. "No, I don't need to know anything about him."

"Yes, you do."

"No, I really don't. And unless you've come for some other reason—"

"I've never had sex with him." Novo's voice was clear, unforced, and calm. "He took me to the club, yes. So I could become a member there. I asked him to do it for me as a favor. I've never once been with that male—and as far as both he"—she pointed at Peyton—"and I are aware, Axe hasn't slept with anybody since that night he first met you."

Peyton spoke fast, as if he were worried that Elise was going to run out of the room and he was going to lose his chance to say what he needed to. "I know this is not my business, technically, but you kind of made it mine when you came to see me."

"And I know you found that key of his." Novo nodded at Peyton. "He told me that Axe made like he didn't know what it was. I don't want to speak for the guy, but when you join the club, you're not supposed to talk about it. You're not supposed to reveal to anyone what the key is, where you use it, what it's about. It's a members-only thing, and if you blab, you're out. I'm not saying that's why he didn't tell you about Allishon's. But it's just something you should think about. Before you shoot him in the foot for apparently lying to you."

Elise's mind started to grind on the information. Even as she didn't want that whole door reopened.

It had been too hard to shut the damn thing in the first place.

Peyton came forward, stopping when he was right in front of her. "It's New Year's Eve. I want to start this next year on the right foot. That's why I'm doing this. See, there are some people who feel like I'm an asshole—"

At that point, Novo muttered under her breath something that sounded like, "Go figure."

"—and I guess . . . I'm kind of thinking I'm one of them." Peyton shrugged. "So yeah, Axe is having a horrible time. He looks half dead. And look, I'm not telling you what to do about this. But you might as well know the truth. What you choose to do or not do . . . is up to you. He's not perfect . . . but he's not like me, okay? He's not worthless."

FIFTY-THREE

Axe never cashed the check that Elise's father sent him.

Nope. He just put it on the mantelpiece above the fire, knowing that at some point, he was going to throw it into the flames. Just not tonight. And not last night, either. Or the one before that.

It kind of felt like his last tie to Elise, and yes, it was pathetic, but that was one bene of living alone—no one else knew the weaknesses of your thoughts, your heart, your little rituals. It was like singing in the shower off-key—nothing you had to share with anybody else.

Sitting in front of the hearth, he was naked and the back side of him was cold, but he didn't care. He hadn't cared about much since Elise had laid down the hammer—

The knock on his front door drew his attention from the flames. "Open," he called out, not giving a shit who it was, and knowing that he could get to his gun if he—

Axe jumped to his feet. Then remembered he was naked, and grabbed a pillow off the old sofa. "Elise?" he said to the closed door. "What the hell are you doing here?"

Her voice was muffled. "Do you, ah . . . do you mind if I come in?"

He shrugged. Mostly because his brain had traffic-jammed and rendered him too stoopid to talk.

Then he remembered she couldn't see him. "Yeah. I mean, sure."

Next thing he knew, she was stepping inside, closing the door and walking forward slowly, like she was thinking he might change his mind at any moment.

God . . . she looked good. Then again, she always looked good. Even when she hated him.

"Look, I don't know. . . ." She cleared her throat. "I don't know how to say this, so . . ."

"G'head. Whatever it is, I'm fine with it."

She'd already dropped a bomb in the center of his chest. So what if she took his arms and legs off as well? And, yeah, yeah, yeah, he should yell at her and get all righteous and shit over the fact that she'd gotten him wrong. But honestly, he didn't have the energy for it.

"I'm sorry."

Axe recoiled. "What?"

"I'm . . . listen, I'm really sorry. I might have misjudged you I think. . . ."

"Wait, *what?*"

She started talking and he didn't really follow. Something about Peyton and Novo coming over to her father's house. The key thing. Membership. Not talking. No sex.

"What?" he repeated.

"Like I said, they came over because Peyton wasn't feeling right about it all. He thought that you were being unfairly maligned by me."

Axe blinked. Then just shrugged. "So . . . ?"

"So, yeah, um . . ." She shook her head. "Can you just tell me why . . . you didn't explain to me about the key?"

"And you'll believe me now?"

"Yes, I think I will."

He dragged a hand through his hair and relived himself standing in that closet of a dead female he didn't know, Elise holding that piece of metal out to him. "I thought . . . I thought you wouldn't understand. You know, that you'd write me off or something. I don't know. I gave up the drugs, but in a lot of ways, I was still self-medicating with sex, you know? Just trying to get out of my head."

"Did you ever hurt anyone? At, the, ah . . . club?"

"Like Anslam, you mean? No. Never. And I was never with Alli-shon. I didn't even know her, to be honest. A lot of people go there." He threw up his hands. "Whatever, I just wanted you to believe in me, okay? I wanted to be the male that I saw you thought I was. And a sex addict was not part of that picture."

"Do you feel any need to . . . go back there?"

"Not since I met you. When I took Novo to The Keys, none of it interested me anymore. I just didn't get juiced like I used to. I wanted to be with you and only you."

"Is that still true?" she whispered.

Axe crossed his arms over his chest. "What do you want from me, Elise? Why did you come here?"

"I'm just . . . I'm so sorry. I jumped to conclusions and I leveled a lot of things at you. And I'm really sorry. My emotions got the best of me, I guess."

"It's okay," he muttered. "I mean, it's cool."

"It's really not." She seemed so sad. "I guess the truth is . . . well, as you said, I'm a better professor than I am a student. I decided every-thing, and you're right, I didn't let you even defend yourself."

As a silence stretched out, Axe wanted to pace around, but, hello. Ass naked.

"I'll ask you again," he said. "Why are you here?"

"Because . . . I love you. That's why."

It took a while for the words to sink in. And what do you know, he

went good and speechless when they did. In his most pathetic fantasies, he had wanted—hell, prayed for—this turnaround on her part.
Had hoped against hope it would be the one miracle he would ever
receive. Was this even real?

Overcome, and highly emotional, all Axe could do was . . . well, he
leaned to the side and got something off the sofa cushions.

Elise came forward as he held out his hand. "What is . . ."

As he gave her the wooden object, he muttered, "It was supposed
to be a bird. I don't know what it really turned out to be. Anyway, I
love you, too."

Her head snapped up, her eyes popping wide.

Axe just shrugged. And then started to smile. "What? Do you
want me to get on your case for wronging me? You're clearly already
doing that yourself—and as someone who can beat himself up a
lot, we'll always be harder on ourselves than we will be on anyone else.
And come on, I've bonded with you. So you could pretty much run
me over with a car, light me on fire, and pitch me off a bridge, and
I'll still take you back. Not that I'm recommending that approach to
reconciliation—"

Elise threw herself at him and hung on to his neck so hard, he
couldn't breathe. But he was good with that. Just having her against
him and smelling her hair and her skin . . . feeling her close, not just
physically, but right in his heart?

Who the hell needed oxygen, anyway.

"I love you," he said again as he began to shake. "God, I love
you. . . ."

It was not at all how Elise thought it was going to go. Not even close.

She had braced herself for all kinds of recriminations. Was pretty
sure that she was going to be kicked out of the cottage on her butt, and
how could she blame him? She had jumped to a whole lot of conclu-

sions because she'd been hurting and feeling so paranoid and betrayed. Heck, she had hit him where it counted, reducing him to a grief strategy.

And yes, that might have been where things had started on her side, but it certainly had evolved into so much more: If Axe had only been a psychological crutch, she wouldn't have missed him as much as she had. As in every second, each heartbeat, and all the breaths in between.

"I love you," she said. "I love you so much, and I almost blew it, and—"

"Shh . . . we don't need to think like that."

"But I have to make amends, and I have to re-earn your trust, and I need to—"

He put her down on her two feet—um, okay, wow. He was oh, so naked and, yes, responding to her presence. And . . . yup, she was responding to his.

"Elise." He brushed her hair back out of her face. "Listen, I'm not going to condemn you for protecting yourself. The truth is, we don't really know each other very well, and trust . . . it comes with time. You were emotional. I was emotional. And . . . shit happens. I don't know about you, but I'd much rather focus on the future than a couple of crossed wires that are really just part of the process."

"Except what if Peyton hadn't said anything?"

"He did, though."

"What if you hadn't let me in the door?"

"I did, though."

"But what if you didn't believe me—"

He put his forefinger gently on her lips, stopping her ramble. "So I'm thinking right now about something Rhage said to me a while ago."

"Was it about professors being idiots in their own subject matter?"

"You're not an idiot. And no, it was about . . . well, that night I saved him in the alley? Afterward? I was freaking out just like you are now. I was all, like, what if I didn't make it in time, or what if this, or that . . . and he said something about there being no reason to beat yourself up over something that was fated to occur. On that theory? Even if Peyton hadn't said something, we would have ended up back together because that just is what's supposed to happen."

"But . . . but . . ."

"Elise. Don't you understand? My door was always going to be open to you. It *is* always going to be open to you."

And then he was kissing her, and laying her out in front of the fire.

Elise was soaring with him even before she was naked, her heart free, the tangle untangled, the path astray now back on course.

Just before they were joined, she inched back. "So your door is always open, huh?"

"Always."

"Really . . ." She smiled at him, thinking if she were any happier, her heart would burst. "Because I happen to be moving out of my house."

His brows lifted. "You are? You don't say. . . ."

"It makes me sad, but it's just not the right place for me."

"You know . . . I could use a roommate. In fact, I was just thinking I was looking for a beautiful, intelligent female who's good with a comeback and a gun."

Elise started to nod. "And I'm looking for a place to stay that's safe, secure, private . . . heated by an open hearth—and that has fireworks every night thanks to a guy who has tattooed half of himself and doesn't mind females who jump to conclusions."

"I'd say we're a perfect match, then."

On that note, he arched his back and filled her deeply. And as she gasped, he gave the knowing smile of a male was who well aware of the effect he had on his female.

"We are a perfect match," she moaned. "But there's just one thing."

"What's that?"

"I don't . . ." She glanced at the hunk of wood he'd given her. "I don't think you're much of an artist."

Axe started to laugh. "I know, right? What the hell is that? I tried to give my dad's thing a shot and I sucked at it—"

"You're sure it's a bird—"

"I don't know—"

As they talked over each other, midnight came and went, a new year beginning, a fresh start happening for both of them.

A fresh start . . . that was going to last two lifetimes.

FIFTY-FOUR

"Wait, this one's for L.W.!"

As Mary sat back in the library with a cup of hot cocoa in her hand and a candy cane in her mouth, she smiled as Bitty rushed over to the First Family with a foil-wrapped present. The girl was dressed in a red taffeta gown that had a green sash, and she looked picture perfect. Except for one thing: She was also wearing, tragically, Lassiter's baseball hat with the reindeer antlers. Which would almost have been okay.

Except it read "The Grinch Can Elf Off."

At least, Mary decided, there wasn't an actual "f-bomb" in there.

The entire household had crammed in around the Christmas tree—well, everyone except the angel, and God only knew where Lassiter was. For the last hour, presents had been passed out, the human holiday being celebrated on New Year's Eve instead of the correct date because, hello, there had been a lot going on.

Rhage leaned in close. "So . . . can you and I play find-my-mistletoe today after the kid goes to sleep?"

Mary felt her body warm up. "Absolutely."

Her *hellren* let out a purr. "And I know just where to put it."

She elbowed him. "Shh, stop thinking like that. We still have a party to get through."

"There's always the bathroom. The pantry. The great outdoors—"

"It's freezing!"

"I'll warm you up, female."

Mary threw her head back and laughed just as Wrath said, "What is it?"

"A Tonka truck!" Beth smiled at Bitty as she put the toy in her son's lap. "Did you buy this with your own money?"

"I did." The little girl was very proud. "You said you thought he'd like one."

George, Wrath's seeing-eye dog, sniffed the thing and gave it a lick.

"L.W.'s going to love—" Beth laughed. "Yup, right in his mouth."

As the King's firstborn started gumming the tires, Bitty danced back to the tree and hunted around. "The last present is for you, Uncle."

Ruhn was two armchairs away, sitting in the self-contained way that Mary was coming to associate with him. He wasn't aloof—on the contrary, he was always open and warm—he just seemed a little over-whelmed by all the people and the shouting and the laughter and the never-ending rotation of inside jokes between the Brothers.

"Thank you," he said quietly.

Everyone went silent as the large flat box was delivered into his lap.

"It's from all of us!" Bitty exclaimed. "I put some of my money into it, too."

"Y'all have been too generous already." The male looked down at the pile of clothes next to his chair. "I don't know how to thank you—"

V cut in. "Yeah, yeah, yeah. Just open it, will ya?"

"Vishous!" Jane hissed over in the corner. "Seriously—"

"What! Come on, I seriously spent, like, hours trying to help Rhage find the right one—"

Butch chimed in. "He totally did. I mean, it was intense, the two of them—"

Rhage shrugged. "But hey, you know, this is an important gift . . . you want to get the color right."

"Is it another sweater?" Ruhn asked. "I have two now already?"

"You should open the box," Rhage said. "G'head, son."

It was funny, Ruhn had been taken under Rhage's wing within a night of coming here, and the two were really sweet together. Ruhn took all his cues from Rhage, learned from him, spent a lot of time with him.

Turned out Ruhn had gone through his transition only fifteen years before.

And Rhage would probably not admit it, at least not anytime soon, but Ruhn was quickly becoming a son to him.

Yup, that was Rhage's boy: Each time Ruhn mastered something else, like working out in the weight room with the Brothers, or signing up for an English-as-a-second-language course to learn to read, or watching another of Rhage and Bitty's god-awful movies, there was pride on Rhage's face.

The universe had given them a BOGO, in essence—

Ruhn opened the top of the box and rifled through the tissue paper. Then he frowned. "Wait, what is this?"

He held up a key fob.

Rhage jumped out of his seat. "Come on, son, you gotta meet her!"

Bitty squealed and started yanking on her uncle's arm. "She's out back—right here!"

"Here, hit the button on the fob—"

"Wait, what—"

As Rhage threw open a set of French doors, the whole household exploded out of their seats and jammed the exit. . . .

To see the most beautiful heavy-duty Ford truck with a blah-blah-something or another for an engine and double cab blah-blah with eight gazillion horses under the hood and yada, yada, yada, suspension, gear-shifting whatever—

All that stuff.

Mary hung back and let them all go, the security lights coming on and giving her a great view of Ruhn's total shock and then tentative excitement.

And then the male was turning to Rhage and not looking him in the face. Rhage knew what he was doing, though, and wrapped Ruhn up in a big bear hug—while Bitty danced around like a firefly.

Yes, Mary thought, this was the best Christmas she'd ever—

"Mary."

Turning at the soft sound of her name, she glanced behind herself. Then frowned. "Lassiter?"

"I'm over here."

"Where?" She looked all around. "Why is your voice echoing?"

"Chimney."

"What?"

"I'm stuck in the fucking chimney."

She raced over to the fireplace and got on her hands and knees. Looking up into the dark flue, she shook her head. "Lass? What the hell are you doing up there?"

His voice emanated from somewhere above her. "Don't tell anyone, okay?"

"What are you—"

An arm came down. A very sooty arm that was encased in a red sleeve that had white trim. Or what had been white trim and which was now smudged with ash.

"You're stuck!" she exclaimed. "And thank God no one lit this fire!"

"You're telling me," he muttered in his disembodied voice. "I had to blow out Fritz's match like a hundred times before he gave up. Fuck, that sounds dirty. Anyway, just remind me never to try to be Santa for your kid, okay? I'm not doing this again, even for her."

Mary stretched a little farther in, but the logs on the hearth stopped her. "Lassiter. Why can't you free yourself by dematerializing—"

"I'm impaled on a hook that's iron. I can't go ghost. And will you just take this?"

"What?"

"This."

He turned his hand toward her and there was . . . a box . . . in it? A small navy blue box.

"Open it. And before you ask, I already cleared it with your pin-headed *hellren*. He's not jel or anything."

Mary sat back and shook her head. "I'm more worried about you—"

"Justopenthefuckingthingalready."

Taking off the top, she found a slightly smaller box inside. That was velvet. "What is this?"

As she lifted the lid, she . . . gasped.

It was a pair of diamond earrings. A pair of perfectly matched, sparkly, diamond . . .

"A mother's tears," Lassiter's slightly echo-y voice said softly. "So hard, so beautiful. I told you everything was going to be all right. And those are to remind you of how strong you are, how strong your love for your daughter is . . . how, even in the worst of times, things have a way of working out as they should."

Blinking away tears, she thought of her crying in the foyer in front of the angel, crying because all had been lost.

"They're just beautiful," she said hoarsely.

Slipping one out of its box, she took out the pearl in her lobe and replaced it with the diamond. Then did the same on the other side.

"Mary!" Rhage said from the open door. "You gotta come see—"

He stopped and then smiled. "So he gave them to you, huh."

"He did." She put the box aside. "But, Rhage, we have a problem—"

"You weren't supposed to tell him!" Lassiter barked.

Rhage frowned. "Lassiter?"

"Fuck you!" came the muffled response.

Mary pointed to the hearth. "Lassiter is in a Santa suit, stuck in the chimney, impaled on something that means he can't dematerialize. So we've got a problem."

Rhage blinked once. And then threw his head back and laughed so loudly the windows shook. "This is the best fucking Christmas present *ever*!"

"Fuck you, Hollywood!" Lassiter yelled from inside the chimney. "Fuck you so hard—"

Brothers started filing in, and Rhage was all over it, reporting the situation—while nearly wetting his pants laughing.

Then Rhage marched over, put his hands on his knees, and hollered up, "How's it feel to be a proctologist, angel! You like that tight squeeze? I'd call you something else but my daughter's in earshot. Starts with 'd' and ends with an 'o,' though!"

"I'm gonna kill you as soon as I'm out of here!"

"You want a Little Mermaid doll to keep you company? Or, wait, I'll send that stuffed tarpon up—"

"Eat me!"

As the two exchanged festive holiday cheer, and the rest of the household gathered around and laughed until they were hoarse, and V decided that maybe they could run a chain from the back of Ruhn's new truck, Mary stepped out of the way and just watched her family.

"Mom?"

Focusing on Bitty, she smiled and stroked the girl's long dark hair. "What, my love?"

"Merry Christmas, Mom." The little girl came in for a hug. "This was the best Christmas ever, don't you think? I mean, I know it's my first, but I don't think it gets any better than this."

Mary tucked her daughter in close, looked at the load of opened presents and the acres of crushed wrapping paper and the utter and complete chaos . . . and found herself filled with such joy, her body and soul became a happy balloon, bouncing in the air even as she stayed with her feet on the ground.

"No, Bitty, Christmas doesn't get *any* better than this."

Bitty frowned. "Are they ever going to get him out?"

Mary laughed. "Yes. But they're never, ever going to let him forget this one. Ever. Yes indeed, this is one holiday everybody's going to remember!"

ACKNOWLEDGMENTS

With immense gratitude to the readers of the Black Dagger Brotherhood!

Thank you so very much for all the support and guidance: Steven Axelrod and Kara Welsh. With love to Team Waud—you know who you are. This simply could not happen without you.

None of this would be possible without my loving husband, who is my adviser and caretaker and visionary; my wonderful mother, who has given me so much love I couldn't possibly ever repay her; my family (both those of blood and those by adoption); and my dearest friends.

Oh, and my WriterDog, Naamah!

ABOUT THE AUTHOR

J. R. WARD is the author of more than thirty previous novels, including those in her #1 *New York Times* bestselling Black Dagger Brotherhood series. She is also the author of the Black Dagger Legacy series and *The Bourbon Kings*. There are more than fifteen million copies of her novels in print worldwide, and they have been published in twenty-six different countries around the world. She lives in the South with her family.

JRWard.com
Facebook.com/JRWardBooks
@JRWard1

ABOUT THE TYPE

This book was set in Garamond, a typeface originally designed by the Parisian type cutter Claude Garamond (c. 1500–61). This version of Garamond was modeled on a 1592 specimen sheet from the Egenolff-Berner foundry, which was produced from types assumed to have been brought to Frankfurt by the punch cutter Jacques Sabon (c. 1520–80).

Claude Garamond's distinguished romans and italics first appeared in *Opera Ciceronis* in 1543–44. The Garamond types are clear, open, and elegant.